Praise for *The Illust...* ....

'A captivating comi.. g ...ge story with memorable characters
beautifully brought to life in a setting dripping with atmosp. '
Daily Mail

'Evocative and enchanting – a future
classic and a star in the making.'
Veronica Henry, *Sunday Times* bestselling author

'Part fantasy, part coming-of-age, the undercurrents
of child neglect and mental ill health pull at you
all the way through this poignant tale.'
Heat

'An enthralling read with a real heart of darkness.'
Abigail Dean, *Sunday Times* bestselling author of *Girl A*

'A bewitching read.'
Woman & Home

'An extraordinary debut... beautiful, dark, haunting and
unforgettable. It is a most wonderfully tender nightmare,
a haunted-house childhood where the landscape gets ever stranger,
a deeply affecting portrait of the climb towards adulthood.
Nostalgic, familiar and yet utterly strange. I loved it.'
Edward Carey, author of *Little*

'I cannot recommend this beautiful, haunting novel
enough! Polly is an astounding new literary voice.'
Scarlett Curtis

'[A] gem of a read.'
Good Housekeeping

'Written in fine, delicate prose, this treasure of a debut takes up the palette of emotions and paints with all the colours.'
Nydia Hetherington, author of *A Girl Made of Air*

'A promising debut novel… full of atmospheric tension.'
Mail on Sunday

'Exquisitely written, stunning, totally unique. Everyone needs to read this.'
Jessica Ryn, author of *The Extraordinary Hope of Dawn Brightside*

'A unique and bewitching treasure to read.'
Woman

'A magical tale, beautifully written, evocative and mysterious, and stitched through with a dark thread that I wasn't expecting. What a wonderful book.'
Anita Frank, author of *The Lost Ones*

'A beautifully written tale that evokes dreams and imagination.'
Daily Record

'Polly Crosby makes sensory magic, conjuring images of such vividness that I'll remember them always. I'll remember Romilly and her father too: I loved them deeply, and they filled and broke my heart.'
Clare Beams, author of *The Illness Lesson*

'Beautifully written… mesmerising.'
My Weekly

'Crosby weaves a magical spell in which dark-edged fantasy collides with everyday life.'
Publishers Weekly

Polly Crosby lives in Norfolk with her husband, son and rescue cat. To find out more about Polly's writing, please visit pollycrosby.com. Polly can also be found on Twitter as @WriterPolly.

The *Illustrated Child*

POLLY CROSBY

ONE PLACE. MANY STORIES

HQ
An imprint of HarperCollins*Publishers* Ltd
1 London Bridge Street
London SE1 9GF

www.harpercollins.co.uk

HarperCollins*Publishers*
1st Floor, Watermarque Building, Ringsend Road
Dublin 4, Ireland

This edition 2021

1

First published in Great Britain by
HQ, an imprint of HarperCollins*Publishers* Ltd 2020

ISBN: 9780008358440

MIX
Paper from
responsible sources
FSC™ C007454

This book is produced from independently certified FSC™ paper
to ensure responsible forest management.

For more information visit: www.harpercollins.co.uk/green

This book is set in 11.5/15.5 pt. Centaur

Printed and bound in Great Britain by
CPI Group (UK) Ltd, Croydon, CR0 4YY

To Matt and Sebastian

Prologue

You probably know me: I'm the Kemp Treasure Girl. Maybe you had the books as a child. Perhaps your dad read them to you in those wilting hours of sleep where books become dreams and dreams become books. Did you look for the treasure, digging in your garden, unsure of what you were searching for?

Mine was an unusual infamy for one so young. Not an all-encompassing, celebrity fame, but one that flattened me into two dimensions and picked out the colour of my eyes and my dress. One that stopped people in the street and made their necks crane back round to gaze at me.

The version of me in the books was my friend. She was always there for me, sharing in my adventures, appearing at the lifting of a page. But children grow up, and as I grew taller and wiser, Romilly Kemp in the book stayed young and innocent, a sickly-sweet imposter who wore my dress and suckled at my father's love, leeching it away until there was barely any left for me at all.

But then I made a real friend. Someone I could trust: someone who knew intimately my deepest, darkest thoughts even if I dare not acknowledge them myself.

But the beginnings of a friendship are like the beginning of a book: you never know how they will turn out until the very end.

PART ONE

One

Braër was an ancient farmhouse. A month of living there had still not unearthed a fraction of its secrets.

As I ran from the house, tugging on unfamiliar wellies, I stared up at its mossy roof and dirty walls. Dad told me that it had probably once been called Brother Farm, but time and the soft Suffolk accent had changed it.

The house itself was long and low and surrounded on three sides by a moat clogged with cowpats and slime. In the middle of the water was an old fountain, and perched atop it was a gargoyle with a sinister, winking face. It ogled me as I ran past, its eyes bulbous and staring.

On the south side of the house, down an overgrown path, stretched a bumpy meadow filled with sagging grass. It was the perfect base for my newly invented invisible army, and the edge of my territory. I could go there on my own, making pretend campfires and having sword fights with prickly bushes, knowing that I was safe, even though I could barely see the house above the long, scratchy grass.

As I set off down the path towards my camp, a sharp whistle brought me back. Dad was stooped in the back door, his huge shoulders nearly touching the frame on either side. Something small and snow-like was curled up in his open palm.

'What is it?'

'I wanted to draw one, so I thought, why not?' he said, planting the tiny kitten into my eager arms, and suddenly it was mine. 'It's a Siamese,' he said, wiping his hands on his trousers, leaving a snail's trail of white fur on the corduroy.

'Is it a girl or boy?' I asked, trying to look through the fur at the correct place.

'A boy.' Dad crouched down, looking at me as I hugged the kitten. Briefly he reached forward and touched my cheek, and I leant into the roughness of his hand.

'Yes,' he said to himself, his voice a growl of love, 'it's that look in your eyes, right there that I want to capture.' He straightened up, his knees creaking. 'I'm going to need to paint him. And you, of course. I have an idea...' he trailed off. Frowning at me, he turned on his heel and entered the house, leaving the kitten and I alone.

I examined his bony body. He was small and soft, and smelt of wee and sawdust. He had pale creamy fur tinged with chocolate brown at each edge. As I was studying him, he uncurled himself, tipping off my arms, towards the moat below us. I caught him by the tail just in time, tucking him back safely into the crook of my arm. He opened his eyes for the first time and stared at me with big, red-blue irises. He was hot and slightly sticky-damp in my hands, and I loved him immediately.

I balanced him on my shoulder and made my way up the two flights of stairs to my bedroom, filling the kitten in on the minutiae of our lives.

'Dad lost his university job ages ago, and he's been trying to work out what to do with himself ever since,' I said, tickling him under his chin as I ran up the second staircase; the tiny, windy one that Dad was forever tripping up on. 'He says we've moved here so he can paint instead of teach art. It's the summer holidays, and I'm going to be nine soon, and Dad says he might have to give me a painting instead of a real present for my birthday, but that's OK because his paintings are like stories made real. He says someone has to make some money, or we'll be living on bread crusts and moat water, so I thought I might sell some stuff outside the house. I found some nice pebbles and I tried to paint them, but I'm not very good at painting. So I wrote poems on them instead, but I'm not very good at poems either, so I dropped them in the moat. Here, this is us.'

I pushed open the three-foot-high door that marked the entrance to my vast bedroom.

The kitten perked up as we climbed through into the huge, bright space. It was the shape of a tent, one of those old-fashioned tents – a huge triangle. And it felt like a tent too: when it was windy outside, the air caught beneath all the beams and vibrated until you felt like there was nothing but thin canvas between you and the sky.

When Dad had first shown me my room, I spent the entire day in there, not daring to believe all this space belonged to me. There were dustsheets over the furniture, and in the corner, a pretty parasol leant against the wall as if the young lady it had belonged to had left it there only moments before. The first time I opened it, it showered dust all around me, and I walked the length of the room, holding it above my head in a sedate manner, pretending I was as posh as its previous owner.

I tipped the kitten onto the bed, and studied him. 'You look like someone important,' I said, 'and important people have long names. How about Captain Montgomery of the Second Regiment?' Montgomery seemed satisfied with his name, and curled up happily on the quilt.

On that first night his mews pierced my dreams. He wrapped his pulsing little body about my head on the pillow, and I found him in my dreams too, popping into existence in the middle of a sweet shop, then a flowery meadow, the little bell on his collar rattling shrilly, announcing his arrival and preceding his loud meow.

On waking the next morning, he followed me round the house, and Dad soon joined us, stooping to sketch us whenever we stopped, wiping his dark hair out of his eyes and grasping his stubby pencil, his knees creaking as he crouched down to get a better angle of us.

Dad's love of drawing had always been a part of him, but since we had moved to Braër it had become an obsession. His fingers, when they stroked the fringe from my face late at night, had the sharp tang of pencil lead on them, and the skin of his face had echoes of paint and pastel, especially under his eyes, where he had rubbed them so often in frustration. I had the feeling that moving to such a ramshackle house had made Dad start to go ramshackle too. His jumpers, once smart, had started to become holey and smattered with the baked bean juice that he sipped straight from the tin.

It was only by the end of the second day of kitten ownership that I managed to shake Dad off, creeping back to hide in my bedroom, the little cat on my shoulder. I shut the door quietly so as not to let Dad know where we had gone. I needed to show Montgomery something secret. In the middle of my bedroom, concealed beneath my bed, was a special floorboard. Below it, in the small dark vacuum, were my favourite things: a musty snail's shell, a rusty bolt with a star-shaped end that I'd brought from our old house, and my most treasured possession: a shiny yellow coin that I had found three days ago in the middle of the meadow, which might or might not be real gold. It had a funny-shaped man's head on one side, and he was wearing a crown a bit like Jesus. I put the coin between my teeth and bit down on it like I'd seen pirates do, but my tooth, which was a bit wobbly, shot with pain. I spat the coin back into the hole and sat, tonguing the tooth so that it spun-danced in my mouth. Montgomery, growing disinterested, squatted nearby, releasing a flurry of wee that trickled into the cracks between the floorboards.

Later, in the slumbering twilight hours of my bedtime, when my tired mouth could no longer accommodate the syllables of my new kitten's name, Montgomery was condensed down to Monty, and then just Mont. I held him close and inhaled his buttery smell.

I lay back, eyes half closed, listening hard for the battalion of soldiers that left the meadow at night to keep their march on the stairs. Their marching tonight was soft, as if their feet were clad in slippers. They condensed into one soldier, a bearded, paint-covered soldier that melted into the form of my dad as he sat on the edge of my bed.

'Sorry for hiding,' I mumbled, turning my cheek so it nestled into the soft corduroy of his leg. I felt his hand on my head. It was big and heavy. I liked it.

'Your hair is awfully tangled; it feels like a bird's nest.'

'I'd quite like a bird to nest in my hair.'

'Then we shall leave it be. What story shall I tell you tonight, daughter-mine?'

'The one about the Rabian Nights.'

Dad's stories were full of colour even though he never had any pictures to go with them. You could smell the hot, spicy night air and the sweating horses as they galloped across the sand. Mont jumped from my neck and landed with a soft thud on the bed. As he began the story, Dad ran a hairy finger along the length of Monty's tiny spine, exploring the kitten's bones as he spoke of strange fruits and spiky plants, turbaned men and glittering jewels. I closed my eyes and I was there, a bearded man with tattooed skin and dark eyes swooping in at me amidst a cloud of fragrant air.

Dad leant forward and kissed me, first on my forehead, and

then on the little mole on my cheek. He left me dozing quietly, my mind on flying carpets and dancing snakes. When he had gone, I opened my eyes and scooped Monty up, wrapping him round my head like a turban, his tail covering my face. My finger inched its way under the floppy skin of his belly to stroke the soft bump of the mole on my cheek, and the light beyond Monty's fur flickered out as my eyelids closed.

Two

'It's done in oil paint. I thought I might sell it,' Dad said, his hand gently stroking the thick swirls of the painting he had unearthed from one of the bedrooms, as if he could manipulate the long-hardened brush strokes. 'This is where we are now,' he said, pointing to a tiny line of black far up at the top left of the painting.

'What's that?'

'It's the roof of Braër House.'

'And are we in that house, too?'

'A version of us is,' he answered, putting me down on the floor.

'Is it the version where Mum still lives with us?'

Dad stared at the little roof in the painting.

'Is there a painting like this one in that Braër?' I continued, unperturbed.

'Yes,' he said finally.

'And which version of me is looking at it?'

'The version that doesn't ask so many questions.'

I wondered if there was a version of me that didn't ask questions at all. It must be a very boring one.

'How old is Braër?' I asked.

'Oh, hundreds of years old. Many, many families have lived here before us. Probably families with children at some point, too.'

I nodded, thinking of a doll I had found in a tattered cardboard box on our first day here. It was missing its hair, and its head and all of its limbs were lying in a mangled heap. I wondered who had taken it apart. They might be grown up now: a famous surgeon, or someone who solved murders by studying dismembered bodies.

Dad's stomach gave a sonorous rumble. 'It must be lunchtime,' he said, patting his belly affectionately and looking around for a clock.

'I'm not hungry,' I said, catching sight of Monty as he trotted past the door.

I left Dad studying the painting, and wandered into the dining room to look for the kitten. The day before I had found a really useful hiding place behind the dining table. The wall down near the floor was crumbly and appeared to be made of hair. Thinking of dead bodies and mummified cats, I had pulled at the hair, hoping for at least a fossilised baby. Instead, a great lump of wall came partly away. I had put my hand in the hole and felt around. The ground inside the wall felt all rough and cold. When I pulled my arm out, my hand and sleeve were black. I had since discovered an old bottle of nail varnish in the upstairs bathroom. It smelt of pear drops and made my eyes water. I was on the hunt for a good hiding place for it. Forgetting Monty, I got down on my knees and inspected the hole again. It was blacker than I remembered. If I screwed my eyes up I could almost see spiders in it, tumbling about, spinning their sticky webs.

Disappointed, I carried my little bottle outside instead. It had rained in the night, and everything sang with the drip of water. I looked out over the straggly remains of the ornamental yews bordering the herb garden, and felt especially small and alone in such a grand space. It was a huge house for just Dad and me, and I glanced back inside, wondering whether to call out to him, to ask if he'd like to come and play. But Dad, I knew, was busy, and so I stepped gingerly forward, into the unknown.

The unknown, it turned out, was wild and wet, and my trainers soon became woven in soaking grass stems. I swept through the garden, admiring my new green shoes, and stopped briefly to gaze into the moat.

I could sense the gargoyle watching me from the top of the fountain even before I looked at him. He was small and crouched like a monkey, perched in the middle of the moat on the fountain's broken remains. I studied the mischievous leer on his face, trying to decide if he was friend or foe.

When we had arrived, a month before, we had unloaded our suitcases into the garden and sat on the bank, dipping our weary feet in the cool of the moat.

'Don't ever go in the moat without me, Romilly. Do you understand?' Dad had said, his toes sifting the pondweed that coated the surface. 'Water can be very dangerous.'

I had nodded solemnly. But now, a month later, and much more worldly wise, I crouched down by the water's edge. The moat didn't look dangerous; there were no crashing waves or sucking whirlpools, only the quiet drip, drip of water leaking from the gargoyle's broken mouth. I had a sudden, strange feeling that Dad would know if I disobeyed him, that the peculiar creature could spring to life and whisper secrets to him. I turned away from the moat, picking my way instead over to the cart shed, where the remnants of roof tiles littered the ground.

I came to a stop at the water butt that stood under the guttering. Mouldy snails floated in the water, covered in a film of green slime and exuding a smell like rotten cucumbers. I held the nail varnish above the water, poised to drop it, mesmerised by the smooth khaki surface. But then a particularly bulbous snail floated past, putrid and engorged with slime, and I changed my mind and dropped down on my knees to look underneath instead.

Here, the grass had grown strong and lush from the constant drip of fetid water, and I crouched down and placed the little bottle there, plaiting the blades over it to hide it completely. I sat back on my haunches and studied the effect.

'What are you doing?'

At first I couldn't locate the voice. For a moment I thought it might be the buddleia tree that covered half the cart shed, its branches gesticulating gently in the breeze. I stood up.

'Who's there?'

'What were you doing?' The voice was more insistent now. It was definitely coming from the buddleia. I looked carefully between the branches. A mop of tawny hair and two eyes were peeping over the wall behind the tree. I flushed.

'Nothing.'

'Didn't look like nothing.'

'It was nothing to do with you.'

'Didn't say it was. It looked like fun, that's all.' The eyes and hair disappeared. I waited for them to reappear, but they didn't. Worried I'd upset this new-found being, I ran to the gate to get a better look.

'Hello?' I asked desperately, peering through the wooden slats. The mop of hair appeared, this time attached to a muddy T-shirt and shorts, and two stumpy legs.

'You look like an animal at the zoo,' it said, 'can I feed you?'

'You don't know what I eat.'

The stranger put a hand in a pocket and pulled out a worm. It dangled there, trying to turn up towards the sky. 'These?'

I backed away. The stranger grinned, throwing the worm on the ground.

'Want to play?'

My stomach contracted. I took in the muddy clothes and a nasty-looking graze to the cheek.

'Yeah,' I whispered in awe.

Stacey was a girl. I hadn't been sure at first. Her hair was short and messy. It hung down at the front like two curtains over her eyes. '*His* eyes,' I whispered, thinking she might have lied and she really was a boy. I wondered how I could check. She had very straight teeth and marks on her cheeks that could be freckles like mine, but were more likely dirt.

We were walking down an overgrown path that Stacey said led to a river. I had never been this way before. I thought back to the water butt and the nail varnish hidden underneath it. I wondered if Stacey had seen me hide it. I opened my mouth to confide, but stopped myself. Perhaps I should wait a while: I would tell her if we were still friends tomorrow.

'Here, want one?' Stacey said, offering me a sweet from a little foil packet.

'Thanks.' I popped it in my mouth, and my lips crinkled at the perfumed taste. I shivered and swallowed quickly, picking the remains out of my teeth.

Stacey was beating the nettles down on either side of the path with a stick. She stopped abruptly and pointed to a giant stinger on our left.

'I dare you to pick it,' she said.

'No.'

'Go on.'

'No.' I twisted my fingers into the hem of my jumper. I didn't like this game. It felt dangerous.

'Fine. I will.' And she bent forward and picked it.

'Didn't that hurt?' I said, my fingers contracting in empathy. She dropped the nettle and looked at me sympathetically.

'Watch what I do,' she said, a smile playing around the corners of her mouth. She moved her hand towards another nettle, and just as she got to it, she placed her thumb and index finger on the underside of the two lowest leaves. Pushing up, she clamped the leaves to the stalk and pulled. The whole nettle uprooted itself and hung from her fingers.

'Ha!' she cried, swinging the plant to and fro and looking at my uncomprehending face. 'The underside doesn't have prickles. Here.' She proffered the nettle to me. I took a step back. 'Fine. Come on, let's go.' Dropping the nettle, she pranced away.

I watched her running, a flush of admiration crossing my face. Setting off after her, I mounted some concrete steps that led to the river.

At the top I stopped. Stacey was already at the bottom, making her way toward the water's edge. I turned and looked back at Braër. I had never been out of the garden before. Not without Dad. My hand went to the mole on my cheek, stroking it distractedly.

'Stacey!'

She turned and raised her eyebrows. Her upturned nose was pink.

'I don't think I'm allowed to go any further.' As I said the words, I felt shame in my tummy. It made me want to go to the loo.

'Well, *I'm* going to look for buried treasure under the bridge.' And with that she turned and skipped towards the water.

I took a deep breath and gripped the railing. Slowly, step by step, I started to descend the concrete steps. Every second I expected Dad to come running up behind me, asking me what on earth I thought I was doing, but he didn't. Letting go of the rail, I ran down the remaining steps and joined Stacey at the water's edge.

She was staring into the grey depths below. The heat of a late spring had dried the banks, and the water had slunk back to reveal foul-smelling mud on either side. We made our way to the bridge, and

Stacey started climbing down the bank, gripping handfuls of marram grass as she went. I looked at my shoes. They were my favourites: plastic trainers with planets dotted all over them. I took a deep breath and followed her.

Stacey was already under the bridge when I reached the muddy bottom. I had to duck to join her in the shadows. A thrill rushed through me as I straightened up under the planks of wood. The river made a roaring sound here as it channelled under the bridge. It looked a lot more powerful close up.

My trainers were sinking into the mud. Every few seconds I had to pull my feet out. The mud made a sucking sound, and a great gassy waft hit me in the face. The planks of wood that made up the bridge above us echoed dully as someone walked across them. Grains of dust fell down onto us.

Stacey was scanning the ground, her eyes bright, her hair tucked behind her ears. Then, she dropped down, her fingers slipping into the mud and withdrawing just as quickly.

When she straightened up, there was a small grey pebble in her hand. The excitement I had felt when she first dived in died at the sight of it.

'It's a stone.' I couldn't keep the disappointment out of my voice. Stacey glanced at me, her eyes glinting in the dark shadows, but kept silent. Pocketing the stone, she continued to look at the ground.

I pulled my feet out of the mud with a slurping sound, and, ducking out from under the bridge, made my way up the bank, wiping dust from my face and clinging to the marram grass to help me up.

When I was at the top I sat down to wait for Stacey. I looked about for the person who had walked across the bridge, but the land was flat and empty as far as I could see.

'Stacey,' I called nervously. Her earthy face appeared below me. One strand of hair was slicked with mud.

'What?' she asked, tucking the muddy lock of hair behind her ear and sniffing noisily.

'That person that walked over the bridge just now. There's no one out here.'

Stacey grinned. She climbed out and joined me on the bank, wiping her shoes on the grass to remove the clumps of mud. 'Happens a lot round here. Some say there's a man lurks near the river, waiting for little girls to kidnap.' She put her hand in her pocket and pulled out the pebble. 'Here,' she said, handing it to me.

I took it. It was lighter than I thought it was going to be. The surface was smooth and greasy. I rubbed it between my hands. It began to crumble. Stacey leant toward me.

'I wonder who dropped it?' she whispered. I could feel the ends of her hair tickling my ear. I rubbed harder at the pebble. It started to break into pieces, disintegrating beneath my fingers. That same putrid vegetable smell hit my nose. It was made of mud, but there was something hard beneath. My tummy twitched as a flat surface met my thumb. A little brooch, its pin long since lost, fell onto my lap, brown and rusty, but solid and round.

'Buried treasure,' Stacey said.

'It's like magic,' I said, 'ghost magic.'

Stacey nodded, her face serious, staring out at the flat fields that surrounded us.

'You need to see the shrieking pits. *That's* proper ghost magic.' She leant back on her elbows and raised her eyebrows, waiting for my reply, knowing it was coming.

'What's the shrieking pits?' I asked obediently in a whisper. The grey sky dropped lower on the landscape as if it were listening too.

She leant in to me and looked me in the eyes. I noticed her left eye had a dark grey slash across its green iris. 'No one knows why they're there. Some say they're millions of years old, ancient holes that have filled up with rainwater. Others say they were dug a hundred years ago: people quarrying for rocks and flint. But sometimes, weird noises come from them. Screams and cries for help. And people see things when they're near them.'

'Things?' I murmured, almost not wanting to hear her answer. I was beginning to regret my trip to the river.

'People. Acting weird. Ladies dressed in old-fashioned clothes.'

'Have you seen them?' I held my breath, my body stiff, waiting for her answer.

'Nah. I don't even know where they are. We should go looking sometime.'

I scratched at the brooch in my fingers, relieved. Flakes of metallic mud fell away. It was pretty, about the size of a pound coin, with a frilly edge and lots of little decorative holes dotted about it, like a doily.

'I think I'm going to like living here,' I said.

'Where did you live before?'

'Dad and me moved around a lot. Before we moved to Braër we were staying in a B and B. And we camped, too.' I had a vague memory of a caravan and strange-smelling tea. 'Before all that we used to live with my mum in London.' I scratched my finger into the muddy ground. 'But she went away.'

'It must be weird, not living with your mum anymore.'

I hadn't thought about it before. I rarely thought about Mum. It was years since I last saw her, she was so far back in my past that weeks could go by without me remembering her at all. Now with Stacey's question, a guilty feeling opened up inside my chest.

'Why did she go away?' Stacey said.

'I don't know.' I put my eye to the holes in the brooch. The world was fragmented, like looking through a thousand keyholes, and I could only see a tiny part of everything so that I couldn't work out what it was I was looking at.

'My dad went away,' said Stacey, 'I don't see him often, maybe five times since I was a baby.'

'That must be strange.' I couldn't imagine not having a dad.

'It's OK. I sort of do have a dad sometimes. It depends who Mum brings home. Sometimes, if I don't want to go home, I go to my gran's instead, and sometimes I just stay out here.' She gestured to the flat fields that surrounded us.

'What, even at night?'

Stacey shrugged. 'Sometimes. Do you still see your mum?'

I shook my head. I tried to picture what she looked like, but all I could see when I screwed my eyes up was a pair of smooth, delicate hands holding onto mine, sharp red nails gripping my skin painfully, a glittering diamond ring crackling with light.

'I haven't seen her since we left London,' I said, 'and that was when I was four.'

'Is she still in London?'

'I'm not sure.' I tried to remember if Dad had ever told me. 'I think she might have left to join the circus,' I said, thinking about a painting Dad was working on at the moment: sequins and colourful feathers and soft, wavy chestnut hair. I had glimpsed it earlier, walking past Dad's study, but he had kicked the door shut before I could see anything more.

'Cool,' said Stacey, 'imagine being with lions and elephants every day.' She pulled at the marram grass. 'I'd love to go to the circus,' she said wistfully, 'but Mum never goes anywhere. She just sits at home, watching TV.'

'Where do you live?'

'On the other side of the village. You know the long road that leads out towards town?'

I nodded, remembering an ugly line of boxy houses we'd driven past when we moved here.

'I live over that way in a little red-brick house.'

It sounded like something out of a fairy tale. I imagined her and her mother, welcoming different dads inside, plying them with mugs of tea and cuddles.

'What was your house in London like?' she said. 'Was it big and spooky, like Braër?'

'I don't know.'

'You don't know much, do you?'

'It must have been quite big, because there were more people living in it.' I had a hazy memory of closing my bedroom door so that I could sit still and quiet and alone in the small space. It was a busy house where I never had a moment to myself. There was always raucous laughter, occasional yelling. Sometimes there were smacks followed by kisses to take the pain away. 'It was very different to Braër,' I said.

Stacey got up from the bank, brushing the dirt from her shorts. I started to hand the brooch to her.

'No, you keep it, it'll bring you luck,' she said. 'People lose things all the time, make sure you don't lose it.' She smiled. She had a pretty smile. It transformed her face.

'You look like a girl now,' I said.

She laughed. 'That's why I don't smile very often. I wish I was a boy sometimes.'

'Why?'

She kicked at the grass. 'I don't know. Boys have it easy. They fight better.'

I glanced at the sky. Behind the low clouds the sun had begun to peer out. We were both squinting in the hazy light.

'I'd better go home,' Stacey said with a sigh. 'Can we play again?' I nodded, squeezing the brooch in my hand.

'Right ho. See you, wouldn't want to be you!' She grinned at me, and then she was off, running across the grass.

I watched her go, jealous of the speed at which she could run, then looked at the watch on my wrist and wished it was more than a plastic toy. Dad would be frantic. I started on my way home, the mud on my trainers weighing me down like an astronaut with moonboots.

Three

I wanted to see Stacey again, but every time I thought about climbing the gate and going looking for her, I felt a sick feeling clenching in the pit of my stomach. Dad hadn't mentioned my mud-encrusted trainers, but they appeared on the washing line the next day, clean and sopping, with muddy drips leaking from the ends of the laces. They took three whole days to dry.

It rained every day for the next week, and I spent my days inside, not daring to venture away from Braër on my own without Stacey.

But being inside meant I was in Dad's line of sight more often. He followed me from room to room, drawing pad in hand, commanding me to stop while he quickly sketched in an outline. On a really wet Wednesday, when the rain was so torrential that the sound drummed into my skull, he managed to corner me, a comb replacing the usual pencil in his hand.

'You really can't carry on like this, Romilly. Your hair is so knotted it's actually growing upwards.' He pushed me onto a stool in the bathroom and set to with the comb, ignoring my gasps and winces as he attempted to tease out the knots.

'Ow, Dad.'

'I'm sorry, but we should never have let it get this bad. It's like candyfloss, for goodness' sake.' He stopped, staring at my hair in the mirror. 'There's nothing for it,' he said at last, 'I'm going to have to get the scissors.' He abandoned the comb, its teeth chewing at my hair, and went marching off.

'No, Dad!'

'I'm not going to cut it all off, I just need to get rid of a tangle or two, that's all.'

I looked in the mirror. He was right: I could see thick, matted areas that looked almost solid. There was a raven's feather hanging from the back that I had stuck in there days ago. I tried to imagine myself with short hair. I thought about Stacey. She had short hair. It suited her.

When Dad came back, I said, 'Does having short hair mean you turn into a boy?'

'Not in the least.'

'You can cut it off then. But keep the feather in it. I like it.'

When Dad let me go, my new haircut rustling around my ears, I roamed the house, turning my head this way and that, liking the way the air breathed on my exposed neck.

It was still raining outside, and I decided I would spend my time indoors wisely. Talking to Stacey at the bridge had brought to mind my mother, so I set out to discover as much as I could about her.

All of Braër's rooms were accessible to me except one: Dad's study, which was locked whenever he wasn't inside. But Dad wasn't very good at security, and he always hung the key on the wall next to the study door. Shaking my head at his lack of ingenuity, I unlocked the door and slipped inside.

This was his painting room. It was a small, square space that hung out over the moat at one end of the house. The walls were dark with mould where the damp had crept in, but the view made up for it: a huge picture window that looked out from the north end of the house towards a meandering stream. Dad had told me there was a watercress bed somewhere beyond the little bridge in the distance, and every time I ventured out that way, I picked a leaf from a different plant and tasted it, hoping for the peppery bite on my tongue.

I looked around the room, searching for vestiges of Mum that Dad might have brought with him: a pair of high-heeled shoes tucked away in a corner, or a pretty scarf hanging from a hook. There *was* a pair of shoes, half hidden under the cupboard near the window, but they were much too small to be my mother's – something a little girl would wear, with large red bows at the toe. I picked them up and examined them, wondering if they had belonged to the same girl who owned the baby doll and the parasol. I turned to Dad's desk, hoping for a letter from my mum, or else a paper knife, engraved 'to darling Tobias, from your loving Meg'.

Instead, the desk was scattered with half-squeezed tubes of paint. A cloudy jar of water stood in one corner, its contents silty and grey like the moat outside. The painting I had glimpsed before was still there: a woman in a sequined leotard with candyfloss pink feathers in her hair. She was riding an animal in the circus ring, but the rest of the painting hadn't been completed, and it was impossible to tell what animal it was going to be. I hoped it would be a dragon, or else a polar bear. Something unusual.

Scattered around the desk were close-up sketches of the same woman's face. They were simple line drawings, but her eyes burrowed into me with a deep wisdom. I gazed back, transfixed. Was this my mother?

'Romilly, what are you doing in here?' Dad's voice, usually so loud and booming, was somehow more menacing in its quietness.

I turned around. He was standing in the doorway. 'Looking for Mum,' I said.

'Your mother doesn't live here.'

'I know. I just wanted to remember her a bit. To find something of hers.'

Dad sighed. 'Well, you won't find anything in here. Out, please.'

I wavered, summoning the courage to ask Dad about the picture, feeling as if a spell had been cast between me and the painted lady. I opened my mouth. 'Is she my—'

'Perhaps I can write to your mother,' Dad interrupted, cutting me off before I could finish, 'ask her to send you something. How about that? You're old enough now to know a bit more about her.'

I nodded, taking one last, long look at the pictures. Was it my imagination, or had the woman's mouth turned up at the corners? Were her eyes more wrinkled, as if she were smiling, just for me?

Dad cleared his throat and stepped aside, making room in the doorway, and I tiptoed out.

'Please don't come in here again,' he said, pulling the door closed and locking it. This time he didn't hang the key on the wall.

As the summer wore on, I hung around near where I had first seen Stacey, hoping she would turn up again, pretending to catch butterflies in my net and keeping an eye out for her watchful gaze between the buddleia's branches.

On a hot, sticky night in July I woke up, pulled from a dream where Stacey and I were wading through a shrieking pit, the echo of a hushed voice still whispering in my ears.

'Stacey?' I said, thinking she might have somehow managed to climb in through my bedroom window. I looked around my room. Moonlight filtered through the thin curtain and lay in bluish stripes across the floor. There was nobody there, and yet the whispering continued, words that I couldn't quite grasp, as if they were speaking another language. I knew that I should be frightened, but the sound was comforting, like little waves lapping at a shore.

I got up and tiptoed to the window, pushing the curtain aside and unlatching it. Leaning out, I could just make out the dark surface of the moat below me, and in the middle, the gargoyle, crouched low over the water. The voice intensified, whispering urgently, and for a chilling moment I thought I saw the gargoyle twist and look up at me, its mouth whispering. I slammed the window shut and ran to my bed, pulling the covers over my head.

The voice died away, and I lay, holding my breath, listening extra hard, but all I could hear were Monty's cat snores.

I thought about the shrieking pits that Stacey was so excited to find. Had the voice come from there, drifting across the fields? I wondered if she had found one yet; if she would tell me about it in a spooky voice next time we met. I reached out from under the duvet, my fingers closing over the little brooch she had given me. I pulled it into the warmth of the covers and held it tightly in my hand, thinking about Stacey, conjuring her up in my mind.

'Stacey, Stacey, come back to me,' I chanted under my breath, clutching the brooch so hard it hurt, my eyes squeezed shut. When I opened them, I half expected her to be lying next to me under the duvet, giggling at my silliness, but of course she wasn't, and I felt embarrassed that I had even tried.

I put the brooch on my bedside table and tried to get to sleep. I would just have to wait until I started my new school, when the autumn term began in a few weeks. The thought made my tummy flip with nerves. But Stacey will be there, I told myself sternly. She will take me by the hand and show me around, calming my fears and introducing me to all her friends. And I'll be able to see her every day.

The chanting didn't bring Stacey back to me, but it did bring another kind of magic.

The circus came to town.

It was to be a treat for my ninth birthday. I stood in the shade of the weeping willow waiting for Dad, and running my hands over the tiny squares of my best dress, a pink gingham one with an elasticated bodice that dug painfully into my armpits. From here I could just make out the moat, and the gargoyle crouched over it.

Earlier in the day, after a birthday breakfast of crumpets and smoked salmon, Dad had given me a painting. It was a portrait of me, standing in my bedroom, with Monty in my arms. Dad hung it on the wall near my bed, and told me to stand beneath it.

'Now, look up at the picture,' he said.

I looked up. The version of me in the picture was standing in exactly the same spot in my bedroom, holding a cat that looked just like Monty, and *she* was turning and looking up at a picture on *her* wall, of a girl standing in a bedroom, holding a cat. I screamed with delight, and Monty scrabbled away from me in fright. I reached up and took the picture down, putting my nose to it, examining every detail. The little version of me was looking up at a minute painting, no bigger than a drawing pin above her head. I got lost staring at it, trying to make my eyes go back and back, wondering how many versions of me Dad had painted, how strong the magnifying glass must have been for him to paint so small. 'Watch out, Roe, you'll go cross-eyed,' Dad had laughed.

'Where are my keys?' His frustrated voice filtered out now from somewhere in the depths of the house. I made myself blend into the willow's spidery branches. He had lost his keys three times this week, and made me search for them every time. This time he could do it on his own.

I had wanted Stacey to come to the circus too, and I had walked to the other end of the village to find her little red-brick house and ask her. But when I got to her road, I was confronted by a long line of ugly houses that all looked the same, the front gardens divided up with nasty-looking wire fencing. I thought about asking someone where she lived, but the only person within sight was a man with no hair sitting on a low wall, smoking a cigarette. An empty pop bottle rattled along the road, and I turned and walked home instead.

I told Dad I wanted to take Stacey to the circus, but he said since we didn't know where she lived, we had no way of asking her. Instead I had asked if Monty could come, worried he would miss us. On the odd occasion that we had gone out before, we had come back to a kitten with no voice from mewing so loudly. But Dad wasn't sure cats were allowed at the circus, and anyway he said Monty needed to learn to be on his own. He was halfway to being fully grown now, and would no longer fit on my head as a turban, but he curled snugly round my shoulders instead.

Eventually, Dad shouted that he'd found his keys and appeared at the back door, a brown parcel in his hands.

'What's that?'

'It's for you. The postman's just dropped it off.'

I sat under the willow and pulled at the string and sticky tape. Out fell a denim pinafore dress with large red plastic buttons like round flying saucers.

'Who's it from?' Dad said, leaning over and plucking out the card that came with it.

I watched as he read it, his eyebrows growing closer together the further he got.

'Who is it?' My voice was muffled as I pulled off my gingham dress, dropping it onto the floor, and stepped into my new pinafore.

'It's from your mother. I must say, I didn't expect her to actually send anything.'

'It is?' I'd never had a present from her before. I looked down at the dress with renewed love, smoothing the denim. It was very grown up. I wondered if my mum had one the same.

'You don't have to wear it,' Dad said, starting towards the car, 'the gingham one's perfectly respectable.'

'But I want to. Dad, where is Mum? Why doesn't she live with us anymore?'

Dad was halfway to the car now. 'I keep telling you,' he called back over his shoulder, 'she had to go away, she wasn't well.'

'Will she come back soon?' I asked, but he was already heaving his huge bulk into the little car. Perhaps Mum would appear at the circus as a surprise, popping up from the middle of a giant birthday cake, or exploding out of a cannon into the audience. I smoothed down my hair with spitty fingers: I wanted to look my best, just in case.

The Circus — so important it required capital letters — was on top of a hill. We parked at the bottom, and as we made our way up the soft grass, a warm waft of animal smells filtered down to us with a hint of candyfloss. Dad took a deep breath in through his nose and pummelled his chest.

'How could you capture that in a painting?' he asked me. I ignored him.

Inside the circus tent it was dark and hot. My eyes took a while to adjust and I sought out Dad's hand, dry and warm round my own. We took our seats halfway up a flimsy stairway. Dad's seat creaked, while mine merely sighed. I couldn't see much over the heads in front of me.

A man in a black-and-red suit made his way over to us, whispering into Dad's ear. I peered round Dad to look at him. He had a tall top hat, and long brown hair flowing down to his shoulders: the ringmaster. As he was talking to Dad, he looked at me and smiled, his mouth glinting dangerously. I leant back in my seat, reaching for a hand to grab hold of, but instead I caught hold of the arm of a woman I didn't know who was sitting next to me. She frowned, removing her sleeve from my grip.

Dad was getting to his feet. He indicated with a nod that we should follow the man in red. We navigated our way back along the row, Dad's gruff voice apologising as person after person had to stand to let us out. The man in red-and-black took us to some seats right at the edge of the ring. These ones didn't creak as we sat down. From here I could see everything. I craned my head back to look at the very top of the tent.

'This is more like it!' Dad whispered as he whisked a toffee apple from a tray held by a grinning clown.

I reached over to the tray and stroked the apples' shiny surfaces, trying to decide which one had the thickest toffee. Suddenly, a stream of water hit me right between the eyes. I looked up, half blinded, to see the clown and my father laughing at me, a dripping plastic flower suspended from the front of the clown's costume.

'Serves you right for putting your sticky mitts all over them,' Dad said, handing me a handkerchief to mop myself up with. I narrowed my eyes angrily at the retreating clown. He was still smiling, but I couldn't tell if it was a real smile, or just one painted on over his sad, thin mouth.

Dad passed me his toffee apple instead, and I blinked the last of the water from my eyes as the lights went down.

A single spotlight illuminated a small circle in the centre of the ring. The ringmaster was there, appearing so fast it was as if he had teleported from right next to us. He opened his mouth as if to speak, but in a flash of fireworks, he disappeared again, and in his place was a woman dressed in glittering pink. The audience oohed and clapped, and the woman bowed, her feather headdress undulating.

I passed the half-eaten toffee apple back to Dad, and he took a bite, the toffee shell shattering with a satisfying crack.

'Isn't she beautiful?' he said, winking, and I nodded.

We made our way out through the milling crowd. Night had begun to fall, and the air had lost its warmth. Dad wrapped his huge jumper round my shoulders. We stopped just outside the tent and looked out from the top of the hill. From here, Suffolk lay flat all around us, as if we were on the only hill in the world. The first lights of houses and streets could be seen against the yellow-blue sky. I stood, a little way away from Dad, on the edge of the hill, looking up at the countless stars. A warm hand slipped into mine, and I jumped at the touch, but when I looked there was no one there. I ran to Dad and hid my face against him, feeling his arms wrap tight around me, and peered back anxiously to check for ghosts.

A horse from the show pranced past us, coming to a stop nearby, its huge, feathery headdress shimmering as it tossed its head. The woman leading it stopped too. It was the woman in pink I had seen in the ring. Close up, she was a strange, glittery creature, but there was something familiar about her. A glimmer of sequined leotard peeped out from beneath a tan belted coat, and I realised that this was the lady in the picture Dad was painting at home. She had the same chestnut hair, set in waves, and the same pink feathery headdress.

'Tobias,' she said, then she looked down at me and smiled, a knowing, thoughtful smile. I retreated further into Dad's jumper.

'Lidiya,' Dad clasped her hand in his, 'thank you for getting us such wonderful seats.' His voice was lighter than I had heard it before, as if the toffee apple had varnished his throat on the way down. They were still touching hands.

'Don't be silly, Tobias. Anything for your pretty girl.' She pronounced it 'preetty', and she crouched down and smiled at me again, the pink feathers on her head nodding at me like insect feelers. From here I could see a great gorge of white cleavage encased in pink sequins. She was like a butterfly that had settled just for a moment. I held my breath, careful not to blow her away. She studied me, her head on one side, then reached up and plucked a feather from her headdress.

'Here,' she said, offering it to me, 'a pretty feather for Tobias's pretty girl.' Her voice wasn't the hushed Suffolk sound that I had heard a lot of recently. Maybe she was Scottish. Or Irish. I took the feather and whispered my thanks.

Later that night I climbed into my bed. Stacey's little brooch was on my bedside table, and I picked it up and put the feather in its place, running my finger round the brooch's rough edge. Dad climbed through my doorway and sat on the bed, watching me for a moment.

'Treasure?' he asked.

I nodded, and he smiled approvingly.

'What story shall I tell you tonight?'

'The one about The Circus.'

And he began. He wove our visit into a story of giant grey elephants and man-eating panthers. I could smell the sparklers, the toffee apples and the elephant poo, which is strange because we had only been at the circus a few hours ago, and I didn't remember any elephants when we went.

Warm arms wrapped themselves around me and lifted me down

into softness. Suddenly I was wide awake, remembering the way the gargoyle had whispered to me a few nights ago.

'Dad?' I said.

'Yes, Roe?'

'I'm scared.'

'Oh? What of?'

'The other night, the gargoyle in the moat spoke to me.'

'Oh really? And what did he have to say?'

'I don't know. It was in another language.'

It was funny how Dad's features sometimes looked a little gargoyle-like. I reached up and touched his cheek, trying to turn him human again. He got up and went over to the window, unlatching it and leaning out, just as I had done. When he came back, his eyes were hidden beneath his brows. 'Our minds perceive things differently at night,' he said. 'Even grown-ups get scared sometimes.'

'Really?'

He nodded. 'Oh yes.'

I yawned, sleepy again. 'Dad?' I said. 'Where did we live, before Braër?'

'We travelled around for a while, don't you remember? Lots of B and Bs and camping. A bit of sofa surfing. But before that, when your mum lived with us, we lived in London, you know that.'

'But why did we travel? Didn't we have a home?'

'No, I suppose not. I think I was trying to work out where I wanted us to be. Trying to find us just the right place, and I think I managed it, didn't I?' He looked round at the walls of my bedroom, nodding to himself.

I nodded back, not yet sure if I liked Braër as much as Dad did. 'What was it like,' I said, picking up the feather and stifling a yawn, 'our house in London with Mum?'

34

'It was a small flat. No room for thinking, or painting. Too many people, not enough space.'

'Why can't I remember it?'

'You were only four when we left. That's half of your life ago.'

'Oh.' But sometimes I thought I did remember it. Sometimes, just as I was drifting off into sleep, I started awake, an image hanging in my mind as clear as if it were suspended in the air in front of my face: a little toy hare, silvery and staring, perched on a shelf high above me. Sometimes when this image came to me, I would feel a hand reaching out from my dreams, patting me affectionately on the arm.

I was suddenly nervous about falling asleep. I grabbed Dad's hand, rough and hairy. 'Dad?'

'Yes, Romilly?' He looked down at his watch, clicking his tongue impatiently.

'Have I been to the circus before?' Memories of the flat were mixing with other memories now. A caravan like the ones I spotted behind the circus tent, a small brown dog, a lady covered in bells…

'Well, yes. When we were travelling we followed the circus around for a while. I quite liked their nomadic life. But it's not the right life for a child: your education suffered.' He got up and stretched, going to the window again to check the latch.

'Dad?'

'Yes, Romilly?' He was exasperated now, I could tell from the rasp of his voice.

'Is that lady at the circus my mum?'

There was silence as Dad padded back to the bed and fiddled with the chain on the bedside lamp. The light went out, and the sky appeared in a rectangle of window, the strawberry moon huge and red.

'No, Romilly,' he said at last.

Stars in their millions fizzed in the blackness of the window, and Monty curled himself around my hands.

'Who is she?' I asked, tracing the soft edge of the feather over my cheek, and wondering if it felt like a mother's loving fingers, but there was no answer. I opened my eyes, searching for his huge shadowy bulk in the dark room, but he was already gone.

Four

I awoke the next morning to the screech of metal on metal, and for an instant I thought it was the gargoyle, cut loose from his fountain, climbing the guttering to rap at my window.

It was a light, bright morning, and I climbed out of bed and peeped outside. I had been half right: Dad was standing submerged in the moat below, a pair of pliers in his hands, attempting to unscrew the bolts that held the fountain in place. The sound it made set my teeth on edge, and I watched his red face, the thick cords of muscle bunching in his neck as he worked.

As the last bolt loosened, he lifted the pliers high above his head and I winced as he brought them down on the gargoyle. The sound rang out across the garden. The fountain began to tilt, swinging down towards the water.

I opened the window, scrambling onto the sill to lean out. 'What are you doing?' I shouted.

Dad looked up, and his eyes widened. 'Get back, Romilly, you might fall!'

I leant back, still looking out.

'It was giving me nightmares too,' he said more quietly, wiping a slick of mud from his brow. He climbed awkwardly out of the moat, the dented remains of the pliers hanging from his hand, as the fountain slowly sank beneath the water.

I spent the morning re-enacting the circus, trying to tame Monty with a whip I had fashioned out of a long strip of willow, but he just looked at me warily and skittered off, chasing the seed heads from a dandelion clock. I shot occasional glances at the place where the gargoyle had been, imagining him rising up out of the moat to haunt me, but there was only calm, still water there now.

In the afternoon, Dad announced that I couldn't run a circus without making toffee apples, and so we shut ourselves in the kitchen, the room filled with the most glorious smell of caramel. In the saucepan, the boiling liquid was hypnotic, popping gloopily like lava in a volcano.

'I think it's ready,' Dad said, peering into the pan, 'grab an apple.'

Obediently, I picked up one of the many apples sitting ready on the counter, a lolly stick implanted vertically into its heart.

'Dip it, girl! Dip like you've never dipped before!'

I lowered the apple into the saucepan, aware of the sugary steam coating the little hairs on my hand, and skimmed it in the golden liquid before pulling it out, round and fat and coated in a layer of glossy mahogany.

We repeated the process with the remainder of the apples, setting them to cool on the side, the molten toffee pooling at their bases. Dad helped me down off the stool, his palms just as sticky as mine.

'Can we eat them now?'

'No, they need to cool first. I tell you what, I have something to show you while we wait.'

I followed him to his study. I hadn't been in there since I had gone looking for evidence of my mum weeks ago. It was always locked now. Dad magicked the key from a trouser pocket, and I waited in the hall while he unlocked the door with a fumble and a click.

'I found this the other day in the little attic space just off your bedroom. I thought you might like to meet her.'

'Her?' I peeped round Dad, intrigued.

His desk was unusually tidy. There were no paints or brushes, and no picture of the circus lady like last time. But what was there was so interesting, the thought of paintings went completely from my mind.

'A parrot!' I said, for there on the desk, staring at me beneath a dusty glass dome, was a green parrot with a big black beak and round yellow eyes.

'She's rather spectacular, isn't she?' Dad ruffled my hair.

'Can I keep her?'

'I don't know, Roe, she's very old, and a bit flea-bitten. Look:' He pointed to the bottom of the jar, where a number of dead insects lay, their legs in the air.

'Where's she from?'

'I told you, the attic.'

'No, I mean before. When she was alive.'

'Well,' Dad settled into the seat behind his desk, looking hard at the bird, 'sometimes they're kept as pets, but originally she would have come from a country far away. Somewhere warm and wet and filled with the raucous chitter of birdsong. In fact—' he shifted in his seat, getting comfortable, and I perched on the edge of his desk, knowing a story was coming, and relishing the thought.

'In fact, many years ago, this particular parrot flew over the Amazonian rainforest, calling out her strange song, but none of the other birds understood her. So one day, as the monkeys chattered and the crickets whirred and buzzed below, she took off from the fronds of a barrigona tree, and began the longest flight of her life.

'On the way she passed swallows and swifts, and even, once, a seven-tailed peacock from the Peruvian mountains.'

'A what?'

'They're very rare.'

'Oh.'

'And then, one warm, balmy English summer's day, she spied this house, and came down to land.

'Now, this was Braër House from a hundred years ago, and a different little girl lived here then. The parrot landed on the bridge, and the little girl said, "Oh, hello," and the parrot found she could understand her: the language she had been speaking all this time was English.'

'Did they have lots of adventures like me and Monty?'

'Well, they would have done, but just as they were beginning to be friends, a witch came to the village, looking for somewhere to stay. She knocked on the door of Braër House, and asked if she might have a bed for the night.

'The girl's father – who was a disagreeable sort – told her to leave. But on her way out, she saw the girl and the parrot. The witch was tired and hungry, and somewhat grumpy, and, feeling spiteful, she cast a spell over the two of them. When the daughter didn't come home for tea, the man went outside in search of her, and there on the grass was the parrot, dead and stuffed and perched in a glass bell jar.'

'No!'

'But that's not all. When he went back inside his house, he found his daughter in the little study at the end of the hall, also dead, also stuffed, in her own, life-sized bell jar, staring out at him, her little hands pressed against the curved glass.'

'But... but the witch wouldn't leave her like that!'

Dad lifted a finger to quieten me. 'Sometimes, the girl's father would come downstairs and the girl and the parrot had changed position.'

'No!'

'The parrot would be standing on one leg, or tucking its head under its wing. And the daughter, well, she was often sitting on the floor of the bell jar, her head in her hands, and once he found her on her knees, her hands pressed together in prayer.'

'What did he do?'

'He decided to open the bell jar, to release his daughter. He imagined that whatever magic was going on, it was contained within the glass, and once the glass was removed, she would resume her original form.

'But he was so desperate to free his daughter, he didn't consider what might go wrong. He tried to lift the heavy glass dome, but it was stuck tight to the base. His daughter was crouched at the bottom, frozen in a cowering posture, her hands above her head as if preparing for the disaster that was sure to come.

'Frustrated, the man found an axe and took it to the bell jar. As the metal bit into the glass, the jar crazed and cracked and began to shatter, falling over his daughter like rain, landing in her hair and slicing at her skin.'

I put my hand to my mouth in horror.

'But his daughter began to crumble too. She cracked like glass, collapsing into a million shards. The man bent over and picked up the largest piece he could find, a fragment of her eye, and he stuck it right in the centre of the fireplace in the drawing room so that she would watch over them always. And then he poured the rest of her away into the moat.'

I jumped down from the desk, pulling the parrot off and carrying it awkwardly into the drawing room. Dad jogged behind me, his arms outstretched in case I dropped it. The drawing room was a large space full of dusty old furniture. Ancient frayed rugs lay underneath spindly chairs with legs shaped like bamboo. There was a huge stone bowl protruding from the far wall that looked like it came out of a church. It had a spout in the shape of a raven's head, and I eyed it beadily as I came in, thinking how similar it was to the gargoyle in the moat.

The fireplace was a huge brick affair, the kind you could walk into and stare up into the blackened chimney above. Monty was sitting there now, transfixed by the echoing caw of the crows perched on Braër's roof. He stood up to greet us, his back end coated in soot.

True to Dad's word, stuck fast in the middle of the mantelpiece was a dark, shiny fragment that looked like flint. I put the parrot on the floor and reached up to touch it, but I was too small, and my fingers brushed the rough brickwork instead.

'What happened to the parrot after that?' I said to Dad.

'The man hid her in the attic because she reminded him of his lost daughter. And that's where she stayed until I dug her out, covered in cobwebs.'

'Have you ever seen her move?'

'Nobody sees her move, Romilly. They only notice it when she's changed position.'

I went over to the parrot again. She was sitting straight-backed and to attention, her head cocked slightly to one side as if she were listening.

'Come on,' said Dad, 'those toffee apples should be cool enough to eat now.'

I hefted the glass dome, my hands barely reaching round it, and carried it, panting to the kitchen table. Dad was levering the toffee apples off the tray with a knife.

'Dad, can I keep the parrot? Can she live in my room?'

He put down the knife and looked at me with a very serious expression. 'You'll need to look after her, she's very old,' he said. 'Here,' he handed me a toffee apple, and I licked it, patting the parrot's glass dome with the flat of my hand as if I were patting a dog.

Dad put his hand on top of mine on the dome, his fingers flexing slightly the way they did when he laid his hand on my head to say goodnight. I licked my toffee apple. It didn't taste like the ones at the circus. It had a slightly burnt flavour, mixed with a smoky smell that felt wrong with all of that sugar.

'What was she called?' I asked between licks.

'Who?'

'The girl who died?'

Dad's hand stopped flexing. 'I don't know,' he said at last.

'And the parrot? Does she have a name?'

'I think it's engraved right here.' He bent and looked at the little curved plaque at the jar's base.

'What does it say?'

'She's called Jasmine.'

I studied Jasmine in her curved glass aviary. She was looking back at me in the same way that the eyes of people in portraits follow you around the room.

I took a bite of the toffee apple, and a sharp pain sent shivers up into the roof of my mouth. 'Ow!'

'What is it?'

Something foreign and sharp was rolling around my mouth, knocking against my teeth. I put my finger in and scooped it out.

A large tooth lay in my palm. On one side was a big, brown hole. The place where it had been in the back of my mouth sang with pain.

Five

After the first day at my new school, I ran down to the meadow to find Dad. The huge beech tree in the garden was beginning to shed its leaves, and they were scattered across the grass like a discarded silk petticoat. I laughed at the tree's nakedness, shaking off the cardigan from my new uniform. The fallen leaves flew up all around me in a cloud of gold, and I pretended I was commanding them, waving my hands about my head like a witch casting a spell.

Dad was sitting on an upended wheelbarrow in the meadow, his sketchbook in hand, his great bushy eyebrows furrowed in concentration. His face was still nut brown from the summer, and I could see little stripes of white all over his forehead where the skin between his wrinkles remained untanned. He looked like a tiger.

I came to a stop near Dad, and he snapped his sketchbook shut as soon as he saw me.

'Young Romilly!' he roared, and I jumped, wondering if he was losing his hearing.

I offered him a bit of the tangerine I had saved from my school dinner, and which tasted of wet toilet paper, and he took it gratefully, munching it, pips and all, the bristles around his mouth frothing juice.

'Rumour has it that this little meadow was an overflow for the churchyard.' He nodded towards the church's high tower, peeping over the hedge.

I looked around the meadow. It was a triangular field bordered on all sides by high yew hedges. 'But there's no gravestones,' I said, feeling a little disappointed. It would be nice to find some human bones.

'Well, that's what rumours are. No one knows if they're the truth.'

I scanned the field again. There was nothing exciting here, unless you counted a huge heap of metal rods and discs piled up by the hedge that hadn't been there the day before.

'Do I have to go to school?' I asked, changing the subject and biting hard on a piece of tangerine. Stacey had not been in my new class. At break time I had searched the playground, but it was only a small school and none of the children milling around on the tarmac were her.

Dad placed the sketchbook on the floor. 'School is important, Romilly,' he said with a sigh, 'and besides, people would berate me for taking you out.' He got up from the wheelbarrow and stretched, his joints cracking noisily. 'Even if I was able to just whisk you out, I really can't have you at home right now. My mind is bursting with ideas on how to make money out of this old place, and you'd be too much of a distraction.'

I looked down, digging my toe into the mound of grass beneath my feet. When I looked up, he had crouched down in front of me so that his eyes were level with mine.

'Just because I can't give you what you want, doesn't mean I don't love you.' His eyes were shiny, as if he had been caught unexpectedly in a ferocious gale.

I nodded.

'And I'm sorry if I'm not always here for you at the moment. It's just, I have so many things to think about right now. Tell you what, when everything in here has calmed down somewhat,' he indicated his head, and I imagined cogs whirring and little hammers tapping,

'I'll be able to focus much more on you, and then we can formulate a plan. Deal?'

'OK,' I said, swallowing my tangerine wedge painfully. 'What are you doing down here, anyway?'

'Attempting to pay the mortgage,' he replied with a chuckle, glancing over at the rods and pipes in the corner.

I looked around, but I couldn't see any money anywhere.

'Is it a project?' I said, running my eyes over the metal rods. We had started a project at school that day, making buildings out of spaghetti and balls of plasticine. Maybe Dad was going to do the same on a bigger scale.

'I suppose it is. But it's stuck right here.' He grabbed forcefully at the top of his forehead, as if he could pull the project right out. He smiled and turned back to his sketchbook, becoming still as a statue as if a light had gone out in him. I stepped forward and waved a hand in front of his face, but his batteries were well and truly dead, and I left him to it, walking back up to the house, in search of something living.

Stacey was sitting on the gate, letting it swing back and forth beneath her. My stomach flipped with joy at seeing her.

'You've had a haircut,' she said. She had a packet of crisps in her hand, and she offered me one from the crackling bag. It tasted far more satisfying than the pithy, leftover taste of tangerine in my mouth.

'Stacey, why don't you—' I started.

But, 'Shh, I want to show you something,' she said, wiping salty potato crumbs from her lips. Jumping down from the last bar of the gate, she took off, not looking back to see if I was following.

She led me through the village to a paddock behind a farmhouse. I hurried after her, intent on asking her about school, but when she stopped, the question fell from my lips. A donkey stood at the fence staring at nothing, its ribs clearly visible under its shaggy coat.

'It's going to die this afternoon,' Stacey said, watching me for a reaction. 'I heard the farmer. They're going to put it down.'

'Why?' I stepped closer to the animal. Its ears twitched, but it continued to stare into nothing.

Stacey shrugged. 'It's old.'

'Has it got a name?' I reached my hand out tentatively, touching the donkey's muzzle. Long grey hairs prickled my hand.

'I think it's called Billy,' she said, climbing the fence and prodding the donkey's flank with a stick. His tail swished angrily. He was chewing slowly, his lower lip working up and down, wobbling gently. A fat strip of hay dangled from between his teeth. I touched the edge of it as it trembled in his velvet mouth, and his lips caressed my fingers. How could such an old mouth be so soft?

'Will it... will it hurt him?'

'Nah, it's quick. One shot to his brain and he'll be gone, none the wiser.'

'Shot? They... they shoot him?' Putting down suggested a gentle collapsing of limbs. I had imagined the vet's hand laid on the animal's side until he bent his aged legs and lay, quietly, asleep. Shooting, on the other hand, was violent and loud: an angry death.

'Can't they give him some medicine to make him go to sleep instead?'

'Not something this big. They have to get them right here, between the eyes.' She formed her hand into a gun shape and touched her fingertips to Billy's forehead. He blinked. 'Got to get the brain. Don't worry, he won't know what's happening.'

But *I* will, I thought.

Her warm, slightly sticky hand pushed its way into mine, and I looked up to see her looking into my eyes. 'It's the kindest thing, Romilly,' she said, squeezing my hand. 'Are you OK? Mum says sometimes I go a bit too far.'

I sniffed, wiping my nose on my sleeve, and nodded.

'Good, 'cause you're my friend and I don't ever want to upset you.'

I smiled, and squeezed her hand back.

'I'm going to come and watch. If I ask, they might let me hold him while they do it.' Stacey's eyes glittered. 'Do you want to come?'

'No,' I said, shaking my head vehemently as I looked into his huge, treacle eye. The whole of the farmland behind me was reflected in it, stained brown like an underwater world. I could see my own tear-filled eyes reflected there too. Billy had stopped chewing. He was looking at me. Carefully I pulled the blade of hay from his mouth and tucked it into my pocket. His warm, sweet breath lingered with me all the way home, and it wasn't until I was curled up in bed that I realised that I hadn't asked Stacey where she'd been all summer.

A week later, I opened the back door of Braër House, and even from this far away I could see something had changed down in the meadow. In the grey dusk, a tall pole stretched up to the sky. It was moving slowly, like the pendulum of a clock.

I ran to the meadow. Close up, the pole was bent slightly like a giant tusk. Dad was standing next to it, gazing upwards, his face sweaty and earth-covered. I watched for a moment, then backed away, not sure I wanted him to know I had been there.

Over the next few weeks, as the leaves turned yellow and red and began to fall from the trees, more giant metal structures appeared in the meadow: great swinging pieces that whorled and arced above your head in the slightest of breezes. Some resembled animals and birds; others were strange collections of metal that looked lighter than paper when they skimmed the grass.

'What are they, Dad?' I finally asked, staring up at the huge structures apprehensively one evening.

'They're mobiles,' he said.

'What are they for?'

'They're not really *for* anything. They just are. You mustn't go in there, Romilly, not without me. They're dangerous. They could flatten you in an instant.'

I nodded, staring in awe at the huge mobiles. I wasn't sure if they were the sort of thing that could fix the boiler or feed us more than jacket potatoes and beans, but I was happy Dad was busy. I couldn't wait to show Stacey.

Six

Dad was watching the weather forecast. A man named Michael Fish was gazing sternly out of the television.

'Earlier today, apparently, a woman rang the BBC and said there was a hurricane on the way. Well, if you're watching, don't worry, there isn't.'

'Well, that's good,' said Dad, looking out nervously towards his mobiles. They were whirring noisily, racketing along in the dark. 'Should have fitted a braking system,' he mumbled, 'hindsight, hindsight.'

'A girl at school said there's been a sighting of a panther near the village,' I said, peering out of the window at the dark garden. The nights were closing in earlier now. Soon it would be bonfire night, and then the run-up to Christmas would begin.

'I don't envy it out there tonight,' Dad said, pulling the curtain closed so I was hidden behind it. I leant my forehead on the glass so I could see through my reflection, expecting to find a huge cat curled up in the grass outside, meek as a domestic tabby.

'She said it escaped from the circus in the summer.'

'That's odd,' Dad said, 'I didn't see one when we went, did you?'

I shook my head. 'Are they dangerous?'

'Could be. Probably not for adults, but maybe little children...'

'I bet it couldn't eat a whole one.'

'No, but it could split you down the middle with its sharp claws and siphon off your insides.' He picked me up, unravelling me from the curtain and hefting me over his shoulder in a fireman's lift.

'Now, a boa constrictor, *that* could swallow you whole. You'd be stuck in his stomach, shouting to get out, his digestive juices working overtime to dissolve your bones.'

We were halfway up to my bedroom now. On the landing Dad tipped me off his huge shoulders and we climbed up my little staircase.

Up in my bedroom it was even wilder.

'It's like being at sea, this,' Dad said, nodding appreciatively at the flurry of wind. It felt as if the whole room were rocking gently. The usual chorus of starlings in the eaves was silent, as if they were listening too.

'Batten down the hatches.' He grinned, pulling the curtains together. They lifted gently, the wind forcing its way through the cracks in the frames.

I had a moment of panic. 'I will be OK up here, won't I?'

Dad chuckled, sitting down on the bed next to me and pulling our game of chess towards him. We had been playing the same game for months now. Most nights I came to bed and found Dad had made his move while I'd been away. Dad studied the pieces.

'You're perfectly safe,' he said, touching a knight, 'the rigging's well and truly tied down.'

'Did you used to be a sailor?'

He laughed again. Getting up, he lifted the stuffed parrot from where she sat on my desk, and placed her next to me on the bed. I had taken the glass dome off weeks ago, disappointed that it had come apart so easily, without the need for an axe. I pulled her to me and Dad tucked us into bed together, her beady eye glaring at him all the while he was doing it.

'Can't I stay up for a bit longer?' I said, yawning. I didn't want to be on my own, stranded at the highest point in the house while Dad was cosily anchored far below me. What if the roof got whipped right off and went whizzing away with me inside it?

'No, Roe, it's very late.' Dad tucked me in and kissed me goodnight, his stubbled beard tickling my skin. Monty jumped up too, somersaulting onto the duvet, tucking his paws beneath him.

After Dad had gone I turned on my side, pulling Jasmine the parrot close for a cuddle, and saw that one of my pawns had been caught. It lay defeated on its side as if the wind had snuck into the room and blown it over. I looked up at Dad's little portrait of me and Monty, the picture within a picture stretching back for all eternity. It didn't look as if the wind was blowing quite so ferociously in their world. In the half-light I thought I saw something else in the picture, a pair of eyes watching me, but then they were gone.

I woke up in the dark, hours later. The room was wracked with noise. It felt like the whole house was swaying. Beneath the wind I thought I heard Monty scream, a pitiful thin wail, dissolving into a sob. I sat up. Monty was sound asleep beside me on the bed. The sound had come from downstairs.

I got out of bed, clutching Monty to me unsteadily as the floor buffeted beneath us. We descended the steps carefully, clinging to the brickwork, the house quaking all around us. On the landing, the crying changed, ebbing and flowing through the house. I peeped into every room in turn, grateful for the cat's warmth in my arms.

In each room the crying sounded different. In the drawing room there were huge, wracking sobs; in the bathroom quiet little whimpers. It was as if a ship full of sad ghosts had been blown through the village and landed, marooned in our house. It wasn't a scary sound, but a sad one, and I came back to the landing heavy with sorrow. I sat down at the centre of the noise, hugging Monty to me fiercely, and with a deep, unknown grief, I began to cry. I curled up on the floor, tears coating my face as I listened to the keening of the thousands of people all around me.

I awoke to Dad's touch, stroking my forehead. I was lying on the landing, my bare feet frozen. A pale sun was beginning to peep round the edge of the window. Something looked different outside. I sat up, trying to work out what it was.

'It's the poplars,' Dad murmured, following my gaze. 'All of them have gone. Completely gone.' There was quiet surprise in his voice.

I looked again and he was right: where a line of tall trees had stood in the distance, now there was only sky. The beech tree in the garden was still standing, but it was like a giant octopus, its branches thrashing like tentacles in the sky.

The electricity was off. With mugs of sugary tea heated on a camping stove we listened to the radio, waiting to hear if my school would be open. I really didn't want to go. Some of the girls had cornered me in the toilets last week and demanded I take off my new shoes, before throwing them in the toilet and pulling the chain. I had told Dad, but he'd just laughed. 'Japes,' he had said, his eyes twinkling.

The radio sounded crackly as if even the radio waves were being pounded by the wind. We both hooted with excitement when my school's closure was announced.

I sat on the low window seat in the drawing room, watching the assault of the hurricane on the village. Not many people had dared to leave their houses, but those who did were walking at a peculiar angle, the wind lifting them on invisible wings.

Stacey turned up at lunchtime wearing her usual shorts and T-shirt, wind-hardened drizzle spattering the denim.

I pulled her inside, away from the beginnings of a hailstorm, and we ran up to my bedroom and knelt by the open window. Stacey put her arm out to try and catch the hail.

'Where've you been?' I asked her.

'What do you mean?'

'I haven't seen you in ages.'

She brought her hand in and licked the little balls of ice from her palm, crunching thoughtfully. 'I was at my gran's house,' she said. 'She says it gives my mum a rest. I'll always come and find you when I get back.'

'Promise?'

''Course. Here, this is better than a promise.' She put her hand out of the window again and kept it there until it was full of hailstones again.

'Shake hands,' she said, slapping her hand into mine without warning and shaking it vigorously. The cold stones crunched between our skin.

'Now we eat whatever's in our hand.' She licked at her palm, slurping up the slush that had stuck there, indicating I should do the same. 'It's like blood brothers,' she said. 'Snow sisters.'

I looked at my palm. Most of the hail had stayed on her hands, but for a fine icy imprint covering my own. I put my tongue to it. It tasted cold and gritty.

'What's this?' Stacey said, wiping her hand on her shorts and picking up a little picture on the window sill.

'It's Mary Mother-of-God.'

The picture had arrived a few days earlier in an envelope addressed to me. It was a present from my mother. Except for the pinafore dress in the summer, she had never sent me anything before. I wondered if this was to be the start of a magical ritual: a gift from mother to daughter every few months.

The letter that had come with it was very short.

'*Mary is the mother of all of us,*' my mother had written, '*and while you have this picture you will never be alone.*'

Why does she think I'm alone? I had thought at the time, I have Dad.

I read and re-read the letter often, running my fingers over the last two words, '*love, Mum*'. Her writing was very pretty. I had taken the picture into bed with me, hoping for comfort, but it had sharp, cold edges, and had ended up back on the window sill.

'Is Mother-of-God her surname?' Stacey said.

I nodded. I didn't tell her who had given it to me. It felt nice to have a secret.

Stacey stood the little picture back on the sill. It was bright and colourful, with a silver frame. Mary Mother-of-God was very pretty, and had a golden circular hat on her head.

'Is your school closed today, too?' I asked.

'I don't go to school.'

I turned to her, 'Really? How do you learn?'

'Mum home schools me.'

'Wow, that's so cool. I wish Dad home schooled me. I asked him but he says he's too busy.'

'It's OK, I suppose. It can get a bit lonely.'

'You can come round here any time you want. If I'm still at school, you can just come and play in my room. Or Dad could draw you.' Dad was always looking for fresh subjects to draw. 'Except he's obsessed with kittens and circuses at the moment, so unless you dressed up like a clown or a cat, he might not want to.'

Stacey laughed.

'Hey, they're saying there's a man-eating panther on the loose,' I said, remembering, 'apparently it escaped from the circus.'

'Who says?'

'People at school.'

'Did you see it when you went to the circus?'

I tried to think back, but Dad's stories were already mixing with the truth, and I couldn't separate what was real and what was fable. 'I don't think so. Dad says he can't remember it, anyway.'

'Maybe it had already escaped,' she said. I could see the excitement building in her eyes, 'wanna go look for it?'

'Nah,' I said, spotting the tops of the mobiles out of the window, 'I've got something even better to show you, come on.'

We ran down the two flights of stairs, the back door slamming forcefully behind us as we went out into the garden.

'This way!' I shouted above the wind, and then I was pushing past her and running down to the meadow, the grass rushing beneath my feet, and she was behind me, unable to catch me up. I was as fast as her now, I realised with a flush of jubilation. We flew over the grass, the gale pushing us onwards. Coming to a stop at the edge of the meadow, we beamed at each other, the wind stealing our voices.

Still grinning, Stacey turned and saw the mobiles, and her smile faded.

'Dad made them,' I said proudly, looking at them with relish. Some had stopped moving, wedged and jammed by the wind, but others were rotating faster than usual, screeching painfully in disharmony. I ducked as a huge steel disc came whirling towards me, missing me by inches.

'They're monstrosities.'

'No, they're not,' I said, 'they're beautiful.' Remembering Stacey's nettle dare, I said, 'I dare you to go in.'

But she shook her head, taking a step back, a look of horrified fascination on her face as she stared at the swinging pieces of metal. A plastic bag flew through the air, catching her shoulder for a moment, making her jump. I laughed.

'You go in if you're so brave,' she said.

'OK, I will.' I shot a guilty glance at the house, but Dad was nowhere to be seen. Taking a deep breath, I stepped in between the structures, my heart hammering.

The roar of the wind in here was like the whistle of an overboiling kettle. The mobiles surrounded me like a pack of hungry wolves, moving stealthily as if they were hunting me. As I reached the middle of the meadow the sound of the wind disappeared altogether. The mobiles were close now, blocking my path at every turn. Across the meadow, in a shadowy corner, something crouched, watching me.

Stacey was shouting. With a shiver, I tore my eyes away from it and looked at her. She raised her arm, pointing behind me. I turned to look, and something slammed into my shoulder, knocking me to the ground.

I lay, pinned to the earth. Slowly, helplessly, the mobile began to drag me along the ground, my face scraping against the soil. My hands scrabbled to grab hold of the grass, my fingers slipping against something shiny in the ground, and then the propulsion stopped and I was being hopelessly, piteously pressed into the earth, an insistent hand driving me deeper into the meadow.

With a crack, a searing pain shot through my arm. The mobile above me came to a stop, whining and creaking, eager to be moving. All the wind in the whole of the Suffolk sky was rushing toward me. I looked for Stacey, but she was gone.

I lay on the ground, the scream of bone juddering in my arm, and I screwed my eyes shut. Something was tickling my face. I squinted upwards. A huge black cat was sniffing me gently, pressing its nose into my ear, its tongue smoothing my forehead with gentle wet laps.

'Do not worry,' it said, its gruff voice full of hurricane. I closed my eyes. A day, a week, a month later, I opened them again. Two faces appeared above me, Stacey's small muddy one stained with tears, and Dad's huge bristly one, white under his dark beard.

I came home from hospital the day after the hurricane. The sky was lemon pale, as if the wind had cleared not only the clouds but had sucked up all the water too to make a weak cordial of the sky. As we walked delicately through the gate, my arm heavy with plaster and bandage, I stopped. Where there were usually branches, gesticulating in the breeze, there was only a vast expanse of sky. Our huge beech tree lay across the garden like some great slain beast, its topmost branches reaching up to my bedroom window as if pleading for help. I tiptoed up to it and laid my hand on a thin branch, marvelling at how quickly things can change: how only a few hours ago it had been high up in the sky, dancing in the wind, far, far out of reach.

In the house, Stacey stroked my white fingers. My arm was broken in two places and the cast was tight on my skin.

She wrote and drew all over the cast, making use of my felt tip pens until a riot of colour gambolled across the white plaster, words hardly readable and definitely spelt wrong, but I loved them. Best of all, Dad said Stacey was allowed to visit me whenever she wanted. I wanted her to come every day.

On the night of my homecoming, Dad didn't come to tuck me in. I whispered to Stacey as she gently fussed around me, tightening the duvet round my body, 'Do you think my dad is going to leave like my mum did?'

'Nah. He's got nowhere to go.' She pulled a tatty pack of Parma Violets out of her pocket and offered me one. I shook my head, remembering their cloying taste and the nauseous feeling it had conjured in me.

'But he's angry with me,' I said.

'No he's not, idiot. He's angry with himself. What sort of dad lets their daughter go into a field of moving metal? It's like something out of *Indiana Jones*.'

'Then why doesn't he come and see me?'

'Grown-ups deal with angry feelings differently to us. He'll come soon, I'm sure.' She lifted my cast gently to tuck me in better, placing it carefully on the bed.

I looked down at it. It was very itchy. I caught sight of a red heart on the white plaster.

'Did you do that?'

Stacey reddened.

'It's OK, I like it,' I said, tracing the heart with my finger. Tiredness overwhelmed me.

'Will you stay with me while I go to sleep?'

She nodded.

'And will you sing me a song?'

'I don't know many.'

'Just a nursery rhyme will do.'

'OK.' Stacey thought for a moment and then began to sing. Her voice was clear and light, as if it were coming from another room.

'Rock a bye baby

'On the tree top

'When the wind blows

'The cradle will rock...'

Long before she had finished, I was fast asleep.

I awoke, hours later. Dad was sitting next to me on the bed. I could still feel the echo of his kiss on my forehead. He smiled at me, touching the mole on my cheek lightly, his eyes crinkling.

'Is it morning?'

'No. It's just gone midnight.'

I stifled a yawn and rubbed my eyes. In the dark, Dad was a soft shadow.

'I need to go to London soon,' he said. 'I'll call and make the appointment tomorrow.'

'Can we go to the British Museum?' I said, the yawn emerging at the same time as the words. I could remember going there when I was younger, and seeing giant stone people. Sometimes they hefted their huge bulk into my dreams, moving infinitesimally slowly, smiling down at me as if I was a tiny ladybird on the floor.

Dad cleared his throat. 'I'm afraid this is a Dad-only visit, Roe. I should be in and out within the day. Will you be all right on your own?'

I could see consternation crossing his brow. I nodded, and he patted my good arm before climbing carefully back down my stairs, leaving me to lie in bed, wide awake, wondering why he was going to the British Museum without me.

Seven

On November the fifth, our small Kemp family stood round a bonfire of raked-up leaves in the twilit garden. Dad doled out homemade soup in mugs, while I stoked the fire. I was wearing the pinafore dress my mother had sent. I had worn it so much, diving into bracken-covered dens and biting at the dull sweetness of blackberries, that holes and stains had appeared across it quickly, prompting Dad to sew patches of fabric all over it until it had become, not so much a denim dress, but a dress-of-many-colours.

'I wish this wind would settle,' Dad said, watching nervously as fiery leaves kept trying to escape into the sky like little comets. 'I've had enough hurricanes for one lifetime.'

Dad had come home from his appointment in London with sweat under his arms and a clinical smell about him that reminded me of the nurses who slathered the plaster onto my broken arm. He brought with him a huge bag of new paints and brushes, which seemed rather silly, since he already had far too many as it was. He had mumbled something about a new painting project, cupping my cheek in his hand and dropping a kiss onto the top of my head, before pouring himself a very large whisky and promptly falling asleep in the snug.

Since then I hadn't seen him use the paints, and I wondered if he had forgotten all about them.

Montgomery picked his way down the path towards us, but shot off in another direction at the sight of the crackling flames. Dad passed me two mugs, steam rising thickly from the soup's surface. I took them awkwardly.

'Why have I got two?'

Sipping deeply at his own mug, Dad swallowed, wiping a line of mush from his moustache. 'I thought your friend Stacey was coming?'

'Oh.' I squinted hopefully past him into the dark towards the gate, looking for her customary bare legs scrambling over the top, but there was nothing there. Perhaps her mum had a new boyfriend and she was staying out of the way with her gran.

'Romilly, I've been meaning to talk to you. I've had a lot of time to think over the last few weeks, and I've decided to write a book.'

'A book?' I blew on my soup, watching how the steam mingled with the woodsmoke. 'What about?'

'It's the painting project I was telling you about. I was thinking of a picture book. Starring you.' He looked hard at me, his eyes glowing like embers.

I swallowed a mouthful of soup rather quickly, scorching the back of my throat. 'Me?'

'You and your cat. I've a publisher interested.'

'Will we be able to buy loo roll and new socks?' I said, thinking of the ripped-up newspaper in the downstairs loo.

'It should help out. I have an idea or two. And a fat advance if I decide to do it.'

I sipped my soup thoughtfully. I couldn't imagine anyone would be interested in a book about me.

'Well, Romilly?' Dad said, scooping my hair out of my scarf. It had begun to grow again after he cut it, and I felt it lift in the breeze as Dad crouched down so that we were nose to nose. 'What do you think, Romilly-Roe? Do you want to be famous?'

Images of glittering evening dresses and flashing camera bulbs lit up my mind. Giant chocolate cakes and expensive teddies. A hazy memory of a be-feathered woman in a pink glittering leotard. I nodded quickly, kissing Dad on his bulbous nose and wrapping my arms round his huge neck.

During the next few weeks, while I was at school, Dad worked hard on ideas for the book. In the Christmas holidays he spent every day locked in his study, only coming out on Christmas Day to baste the turkey and pour himself another glass of port. Whenever I dared knock on his door to ask if he wanted to pull a cracker or listen to my rendition of 'Jingle Bells', he said, 'Not now, Romilly,' and closed the door smoothly.

By early spring, he had emerged from his study as if from hibernation, blinking in the pale spring light, his hands and face covered in dabs of orange paint like some undiscovered new species. He made up for hiding away by playing hunt the Monty-cat with me all over Braër's sprawling rooms. One afternoon he strode from the kitchen bearing a huge strawberry jelly on a dinnerplate. It was so large and wobbling that when Monty jumped onto the table to sniff at it I could see his whole body, wibbly and faintly pink, through its transparent side.

I forgot about the book after that. Stacey came to call often, and as the evenings got lighter, I was allowed to stay out later. We explored the countryside, roaming like wildcats through the gorse and the reeds.

For my tenth birthday, Dad hosted a tea party by the moat for Stacey and me. He dressed up as a butler, sweating in a too tight suit and calling us both 'Ma'am' whilst he served us scones with clotted cream and dollops of plum jam that we had made in great batches the previous summer.

A few days later, he came home from a trip to London with

a bottle of perfume for me, and armfuls of carrier bags bearing the word 'Harrods'.

'The book's finally out, Roe!' he announced, whipping a copy out of one of the bags. But before I had a chance to take it, he roared, 'Go and get your best frock on, it's time for a banquet!' and he pulled a huge bottle of champagne out with a flourish, like a magician pulling out a bunch of flowers.

I raced upstairs and pulled on my denim dress. It had ripped on a bramble the previous week, but Dad had sewn a patch of flowery material over the hole. It was almost more patch than denim now.

When I got back downstairs, my stomach rumbling for the feast to come, Dad was still unloading bags of food onto the table. There was a whole plate of cheese, one of them so ripe it wobbled like the strawberry jelly and stank like my trainers. There were little cakes arranged delicately on a tiered plate, each one smelling different, each no bigger than a tiny bite.

'What's happened to the oranges?' I said, pointing to some small, egg-shaped oranges in the fruit bowl.

'That is not an orange,' Dad said importantly, 'That, is a kumquat.'

'Are they nice?'

'No idea. Expensive though.' He sat down and began to pile his plate with food.

'Why is everything expensive always so small?' I said, looking at the little pot of fish eggs called caviar.

'Rich people like small things,' Dad said, fiddling with the wire round the champagne bottle, 'it makes them feel bigger than they are.'

'Then why is the champagne bottle so big?'

With a pop that hurt my ears, the cork ricocheted off the ceiling, and white fizz flowed over Dad's hand. 'Because one can never have enough champagne,' he said, licking it off his knuckles. 'This is called a magnum.'

I mouthed the word, liking the way it felt as big and round as the bottle it described.

Dad cleared his throat, 'To our joint venture,' he said, lifting a forkful of chocolate cake into the air. I lifted my spoon of caviar to meet him, and we clanked our cutlery together. The caviar tasted of chocolate and salty fish as I licked it off the spoon.

In the middle of the table was a bowl of baked beans.

'What's so special about baked beans?' I asked, sticking my finger into the bowl and sucking on it loudly.

'It's to remind us that whatever success we may achieve, we should never forget where we've come from. And besides,' he said, plunging a spoon into the beans and shovelling them into his mouth, 'I do love baked beans.'

We toasted the book's publication, Dad with the only champagne glass we owned, me with a trickle in my polka dot mug, the bubbles rising up my nose and making me sneeze. I gulped it down, feeling the sharp-sweetness hit the back of my throat.

Later, as Dad filled his glass to the brim for the umpteenth time, his eyes taking on a dark brightness, the champagne swelled over the edge of the glass like a fountain, and I angled my mug to catch the excess flow. As I took a deep sip, the bubbles shivered over my scalp like a heady witches' brew, and I gazed into the golden depths of the mug, seeing a minute world within: parrots and monkeys and panthers made entirely of bubbles. I blinked, my eyes suddenly unfocused. When I raised my head, I thought I saw the echo of a panther creeping past the window, and the champagne in my mouth tasted bitter.

I would never forget the first time I saw the finished book. Dad had been quite secretive while painting the original pictures for the books, locking himself in his study to paint, and I had only been allowed glimpses of them. So to see myself in a book for the first time, to smell the pages and touch the shine of my hair and the pink blush of my cheeks, was like magic.

The book was called *Romilly and the Kitten*. I had my very own copy, and Dad had signed his name inside the cover just for me. The first time I opened it, it crackled stiffly as if I was the first person ever to glimpse inside. The front cover was a swathe of gold. It was designed to look like a portrait, with a decorative gilt frame around the edge, set with rubies and sapphires. The picture in the frame was a startling likeness of me, standing looking inquisitively out, with Monty cradled in my arms.

Inside the book, every page was crammed with objects and colour, and I recognised it all: there was Braër House, with its crumbling chimney and mirror-still moat, and here was our marvellously retro kitchen, where I recognised the polka dot mug I drank my tea out of, and the cracked egg cup shaped like a yellow chick that Dad liked to eat his boiled egg from.

On every page, I was wearing my denim pinafore with the flying saucer buttons, accompanied by bright red tights. In Dad's paintings, the red-and-blue clothes did wondrous things to my auburn hair, sending flecks of light spinning and radiating from me as if from an angel. But somewhere deep within the printing process the colour of my hair was lost to be replaced by a vulgar crimson that matched my tights.

Still, Romilly on the page looked a lot like me: the same white skin, the same dark eyelashes. The same blue eyes. Even the heart-shaped face of the 2D Romilly mirrored mine – Dad never did things by halves.

It wasn't until I had owned the book for a few days, gorging on the pictures, that I realised there were words hidden in each one. They littered the page in twining calligraphy, swirling through the wallpaper in the drawing room, caught in the knotted grain of the beech tree. Words like *willow* and *roses, teapot* and *parrot*. And once you found the words, it set you off on a hunt for the corresponding objects. My stuffed green parrot was to be located perched on the desk in my bedroom. The roses were sitting in a vase on the kitchen window, their pale pink petals so thin you could see the sunlight pouring through.

After a few weeks it felt normal to be in a book: surely every child had their own adventures hidden within jewelled covers? After all, there was Christopher Robin, and Alice and her Wonderland. They were my new friends, people who knew exactly what it was like to be me.

Stacey wasn't very interested in the book. She said it was because she couldn't read very well, but I think it was more likely that she was jealous. Occasionally I would persuade her to look at it with me, feeling a rush of happiness as her eyes grew round with wonder at all of the tiny, perfect details. Sometimes I felt the heat of her gaze on me as we pored over the book, her eyes enviously flicking from Romilly on the page to Romilly next to her.

The book sat on my bedside table, and the clanking of the pipes under the floorboards finally ceased because now there was enough money to fix them, and Dad's face grew flushed from the crates of wine that appeared in the pantry.

The initial excitement of seeing myself in a book faded, but Dad enjoyed the publicity. Sullen and hermit-like at home, he came out of his shell when signing books and talking to the public. To my surprise, despite the book being full of colourful pictures for children, it was mainly grown-ups in the queue, lining up to question Dad about the different images, asking what they all meant. Dad would grow, if possible, even bigger in his chair as he swelled with pride at the compliments and smiling faces, pulling me over to wrap his arm around my shoulder for a photo. I spent a lot of time practising my signature, perfecting a heart over the *i*, and ending my name with a little curlicued flourish, just in case anyone ever asked me for an autograph.

A few months after the book was published, in the dwindling light of a late summer's evening, Dad and I sat on the edge of the moat, dangling old crabbing lines into the filmy water.

'It's a funny sort of fishing,' I said, turning to Dad, who was concentrating on his own string, his fingers nimbly pulling it up, inch by inch. 'If we can't eat what we catch, why are we bothering?'

'Well, we're fishing for the past.'

I frowned, looking at my own crabbing line. I tugged at it, but the weight at the bottom seemed to have got stuck on something.

Dad was pulling his line in, leaning precariously over the water, wrapping the string over the handle until the weight – a giant magnet in the shape of a horseshoe – came smoothly out. Dangling from it was an old door hinge, half covered in mud. He pulled it in and looked at it with fascination.

'We definitely can't eat that,' I said.

'I know, but isn't it wonderful? Think of the door this came from! Who went through it? How long ago did they die?'

I turned to my own line, and tried again to pull it up, prickling with anticipation at my own catch.

Over my shoulder, I could hear voices. I turned to see two boys climbing the gate into the garden. They hadn't spotted us yet.

'Intruders,' Dad whispered, frowning, and he heaved himself up and strode towards them.

I turned back to my crabbing line, tugging hard. With a twang, it came away sharply from whatever it had caught on. In surprise, I dropped the handle and it slipped from my grasp and slithered down the bank to be swallowed up by the moat, gone forever. As the water stilled, I saw, just beneath the surface, the cunning face of the sunken gargoyle, watching me. The ripples of the water made its mouth look like it was whispering. I got up quickly and followed Dad.

He was over by the gate, brandishing the muddy hinge above his head. 'What on earth do you think you're doing?' he was saying, a wild look in his eyes.

I peered out from behind his broad back. One of the boys looked a few years older than me, the other a year or two younger. They were looking down at their feet. The older one was unsuccessfully hiding a spade behind his back.

'Trespassing!' Dad said, glowering at them.

'We're just looking for the treasure,' the smaller one said.

'David, shh!' The taller one with the spade elbowed him.

'It's the truth,' David whispered. Then he spotted me standing behind Dad, and his face lost all its colour. 'She looks just like her pictures,' he said.

'I *can* hear you,' I said, growing brave, shielded by Dad's huge bulk.

'Enough of this,' Dad said. 'Romilly, don't be rude.' He turned to the boys, 'What do you mean, "treasure"?'

'You know, the secret code. Things hidden in the book.' The taller boy's voice was on the verge of breaking. It wavered between deep and squeaky, and he looked at Dad warily as he spoke.

Dad sighed and rubbed hard at his face with his hands. Then with a flourish, he waved the muddy hinge in the direction of the garden. 'Go on then,' he said, 'search away, but I promise you there's nothing to find.'

The boys tiptoed away, giving Dad a wide berth before running off across the garden.

'Rapscallions,' he muttered.

'What were they talking about?' I said.

'Goodness knows, Romilly.'

'Is there something buried here?' I was looking at the garden with new eyes, every grassy hummock turning into pots of gold.

'Only ghosts,' Dad said soberly, laying his arm across my shoulders as he surveyed the garden.

I followed his gaze. The grassy hummocks suddenly looked like little graves all around us.

'You can't bury ghosts.'

'Well, technically you can lay them to rest.'

'That doesn't make sense.'

'It's a figure of speech. It means letting go of things that worry you or make you sad.'

Dad was still looking out over the garden. His hand on my shoulder had tightened, digging into my skin until it hurt. 'I ought to let her know,' he said quietly to himself.

I pulled away and looked at him. 'Let who know?'

'Sorry?'

'Is there treasure buried here?' I said, trying to make sense of his riddles.

'Not as far as I know.'

'But what did the boys see in the book, then?'

He shook his head as if coming out of a trance, his eyes almost hidden by his furrowed brow. 'I don't know, Romilly,' he said at last, but something about the way he said it made me question his honesty. He lifted a hand and rubbed it over his mouth. 'Excuse me, I need to...' he broke off, patting me on the shoulder. 'Keep an eye on them, would you?'

I followed the boys at a distance, careful to keep out of sight, wondering what Dad had been talking about. The garden was so big and so wild that it was easy to drop down behind bramble bushes or old piles of logs every time they turned my way. I studied them meticulously: they must be brothers; they both had the same upturned nose. The older one had ducked into the space under the weeping willow. I could see his feet circling the bare earth.

'This'd be a great place to dig,' he was saying to the younger boy who had followed him in.

I crept closer, listening intently.

'We can see your feet,' the older boy said.

I parted the willow's branches. 'It *is* my garden,' I said, 'I'm allowed to be here.'

'Yeah, but do you have to earwig in on other people's conversations?'

The circle of shade was cool on my bare feet. I sat down and watched the two boys. 'My dad says there's ghosts buried here,' I said.

'Don't you mean skeletons?' the older boy said. 'You don't bury ghosts.'

I shrugged. 'I'm just telling you what he said. I thought it might help you find the treasure. Are you going to dig, then?'

'Not with you looking at us like that.'

'Suit yourself,' I picked up a stick and trailed it idly in the earth. 'What are you looking for, anyway?'

'We told you: treasure.' The older boy was pacing the small circle now, prodding the ground with his toe.

'But how do you know it's here?'

'We don't.'

'Then what are you doing here?'

He shrugged. 'It's fun looking, isn't it? Have you got any tips?'

I shook my head.

'But you're his daughter. You're the star. You must know something.'

The star. I bristled at the word. 'I don't. What do you mean, *treasure*, anyway?'

'I only know what the man on the news said, that there's treasure buried in the book. Grown-ups are leaving their jobs to hunt for it.'

A shiver ran down my spine. 'What? That's crazy. You can't bury treasure in a book.'

'No, the book holds the clues. We think there's going to be another book, and it'll have more clues in it. Maybe he'll make loads of them and we won't be able to find the treasure until we've got all the books.'

'Don't forget the spooky lady!' the younger boy piped up.

'What spooky lady?' I said, but before the boys could answer there came a rattling sound from the garden, like old bones knocking together, and we all jumped. I peeped out through the branches and saw it was just Dad clicking the old gate shut, a letter in his hand.

The older boy let out a breath. 'David gets freaked out by the spooky lady near the end of the book. You know, the one without a face?'

I tried to picture each page, but I couldn't think of anything that matched their description. 'Sounds creepy.'

'She is!' David squeaked, his eyes huge in the growing dark. 'She just turns up on that page, and then disappears again.'

'And she's got no face?'

'Well, no, but not in a freaky way,' the older boy said, 'it's just, she's sort of in shadow and you can't see her eyes. There's no mention of her in the story either.' He stopped suddenly, crouching down on the ground, leaning on the handle of his spade.

'What is it?'

'Look here,' he said, reaching down to touch the earth.

I got up, bringing the stick with me.

'Is it treasure?' the young boy piped up, but he fell silent as he saw what his brother had found.

We all stared at the ground.

'Do you think it belongs to a dog?' the younger boy said.

'Nah, it's way too big,' said his brother, 'maybe a wolf, or a bear—'

'Or a panther,' I said, looking at the huge paw mark in the bare earth, a tingle of excitement trickling over my skin.

They both looked at me.

'Where would a panther come from?' the older boy scoffed.

'It's no more unusual than a bear. And besides, there've been sightings round the village for ages now.'

'A panther,' the little boy whispered, his eyes huge in his small, pale face.

The trailing branches of the willow began to shimmer and rustle all around us, and we looked up, trying to see past them. The garden seemed to have grown larger and wilder in the last few moments. My hand flew to my mole, stroking it anxiously.

'Romilly!' Dad's shout channelled through the willow's leaves, breaking the chill that had settled over us.

'It's my bedtime,' I said, getting up and brushing the soil from my dress, 'let me know if you find any treasure. You know where I live.'

That evening, after Dad had said goodnight, I sat in bed, my thoughts lost in shadows of panthers and ghostly women. I turned the pages of *Romilly and the Kitten*, trying to find the scary lady the boys had spoken about. It took me two searches of the entire book before I found her.

Just as they said, she was on one of the last pages. It was a picture of the garden in full summer bloom. Monty and I were sitting on a swing tied to a branch of the beech tree before it had fallen. In the distance, on the path that led to the meadow, was the silhouette of a long-haired woman. The boys were right: there was something sinister about her blank face that stirred an uneasy feeling inside me.

But what kept me awake that night was not the shadows of her face or the lack of features, but the fact that I couldn't work out which way she was going; away from us and down to the meadow, or creeping towards us as we swung under the beech tree, oblivious.

In September I started back at school, but right from the first day, something had changed. On the way in, as I was approaching the school gates, I noticed a man holding a camera. The girls around me smoothed their hair down and licked their lips, but to my surprise, the man lifted it to his eye as I got closer, and began to take photos of me. When the girls saw who it was aimed at, they flounced into their little groups, frowning at me, whispering and pointing.

'Romilly!' the man said. 'Over here, Romilly, look this way, darling.'

I dropped my head and hid behind my hair, which was thankfully long enough now to conceal my face.

The man was there again as I came out that afternoon, and again the next morning. By the next week there were two more, all with huge cameras that clicked and flashed at me like giant black insects. The headmistress stood like a sentry each day, shepherding me inside, but I caught the look on her face as she took me to my classroom, a scrunching of the brow that lay somewhere between frustration and pity.

At home one evening, as I was scooping up tomato soup, Dad said, 'I had a call from school today.'

I laid my spoon down, my appetite gone.

'Why didn't you tell me there were photographers at school?'

'I didn't want to worry you. You're busy. You're…'

Dad sighed, running his hands over his face. 'Romilly, I'm never too busy that you can't talk to me. Christ, I had no idea it had got to this point.' With a jerk, he stood up from the table. 'I need to think about this. I need to—' Without finishing, he strode from the room, and I stared at the congealing soup in my bowl, feeling very small.

When Dad didn't return, I got up slowly and tiptoed to his study. I knocked softly on the door. There was silence for a long time. I stood in the dappled light trickling in from the hallway window. Eventually the door creaked open and Dad stood there, blinking in the light. It took him a moment to focus, as if he were coming out of a trance. His beard had grown recently until it covered almost all of his face, and his teeth flashed within the dark stubble like a sly beaver.

We observed each other for a long minute. Then Dad placed his hand on my head, cupping my skull like he used to.

'I don't want to go back to school,' I whispered. His grip tightened ever so slightly. Then he cleared his throat and nodded slowly, a smile lifting his sad face just for a moment.

'OK,' he said lightly, 'understandable. It's overrated anyway. We'll home school you.' He shrugged, then he turned and walked back into his study, closing the door softly behind him, leaving me blinking in surprise in the hall.

Eight

Addressing me over a meagre lunch of cold potatoes and salad a few weeks later, Dad said, in his most pretentious voice, 'Character is destiny, Romilly!'

He had the *Times Literary Supplement* open at a two-page spread, all about his book, and his fingers were covered in newsprint from smoothing the creases in the pages so often.

Meals were now often the only time that we met, we two Kemps, coming together from the furthest points of the house and garden, descending upon the lime green kitchen to inhale whatever was in the fridge before peeling away back to our thoughts and projects. I had been home schooled now for nearly four weeks. I knew this because I ticked off each day on my calendar. Dad's idea of home schooling was quite free range.

Dad grabbed the tomato sauce from the table and liberally slathered his salad with it.

'Heraclitus knew his stuff, Roe,' he said, shaking the ketchup so hard that it splattered against the wall. 'Just think about it. You, and only you, will determine what happens in your books. Whatever you do, wherever you go, that's what I'll write about.' A piece of potato skin had lodged itself over a front tooth as he talked. I giggled. 'You'd like that, wouldn't you? To decide what happens to you in your stories? Rather like being a god.'

I opened my mouth to speak, but he carried on, enjoying the sound of his own voice.

'And since we're talking gods, there's nothing wrong with having a god complex. Nothing at all.' He drew himself up to his full height. 'I am those pictures, and they are me, after all.'

'But aren't the pictures of me?' I asked, a lump of cold potato bulging in my cheek, my eyes so transfixed by the length of his black eyebrows that I only just noticed the flash of laughter cross his face before he resumed an imperious expression once again.

After I left school, I began to forget about the fame that came with the book, and apart from the odd flash of a camera aimed at us when we were walking to the shop in the village, I hardly noticed any change. As autumn took hold, Stacey and I spent much of our time out in the countryside, exploring the marshes and fields. The press hadn't yet cottoned on to the fact that I was home schooled, so we were rarely bothered.

But one chilly December day, something happened that revealed the double edge of my fame.

I was holding tightly onto Dad's hand as we sped along the pavement in the local town. We were in need of a ham hock, and the butcher's was about to close. The streets were lit by a myriad of tiny multicoloured Christmas lights, making the wet pavement come alive with a hundred kaleidoscopic colours. I stopped to look in the window of a bookshop, spotting a flash of Dad's book inside.

A gnarled hand shot out and pinched my shoulder from behind, and I turned to find a squinting old woman leering down towards me, her skin like almond paste.

'Where's the treasure, Romilly?' she whispered, her eyes twinkling.

Dad, having noticed I was lagging behind, politely peeled the hand from my shoulder and pulled me away the way we'd come, the butcher's forgotten, looking back occasionally and frowning. I'm sure she was just a kindly old lady and nothing more, but still my dreams contained her for weeks, her bony fingers clutching at my shoulder, pulling me further away from Dad each night.

The darker evenings of winter meant an earlier curfew, and I consequently didn't see Stacey as much as I would have liked, but Dad agreed that we could have a sleepover so that we could catch up properly. He needed to go away to London for a night, and Stacey said she would stay with me at Braër and keep me company.

It was a Wednesday, and Stacey and I settled ourselves in the smaller sitting room that we called the snug, eating pot noodles and waiting to see Dad's face on the TV. It was a treat for me to be allowed up after eight. Usually I would hear the reassuring *Wogan* theme tune from upstairs, tucked up in bed. Tonight it felt alarmingly loud.

Dad was to be interviewed between a man called Paul McCartney and a woman called Debbie Allen. We scooped ribbons of noodles into our mouths, Monty snoring quietly between us, half listening as Mr McCartney talked about heather and hills and living on a farm. I wondered if *Wogan* was actually a farming programme and Dad would come on to talk about Braër's ancient working past. My eyelids began to droop.

Eventually, the man disappeared from the sofa, and Mr Wogan turned his tanned face to the screen. For a moment the TV was silent, and all I could hear was the flow of water in the pipes of Braër's walls. All of a sudden the house felt very empty, and I grabbed Stacey's hand for reassurance.

Mr Wogan was speaking again. 'Now, there are certain books that capture the hearts of young and old alike. My next guest is both author and illustrator of just such a book.'

Stacey squeezed my hand, grinning, and my stomach lurched. Mr Wogan continued, 'And yet this book is slightly different. It is about a girl, but not just any little girl: it is about the author's very own daughter.' I planted a kiss on Monty's head, and he woke up, meowing loudly in return.

'Yet some people say it is not just a book.' Here, he raised his eyebrows and gazed more sternly at us sitting at home. 'No. Some people say that hidden within its pages is a treasure hunt! Please welcome warmly, Tobias Kemp!'

And as the applause and the theme music exploded through the TV, there was Dad, bounding into the studio, a hastily put together suit flapping as he ran, orange tie flitting through the air.

Stacey squeaked with excitement and my stomach gave a small leap. Dad was here in the room with us, his body shrunk to the size of a mouse, gallivanting across the little TV screen, while really he was far away in London.

'Did you know about the treasure hunt?' Stacey said, looking at me accusingly.

'No. Well... not really.'

'Liar. Why didn't you tell me?'

'I didn't know. Honest!' I looked at the tiny-Dad on TV, and suddenly wished he was here in the house with us. 'Stacey, I'm scared,' I said in a small voice, my tummy squirming.

Stacey reached for my hand again. 'Don't be. I'm here. And Monty will protect us.' She smiled, and I felt a little better. 'Besides,' she said, 'if you went on TV, everyone would know who you were. It's safer that you're here.'

She was right. We had discussed the idea of me going on the show with Dad. The producers had been very insistent about it. I had ironed my denim dress, which was getting very short, and Dad had bought a new pack of red tights in preparation. But then, a few days before we were due to go, I had been on my own down near the meadow, dipping my hand into the frost-covered grass and picking out fallen pine cones to make into birdfeeders, when I had sensed movement out of the corner of my eye. Not the predictable movement of the mobiles, but a swift jolting twitch that made me scan the length of the yew hedge. It took me a while to locate it, but eventually my eyes settled on the gleam of a dark camera lens poking through the leaves. Above the hedge I could just make out the top of a woollen hat.

'Can I help you?' I'd asked politely. Dad always told me to be polite.

'Are you Romilly Kemp?' The voice had come through the hedge, slightly gravelly as if some of it had got stuck in the sharp branches.

As I'd taken a step back, the lens stayed trained on my chest. 'I...'

At that moment I'd heard Dad's voice far away at the house, calling me in for lunch. The man was still crouched on the other side of the hedge, breathing deeply, the hedge jiggling as he panted. I'd turned and ran.

At the house I'd told Dad, and he'd pulled me inside and shut the door.

And so, Dad had gone to *Wogan* on his own, and I sat locked up at home, safe in the cosy snug with Stacey, watching with wonder and only a tiny bit of resentment as he gazed back at me from the other side of the screen.

'Now, Tobias,' Mr Wogan began, 'your book has been out for a while now. What gave you the idea of writing it in the first place?'

Dad uncrossed his legs and cleared his throat. He looked nervous. His beard had been trimmed, and it looked too neat.

'Well, it was really when we moved to the country. I had decided to make a living as an artist, but then I saw this advertisement for a Siamese kitten, and it all went from there.'

As he spoke, the screen changed to a montage of Dad's pictures from the book: paintings of Braër; Monty up a tree; me sitting on my bed. I yelped with excitement.

'So Montgomery the cat is real?'

Another painting flashed up on the screen, this time of Monty as a kitten curled in Dad's hand. The audience gave a collective 'Aah'.

'Yes, he's very real. But he doesn't talk in real life.' The camera flashed back to Dad and the audience laughed. 'It was all about the cat's relationship with my daughter. All these stories popped into my head.'

'And where do you create your books?' The picture zoomed in on Mr Wogan, a smile flickering over his lips.

'At the moment I do it all in my study, but I'm hoping to build a writing shed soon. I need silence and no distractions. It's a tiny room: barely a broom cupboard, really. If I can't move, I get on with my work. I sit squeezed in between a desk and a plan chest.'

Wogan smiled again. 'Oh bless.'

'The room hangs over the moat. You have no idea how cold it's got in the last few weeks, I can see my breath at times. But I have a little gas heater to keep me snug. It smells a bit funny, and I'm sure it's played its part in my more surreal paintings.'

There was an appreciative murmur from the audience.

'Am I to take it that you're making a sequel, then?' said Mr Wogan.

'Well, I'm hoping it'll be the second book in a series, yes. If people keep buying my books, that is.'

The audience laughed again, warming to him, and Dad beamed.

'And I understand that some people think there is a treasure hunt hidden within the pages of your book. What are your thoughts on that?'

'We've certainly met a few interesting people carrying spades and maps in the last few months.' Dad's eyes twinkled.

At this Mr Wogan coughed and dropped his eyes. 'But Mr Kemp,' he repeated, 'are there clues hidden within your book? Have you set up a treasure hunt, and if so, what is the treasure?'

'There are things hidden in the book, of course.'

'Told you!' Stacey hissed at me. She wasn't the only one: the audience had got noisier; a hum of excitement filled the studio.

'For example,' Dad continued, 'I have painted a tiny mouse on each page to find, and there are countless pictures and words that are hidden throughout the book, for those who can't get enough of searching. But I have not *deliberately* written a treasure hunt into my story. I have not gone along to a secret location and buried some gold for any Tom, Dick or Harry to find.' He was enjoying himself now, warming to his subject, his eyes glittering. 'If my readers have studied the books and found that x plus y equals z, then I think they have found their own clues.'

'An interesting answer if ever I heard one,' said Mr Wogan, his tanned face deadpan. 'Do you think that with all that is going on in our world at the moment – take Terry Waite's hostage situation in Lebanon, for instance – your books are some kind of distraction? A reprieve from the real world, if you will?'

Dad considered this question. 'If my books can offer any hope of a better world, then I must be doing something right. As Einstein said, "Joy in looking and comprehending is nature's most beautiful gift."'

Mr Wogan nodded as if he understood. I looked at Stacey, puzzled, and she shrugged.

'Now,' and here, Mr Wogan's gaze became stern as he turned to face Dad again, placing his hands together and resting them on his knees, 'I understand you have had a few issues regarding your privacy. I suppose when one paints one's house and family into a book for all to see, one is bound to expect visitors.'

Here, Dad looked down at his own hands held tightly in his lap. 'This is really the reason I wanted to come on your programme tonight,' he said. 'I had not expected that people would actually buy my book, and I had not expected the fame that went with it, both the good and the bad.'

'And is there something you would like to say to those who might be thinking of paying you a visit?'

Dad looked up. He seemed to be scanning the audience, then he turned his eyes to the camera. He seemed to be looking straight at me.

'Please give us our privacy,' he said, his voice strained. 'There is no treasure hunt. Please let my little girl live a normal life.'

Wogan's voice was soft as he began, 'Do you not think, Tobias, that you have lost yours and your family's right to privacy by using your child as the main character in your book?'

'I think,' said Dad, looking down at his hands again, 'I think that in writing this book, I have provided for my daughter's future in a way I could not have done if I had sat in my study painting pictures of flowers and landscapes.'

When he looked up, I swore I could see the cameraman reflected in his eyes. The television studio audience were silent.

'Thank you, Tobias Kemp.' And Mr Wogan stood and took Dad's large hairy hand in his own tanned one, as the audience clapped, and music swelled out from the TV and into our room.

Nine

Following the first book's success, the second book, *Romilly and the Circus*, came out the next summer, just after I turned eleven. In this story, Montgomery had come to the circus with us, and there had been tigers, and elephants and a talking poodle called Tula. Dad held a joint birthday party for me and the second book. It wasn't as much fun as my tea party the previous year: there were no costumes or funny names this time, and my birthday cake had a picture of his book on it.

I noticed at once that even though Monty seemed to have changed into a full-grown cat in the second book, I still looked exactly the same. When I told Dad how unfair it was, he laughed, continuing to slap paint onto the canvas in front of him as if it was all a big joke. I went into the hallway and looked in the mirror, doubting for a moment that I was growing up at all, but the face that glared back at me was definitely different: it had lost its plumpness, becoming instead more angular and feline.

With the new book's publication there was renewed speculation that the books contained a treasure hunt. Occasionally people came and knocked on the door. Some wanted to look around, searching the house for clues. Others wanted autographs, or a photograph of me and Monty. Dad would answer the door and call me downstairs, chatting enthusiastically to them while he waited, cleverly dodging the question of whether or not there was any treasure.

I observed these people silently from behind Dad's back. Many of them were families with children, but quite often it was just a solitary adult, clutching a map or a copy of the book. To me, the treasure hunt felt the same as believing in fairy tales or ghosts — something you did as a kid. But when an adult so very obviously believed, I began to wonder just what Dad had put in his books to ensnare them.

July was particularly rainy, and I spent long hours indoors, poring over the book's contents, folding down significant pages, and making notes to try to crack the code hidden within.

On the centre pages — a huge landscape depicting the circus on top of the hill, complete with horses and giraffes and a whole village full of colourful caravans — I found the ghostly lady again. She was far off in the distance, away from the crowds who were queuing to get into the circus. This time she had her hands to her face, as if she was holding onto an unimaginable sorrow. I stopped at the page and looked at her. She wasn't scary in this picture, merely sad. I couldn't understand how she could be so unhappy when all around her was colour and light and fun.

My favourite page was a picture of the interior of the circus. It was the painting I had seen Dad working on in his study a couple of years ago. Cantering round the ring was a gleaming white horse, pink feathers crowning its head. A beautiful woman balanced on its back, one dainty leg lifted in a perfect arabesque, a feather headdress sitting jauntily on her head.

It was the lady we had met at the circus, the one who had given me the feather to take home. I often thought about our outing there, the shyness I had felt when she plucked the feather from her hair and gave it to me, how awestruck I was by her beauty. With mortifying embarrassment, I remembered how I had asked Dad if she was my mum.

I noticed something else in this particular picture, too: Monty was in the ring as well, getting in on the action as he always did in Dad's books. He was galloping along behind the horse, the circus lighting giving everything a coal black shadow. I blinked when I first saw it, not quite daring to believe what I was seeing. For Monty's shadow was huge and monstrous, the exact size and shape of a prowling panther, creeping stealthily across the circus tent walls. I thought with a shiver of the paw print under the willow. Did Dad put this picture in the book because I told him about the loose panther? Or was I reading too much into it?

I thought about the day I broke my arm, when the panther visited me in the middle of the mobiles. I hadn't told Dad about our encounter. I didn't think even he, who was the most imaginative person I knew, would understand that.

I studied the page again, searching for the swirling, camouflaged words hidden within the picture. I ran my finger over each one:

Elephant, feather, horse, Lidiya.

Lidiya. The unusual name registered somewhere at the back of my memory, along with the taste of toffee apples and the smell of animal sweat. Lidiya, the pink-feathered horsewoman. I remembered when we first saw her in the circus ring, when Dad had leant over to me and whispered, 'Isn't she beautiful?'

Where was she now? What town had the circus pitched up in this week? I hadn't seen the pink feather she had given me for a long time. I hoped it hadn't got thrown away by mistake. I looked at the version of Lidiya in the book. She seemed more mythic beast than human being, smiling wryly out at me from the pages like a siren, her glimmering sequins catching the bright spotlights.

The rain that had plagued the beginning of July had finally ceased the day before, and it was a beautiful, sultry day. I reluctantly left the books inside and went out, onto the bridge, feeling the sunshine warm my skin. Dad was nowhere in sight – probably off for one of his bracing morning walks that often lasted well into the afternoon. Monty wove round my feet, leaving a slick of cat hair on my legs.

In winter and spring, the moat sometimes flooded over the garden, leaving no room to play, but in the summer it receded to a still, glassy surface that encircled Braër's walls. I looked down at my reflection in the water, as clear as if I were looking into a mirror. Dad had given me a nautical compass for my birthday. It was a beautiful old brass instrument with a flip-top glass lid and a star-shaped design on its face. I wondered if he had given it to me to help me search for the treasure, and if so, whether it was buried deep beneath the moat's surface. I had plans to make a raft to use it on, and had hoped Stacey might come by to help now that the weather was improved. I hadn't seen her for weeks. She knew the second book had come out, because whenever we met up it was all I had talked about. I wondered if she was avoiding me: if I had unintentionally bored her.

I decided Monty would have to be my accomplice today. I had already wound long strips of willow round branches I'd broken off the fallen beech, pulling them tight and knotting them together, but still the raft sagged a bit in the middle.

I lifted Monty up and plonked him onto it, and he stood like a worthy sea-dog, wobbling obediently. I glanced surreptitiously behind me: we had heard rumours of evil cat-hunters in the area, preying on beautiful felines and turning them into fur coats, and we needed to escape on the raft before they caught up with us. I took hold of the edge and pushed it towards the water.

The gate creaked open, and a woman in a long coat and heels clicked into the garden. I eyed her suspiciously, grabbing Monty and hugging him close. The stranger stopped at the gate. She was carrying a battered leather case. Perhaps she was a cat-hunting version of Cruella de Vil, on the search for the perfect fur coat. Her case might be full of catskins, I thought, sending daggers at her.

She took a few steps towards me, and stopped again, and the leather case fell from her hand and landed on the ground with a clatter. Monty jumped from my arms in panic, scratching the back of my hand in his haste to get away. I shot the woman an angry look. She was still standing there, staring at me. Close up, her long coat was definitely not fur. It was wool and quite scruffy. We observed each other in silence.

She bent to pick up her case, and I noticed that she had long red nails. Something about them made my heart begin to stammer in my chest, and I put my hand to the mole on my cheek, wishing that I had Monty's soft body back in my arms to cling onto.

The woman straightened up, still looking at me strangely. She opened her mouth to speak.

'Romilly?' she said, and I swallowed and began to cry.

Her name was Meg, and she was my mum.

She was showing me the contents of her case, balanced on Dad's bed. No furs or skins inside, but a shiny new school satchel for me, with my name written neatly on a piece of card slotted into the front. I hadn't the heart to tell her I didn't go to school.

I worried where Dad would have to sleep if Meg was to stay in his bed. I didn't quite dare call her Mum, as if I didn't yet believe she was real. I decided to offer my bed to her. I had dreamt of having a sleepover for years, and a sleepover with my mum would be extra special. I opened my mouth to ask her, but no sound came out.

She leant towards me and picked a white cat hair from the front of my T-shirt. I flinched as her red nails scraped against my ribs.

'I brought you something else,' she said. Digging around in her case, she pulled a pinafore out, the exact deep denim blue as the one I was wearing now, the one made famous in Dad's books.

'I thought this one might be getting a bit small for you,' she said, stroking one of the patches Dad had sewn on, 'and I was right, wasn't I? Look at how you've grown.'

I looked down. The dress was barely covering the tops of my legs. I tugged it down, embarrassed. The new dress had the same huge red buttons like flying saucers hanging from the straps. I stroked one of them, enjoying the shine of plastic on my fingers.

'Do you like it?' She was smiling at me. Her eyes looked sad, but maybe that was just their shape.

I didn't dare answer. I nodded instead.

'It's for you, go on, take it. I know it doesn't have the patches on it like the one you're wearing, but maybe we could do that together: a sewing project, just the two of us. And here, I brought some new tights too. It won't be long until autumn's upon us. Do you do that often?' she said, nodding at my hand. I realised I was scratching my bottom without noticing it. It had started itching a few days before. I pulled my hand away, my face reddening.

From the doorway, Monty chirruped nervously. He wasn't used to strangers.

'And who is this?'

'Captain Montgomery of the Second Regiment.' My voice came out all squeaky, and I blushed.

A soft peal of laughter escaped her as she bent down and reached a hand out, coaxing him forward.

'Well, hello there, little man. Have you been keeping my Romilly safe all this time?'

My Romilly, I glowed at the term. Monty swayed his head drunkenly like a cobra, transfixed by the soft singsong of her voice, before flopping over to expose his belly, his whiskers gently pulsing.

'Romilly?' Dad's bellow, newly energised from his walk, charged up the stairs, breaking the cat-spell. I stayed silent, looking at Meg. Her eyebrows were drawn together and a pink tinge had appeared at the centre of each cheek. She put her finger to her lips and winked conspiratorially.

We went out onto the landing and looked over the banister. Dad was crouched in the hallway, untying his shoelaces. My mother began to descend the stairs so quietly it was as if she were floating. Monty trotted after her, but I grabbed him by the scruff and pulled him back. We hung over the banisters and watched.

From here all I could see was the top of Dad's head. As my mother reached the bottom she sat down on the last step and reached out a hand to him. He looked up and stopped. They observed each other, as still and calm as the moat outside. Monty wriggled in my arms and I clamped him tighter to me, somehow knowing that downstairs belonged to a different time now – one that stretched back to when Mum and Dad last saw each other, when I was four and small and unknowing.

It felt very strange to wait for not one, but two goodnights. I lay in bed, imagining my mum curling up under the covers with me, the chocolatey promise of a midnight feast when we woke up. In my head she became a princess, waltzing into our lives to magic everything bad away.

When she climbed through the doorway to say goodnight, I was surprised to see that she looked perfectly normal: no glass slippers, no sparkly tiara on her head. She lifted her head and craned her neck back, gazing into the shadows of the arched roof.

'What a bedroom,' she whispered, as if she were in a cathedral, and she lay down next to me, looking up at the vast space above us.

A rhythmic clicking started up somewhere above our heads.

'What's that?'

'It's Mr Deathwatch-Beetle. He's chatting to his wife.'

'Lord, we have those, do we?' she said, as if she had decided to join us in this huge house, not aware that it belonged to Dad and me, and she'd need to ask first.

'Dad says they make music to help me sleep. Once I woke up and one was extra loud because it was actually sat on my ear.'

My mother shuddered and laughed all at the same time. 'I thought they tapped on wood to make the sound?'

'My ear must be made of wood then,' I giggled.

'When did you lose that tooth?' She was looking at my smile strangely, as if it scared her. I ran my tongue over my teeth, and came to the gap where the toffee apple had pulled one out.

'A while back,' I said, tonguing the hole.

'Oh.' She patted my cheek, frowning as she did. 'Well, goodnight, sweet,' she said, leaning in to hug me. It was our first hug, and it felt right and wrong, all at the same time. She was a lot thinner than Dad, and a lot more brittle, and her chin clunked against my collarbone. But she smelt nice, like exotic flowers, and I thought of Jasmine the parrot, sitting on my desk, and the rainforest that she had come from.

I lay in bed, my finger pressing into the hole where my tooth had been. It had never occurred to me that another tooth wouldn't grow in its place eventually, but now I thought about it, it had been a long time since I lost the first one. My finger revolved around inside my mouth, finding rough bits on my other teeth. They swelled with pain when I pressed them, and I withdrew my finger quickly.

I turned my attention instead to the itch that had begun in my bottom, enjoying the relief that raking my fingernails across the skin brought.

When sleep had nearly found me, I heard their voices drifting up from downstairs, bringing me back to consciousness. I crept out of bed and tiptoed down the curved staircase onto the landing below, sinking onto the top step and rubbing my bottom against the carpet to sate the itch. Mum and Dad were in the kitchen, their voices quite audible.

'Worms,' I heard, and I wondered whether they were off for a late-night fishing trip in the moat, which was pointless because I'd never seen a single fish in there, but then my mother's voice carried on, louder than before.

'She's got worms, Tobias! Her nails are so long, lord knows what's stuck under them.'

I looked down. I had been digging in the earth by the cart shed yesterday, and my hands were a rusty brown from the soil. My finger-nails were long and bendy with a line of thick black dirt underneath each one. My bottom on the stairs was painful now, and my hand inched automatically closer, desperate to scratch at it. It wasn't such a nice feeling anymore; raw instead of tickly, making me want to scrape harder, tearing the soreness away.

Mum carried on below.

'I haven't seen her wash her hands since I've been here, and when did she last have a bath? And her tooth! Does she go to the dentist ever? The poor mite, Tobias, the poor little mite.'

There was silence now. It filled the house, drifting up the stairs like a ghostly smog, enveloping me until I thought I had become deaf.

'I love her ferociously.' Dad's voice broke through the silent mist, quieter than I had ever heard it before, and I strained to listen. I imag-ined Mum, grown to a huge monster, towering over him as he shrunk to the size of a mouse.

'Why didn't you call me?' Mum sounded angry. 'Why didn't you let me know?'

I hugged Monty closer.

'I wasn't aware you were allowed out on day release from those places.'

'Of course they let you out: I checked myself in, didn't I? I can check myself out.'

'You're out for good?' There was disbelief in his voice, and I felt my mother bristling, out of sight in the kitchen below.

'Careful, Dad,' I whispered into Monty's fur.

'I'm glad you have such strong belief in my ability to stay well,' she said, her voice cracking, almost as if she were crying. 'How could I stay there after I got your letter? I've worked so hard since then to get better.'

'You're cured then?'

'Cured? What does that even mean, cured? It's not something that's going to go away, Tobias. But I need to be here now. To look after our daughter: what she needs now is love and care.'

'She has it. I loved her enough to write to you when I... when...' His voice faltered and died.

I felt the silence flow in like a tide in the house, flooding past me, then receding back until the tick of the grandfather clock in the hall became audible again.

Their voices began again, getting louder, battling against one another, and this time I imagined them as yowling cats, circling each other round the kitchen table. Dad was a battered Tom, saggy and shaggy with half an ear torn away. Mum was black and sleek like a witch's cat, with magic in her heart and sharp, sharp claws. Dad didn't stand a chance.

I got up and ran down the remaining stairs, barrelling through the hallway and into the kitchen, where the cats dissolved back into my parents, and I charged at Mum, my hair flying behind me, my arms outstretched as I ran with full force into her, reaching up to scratch at her face.

'Daddy needed you!' I shouted. 'Who cares if there's worms in my arse and dirt and no baths? I've got a cat and a big bedroom and the best dad ever. And I don't need a mum. You're not a princess, you're an imposter, you're... you're Cruella de Vil.' And I sank my nails into her cheek, feeling with satisfaction the skin catch momentarily under the force of my swipe, before running out of the kitchen, and back up the two flights of stairs to my bedroom, where I threw myself onto the bed and burst into tears.

I slept late the next day. I don't know what woke me, only that I had the feeling someone had been whispering to me just before I woke up. I looked around my bedroom, blinking. Mid-morning light flooded the cavernous space. My face felt tight from the tears that had dried on my skin the night before. I sat up, the echo of the half-dreamt whisper still in my ears.

My eyes felt scratchy. I looked around for Monty to cuddle, but he was nowhere to be seen. I could smell coffee and tea and toast, and I curled myself up in my quilt and pretended to be on an island far away from all grown-ups.

Dad put his head round the door, and I burrowed further into my quilt. He didn't say anything, but I felt the weight of him pinning the quilt to the bed as he sat by me. Then his hand was on my back, stroking in rough circles. If I were a cat, I thought, I'd purr. Instead I began to sob, and I pulled myself out of the quilt and wrapped my arms around his waist, burying my face in his dressing gown.

'Why is she back?'

'Because she loves you.'

'And because she loves you?'

'We... need looking after.'

'Will she stay this time?'

Dad didn't answer. Instead, he pulled a bottle out of his dressing-gown pocket and unscrewed it, tipping the contents into a spoon and holding it in front of my mouth.

'She went out early this morning and got you this.'

'What is it?'

'Worm medicine.'

'Is it made of worms?'

'No, it gets rid of them. Open up.'

I opened my mouth and he tipped it in, the cold metal of the spoon singing against my teeth. The medicine tasted chalky and sour and I swallowed, accepting a sip of Dad's sweet coffee afterwards to take the taste away.

'Don't tell me you're allowed coffee now too?' My mother's smiling face poked up from the stairs below, the scratch on her cheek red against her pale skin. I pulled the quilt back over my head, embarrassed by my behaviour the day before. It was quite hard to breathe under there.

'I want Monty,' I said, deliberately sounding babyish so they wouldn't tell me off for what I had done.

'We'll go and look for him,' Meg said, and the bed creaked as Dad got up too. I listened to their departing footsteps, quickly pulling the quilt off my head and sucking in huge gulps of air.

'Monty,' Dad shouted, from far off at the front of the house. We were all looking now.

'Monty!' I called. I was wearing my pyjamas still, my feet stuffed into wellies,

'Monty,' my mother sang. I stopped at the edge of the moat. A thick bubble popped gloopily on its surface, as if something were breathing far down below. Was it the gargoyle, awake from a deep slumber, or my Monty-cat, racing through the last of his nine lives? I remembered my mother's battered case of catskins, and for a moment everything shivered as I teetered on the edge of the moat.

'Whoa there,' my mum caught me and pulled me away, her hand gripping my arm.

And then we heard it, from far away, a high-pitched cry.

'Monty,' I whispered, and I was off.

I raced towards the sound, through the garden, past the willow, towards the meadow. Monty's cry was louder here, and I stopped at the meadow's entrance, trying to see him between the mobiles and the hummocks of long grass. It was a hot, sultry day, and the mobiles were still. I followed the sound, close now, a keening cry I'd never heard him make before. I lifted my foot to take another step.

'Stop!' My mother's voice, breathless behind me. It had lost all its singsong lilt. It was commanding, and I did as she said, one foot in mid-air.

'Look, just ahead of you. Careful, Romilly.'

I looked. Just in front of me, hidden by a mound of grass, was Monty. My tiny half-kitten half-cat, lying awkwardly, one of his front paws raised as if he were waving. The sound he made was terrifying. He was so still I had almost stepped on him. Then he began thrashing about, his tongue out, panting, his little body convulsing.

And then I saw the wire. Almost invisible, it ran from his leg to a stick that had been pushed into the ground, and it was taut, pulling tighter around his leg each time he moved. His pure white leg wore a ring of red as if he had dressed up in a ruby bracelet.

'Monty?' I asked, not understanding. I dropped down by his head and stroked him carefully, and still he wailed. It was a pitiful sound, full of pain, and I couldn't think above it. I slammed my hands over my ears and shut my eyes, listening instead to the catching of mucus in my nose.

I sensed somebody crouching next to me and opened my eyes just a crack. My mother was there, lifting Monty gently. He didn't struggle, lying limply in her hands as she placed him closer to the stick so that the taut wire relaxed, though it was still pulled tight around his leg. His mouth opened wider as he cried, silent to my blocked ears. The sound of my panicked breathing got louder in my head.

My mother gently pulled my hands from my ears, and the full horror of the sound he was making penetrated deep into my head and down into my ribs. She drew my face away from him so that I was looking at her.

'Romilly. Look at me. I need your help. Focus on me.' Her face was serious and full of concerned love, and I knew in that moment that I could trust her. I did as she said, trying not to turn and look at my poor mutilated kitten. Her face was pale, with freckles on the nose and cheeks, just like mine. Just like me.

'You need to hold him still. I can help him, but he must stay still. Do you understand? If he goes running off after I release him, we may never see him again. Can you help me?' She was looking at me with such ferocious intensity that I nodded my head vigorously, desperate to show her I could help. I reached down to Monty and held his body securely, the sound of his pain filling my head until even my thoughts disappeared and the whole world shrunk down to my shaking hands clutching at the white fur.

My mother was whispering to him, her voice like a lullaby as she looked closely at his leg. His tiny broken paw twitched involuntarily, shaking droplets of blood onto the grass.

Then she took a pin from her hair and eased it gently under the wire around his leg and Monty screamed. But then I saw that the wire was loosening, and Monty was trying to scramble up, pulling his mangled leg free of the noose. I held on tight amid a flurry of white hair. His eyes were bigger than I had ever seen them. He clung to my jumper with his one good front paw, his claws knitting themselves into me so hard that it hurt, but it was a good hurt and I didn't complain, I scooped him to me and dropped kisses on his head, his nose, and his cold, cold ears, my pyjamas painted with his blood so that we both were dressed in trembling rubies.

The stitches were huge, puncturing his shaved skin like wiry teeth.

'But he might not be here at all if your mother hadn't thought so quickly,' Dad said, sharing a quick glance with her as he tried to strap Monty into the wheelchair he had built for him. It was an ugly contraption made out of wood and leather, using the wheels from my old toy pram. The strap was meant to secure around his chest, supporting the front of his body and stopping him from tipping over on his one remaining front leg. As Dad tried to pin him down, Monty twisted away and staggered across the room. His new three-legged walk was clumsy, like a drunken hare, and he came to a stop at the other end of the room, staring warily at the strange invention in Dad's hands.

We were in the drawing room, watching him to make sure he didn't over-exercise. Dad and I rarely used this room. It was full of a mishmash of furniture that had come with the house, pieces that Dad called eclectic and my mother called junk, but there was a twinkle in her eye when she said it.

Monty kamikaze-rolled towards us across the parquet floor, forgetting he was missing a leg, and somehow managing to pounce on a spider in the process. I watched with pleasure as he chewed it, the legs poking out of his mouth.

'Who do you think set the trap?' I said, wincing as I remembered the wire squeezing his leg so hard that the skin parted like butter.

'I don't know.' My mum was examining the little posy of dusky pink roses I had picked to say thank you for saving Monty. They were the exact rosy blush of her cheeks, and they were almost as pretty as she was. I hoped she would put them in a vase by her bed.

'I expect whoever it was didn't mean to catch a cat,' she said, 'they were probably after a rabbit. My grandfather used to catch them like that all the time.'

'Whoever they are, they're mean. I hope they get their leg caught in a trap.' Maybe Dad could make one. A human-sized one with sharp, bitey teeth and an electric saw to cut through the bone.

Monty was trying to climb the velvet curtains now. The movement caused a flurry of moths to take off like papery snowflakes. The claws of his one front paw attached themselves to the material, and he hung there, unable to unhook himself. He stared at us silently. Mum got up to help him, leaving the roses abandoned on the floor.

'He's healing well, your Captain Montgomery,' she said. 'He was very brave. We should give him a promotion.' She placed him in my lap and dropped a kiss onto my head at the same time.

'What's higher than a captain?' I asked, feeling a blush of affection for my mother. I ducked my flaming face on the pretence of checking his stitches. They felt bumpy under my fingers. The shaved skin was puckered, like the frill of a snail's body.

'Hmm, I think it's a major.'

'Major Montgomery of the Second Regiment,' I whispered, trying it out for size.

'Romilly my girl,' Dad said, putting his hand in his pocket, 'I almost forgot, this is for you.' He pulled out something small and brown, swinging from his hand, and dropped it into my palm. It felt soft, nestling in my hand like a little mouse. A keyring loop hung from its top. I turned it over. It was an animal's paw, the little pink pads hardened and shiny.

'Oh, Tobias, no,' Meg said, and with a shiver I realised it was Monty's hurt foot. It dangled from my hand, gently twirling.

'What?' Dad said, shrugging. 'The vet would have thrown it away. Look.' He bent down and touched the silky fur, his finger nearly as big as the whole paw. 'I soaked it in salt water so it's preserved. You can just see the edge of his leg bone poking out of the skin there.'

I stared at it with fascinated revulsion, marvelling at Dad's tiny stitches holding the crisp skin closed. I held it out to Monty, who sniffed it, burying his nose deep into the crevices of the pads as he caught his own scent. I wondered if he knew what it was.

'Romilly, you don't have to keep it.'

'Monty likes it. And if he likes it, it must be OK. Besides, I'm eleven now, that's plenty old enough for something like this. Mum, how can a part of him be dead, but part of him still be alive?'

Monty was rubbing his cheek against the paw now, purring loudly. He tried to bat at it, forgetting he only had one front leg and rolling over onto the rug again.

Mum was silent. I looked up.

'You called me Mum,' she said.

Ten

The day after Monty came home from the vet's, I bent down underneath the water butt, looking for the nail varnish I had hidden there two summers ago.

Mum's long nails were one of the only things I remembered about her from before: the sharp, pleasant-painful feel of them as she held tightly onto my hand. This morning, I had tried to cut the end of my own nails into sharp points, but Mum caught me and made me cut them straight, so now they were short and blunt. They would look much better with varnish on them, I thought. Much more grown up.

The grass had grown since I'd hidden the bottle, but it was still there, the bleached white shoots twisting around its lid. I pulled them off and gazed at the bright, viscous liquid within, considering whether it was too old and gloopy to work.

'What've you got there?' The voice startled me. I stuffed the nail varnish behind my back and turned around.

It was Stacey. She was dressed in her customary shorts and T-shirt. She looked cleaner than I had seen her before, as if her mum had managed to dunk her in a bath, though I thought it more likely she had just gone for a swim in the river.

'Have you been at your gran's again?' I said brightly, knowing deep down that it was the publication of the new book that had put her off coming to see me. I always felt slightly embarrassed when we looked at the books together, as if I should feel guilty that I was famous and she was not.

'I've been around,' she said. 'I haven't seen *you* in ages either. You never go out to play anymore.'

I had thought I was getting a bit too old for playing. Stacey was the kind of girl that would continue to play all of her life, without caring who laughed at her. I reluctantly pulled the nail varnish out from behind my back to show her. I was reminded of the first time I had met her, when I had been standing right here, having just hidden the same bottle under the water butt.

'That's a bit of a girlie colour,' she said, her nose turning up at the end.

'I *am* a girl,' I said, looking down to check the pink decoration was still stitched into my jeans, and seeing as I did so my reflection in the water butt. The surface was oily and syrupy-black, and for a second the sightless face of the shadowy woman reared up at me.

'You all right?' Stacey said, looking at me curiously. 'You look like you've seen a ghost.'

I looked at the water again, but it was only my own reflection. 'I'm fine,' I said. 'Your hair's different,' I added.

'Cut it myself. But it's hard to reach the back of your own head.' She patted a few straggly bits on her neck.

'Why didn't your mum do it?'

'Too busy I s'pose.'

She stepped closer and peered into the water butt. Her nose wrinkled at the smell. It had rained throughout the end of the summer, and the tank was nearly full of water again. With lightning speed she dipped her hand in and pulled out a snail that was attached to the side.

'Guess what?' she said.

'What?'

'I saw a ghost in your garden earlier.' She was rolling the snail between her palms, smoothing it like a ball of plasticine.

I glanced at her, trying to work out if she was telling the truth. She looked serious. 'What did it look like?'

'It was a lady. Baggy jeans and a sort of smock top. Big wooden earrings that looked like parrots.'

'That's not a ghost. It's my mum.'

'But you haven't seen your mum in years.'

'I know, but she's back.'

'Parents don't just come back.'

I felt bad for her. Her dad may never come back, but it didn't mean my mum couldn't.

'Yes they do. Sometimes.'

'You're lying. I don't believe you ever had a mum.'

'Just because you've never seen her, doesn't mean she doesn't exist,' I said. 'I've never seen your mum, but I know you have one.'

Stacey didn't answer.

'Where was it, then?' I said, relenting, 'this ghost you saw?'

She pointed to the compost heap next to the cart shed. Something dusky pink sat on top. I got up for a closer look.

It was the roses I had given to Mum yesterday. I picked them up and stroked one of the velvety petals, watching a tiny beetle as it crept along a stem. Why would she throw them away when they were still so fresh?

'We could make a potion,' Stacey said just behind me, making me jump. She reached round and grabbed the flowers from my hands. 'Petal potion,' she said, 'like the old gods used to make.'

'What old gods?'

'I dunno. Flower gods? Get some water from the moat, would you?'

As if under her spell, I turned and walked to the moat. I rooted around in the grass for a vessel to put it in, kicking at a few broken flower pots before finding an old jar that was almost whole. It must have been left over from one of Dad's outside painting sessions: the inside was a pale green-blue as if he had been painting the sky. I rinsed it in the moat, and scooped the water into it. When I held it up to the light I could see a whole world swirling within: little dancing insects spiralling through the water, drifting flakes of green algae, and a peculiar little thing with feelers, its body encased in tiny stones, sinking down, down, and settling at the bottom.

Stacey was roaming the garden, looking for a potion-making spot. She ducked under the willow and I followed her, placing the jar right at the centre of the dusty brown circle.

'After this, let's race snails,' she said, her mind already cantering forwards to the rest of the day.

'OK,' I said begrudgingly, watching her tear at the petals of my mother's roses and drop them into the jar. She scooped a handful of potion out and, pulling roughly at my arm, sprinkled it over us both.

The shock of the cold water raised goosebumps on my arm. We both lay back, gazing up at the willow, its green fringe splayed out all around us in a perfect circle. We could do anything in here, I thought, and no one would know.

'Come on,' Stacey said, pulling herself up, her arms covered in fragments of pink petal. She took my nail varnish from her pocket. She would make a good pickpocket: I hadn't seen her take it.

'We could paint this on the snails,' she said, holding it up, 'we can number them so we know which one wins.'

Kicking over the potion, she ducked and ran out from under the willow. I held back, watching as Mum's rose petals and countless living beings cascaded out of their world and flooded across the bare earth.

I found her at the water butt. She was staring down into the slimy depths. I looked doubtfully at the shells bobbing on the surface.

'Wouldn't it be cruel, painting nail varnish on them?'

'They're only snails. They don't have brains or anything.'

I looked at my precious bottle of nail polish, then at Stacey with her terrible haircut. Her eyebrows were raised and her mouth was pursed. She looked like she was holding her breath in anticipation.

'OK,' I said grudgingly.

'Cool. Snail varnish!' She dropped onto the grass by the brick wall and wedged her fingers round one of the bricks.

'What are you doing?' I said, kneeling down beside her. Ignoring me, she levered a brick out, bending low so she could see into the small hollow she'd opened up.

'Whoever wins gets this,' she said, pulling out a small round badge and handing it to me. On its rusty face was a little squirrel dressed in a colourful suit. The words 'The Tufty Club' were written round the edge in black.

'How did you know it was there?'

She shrugged again, replacing the brick with practised flair. I wondered what other secrets she knew about Braër.

'What's the Tufty Club?'

'Dunno. But it's the only prize we've got, unless you want to bet this nail varnish.'

I grabbed the little bottle from her and held onto it tightly.

'Thought not. Tufty it is.'

We scooped up a handful of snails each, me placing mine on the grass quickly and wiping my hands on my T-shirt, Stacey seeming to relish the feel of the slime between her fingers.

We decided to paint a picture on them instead of a number. My snails had stars on them. Stacey's had faces that looked more like fried eggs.

The first pair of snails went in opposite directions, but the second pair began to race. Slowly they crept over the grass, picking up tiny crumbs of dirt on the way. Stacey's snail climbed a long blade of grass which buckled forward, propelling it into the lead. She knelt as close as she could, her head bent in silent support of her snail. But the shock of its tumble from the grass had sent it into its shell, and no amount of prodding would coax it out. My snail gambolled forward, joyfully crossing the dandelion finish line.

Smash. Stacey's fist came down on its shell.

Crunch. Her shoe thudded on top of her own snail. Getting to her feet, glistening snail shell hanging from her knees, she stood over the snails, her face snarling, then she turned with a whirl and ran from the garden.

'Stacey!' I called, jumping up to run after her, but she had gone. Seeing the two mashed snails in the grass I sank down to scoop them up, the smell of nail varnish in my nostrils, tears dripping onto them as I watched their slow, silent death throes.

Eleven

'Dad?'

'Ah, there you are, Roe. Grab the other end, would you?'

I took hold of the end of the plank of wood and lifted, holding on fast, feeling my arm muscles shudder at its weight. There was a piece of snail shell on my sleeve still, I could see it hanging by a thread. I went to pick it off, hefting the wood into my other hand, but my knees wobbled under the weight of it and I left the shell dangling where it was.

'Hold tight, Romilly, please don't drop it.'

'Dad?'

'Yes,' he said distractedly, trying to manoeuvre the plank towards the ground and simultaneously pick up a hammer and nails.

'How can you tell if someone's real and not a ghost?'

Dad lowered the plank to the ground, and gently spat a couple of nails onto the grass while he thought. My arms felt like they might fall off. I lowered my own end to the ground too, and began to pick out the splinters in my palms, brushing the piece of shell away as I did so.

Dad had spent a lot of the summer erecting a shed in the garden. Small yet grand, it had a crenulated roof and faux marble pillars at the entrance. Above the door was a little cut-out of a wooden circus tent, its flaps folded back. If you looked really closely, you could just see an elephant inside balancing on a big red-and-yellow ball. The shed was to be his painting studio. During its construction, he was often to be seen standing back and contemplating it, or else pacing out the space inside, sketching the layout of armchair and drawing board.

Now, he sucked on a fragment of leftover nail in his mouth as he contemplated my question.

'Is it if you can't touch them, is that how you know?' I asked hopefully, poking him gently in the belly to demonstrate he was real.

I thought about what Stacey had said about my mum. I trusted Stacey's judgement, but Mum couldn't possibly be a ghost. And yet there *was* something otherworldly about her, a sort of glassy sadness that made it hard to love her.

There had been a moment – after she saved Monty from the snare – where everything felt exactly right: we were like a proper family all of a sudden, sharing in silly stories and laughing with each other, just like you see on the TV. When she came upstairs that evening to kiss me goodnight, she hugged me so tightly, it was as if she couldn't quite believe I was real. Each hug she gave me felt better than the last, like she was learning from scratch how to do it.

But then last night, as she leant in to kiss me goodnight, her ruby red nails pinned the pillow on either side of me, and a long-forgotten memory flitted across my vision: a red-nailed hand swooping sharply towards my cheek, so fast that I had no time to duck out of the way. As her lips kissed my cheek, I flinched, the memory of the pain so sharp it was as if she had hit me for real.

Mum paused, frowning. 'What's wrong?' she said.

But how could I put into words the memory, if memory it was? I think she saw the fright in my eyes, because she drew away, saying goodnight in a flat voice, before climbing back down the stairs.

I had wanted to jump out of bed and follow her, throwing myself into her arms for a hug the way I did with Dad, but there was something about Mum that stopped me doing anything too spontaneous, as if she might be frightened by the sudden movement and run away, never to be seen again.

Dad was still considering my question. He had picked up the hammer again and was turning it in his hands. 'But if you went round prodding people to check they were real,' he said, 'you'd end up in prison.'

I loved this about Dad. He always gave my questions some real thought. He was looking at me while I thought about all this, his brow creased.

'Look,' he said, 'relationships need give and take, Romilly. Even mother-daughter relationships. Perhaps you need to make the first move with your mum – show her you care. Why don't you thank her for all the nice things she's done for you? That would be a good start.'

I racked my brains for things I could thank her for. There wasn't a huge amount to choose from. And then I remembered my little picture of Mary Mother-of-God. I had never had the chance to thank her for it when she sent it. I would do that.

'She's as real as the rest of us, your mum,' Dad said. 'I know she might not be what you were expecting, but she's your mother, and that counts for a lot.'

I shoved my hands in my pockets, feeling guilty.

'I don't know if there is a way to tell if someone is definitely real or not, Roe. The most real people are sometimes not really real at all, and the most mysterious and other worldly people are sometimes more real than you or I.'

'I am real, aren't I?' I asked quietly, pulling my hands out of my pockets and looking at them, and wondering if it were possible to touch one's own skin to prove your realness.

'You're as real as I am.' He bent down and dug his finger into the recently excavated mud that surrounded his shed. Straightening up, he lifted his hand and swabbed the mud down my forehead and over my nose and mouth, coming to a stop on my chin. I could smell the mud's cold tang, and feel its grit on my teeth. I stood still, focusing on a small crumb of wet earth on the end of my nose until my eyes crossed.

'You're as real as that earth on your skin. And it's made from millions of leaves and insects, millions of years old. Nothing is more real.' He smiled at me. 'Close your eyes. Can you feel it still, even if you can't see it? Can you smell it?'

I did as I was told, my world shrinking down to the slick of cold wetness on my face. I nodded, feeling not like a human any more, but a relic, ancient and petrified. I didn't know if I felt real at all anymore.

In the house, Mum was sitting on the velvet sofa, rolling up a ball of wool that Monty had chased across the rug. A pale sunbeam slanted across her face, making a slice of her shimmer. I watched her for a moment, trying to pluck up the courage to talk to her.

'Mum?'

She looked up and smiled.

'Thank you for the picture of Mary Mother-of-God,' I said, kneeling down on the rug by her feet.

'What?'

'The lady with the golden hat? You sent it to me just before the hurricane broke my arm. When I was nine.'

She set the wool on her lap. 'You did get in a lot of scrapes before I came along, didn't you?' she said. 'I don't remember sending you a picture.'

'You did. You said that she would look after me until you could. And she has.' I wanted to convey how comforting the little picture had been, but Mum was frowning.

'I think I'd remember doing something like that. And why would I send you a picture of the Virgin Mary? I'm not religious. You must have got it from somewhere else.'

'I didn't. You sent it. And you sent me the denim dress, the first one.'

'I admit, I did send that – I remember the nurses helping me order it – but not the picture.' She was looking at me warily. She put a hand to my forehead, and I jumped at the touch. 'Are you sure you're feeling all right?' she said.

I shook my head, pushing her hand away, searching around for a way to explain. 'You wrote me a letter,' I said. 'I can go and find it. . .' I started to rise.

'Don't be so silly, child. I remember the autumn you hurt your arm. I wasn't in a good place. I could never have written a letter back then, let alone send things, I wasn't well enough to get my own breakfast.' She narrowed her eyes. 'Is this a trick?'

'No!' I felt like I was in sinking mud, slowly being swallowed up: this conversation had layers that I couldn't understand. 'Mud!' I blurted out, clinging on to Dad's explanation.

'What?' Mum said, the word coming out in a huff of air.

'Dad says I'm as real as mud.' I sank back down onto the floor, and picked up a strand of wool, curling it into a ball to help her. 'We were talking about how you can tell if someone is real, and Dad said I'm as real as mud.'

Mum looked as if her patience was wearing thin. She took a breath, her eyebrows rising. 'Well, mud is very real.'

'He said I was as real as him, and he's very real. But mud isn't very real, is it? It doesn't breathe.' I was getting confused now, forgetting his explanation that had made perfect sense moments ago. I wrapped a dead daddy-long-legs up into the ball of wool, a little surprise for next time Mum did some knitting. I imagined with pleasure a jumper embellished with delicate lace-wings, a few long spiny legs here and there for good measure.

'You mean mud isn't very *human*,' Mum said, plucking the ball of wool from my hands and picking out the bits of daddy-long-legs she could see before giving it back. 'It's definitely real. And it does sort of breathe.'

'Can someone be human and not real?' I picked up a dead fly and tucked it inside the wool.

'Romilly, will you please stop putting dead insects into my wool. It's disgusting.' She grabbed the ball again and shook the fly out onto the floor. The ball of wool slipped from her hands and unrolled across the rug. 'Now look what you've made me do,' she said, exasperated.

The dead fly came to a stop near Monty, and I leant over and flicked it for him. Mum put a hand to my forehead again. Bits of dried mud flaked away and floated down in front of my eyes.

'You're a bit warm, do you think you might stay inside now? There's a chill in the garden.'

'But I want to go and find Stac. . .' She looked up, eyebrows raised. 'I want to go and play outside,' I finished lamely. Mum didn't approve of Stacey, which was unfair since she hadn't even met her yet. Mum didn't approve of much, it turned out, except manners and early bedtimes. I looked out of the window and sighed. I wanted to go and see if Stacey was all right after the snails outburst.

'Please?' I said. 'Please can I go back outside? Just for a little while?'

'I don't think so, Romilly, not today. You might catch a chill: your chest's sounding a little gritty.' She had picked up the ball of wool again.

I tried to focus on my breathing, but it sounded perfectly normal to me. 'But I need to check something,' I said, picking at the desiccated pieces of insect on the rug and wondering when they would turn into mud.

'For goodness' sake. No means no!'

'Dad'll let me,' I said, starting to get up.

She looked at me with ill-concealed anger. 'I'm here now, and I say you're to stay inside. Sit. Down.'

Deep in my chest, a white-hot rage opened up, goading me. 'Why did you leave us?' I asked.

She held my gaze for a moment before looking out of the window at the moat, her hands stroking the wool. 'You need to ask your father that,' she said, and at her answer, the rage and the injustice and the unfairness of it all bubbled up inside me, and I couldn't hold the words in any more.

I looked down at the rug and whispered, 'You're just a ghost.' I let the words pour out into the red and black threads, forcing my anger into their pattern, shooting it out like lasers from my eyes.

Mum dropped the ball of wool. 'What did you say, young lady?' Her voice was icy.

'Nothing,' I said quickly. A little bit of warmth trickled into my pants.

She picked up the wool again, spooling it angrily in her hands, not taking her eyes off me. 'How dare you,' she said. 'I come here to look after you. I've been nothing but nice to you – despite everything that happened – and yet you're so insolent. So rude.'

With each word she spoke, it was as if she was picking away at our relationship, attacking it in the same way that she attacked the knots in the wool, pulling and stabbing. I was mesmerised by her hands, by the sharp, red nails plunging into the soft wool.

And suddenly those sharp talons were coming towards me, gripping my arm, squeezing into my bare flesh until I thought my skin would break apart.

My pants suddenly felt very warm as a wet torrent of urine was released.

Smack! A sharp pain cascaded across the backs of my legs, and without warning I was lying on the floor.

'Look what you've done – soaked the rug.' A hand grabbed at my wrist, sharp nails digging into the bones of my arm that had so recently healed, and I was being dragged back onto my feet and pulled along. Glimpses of Braër's hall rushed past me as I half-ran behind Mum, and then we were in the kitchen and I was being pushed into the pantry, and the door was shutting, and I was alone.

It was cold in the pantry, and I shivered as I got to my feet, the smell of urine mixing with the years-old dried herbs that sat in jars on the shelves. I could still hear my mother on the other side of the door. I put my eye to the keyhole and I saw her, pacing. She was whispering to herself, her hands to her face, and then her knees buckled from under her and she let out a strange guttural moan, collapsing like a broken marionette onto the floor.

'Mum,' I whispered, 'Mummy? Are you all right?'

She lay on the floor, silent now, her hands still over her face as if she couldn't bear to look at anything. Then she pulled herself up and brushed herself down, and, without looking at the pantry, walked out of the kitchen.

I stood up and looked around me. There was a small square grate at the back of the little space. I reached up on tiptoe and wiggled my fingers through its lattice pattern, hoping someone would see and come and rescue me.

My arm was aching from being so high up and my fingers were growing numb and tingly, when, 'Who's there?' came a familiar voice. Relief flooded through me.

'Stacey?' I whispered.

'Romilly? Why are you sticking your fingers out like that? I thought they were a bunch of worms.'

'Stacey, help me.'

'What are you doing in there?' she said, her voice so close now I could feel her warm breath on my fingers.

'Mum shut me in the pantry,' I whispered. 'Can you come and let me out?'

'I don't think I'm allowed in your house. I don't think your mum likes me.' She sounded scared.

I tried not to whimper. 'Then can you find my dad? He'll be able to let me out.'

'I'll try,' she said, and I felt the tips of her fingers briefly clutch at mine. I jumped at her touch.

'Stacey?' I whispered urgently, but she was gone. I sat down on the floor and waited.

A high, breathless child's voice lingered in my ear, whispering me awake. I lifted my head, my cheek creased from the tiles on the pantry floor. I was shivering with cold.

The voice was still there, a soft caress in the hard, cold room. The pantry was dark, despite the light trickling in from the grate, and I shifted around, trying to get my bearings, looking for the source of the whispering voice.

'Stacey?' I said quietly, cautiously, but there was no answer.

I was alone.

My stomach rumbled. How many meals had I missed? Maybe I would die in here, I thought with a gulp. I remembered that it was important to drink if you wanted to stay alive, and I got up gingerly and started feeling along the shelves, running my hands over the glass bottles and jars. My fingers found a fat, brown bottle. I squinted in the gloom at the label, sounding out the letters. The first word was 'malt', like Maltesers, I thought, licking my lips. The second word was longer and alien to me. I wished that Dad has spent more time on my spellings: I couldn't get past the first three letters, *v i n*. I held the heavy bottle in my hands, trying to decide. Malt was nourishing, Dad said, like the Ovaltine he made me before bed.

I unscrewed the cap. Immediately its acrid smell hit the back of my nose, making my eyes fill with water. I held the bottle away from me, listening to the world outside the pantry, hoping to be rescued before I needed to drink. I thought I could make out the sound of footsteps far off, then mumbled shouts and a door slamming. Then silence. My mouth was dry. I screwed up my nose and took a deep gulp from the bottle.

An acidic fire hit my stomach, and I choked, the spray of liquid exploding out of my mouth as I simultaneously tried to breathe in. There was a whole family of spiny hedgehogs in my nose, scrambling to get out, and a cactus pulsing in my brain. I shook my head, trying to swallow through the pain, and then footsteps were coming closer, and the pantry latch was lifting, and the door was opening and Dad's huge silhouette was standing in the light, scooping me up and hugging me close.

'Romilly,' he roared, 'oh, my darling child.' And I could hardly breathe I was so relieved.

My parents were arguing again. I was in bed, pretending to be asleep. I had fresh pyjamas on and Monty was lying in my arms.

Mum and Dad's voices were far away, as if they had shut themselves in a room so I wouldn't hear. I wondered if they were in the pantry. Then a door downstairs opened and Mum's voice was clear as a bell.

'. . . nothing wrong with you. It's all a lie.'

I could hear her coming up the stairs now, Dad's heavy footsteps following behind. I pulled the duvet over my head, hoping they weren't coming up to my room.

'Why would I lie?' Dad's voice now, booming deeply through the duvet. 'I didn't want you to come, you know. I only wrote to let you know. You're just here because the books are doing well. Where were you when she was younger, eh?'

'How dare you. You know exactly where I was, not that you ever visited. Not that you ever brought her.'

'What good would it have done her to see you in there?'

'What about me, Tobias? What about the good it would have done *me*?' Her voice was so high-pitched now it was almost a scream. Suddenly it dropped. 'I can't do it, Tobias, I can't look after her. I've tried, I really have, but she's such a strong-willed child.'

'Like her mother, then.'

'And when I look at her, I see...'

'You're just seeing what you want to see,' Dad interrupted, his voice was quieter now. 'And you can't blame her, Meg. She was four years old.'

'I can't stay here. It's so claustrophobic, so isolated. And I can't be around her, not after...' I strained to listen, but Mum's voice was becoming quieter too, almost as if she were whispering.

Dad's voice boomed in response. 'No! That won't happen. She stays here with me. You can stay, or you can go, but Romilly goes nowhere.'

'You want me to leave her to run wild with you? After all you've told me? She could get abducted by a paedophile, or hit by a car.' Mum's voice was high-pitched again, like a shriek.

'She's not destined to die, you know, Meg. Let her dream her dreams and live her life if it makes her happy. She never wet herself before you came, and she damned well won't do it once you're gone. Go back to your facility and your five o'clock therapy meetings, we'll be fine without you.'

Their footsteps drummed back downstairs and I curled up in a ball, relieved they were going further away.

When I woke, Mum's voice had disappeared, and Dad was quietly climbing through into my bedroom. Monty stretched and chirruped in welcome. Dad pulled me into a gentle hug.

'I'm sorry I wet myself,' I mumbled.

'Don't be sorry.'

'Where's Mum?'

'She's gone.'

'Gone where?'

'Just gone.'

I plucked at a loose thread on my cotton duvet, it came smoothly out, leaving a long line of nothing behind. 'What's a facility?' I asked.

Dad sighed and rubbed at his beard. 'It's a... a place you go to live when you're not well.'

'Is it haunted? Do ghosts live there?'

'I don't think so. Actually, probably.' He snorted quietly under his breath.

'Will she come back?'

Dad paused, drawing circles on the duvet. Finally, he said, 'No.'

'Never?'

'I don't think so.'

I dropped my head and looked hard at the duvet, my eyes swimming.

'I can't let her come in and out of your life as she pleases, Romilly, it's not fair on you. You need routine, and she can't give you that right now.'

'Can I visit her? At her facility?'

'I don't know. When you're older, how about that?'

I nodded. It was strange. I had thought that if Mum left, then Dad would become the huge, roaring Dad I knew so well, but instead here he was cowed and shrunken like a little mouse on the end of my bed. I hoped that time would restore him, or else I might find myself shrinking with him, until we slipped between the floorboards of my bedroom, never to be seen again.

Twelve

As autumn turned to winter, we settled back into our old, familiar routines. Dad was often in London doing interviews in preparation for his third book, which would be out the following summer. On the days when he wasn't at home, I spent the time pulling out the few belongings Mum had left behind: an old red lipstick; a gossamer-thin scarf that I found hidden down the back of the sofa; a book about raising children. I gathered these things together and investigated them thoroughly, trying to find a clue to where Mum had gone. Before Dad got home each time, I hid them all away in my room, sensing that it was easier to pretend she had never been here at all than to explain what I was doing.

In early December, Dad came home from London with a shiny new toy.

'It's a metal detector,' he said, brandishing the long instrument in front of him like an elephant's trunk. It had a round disc at one end and a handle at the other. 'They're all the rage in the city – people are using them on the banks of the Thames to find bits of history. It's called mudlarking. I thought we could try it here.'

'Do you mean in the moat?' I had visions of standing up to my neck in pongy moatwater, tripping over the sunken fountain as I tried to wade through the mud, while Dad directed me, dry and comfortable from the bank.

'No! On the parsnip field behind Braër. Don't worry, you'll stay perfectly dry. Come on!'

The metal detector swung from right to left across the churned-up earth. We had heard it beep only once, when Dad dropped his keys underneath it to check it was working. In Dad's hands it looked graceful, its swan neck curved toward the ground, listening intently for something we humans couldn't hear. I had tried to hold it earlier, but it was surprisingly heavy, and it crunched along the ground, scraping at flints and old leftover parsnips.

'What kind of treasure are we looking for?' I asked, picturing an Aladdin's cave just beneath the field's surface. I half wondered if this was Dad's way of showing me where the treasure from his books was buried. I resolved to come back alone another day and dig.

'A gold torc would be nice,' Dad said, 'but even a ring-pull would be quite fabulous at the moment.' He wiped a hand over his damp brow. 'You've got to remember, Roe, that these things take time: it only takes three digs to bury the treasure, but it can take a thousand to find it.'

I remembered the coin I had unearthed in our meadow, before the mobiles were there, trying to think if it was still in my floorboard caddy.

After a while, I grew cold and bored, standing with nothing to do while Dad patiently swung the machine over the ground. I wished Stacey was here. Things were always more fun with her around. I looked out over the field. It was chocolate-dark against the white, wintry sky. It looked as if it were about to snow.

The metal detector beeped, making me jump.

'Ready with the spade, Roe?' I nodded, lifting it high so it glinted in the winter sun. Dad moved the detector carefully over the soil, back and forth, locating the treasure.

'It's small. It might be a jewelled amulet, or a filigree brooch. Or a Celtic ring belonging to Boudicca herself. Dig, Romilly, dig!' I did as I was told, and plunged my spade into the soil. It was surprisingly hard work. I dug for what felt like hours, my hands growing red raw from the cold, pausing now and then for Dad to run the detector over the hole.

Something silver winked in the sunshine. Dad grabbed the spade from me and sliced into the loam, barely missing my fingers. Dropping the spade, he leant forward, easing the treasure out from its burial site.

'What is it?' I asked, trying to work out what the little crumple sitting in his palm could be.

'It's a chewing-gum wrapper,' he said, frowning at the damp silver thing in his hand. I lifted it carefully and smoothed it out, pressing it into my pocket. Treasure was treasure, after all.

On the way back through the field, our noses red and dripping, Dad said, 'It's not really finding the treasure, Romilly, it's digging with all your might in the hope that you might glimpse something sparkling deep in the soil. That's the reason for all this folly.' He waved his arms around, indicating the field and the metal detector.

I nodded, not really knowing what he meant, but liking it anyway. 'What's the treasure in your books, Dad?'

He was silent for a moment, looking down at the clods of earth on his boots as we strode across the field. 'It's complicated, my love,' he said eventually.

'Complicated how?'

Dad sighed. 'There's... something hidden, but—'

'... But, it's not gold or jewels.' I tried to keep the disappointment out of my voice, but I could hear the tears catching at the back of my throat. 'It's not proper treasure at all.'

Dad stayed silent, stepping carefully over the ploughed furrows.

'Why won't you tell me?' I said. 'I promise I'll keep it a secret so everyone can still keep searching.'

He stopped, so suddenly I nearly bumped into him.

'If I told you,' he said, 'it wouldn't be a treasure hunt for *you*, would it? What would be the point of going to all this trouble, just to spoil it for my own daughter?'

Once home, we sat thawing in the kitchen, drinking hot chocolate and eating boiled eggs and soldiers. I pulled Dad's two books towards me, flicking through the pages as I ate. Dad cleared his throat and lifted his spoon in a toast, the golden yolk dripping down the handle toward his thumb.

'This moment right here, watching you read those books,' he said, 'is the very pinnacle of my career, and it is thanks to you, daughter-mine,' here he winked at me and belched quietly under his breath, 'for making this dream become a reality. May the Kemps go marching on.'

And he opened wide and swallowed the last morsel of egg, surveying the crumby mess of our shared tea as if he were a king presiding over his land.

I chewed my last mouthful of soldier thoughtfully. I was quite used to his speeches by now, and I knew from experience that it was better to ignore them, otherwise he wouldn't stop.

'Is it really me in this book, Dad?' I said, changing the subject.

Dad's spoon fell onto his plate with a clatter. 'Butter fingers,' he said crossly, 'what do you mean?'

'It's just, you started them when I was nine, and the girl in this second one looks exactly like the girl in the first one: she hasn't grown up like I have. I'm eleven now, and,' I wrinkled my nose up and studied me-in-the-book closely, 'in this book I don't look any different.'

Dad pulled his glasses onto his nose. They were a new addition to his face and I was having trouble getting used to them. 'I suppose you're timeless,' he said at last, smoothing the pages.

'Does that mean I'm really old?'

'No, it means… it means I've captured a glimpse of you and held it in these pages, like a flower pressing, and now you'll stay that way forever in time.'

'But I'm going to be twelve soon, and then I'll be a teenager after that. I don't always want to look like her.' I jabbed my finger at the little girl in the book.

A flash of irritation crossed Dad's face, but then it was gone, like a pebble dropped deep into the murky moat.

'Oh, don't worry, I can't stop you growing older, however much I'd like to. Look, here's you looking contemplative on the bridge.'

'What does contemplative mean?'

'It means deep in thought, I suppose. But you're not, darling, not usually. It's known as "artistic licence". And look, have you found the little mouse on every page yet? Monty's trying to catch them all.'

'Monty only ever manages to catch spiders. He's more of a purrer than a hunter.' The real Monty was sitting on the table between us, looking down at the book. I wondered if he knew it was a drawing of him.

'Thank God he's not a hunter, otherwise I'd be painting blood and viscera into every scene.' Dad chuckled to himself.

'Monty looks even more furry than in real life.' I stroked my cat's doppelgänger, surprised at how smooth he felt on the page.

'He's a very soft cat, your Monty,' Dad said, stroking Monty's fur covetously, 'you know, you could have him made into an elegant stole once he's dead, you could wrap him around your shoulders when you're an adult, then he could go with you wherever you went.'

I looked at Dad's face, trying to work out whether he was joking or not, and then I remembered Dougal, his Jack Russell who stood eternally and stiffly in a glass cage in Dad's study, and I felt a bit sick.

'Do you like them, Roe, the books, I mean?'

'They're wonderful.'

'Because you're the reason I made them, you know. It's your story, and it's—'

'Dad, my mole's on the wrong cheek.' I had paused on my favourite picture. It was a close-up of my face, framed by my blazing red hair. I had never noticed before. I put my finger to my actual cheek and felt the bump on my skin.

'What?' Dad said, leaning forward again, spilling his hot chocolate. 'No, it isn't.'

'It is, look, it's on my right cheek, not my left.' I lifted my face to him and he ran his thumb across my cheekbone, as if seeing was not quite enough.

'Oh, that's the printing process, Romilly, it flips things over so you see the mirror image.'

'But wouldn't words be flipped too? And they're all the right way round.' I began flicking through the book, trying to find images of me close up enough to see my mole.

'It's back-to-front in the original paintings.' Dad had got up and was looking over my shoulder. 'All artists have to learn how to write back-to-front; they teach it at art school. That and the art of procrastination.'

'But then my mole would have been flipped too.' My mind was working so hard flipping and swapping back and forth that I couldn't remember which cheek my mole was actually on, let alone the me on the page. I touched my face again, running my finger over the reassuring mark.

Dad remained silent, frowning at the picture.

'And look,' I said, scanning my face on the last few pages, 'it's on my right cheek here, but here it's on my left.'

Dad pulled the book towards him, his brow furrowed. He turned back to the first painting I had looked at, the close-up of my face shrouded by my auburn hair, and his hand went to the mole, touching it delicately as if the girl in the picture was alive.

'Did you forget, Dad? Couldn't you remember what I looked like?'

He lifted his eyes to me, and in the dark of the kitchen they looked sunken, as if he had aged ten years. 'I could never forget what you looked like,' he said, 'you're my reason for carrying on.'

I studied his face, not sure if he was joking or not. He seemed serious enough. 'Can I see this painting of me, Dad, the original?'

He sat back down and dabbed at the puddle of hot chocolate on the table. 'I'm afraid not, Romilly, it's still with the printers.' He smiled at me and touched my cheek again, the other one this time, leaving a sticky chocolatey smudge.

It was a couple of days later, when I looked in a mirror, that I noticed he'd left a chocolatey mole-shaped dot on my right cheek, exactly in line with my real mole, so that I was symmetrical. I covered up my real mole and gazed deep into the eyes of the reflection Romilly, wondering who she was.

The beginning of December had been mild, and it wasn't until Dad suggested we make Christmas decorations that I began to feel that fizz of excitement that builds on the darkened evenings that lead up to Christmas.

Together we made decorations for the tree, gluing little top hats onto blobs of cotton wool to make snowmen. Dad painted a set of angels made from meticulously cut baked bean tins. They were curved and smiling and weirdly threatening, as if their divine blue eyes could penetrate your soul. In contrast, my own angels were simple paper creations, grinning vacantly at their superior metal cousins.

'You know, Romilly,' Dad said, picking up a sprig of holly and twisting it with gold wire, 'holly was often brought inside a house in pagan times to ward off evil. It's said that it stops witches from entering your dwelling at night and casting a spell on you. It's always a good idea to have some nearby. For safety's sake.'

I paused from gluing the wool onto an angel's head, a sticky thumb holding it in place. He winked at me and raised an eyebrow, and I giggled.

January brought with it frosts so hard that the water in the toilet froze solid. Stacey came, and took great delight in peeing straight onto the layer of ice, watching it steam and melt beneath her.

'One tip,' she called to me from behind the half-closed toilet door, 'never eat yellow snow.'

In the evenings we put tea lights in jam jars in the garden so we could play out in the dark. I was allowed to light my own fires in the garden now. Dad showed us how to find the tiniest twigs that had fallen and died, caught in the branches of trees. These were the heart of the fire, around which we layered bigger and bigger sticks, the pile growing into the shape of a fat tepee.

When the flames had roared and begun to die, and the charred sticks had scattered, we laid baked potatoes on the glowing embers, pulling them out far too early and biting into their crispy black skin. The centre of my potato was hard and cold, but it tasted of smoke and excitement.

'Are you ever going back to school?' Stacey's voice was muffled over the popping of the fire, her mouth simultaneously chewing and talking.

'I doubt it, it's much more fun staying at home.'

'What's your old primary school like in the holidays? Do the teachers live there?'

'Of course not! They live... somewhere else.' My time at school felt like a lifetime away. I tried to remember if my teacher had ever mentioned where she lived. Perhaps she did stay at the school, curled up in the leaves on the playing field like a hedgehog and hibernating until spring.

'So there's no one there right now?'

'I don't know,' I said doubtfully, picking up a stick and stirring the embers so they caught and fizzed once again, 'why?'

'I'd like to go to your school.'

'It's not my school anymore,' I said, realising with a jolt that I hadn't been to school for over two years.

'Not to be taught, stupid, I mean go *now*. To see what it's like.'

I swallowed a mouthful of potato. It was a hard bit and it caught in my throat. 'I don't think we're allowed.'

'Course we're not allowed, that's why I want to go.'

'What, right now?' My mind was trying to think of reasons not to, but all I could come up with was, 'There might be ghosts.' I knew I sounded pathetic, and I wilted inwardly, knowing she had won.

'Yeah! I bet there are. There was a boy who went to your school once who drowned in a well. Maybe his ghost is there still, pulling up the bucket to try to find his long-dead body.'

'There isn't a well at my school.'

'Course not, they filled it in with stones and earth so no one else would fall in, but you can still make out the circle if you look close enough. Somewhere in there, his bones are rattling about, working their way to the surface.'

I didn't know if she was telling the truth or not. I tried to look into her eyes, but they were masked by the reflection of the flickering flames.

'OK, let's do it,' I said grudgingly.

The school felt familiar, as if I were recalling it from a dream rather than a real memory. It was a Victorian, red-brick building. It loomed out of the dark like a gothic manor house.

'Stacey, I'm not sure…'

'Come on, it's OK,' she said, taking my hand in a rare moment of empathy and leading me through the high metal gate that led into the playground. We had brought a tea light each to light our way, wedged into scraped-out baked potato skins. The liquid wax swayed and splashed in its hot tin holder, coating my thumb in a painful layer of warmth, and setting immediately.

I stepped forward and tried the door, but of course it was locked. We stood on the step, thinking for a minute. 'I know,' I said, inspiration taking me, 'the girls' loos! The windows are always open 'cause they smell so bad.'

We rounded the south side of the building, and sure enough, there were four large windows. The top pane of each was open a fraction. An eerie light filtered out, casting rectangles on the ground.

'I'm going in first,' Stacey said, to my relief, putting her tea light on the ground. 'I'm going to need to climb on your shoulders.'

'OK.' I put my tea light with hers and crouched down by the wall. She climbed on. She was much heavier than I had imagined. I stood up slowly, the world made out of little popping stars. The soles of her trainers ground into my shoulders, pulling on my hair as she manoeuvred herself into a standing position. I struggled to stay still, and then there was lightness and she was gone. I looked up. The top half of her body was inside the window, but her legs were still sticking out. They were flailing about as if she couldn't quite squeeze through.

'Are you OK?' I whispered as loudly as I dared. Her legs kicked violently against the glass, and I thought for a moment she was going to break the window pane, but then with one last flounder she was through.

Her voice came floating out of the open window, echoing as if she were far away, 'This isn't the girls' bogs, it's the boys'. And it stinks! *And* there's poo on the wall.' The voice was getting quieter, as if she were walking away.

'Stacey, what about me?' I said, waiting in the quiet. And then a voice around the corner went, 'Psst!'

She was standing at an open door I had never seen before, as if it had just been magicked into existence. 'Hurry up then,' she said, as if I had been dawdling.

I took her into my old classroom and showed her where I used to sit. She pulled the chair back and sat down, looking intently at the whiteboard. Moonlight filtered through the huge windows, making everything pale blue. Glittering stars and papery snowflakes twirled from strings in the ceiling.

'Do you think your dad's treasure could be hidden here?' Stacey said. It was the first time since Dad went on *Wogan* that she had shown any interest in the treasure hidden in Dad's books.

'What made you think of that?'

'It just feels like everybody in the world is looking for it now. Shouldn't we be, too?'

I looked round at all the trays and cupboards. 'The school isn't in any of the books,' I said doubtfully.

'But that would be the brilliance of his plan!' she said. 'And anyway, he hasn't written all of the books yet. Maybe the next one will be *Romilly and the School*.'

'Sounds a bit dull. What's fun about school?'

'Good point. We should have a look at your dad's books. See if we can spot something everyone else has missed.'

I nodded excitedly at her enthusiasm, my mind already flicking through the pages, showing her my favourite pictures, talking through my theories.

'What do people do in school, anyway?' she said, picking up a pencil and idly scratching her name into the desk. I found her some paper and pushed it in front of her.

'Just do some writing,' I said, and she set to right away, practising her letters, scribbling on the paper, her hand shielding the words.

While she worked, I strolled around the room, wondering if she might be right, if this could be the setting for the next book.

It was strange, being in the classroom again. Whenever I had thought about my time at this school, the memories had been filled with the ring of my classmates' voices. Now, at night, with just the two of us here, I wondered if I had dreamt it all.

I remembered with a shiver the child's voice that sometimes woke me at night, talking so fast and so softly that it sounded like it was speaking another language; a language I had learnt years before but since forgotten. In the silence of the room I thought I heard it here, whispering at me desperately through the dusty air.

'What do you want?' I whispered back to it, straining to hear a reply, to distinguish the voice from the low hum of the boiler, the swish of trees outside.

'Are you OK?' Stacey was looking at me strangely.

'I'm fine,' I said, listening intently, but the voice had gone, melting into the quiet of the classroom as if it had never been there.

Stacey was still looking at me peculiarly. I spotted an old, worn dictionary lying on a bookshelf. 'I was just looking for this,' I said, picking it up and waving it at her. I didn't want to let on how spooked I felt. I flicked through it, navigating past torn, well-thumbed pages covered in great scrawls of crayon. The book settled open, and

I looked down. Whether by coincidence or whether by choice, it had opened on 'treasure'. I put my finger under the definition, reading slowly.

treasure
I precious metals or gems. 2 a thing valued for its rarity. 3 *colloq.* a much loved or highly valued person.

If the treasure in Dad's books wasn't gold and jewels, then it had to be either 2 or 3. I tried to think of anything rare and of value we owned. The only thing I could think of was the original paintings from the books, but it couldn't be them because I already knew exactly where they were, and Dad had said the treasure hunt was partly for me. That left number 3, but I couldn't see how Dad was hiding someone he loved in his books, except for me, of course, but I wasn't hidden: I was painted there for all to see. Then the shadowy woman came into my mind. Was she what Dad was hiding? Was she the treasure? She was the opposite of what I imagined treasure would be. Gold and jewels reflected light, sparkling at you until your eyes were dazzled, but the shadowy woman sucked it in, absorbing light and happiness like a black hole. If she was the treasure, I wasn't sure I wanted to find her.

I looked up from the dictionary at the large, dark classroom, trying to figure it all out. A lone papier mâché dragon hung from a beam above me, a stringy piece of tinsel dangling from its wing. It winked at me, its nostrils flaring. I quickly looked away. The boiler in the corner clunked loudly, making me jump.

I looked over at Stacey. She had stopped writing and was staring around her, mesmerised by the twirl of paper decorations above our heads.

'Shall I be the teacher?' I asked, breaking the silence.

'OK,' she said uncertainly, and I felt a sudden power over her, knowing how out of place she must feel in the school.

'How about…' I said, thinking on the spot, 'how about we do a spellings test. I'll tell you words and you can spell them.' She began to shake her head, but, 'You can't be at this school and not do spelling,' I added imperiously.

'OK,' she said, picking up her pencil and waiting, poised, for the first word.

I thought for a moment. 'Up,' I said. Her face relaxed and she scribbled the word onto the paper.

'In.' I rattled through all the two-letter words I could think of, moving onto three-letter words, watching her face to judge her reaction, trying desperately to think of words she could spell.

After 'cat', 'dog', and 'bum' I decided that was enough, and asked her for the paper so I could mark it. Stacey approached the desk warily and handed it to me. The paper was creased and smudged. I took it and pretended to look over the tops of my (invisible) glasses. Her writing was scruffy and huge. There were no joined-up letters. Everything was spelled correctly though, except 'bum', which she had spelled with an *a* instead of a *u*. I ticked it anyway, feeling guilty for making her do the test in the first place.

She took the paper from me and her face lit up at all the ticks.

'Are these the kind of words you did in your spellings tests?'

I tried to think back to my short time at school. I couldn't remember any spellings tests. I couldn't remember much about school at all. 'Yeah, sort of,' I said.

'Will you teach me to write one day? And to read?'

'Doesn't your mum do that?'

'She used to but she says she's too busy now. Would you?'

I thought for a moment, daunted by the size of the task, not sure I knew much more than Stacey, but how could I say no? I nodded and she launched herself across the desk and hugged me. I'd never been hugged by her before. It was the kind of hug that squeezes the air out of your lungs. It felt good.

Thirteen

Dad announced at the beginning of the new year that the 'Great Outings' would begin: days out to museums and art galleries that, in his words, 'will enhance your appreciation and understanding of the world that surrounds and enriches you.'

It felt like a good opportunity to spend some time away from Braër: the fans that had come out of the woodwork after the second book was published had slowly drifted away, and, with the third book not due out until the summer, we were almost guaranteed some quiet, uneventful trips.

Over the spring, we visited many cultured settings, travelling by car and bus and rail, sometimes too tired from the journey to fully appreciate the places when we got there.

In the summer, as a finale to our cultural tour, Dad announced that for a twelfth birthday treat we would be going to the British Museum. I was overjoyed: I had been asking to go for years, my mind full of hazy memories of the weird and wonderful collections inside.

Dad insisted we go incognito. On our last trip away, we had encountered a very earnest young woman who had been quite insistent that it was shameful and wrong for my father to put me in his books. Her ringing voice had followed us throughout the museum until we had to be escorted out of a back door for our own safety. I felt very silly as we stood on the steps of the British Museum, wearing an identical baseball cap to my father, but no one cast a second glance our way.

From the outside, the museum seemed as if it had been made for giants. Huge, resplendent pillars stood at the front as if they were holding the place up. I wrapped my arms around one, and Dad joined me, but even then, we could hardly reach halfway round, and I wished our little family was bigger so that we could make a proper circle.

Inside, the museum echoed beneath my feet. Dad and I stopped in the entrance hall, feeling the cool, dusty air hit us, a welcome change from the sizzling heat of the pavements outside. Ahead of us, a strange green light filtered through, as if we were about to enter an underwater world.

'Come on,' Dad said, setting off without me.

The hall opened out onto a vast, bright circle, the curved glass ceiling above us criss-crossed with a lattice of triangles. Dad chuckled as I gaped up at it, awestruck.

'Got your sketch pad?' he said, and I nodded, not daring to speak in the huge, echoing room.

'Pencil?'

Check.

'Charcoal?'

Check.

'Right. Meet you back here in two hours.' And he set off at a brisk pace, climbing a curved staircase ahead, leaving me alone in the eerie, pale green light.

At least now I was alone, I could go and find the museum shop for a brief respite. I looked around, searching for a sign to show me the way, and set off down a brightly lit walkway, trying to remember coming to this museum before, my memories as small and diminutive as my former three-year-old self.

I took a corridor, turning left, then right, until I found myself in a vast open space filled with towering stone giants. They seemed made for the museum, fitting perfectly into the high-ceilinged rooms. I imagined them coming to life once the museum was closed, roaming the halls, Egyptian statues shaking hands with Mesopotamian beasts. There were lots of stone animals here: lions and strange wild things that looked like dogs. I paused by a sleek, muscled panther. Its eyes bored into me, and I put my hand warily over its huge paw. 'You don't scare me,' I whispered.

As the day wore on, I began to feel thirsty, and I turned back, retracing my steps. I came to a long, gloomy room that I hadn't been in before. It housed row upon row of Egyptian mummies, standing next to each other in silent ranks, and as I passed between them it felt like they were waiting for something, like an army on the eve of a great war. It was an eerie room, and it made me uneasy. I took the first staircase I came to, and began to climb, looking back to check they weren't following me.

When I reached the top, I looked around to get my bearings, my loose hat tipping down on my nose. I pulled it off and threw it in a corner.

I walked and walked, looking into rooms but not really seeing anything, beginning to think I might never find my way out. There were signs everywhere, but none of them said 'exit'. I began to panic. The only windows were in the ceiling, and I had no idea what level I was on, or which direction I was facing. I looked for Dad in each room I came to, but there were large men in baseball caps everywhere: we had chosen our disguise well.

I stopped in the middle of a long room filled with the glistening skins of long-dead bodies, trying to get my bearings. No other visitors had reached this room yet, and the silence was absolute. I stood, trying not to panic, listening to the sound of my breath as it got lost in the wide space. I became aware of another sound: the tap, tap of footsteps between the display cases.

I swung round, suddenly frightened, and I was confronted by a thin, leathery body in a glass cabinet directly in front of me. My breath left me in a cry of shock.

'It's only the Lindow man,' came a treacly voice behind me, 'there's no need to fear him.'

A little old woman was toddling towards me. She looked like countless other little old women I had seen, except perhaps a touch more glamorous. She was wearing very high heels, tap-tapping on the wooden floor towards me. I wished I still had my cap to hide under: she looked like she recognised me and, worse, she looked like a Hugger. The Huggers were my least favourite kind of fan; not content just to wrap their arms around me, sometimes they pinched me through my clothes, as if seeing the tears and confusion in my eyes finally convinced them I was real.

I hid behind my hair, willing her to go away, and steeled myself as she came closer: sometimes people felt the urge to claim some talisman from me too – the sting as a hair was snatched from my head or a tug on my coat resulting in a stolen button. But this particular person came to a stop about a metre from me, standing neatly with her hands clasped.

'Romilly Kemp,' she said in a voice like melted toffee, and she smiled, showing a perfect set of pearl-like dentures.

Her name was Beatrice, and she was a museum volunteer. We walked down a staircase with gold flowers on the handrail, and she showed me where the shop was, and bought me a cup of tea at the café. Then she took me round, explaining different exhibits.

There was something nostalgically childlike about Beatrice, and something very old-fashioned too. When I stopped to eat my packed lunch, she sat cross-legged on the floor next to me, not on the bench nearby. Seeing her sitting there like that pulled at a memory, as if she was a character from a book I had read many times when I was younger, and still had a blurred recollection of.

'Will you come to my house? I think my dad would like you,' I said between mouthfuls of Wotsits. This was praise indeed. Dad had grown suspicious of most people recently, especially the strangers who turned up at our house unannounced.

'If you really think I'd be welcome,' Beatrice said with a trill of laughter that sounded like a little girl's, 'then I'd be delighted.'

'Do you know where we live?'

I spotted Dad coming out of a room at the far end of the hall, his face like thunder. I suddenly wondered whether I was allowed to ask people round. I took a few steps away from her, in case Dad looked our way and saw me talking to a stranger.

She nodded, a smile stretching across her pretty face. 'I think I can find your address,' she said.

It was a silly question: everybody knew where the Kemps lived.

Two weeks later there was a knock on the door. Dad and I raced each other to the hallway, me in case it was Stacey, Dad, in case it was a treasure-hunting axe-murderer. Beatrice stood there, sparkling on the step like a cut diamond, a plant pot in one hand and a cake tin in the other.

'Beatrice!' I said, flinging my arms around her. When I stepped back, there was a chill to the silence. Dad's face was closed, his eyebrows drawn together.

'How did you find us?' he said.

'Meg,' she said simply, and my ears pricked up at the mention of my mum's name. I looked from one grown-up to the other, confused.

'You have two picture books out, Tobias,' Beatrice said. 'And you were on *Wogan*, for goodness' sake. It wouldn't have been difficult to find you, even without insider knowledge. But I expect you know that: I expect you get all *sorts* of visitors.' In the dappled light from the moat, Beatrice's face suddenly looked too made-up – like a clown. I wondered with a chill who she was underneath the lipstick.

Dad's voice was controlled, as if he was struggling to contain unseen anger. 'That doesn't mean you can just turn up,' he said.

'She didn't,' I piped up in a small voice, 'I invited her.'

Dad blinked, his forehead uncreasing. 'How?' he said.

'The British Museum,' Beatrice said. 'I volunteer there. I did hope that one day I would bump into you. I know how much you used to love it there. Before.' She smiled at me, lifting a hand and touching my cheek with tea-soft fingers. 'She's so very like Meg, isn't she?' she said.

I took a step back, my stomach somersaulting.

Dad rubbed a hand over his face. 'Romilly,' he said stiffly, 'I'd like you to meet your grandmother.'

I turned, my mouth gaping, and looked at the little old lady who was no taller than me.

'Close your mouth, dear,' she said.

Over tea and cake, my dad and Beatrice talked. They had much to catch up on. Beatrice was my mum's mum, and Dad hadn't seen her for eight years.

'What happened eight years ago?' I asked, shovelling a large slice of coffee cake into my mouth.

'Manners, dear. Don't talk with your mouth full,' Beatrice said, wiping a wet crumb from her cheek.

As they talked, I looked at my grandmother. There was something

146

about the flick of her thin wrist as she lifted her teacup, the quick turn of her head that reminded me of the bird-like fragility of my mother. I wondered; did she see any of her daughter in me? Or any of herself, for that matter?

As I looked at her, trying to see the wrinkles under the powder on her face, it felt as if I had known her for a long time. How many times had we actually met before? Why had we stopped seeing each other eight years ago? What had she done? Had she been locked away in an institution like my mum? And did that mean that one day I would be, too? I forced myself back to their conversation, pushing away any thoughts of what my future might hold.

'It's actually... a relief to see you,' Dad was saying. 'It's hard, raising a child on your own.'

Beatrice nodded. 'Especially under the circumstances,' she said, sipping her tea.

I sat stiffly on the sofa, my mind playing over answers to the questions in my head. Dad took sympathy on my silence, mistaking it for boredom, and told me to go out in the garden while they caught up.

Beatrice had given me a plant called a forget-me-not. It was a cloud of little blue flowers. 'It'll need to live near water,' she had said, and so I took it out and knelt by the moat, excavating a small hole and patting the earth around it with care.

I spent some time balancing on the fallen beech tree, my toes clinging to the smooth wood where the bark had begun to peel away, walking a tightrope and trying not to fall. As I practised, I wondered if Mum knew her mother was visiting us. I hadn't thought of my mother for a while. It was easy to forget someone if nobody talked about them. I had spent a year trying to forget her. Remembering her now, I realised my memories were not tinged with sadness at her leaving us anymore, but with anger. How dare she march into our lives and swan out again so quickly? I hoped Beatrice wouldn't do the same, and I vowed not to trust her so easily, just in case.

A red-and-black butterfly flitted past me, settling on a lavender bush under the buddleia. I jumped down from the tree trunk (perfecting my roly poly on landing) and tiptoed towards it, a hand stretched out in front of me, trying to coax it onto my finger.

'Don't touch them, whatever you do!' Beatrice's voice, old and scratchy, shot through the air towards me. Instantly my hand dropped down by my side. The butterfly soared high above my head. I squinted my eyes as it disappeared toward the sun and focussed instead on the tiny woman daintily picking her way in high heels towards me. A little way away she stopped and reached into one of the many pockets about her quilted jacket. Pulling out the sharpest pair of tiny silver scissors, she stepped toward me and laid them in my hand.

'I never go anywhere without these so that I can snip the horrible little buggers in half. They fool you into thinking they're butterflies, but they're not. Watch out for them, they're nasty.'

In the days that followed, every time I caught a flash of red peppered with black in the air, a little shiver touched my shoulders and I would visibly recoil, looking at the murderous little insects with fascination.

Holding the scissors in my left hand, concentrating on not stabbing myself as Dad had taught me, I grinned at Beatrice and started my sentry duty around the garden, seeking out dangerous-looking insects, unsure if I were brave enough to cut them in half. What if they stung you like wasps, or burrowed under your skin? Or maybe they aimed for your throat and strangled you to death with their feelers. I shivered with frightened pleasure.

The garden in summer was made up of smells. Each bed of hot, crumbly soil held tangles of roses and lavender, papery dry in the July sun. Beatrice herself smelt of something a bit like summer turning to autumn, as if she were preparing herself for a long lie down. The tips of her fingers looked as if she had dipped them into tea. She didn't smell like old people normally do, and she radiated colour. Her eyes were ringed with blue powder and her lips wore a bright fuchsia pink smile. Her hair had been yellowy white at the museum, but today it was the shimmering violet of the tiny butterflies that settled on the buddleia in the garden. She smelt particularly of lavender, standing in the middle of my garden, and I wondered if the smell had made her hair change colour.

'Do I have to call you Grandma?' I asked as we wound back up through the garden after showing her the mobiles.

'Not if you don't want to. I'm Beatrice, or Bea, either will suffice.'

'Why haven't you visited before?'

'Family relationships aren't always easy. People tend to take sides. They get angry and then, when they realise they've made a mistake, sometimes it's too late.'

'Did you volunteer at the British Museum just so you could find me?'

'Not only because of that. When you're as old as me, volunteering is a good way to fill up your time. But yes, I was keeping an eye out.'

'I'm glad you were there the day we went,' I said, linking arms with her.

'Me too, dear.'

'Bea, you won't leave us like Mum did, will you? I don't mean you have to live here or anything, but I *can* see you, can't I? Whenever I want?'

Beatrice turned to look at me. 'Of course you can. In fact, why don't we write to each other, too? That way I can keep abreast of everything you do.'

'I'm not very good at spelling,' I said doubtfully.

'Practice makes perfect,' she said, squeezing my hand. 'Your father tells me you're happy living here. A proper free-range childhood.'

'It's lovely.'

'You don't miss London? Or get lonely, not going to school?'

'I don't really remember living in London. And I have Dad, and my friend Stacey.' I patted the beech tree. 'Sit down. I want to check something.' Mention of Stacey had reminded me of the nail varnish I had hidden by the cart shed. 'Do you like nail varnish?' I called to her, going over and ducking down by the water butt to search for the pink bottle, unsure if I had replaced it after the snail incident last summer. It was exactly her colour, I thought.

'I used to love it, but now my nails crumble and my hands are too shaky to paint it on. Do you like it?'

I got up, unable to find the bottle. 'I like it on snails, but it smells too weird to put on my nails.'

Beatrice nodded in agreement. 'That rhymes,' she said. 'Did you know that I'm an author too, like your father?'

'Really?'

She nodded. 'I used to write stories about a group of little ghosty children. I based all the books in the garden of the house I used to live in. Your mother grew up there, too.'

'Was it like Braër?'

She looked about her, and I thought I saw her eyebrows twitch at the wildness of the garden. 'No, not exactly,' she said. 'It was quite a large house. You might call it a mansion. The gardens were large and very neat. Nothing like this.' She put her hand in the pocket of her waistcoat. 'I have the first book here. I thought you might like to see it.' She pulled out a small paperback and handed it to me.

'Thank you.' I took the book and flicked through, disappointed that there were no colour pictures in it. 'It's very different to Dad's,' I said, not very kindly. There weren't many pictures in it at all.

'I wrote it forty years ago, so it *will* be different.' Her voice was fuelled by a creamy sweetness.

I stopped on a black-and-white drawing of a fountain in a formal garden. It was a huge, intricate structure, depicting woodland animals gathered around a pool in the shape of a giant leaf. One or two were dipping their heads to drink. Beatrice had gone quiet. She was looking at me, the smile gone.

Among the animals was a hare, sitting quietly next to a baby deer, its nose twitching. The fountain reminded me of something. I tried to remember where I had seen it before. The drawing was very different in style to Dad's pictures, it was quick and full of movement. I could almost hear the drip, drip of water trickling from the fountain, almost see the animals move slightly out of the corner of my eye. I thought of the gargoyle fountain that Dad had sunk beneath the moat's surface.

'You keep it,' Beatrice said, nodding at the book. 'It's a first edition, it'll be worth something one day, when I'm dead and gone,' she chuckled. 'But don't let that stop you enjoying it.'

I closed the book and looked at it anew. It felt special in a way I couldn't put my finger on.

'Did you ever base the characters in your books on real people?'

'You mean like your father has with you?'

'Sort of.' I was thinking of the circus lady. Real life and fiction seemed so inextricably stitched together that I had begun to think that every character in his books was a real person. I thought of the shadowy woman again.

Beatrice was looking at me strangely again, as if she was trying to read my thoughts. 'I think there is always an element of realness about the characters in one's books,' she said, 'even if it's a subconscious decision.'

I nodded, not quite sure what she meant. 'Did fans of your books ever come to your house?' I said, flicking through her book, coming back to the picture of the fountain.

'Oh gosh, yes, people did visit on occasion, and not everyone that came by was very nice. Sometimes I felt just like one of my little ghosts, trapped in the house by my writing, surrounded by my stories. I sold the house in the end, after your mother went off to boarding school. I couldn't live amongst the fame.'

'Did my grandfather live there, too?'

'He did, darling, but he died very young, leaving me to care for your mother and the house all on my own. In the end, I decided to put all my love into your mother: the house is owned by a charitable trust now; open to the public. Perhaps we could go sometime.'

I nodded. I thought about how I would feel selling Braër and moving away. I wasn't sure I could do it, or where I would go if I did.

It wasn't until she had gone that I realised Beatrice had not once mentioned a treasure hunt, and I loved her for it.

Fourteen

Having spent the beginning of summer rarely seeing Stacey and thinking we were just too different to be friends anymore, she appeared again soon after my twelfth birthday on the last day of July, and it felt as if she had never been away. She had had a growth spurt since I last saw her, and her hair had grown to her shoulders, where it sat in mousy waves.

As we wandered out of the village, we drifted back into our old roles, daring each other to cross the rickety planks that criss-crossed the dike we were walking next to, a thrill of danger in the air. We took a new route, heading out towards the train station. I had only ever been there before with Dad on our trips to London. It was hardly more than a single platform. As soon as we got there, Stacey sat down and began removing her shoes.

'What are you doing?'

'Just do what I do.'

Feeling a frisson of nervous excitement that I only ever felt when I was with Stacey, I bent and untied my trainers, and went to join her on the edge of the platform, my toes clinging to the edge. I looked down at the rails below. It was a pure, hot summer's day, and the train tracks shimmered beneath us.

'Stacey, this feels dangerous.'

'Shh, it's coming, can you feel it?' she said.

'How do you *feel* a train?'

'Listen with your feet.' She nodded down at our bare toes clamped to the concrete.

We fell silent, and I concentrated. Sure enough there was a faint vibration buzzing into my heels and up through my ankles. I strained my eyes, but all I could see was miles of train track disappearing off into nothing.

A curious thing was happening to the tracks. A sort of whipping sound, as if cables were being snapped together, and then the sound melded into a rhythm of electronic staccato – whip-whip, whip-whip – and I was swaying with the sound, absorbed by it, teetering on the edge of the platform. It felt dangerous. More dangerous than anything she had ever dared me to do before.

'Stacey, I…' The wind was whipping up too, stealing away my words before I had a chance to finish them. A newspaper blasted towards me across the platform, catching on my foot long enough for me to read the words, *Terry Waite Alive!* before it was swept away onto the track.

And then, without notice, it was there: the train rushed past my nose as if it had jumped from another dimension, carriages of goods flashing by in an endless panorama of colour. The force of it rocked me back on my heels, pushing me away from danger, and then we were twirling on the platform, drunk on adrenaline, huge gulps of laughter rising from our bellies, our hearts going as fast as the train as it sped swiftly away.

'Told you,' said Stacey, her eyes glittering. And then they flicked away from me and her face changed. I followed her gaze. Far off, at the other end of the platform, a figure stood. Where it had come from I couldn't guess, the platform was an island in a sea of flat fields, we'd have seen them coming a long way away.

Stacey stepped closer to me so that our hands brushed. The figure was very still.

'It's a phantom,' she whispered solemnly, taking my hand properly, her nails squeezing into my palm. My skin prickled.

'It's not,' I said, as whatever it was took a step towards us. Somehow I knew a ghost would be less scary; less real. It was holding something in its hand. It looked like a shovel.

'D'you think it's a grave digger?' Stacey's palm was sticky in mine.

'I don't know. Come on.' I began to pull her away, back towards the village and safety.

'But I want to see!' she said, planting her feet firmly on the ground.

The figure moved closer. It looked like a man; a very tall man with slender arms and legs. He was definitely holding a shovel. Round his neck he had a camera with a long lens attached to it. He lifted it to his eye, training it on us.

'Stacey,' I urged, pulling at her hand desperately.

'Wait,' she said, and I knew that to her this was just another game, like gambling our lives with the trains. The man raised his hand.

'Come on,' I pleaded, giving her hand a yank as the man began to stride towards us, but she wouldn't budge. He broke into a sprint, the spade and camera swinging awkwardly by his side. Stacey stepped in front of me, spreading her arms as if to protect me. The man came to a stop right in front of us. He tilted his head and eyed me behind my protector, and without warning, his hand shot out and he grabbed my wrist.

'Hey!' Stacey shouted. My own voice seemed to have disappeared.

'Romilly Kemp,' he said, squeezing hard. Something about the way he said my name was familiar. The lens of his camera winked in the sun, and a memory came to me of bushes shaking, of the same gravelly voice. And with his words it was as if the spell was broken:

Stacey pushed me away, breaking the man's grip, and we began to run, sprinting over the platform, through the gate and down onto the road, the man standing still and statuesque behind us.

When we had run far enough away to feel safe, we stopped to catch our breath and turned back to the station. The man was still standing there, watching us. His voice drifted across to us, two words carried on the wind like little gravelly ghosts, as if he couldn't reach us himself, but his words could.

'Romilly Kemp,' they whispered, 'Romilly Kemp,' and we turned and ran faster, leaving our shoes behind.

'Why do you think people follow you?'

We were sitting at my desk beneath the circular stained-glass window at the end of my bedroom. *Romilly and the Kitten* was laid out in front of us. Stacey had a copy of her own – Dad had signed one and given it to me to pass on to her a few months ago, around the time that she began to show more of an interest in the treasure hunt. In the short time she had owned it, it was already more thumbed than any book I had ever seen. When I told Dad what a state it was in, he said with a serious face, 'That's the very best proof there is of a well-loved book.'

'Maybe they think I know where the treasure is,' I said. 'They think because I'm in the books I must know.'

Stacey had her finger under a word. 'But you don't.' There was a question in the way she said it, even though I'd told her a million times.

'I don't,' I said. I hadn't told her what Dad had said the day we went metal detecting, that it wasn't necessarily a search for gold and jewels, that it was as much for me as it was for the public. Stacey was only just beginning to find the idea of a treasure hunt interesting. I didn't want to dim that excitement by making it seem less fun. I imagined her hopeful face dropping as she realised there might not be any precious riches to dig up at all.

I was beginning to see what Dad had meant when he said it wasn't just about finding the treasure, but about the excitement and anticipation of searching for it. Every time we looked through the books now, or walked out in the fields, kicking at the earth with our toes, I saw that gleam of excitement in Stacey's eyes, worlds of possibility reflected in her face. No real friend could dampen that with the truth.

And yet sometimes, just as I was about to go to sleep, I felt I was beginning to understand what Dad wanted me to see. An illustration from the book would fix itself in my mind, and it was like it was reaching out and taking me by the hand to lead me down a long corridor of memory, back to London, back to my early years. But whenever I started to follow, feeling that warm, familiar hand in mine, the corridor disappeared, and I found myself in bed again, alone, staring up at the ceiling.

Stacey was gazing absently at the little circular window. I noticed she had the Tufty Club badge pinned to her T-shirt, and for a moment I felt annoyance that she should be wearing it when it was rightfully mine. I looked back at the book and cleared my throat.

'Come on, you know this word.'

Stacey blinked and turned back to the desk. '"Monty was a... cho... choc-o-late point Si... a... mese kitten with cross eyes and a kink in his tail, but to Romilly he was perfect." What's a chocolate point?'

'It's his colouring.' I picked Monty up by the scruff from his sentry position at my feet, and dangled him into my lap where he curled up contentedly and closed his eyes. I pointed to his ears and his tail, 'All his pointy bits are chocolate-coloured. See?'

'Do you think Monty knows what the treasure is? Maybe he swallowed it.' She giggled. We looked at him asleep on my lap, and then at his doppelgänger curled in Dad's hand in the book. There was a silver bell on the kitten's collar. Somewhere in the jumble of my thoughts I remembered the real bell and the shivery sound it made. I hadn't seen it in years.

Stacey turned the pages, flipping through them so that the paper fanned our faces.

'What are you doing?' I asked.

'Why are you always running away from things?' she said, stopping at a random page and pointing.

Along the top of the page, above the main illustration, was a tiny silhouette of me. I was running, my hair flying out behind me. The silhouette of a lion was galloping along behind me, his jaws wide open. I had my head turned and I was looking at the lion, as if I was calculating how long it would take for him to catch up. There were pictures like this on the top of every page. They were so small that you'd need a magnifying glass to see them properly. Fortunately, Dad had bought me one for just that purpose, and I pulled it out and handed it to Stacey. She held it over the lion, and his tiny, sharp teeth came into view.

She turned the page, and there I was again, this time running away from a dragon, its black fiery breath licking at my heels. The next page had a panther, the one after that a wolf.

'I suppose it *is* you?' Stacey said. 'This one could be Red Riding Hood. Maybe they're all fairy tale characters?'

'They look like me.' I bent to study the slope of my nose, the cut of my hair. It troubled me that Dad thought I would always run away from these beasts, that I wouldn't turn and fight. Maybe he wanted to instil a sense of danger in me, I thought doubtfully, a fear of the wilderness that Stacey and I so often marched across together.

On the next page, a gaggle of geese was chasing me.

'That's just silly,' Stacey said, 'what's even scary about a goose? You wouldn't run away from them, would you?'

I felt my face flush. 'Of course not.'

It got even worse in *Romilly and the Circus*. Dad had turned it into a comedy: he had me running away from butterflies, birds and even a tiny mouse.

'Your dad does know you, right?' said Stacey, 'I mean, in real life you're almost as fearless as I am. Look at how you stood on the platform earlier when the train came past. Your nose was about an inch away from it, but you stayed put.'

I shrugged. Maybe Dad didn't know me at all. After all, he spent most of his time locked away, painting his pictures.

'All the main pictures in the books are exactly like you,' Stacey said, pointing to the colourful pictures of me and Monty on each page. 'Look: you're going on adventures, finding things out. But these little silhouette pictures at the top are the complete opposite. It's like he thinks you've got split personality disorder or something.'

She was turning the pages angrily now, and I sighed inwardly, wishing she would forget it. I didn't like it when she got like this, working herself up over something that didn't really matter. She was liable to explode if I didn't find a way of calming her down.

My eyes fell on the open page of *Romilly and the Kitten*, and inspiration struck. It was the close-up of my face, the one Dad had said was a printing mistake, showing my mole on the wrong cheek.

'I forgot about this,' I said to Stacey, cutting her off mid-rant, 'I spotted it last winter. Dad painted my mole on the wrong cheek. He said it was to do with the printers, but half the pictures are the right way round, and half are wrong.'

Stacey looked at the page, her brow furrowed.

'It's probably just one of Dad's lapses of attention,' I said, beginning to close the book.

'Wait.' Stacey's hand slammed down on the paper.

Oh goodness, I thought, I've stirred her up even more.

She was looking intently at the mole, her eyes flashing from me to the open page before her.

'It doesn't matter,' I said, not liking the laser-like beam of her eyes on my skin.

'What if it's a clue?' she said.

'How can a mistake be a clue?'

'What if it's not a mistake?' Stacey bent her head again, looking this time through the magnifying glass. Her breath smelt of Parma Violets as we peered through the lens together.

'It *must* be part of the treasure hunt,' she said. 'It's got to mean something. But what?'

'I don't know...' I scoured my brain for inspiration. 'Maybe you can connect the moles like a join the dots game, and X marks the spot?'

Stacey nodded, her face serious, unaware I was joking.

There was a knock on my door and Dad crawled through, heaving a basket of washing with him.

'Hello, hello. What're you doing?'

'We're trying to work out what the treasure is,' I said, glad of the distraction.

'Not you too. I've just taken delivery of thirty-three long and boring letters, all thinking they've found it. Found what, I ask you? Bloody fools, the lot of them.' He turned the washing basket upside down on my bed. Crumpled clothes landed on the duvet, smelling slightly fusty.

'Is that what you were doing when you lost your shoes this morning, Roe,' he said lightly, 'looking for treasure?'

'No, we were just playing,' I said.

'And did you lose your shoes too, Stacey?'

Stacey looked down at her bare feet. They were black at the edges. She giggled.

'She did,' I said, 'but it doesn't matter 'cause it's summer, and her mum says if you work it right you can turn your feet into leather, and then it's like wearing a pair of shoes, so that's what she's going to do. I might try it too.'

'I've been practising round near the gorse,' Stacey said, 'and I can only feel the prickles if I really stamp on them now.'

'But couldn't you wear another pair of shoes, Stacey?' Dad said.

Stacey looked at Dad as if he'd gone mad.

'Couldn't she find another pair?' he said, looking at me.

'Where would she get another pair from?' I asked. Stacey only had one pair of shoes. Now they were gone, I couldn't imagine her wearing any others.

'Good point. I'm sure Roe's got an old pair you can have. Or else you could tie your feet up in plastic bags.' He chuckled.

'I don't think my mum would like that,' Stacey said, very seriously. 'And I like having bare feet.'

'Romilly, while I've got you here, I wanted to remind you about our boat trip tomorrow.'

'You've fixed it then?' The rowing boat had lain in the garden for years, its warped wooden planks like the remains of a beached whale. Last time I had seen it, it had been more hole than boat.

'I have! And I've tested her too. We won't sink, I promise. I've given her a name as well. I thought I'd call her *Panther*, after the one that escaped from the circus. I'm not sure there'll be enough room for Stacey, it's a two-man boat, but you can both go out in her another day.'

'I don't really like boats,' Stacey said, 'I prefer swimming, it's safer.'

But Dad wasn't listening. He had picked up my picture of Mary Mother-of-God, frowning. 'What on earth is this?'

'It's Mary,' I said. 'Mum gave her to me. She told me Mary is the mother of all people. She protects me.'

Dad stifled a snort that quickly became a cough, standing the picture back on my bedside table. Mary gazed out of her frame serenely. I wanted to tell him that she climbed out of her portrait on the nights he forgot to come and say goodnight, and wrapped her motherly arms around me. Instead I turned back to the book and to Stacey.

Dad picked up the empty clothes basket and nodded at the messy pile on the bed. 'Make sure you put those away, Roe,' he said, turning to go downstairs. He paused on the top step. 'I almost forgot, you had a letter today, it's on the bed, next to the washing.'

I got up and found the letter, balanced on a pile of T-shirts. It felt stiff, more like cardboard than paper. There was a small, hard lump in the corner of the envelope. I ripped it open. Inside was a birthday card with a picture of a circus clown on the front. He was juggling balls that spelt out, 'Happy birthday!' I opened it up.

It said,

Dear Romilly,

Happy belated twelfth birthday, my darling daughter.
I'm so sorry I wasn't able to be with you to celebrate your special day, but I'm sure next year I will be allowed to come. Until then, I thought you would like these earrings. I understand you have recently met your grandmother. These earrings belonged to her mother — your great grandmother — and they are real emeralds. Maybe next year I will be able to come and see you wearing them.

With all my love,
Mum

'What is it?' said Stacey, noticing I had gone quiet.

I tipped the envelope upside down, and a pair of earrings dropped into my hand.

'Wow, they're beautiful,' Stacey breathed, lifting an earring up to the light so that drops of green light flickered over the walls, 'are they real gold?'

'I dunno.' I examined the remaining earring. The bit that went through your ear was bent out of shape.

'I didn't know you'd had your ears pierced,' Stacey said.

'I haven't.' I touched one of my earlobes. It felt soft and warm. I wasn't sure I wanted a needle jabbed through it.

'Does your mum have pierced ears?'

I tried to think back to when I saw her last summer. I had a hazy memory of birds hanging from her ears as if they were flying. 'I think so,' I said, rubbing at my ear and wondering if I was brave enough to be like her.

'You're lucky, having a mum that gives you such special birthday presents.'

'Even if they are a few weeks late.'

'I didn't know she'd given you this, too,' Stacey said, holding up the little picture of Mary.

I took it from her and looked at it properly for the first time in a long time. With a rush of remembered fear, I recalled the last time I had seen my mum, the day she had denied giving me the picture. The flash of the hallway as she dragged me into the pantry. The taste of vinegar on my lips.

I placed the picture in a drawer and pushed it closed tightly. I thought of the way my mother had collapsed like a dying flower after she locked me in the pantry. Why would she write to me now? I tried to bend the earring's hook back into place, but it refused to move.

'My mum's never given me anything,' Stacey said, rubbing her bare feet on the chair's stretcher, leaving a brown mark. 'She was angry when I came home without my shoes earlier,' she said.

I put the earring down. 'Didn't you tell her about the phantom?' I said, remembering him standing there, tall and frightening.

'I did, but...' she pulled back her sleeve. Her wrist was like a green rainbow, as if some ghoulish ghost had got inside her and spread its badness under her skin.

'Was that because you forgot your shoes?'

She nodded. I pulled my own sleeve back, remembering where the man had grabbed me. There was a pale red mark there now. Luckily Dad had believed me when I told him it was from wearing a bracelet too tight.

I lifted my hand and we put our wrists together, the red touching the green like some strange magical connection we didn't really understand.

Fifteen

The oar made a slap, slapping sound as it hit the water, dipping into the soup-like moat and coming back covered in slime. There was a thin trickle of water in the bottom of the boat, near our feet, but Dad had assured me it was from the unseasonable summer rain the night before.

'Is all the river like this?' I asked, wrinkling my nose at the frog-skin smell dislodged from the moat's depths, my eyes tracing the water for signs of the gargoyle.

'No, no, Roe, once we get out from the moat and under the bridge it's much clearer, I promise.'

Monty stood at the front of the boat, his front paw poised on the helm, his tail erect. For once he was silent. As we approached the bridge, he bunched his body up and took a flying leap, just catching the wooden slats with his back claws. He pulled himself up almost unscathed, the end of his tail dangling pondweed.

'Bye, Montgomery!' I called as we drifted beneath the bridge, my voice echoing. His replying meow echoed back, louder than normal, and then we were out the other side, and the water was beautifully, fantastically clear.

'What do you think?' Dad said, propelling the oars with relish, his huge hands bunched like grappling hooks round their handles.

'It's like another world,' I said, leaning over and looking deep into the water. Here and there, the setting sun pierced its depths, filtering through the weedy fronds and catching at the scales of a million fish. I crouched low in the bow, tingling as the tips of a weeping willow trailed its sad fingers over me. The wind rustled in the trees above our heads, and Dad sighed happily.

'Psithurism,' he said.

'Sith-you-who?' I said, not really listening. Early green conkers plopped into the water, sending crystal drops into my lap.

'It means the sound of the wind in the trees. Ow!' A conker landed on Dad's head before rolling around in the bottom of the boat. 'Your mum loved conkers,' he said, picking it up and trying to prise the green shell away. 'She used to collect them on Hampstead Heath. She said we would never have spiders in the flat as long as there were conkers.'

I hadn't heard Dad talk about Mum for a long time. As soon as she left us, the subject of her quickly felt out of bounds. Yesterday's gift of the earrings had unnerved me, plunging me back into the final days of her stay, but now my memories were beginning to blur, like the soft edges of an unfocused photograph, and I wanted to try to love the memory of her, to remember the good in her, whatever else she had done. I listened with rapt attention, clinging on to every word.

'She's a complicated woman, Meg,' Dad said, more to himself than anyone, 'but she could be so loving when she wanted to be. She adored you, Romilly. I'm sure she still does, in her own way. When you were little, you were her energy, her purpose.' He began pulling harder at the shell. 'I'm sorry she hasn't been a better mother to you. Perhaps when you're older you could have a better relationship with her, a more balanced one, if you wanted.'

The shell came away in his hands. A young white conker dropped to the floor of the boat. It looked wrong, obscene in its nakedness. Dad picked it up and let it fall over the side.

'Do you know the story of the Crystalfish?' he asked me, resting an oar and letting the boat drift perilously close to a sandbank.

'Is it one of *your* stories?'

'It is, but I don't think I've told it to you before. Would you like to hear it?'

I nodded. Dad hadn't told me a story in a long time. I thought that he might have stopped for good. It was a worrying idea, mixed up with the feeling that my childhood was nearing its end. Relieved, I settled back on the wooden seat and listened.

'There used to be a fish that lived in this river. She was small and insignificant, except for one thing: she had a diamond growing on the side of her body, just beneath a fin.' He picked up the oar and began pushing it into the sand below us, stirring it up until the water lost its clarity and we were floating on a cloud of glittering gold.

'On grey days, the little fish was safe, but on sunny days the sun would find the diamond and set it sparkling.'

'Was it some sort of treasure?' I was getting too old to believe in Dad's stories, but I couldn't help be sucked in, especially when they contained treasure in some form or another, as they invariably did.

'It was a treasure, but it was also a curse. On days when all the other fish would bask in the warmth of the sun, she had to hide in a rotten old boot for fear of being caught.'

'What happened to her?'

Dad looked sad for a moment, dipping his finger into the settling water and sucking on it thoughtfully.

'I'm not sure. I think that's up to you. It's your story, you know. How do you want it to end?'

Having ownership of the story felt like a big responsibility. I stared at the surface of the water. For a moment I thought I saw something glittering below. 'Can I think about it?'

'Of course.' Dad lifted the oars and began to row. The water sped beneath us. A streak of electric blue flitted past us, and Dad lifted his hand to point.

'Kingfisher!' As he said it, the oar careered out of his grip and fell onto my outstretched hand, sending it smacking into the side of the boat. A dart of pain shot through my fingers.

'Oh, Romilly! Oh, my dear!' Dad looked wildly about as I stared, repulsed yet fascinated as blood spread along the lines in my hand like a flower blooming.

'It's OK, it's only a small cut.' I held my hand over the side of the boat, letting the blood drip into the water. The red dispersed into the gold, and I thought of the fish who would feast on it tonight.

The water beneath us was still as glass now. I leant over the edge, looking at my reflection, my hair so long now that it dangled almost to the water.

'My hair's tickling my twin's face.'

'What?'

'Look, it's me with my mole on the wrong side, just like the pictures of me in your books.'

Dad made to pick the oar up, and it tumbled out of his hands and into the water, sending my reflection into a thousand dancing particles. The girl in the water disappeared. I wondered if she'd swum down to search for the Crystalfish.

'Hark,' Dad whispered, reaching for the sodden oar and turning the boat around to start the journey home, 'I think I hear monkeys.'

I smiled and closed my eyes, and sure enough there was a chittering in the trees that could be monkeys or could be crows.

'Look,' he said, pointing at a stick in the water, 'a snake swimming to the mangroves!' It was getting dark now, the sun almost gone, and it was very easy to believe we were on an Amazonian tributary, drifting through dangerous waters.

'Do you hear that?' I said, joining in. 'A dangerous beast!' Far away, Monty's plaintive meows could be heard, welcoming us home.

I could see the lights of Braër now, and the silhouette of the bridge before it. Everything around us was familiar but oh so different.

'I think I know how the story ends,' I said, pulling my cardigan around me. Even now, in early August, the nights were drawing in earlier, bringing with them a cool wisp of the autumn evenings to come.

I cleared my throat, trying to form the ending in my mind. 'Maybe one day the sun set and it was forever night,' I said, 'and when the moon was full, the Crystalfish came to the surface, knowing she was safe. She stared at the bright round light in the sky, and she was happy and sad all at the same time.'

Dad was silent for a long time, then he stretched as if he were coming out of a reverie, and nodded as we sped under the bridge.

'We're home,' he said quietly.

Sixteen

A few weeks later, in the final days of the summer, I stood in the dining room with Monty in my arms, watching a group of sightseers walk past the house.

In July, Dad's third book, *Romilly and the Windmill,* had been published. In the intervening weeks, more and more visitors had arrived at Braër, searching the village for the windmill in the book, in the hope that it contained unknown wealth and riches.

Dad developed an entry system to the garden on weekends, cordoning off areas with thick twists of red rope attached to golden balustrades, careful to keep the tourists away from the house. He sat at the gate, shaking a money tin as people filed in.

On busy days I often stayed inside, forced out occasionally by Dad as a treat for special customers. Sometimes I quite liked it: the people I met were on the whole friendly and interested. But at times the stares I got were too much, and I preferred the dark of Braër's rooms, losing myself in the books, or playing with Monty, who, unnerved by the arrival of unfamiliar people on his territory, stuck to my side like glue.

The inspiration for the windmill in the pictures was a windpump on the edge of the village, far away across the marsh, surrounded by reeds. The reeds grew so tall in summer that I could hardly see the pump at all from my bedroom window, but when they were cut in the winter it stood, solitary and dignified, alone on the bare horizon, its sails stretching up to heaven and down to the ground.

Dad had told me that his editor said a windpump didn't sound as romantic as a windmill, so for the purposes of the book, a windmill it had become. Why they needed to add romance to it I didn't know.

Stacey hadn't been around for a while — I supposed she was staying at her gran's again. But she had kept me company many times earlier in the summer while I was trapped in the house. She always had great ideas to keep us busy: making jelly with coins in it and trying to fish them out with a spoon, or creating marble runs out of old loo roll tubes and racing them down the two flights of stairs. Without her the house was very dull.

I went over to the dining table where the new book lay. It was an old table, made of oak, and on one of its legs a little mouse had been carved, running up towards the top. It reminded me of the mice in Dad's books, and I wondered if he had got the idea from there.

We had taken delivery of the proof copy of *Romilly and the Windmill* late last year. I loved the magic of seeing a book before anyone else: of being one of the first to try to decipher the codes within. Dad never let me see the paintings before the book came out, so when the proof arrived, it was the first chance I had to examine the pictures.

On the front cover was a majestic windmill, its huge sails made from stiff, gleaming cardboard, pinned to the book in such a way that you could make them turn. At each quarter turn, a different picture appeared in the window of the mill. It was my favourite book so far. Already the pages were looking tired from all the thumbing, the mill's sails bent from the countless times I had pushed them round and round.

There was a picture near the end of the book that showed the inside of the windmill. But instead of the usual machinery for grinding flour, Dad had turned it into a mini circus ring. Little harvest mice dressed as clowns juggled acorns, and a large scrawny rat dressed as a ringmaster, with a sharply pointed nose and huge yellow teeth, had his hands in the air as if he were directing it all. At the centre of the ring, a pure white mouse in a glittering sequined leotard rode on the back of a lithe and elegant hare. Tiny pink feathers nestled around the mouse's ears, and her tail was curled in such a way that it formed the shape of a heart.

I had thought Dad's obsession with the circus would come to an end when *Romilly and the Circus* was finished, but here he was, creating a whole world within the windmill. I wondered what part the circus would play in the next book.

I turned the pages awkwardly, holding onto the cat with one arm and flicking through with the other. I came to a picture of me looking in a mirror. It was cleverly painted so that you could see the face of both the real Romilly and her reflection. Dad was still getting my mole mixed up, I noticed. He often painted it on the wrong cheek, even in this, his third book. The reflection Romilly looked out with the mole on the correct side, and I thought maybe that was the real me, hidden away in a mirror world, trapped behind glass so nobody could get at her.

Monty dropped from my arms to the table, landing on the book, and I ran my hand along his back, grateful for his constant companionship. He had healed well after his accident, and now walked expertly on three legs. He had grown into a huge cat, long-limbed with a tail as long again as his body. It was good for balancing, which was important because, inspired by Dad's books, I had been trying to teach him some circus tricks. I had pilfered one of Dad's red ropes from the garden and strung it from one side of the drawing room to the other, trying to make him walk across it like a tightrope. For a cat with four legs this would have been hard, but for Monty it was near impossible. Still, he tried hard, wanting to please.

'Come on,' I said, scooping him up with the book and carrying them back to the drawing room. I balanced him once again on the rope, his claws clinging tightly onto the twisted fibres. I stood at the other end, a piece of cheese in my hand, watching him wobble.

'Come on, Monty, come on,' I crooned. He took a step forward and immediately rolled over, swinging from the rope by his claws. I tutted and lifted him back up.

'Romilly,' Dad said, bursting into the drawing room. 'There are people in our garden!'

'There are always people in our garden. You invite most of them in yourself.'

'No, no, you don't understand, come and see.' He bent to look out of the window, beckoning. 'There's more of them now, look!'

I peered out of the window. It was indeed very busy. A group of Japanese tourists were wandering around, looking lost. 'They're tourists, Dad. Beatrice says they bus them into the village now and again. It's part of a quirky tour of Britain or something.'

'Tourists? What do you mean, "tourists"? I don't want any bloody tourists here.'

'Really? You're normally sat at the gate shaking a tin for admittance.'

He swung round and rushed to the front window, where a group of men were walking past, cameras hanging from their necks. 'Am I?' He looked back at me. 'Since when have you been conversing with Beatrice, anyway?'

'She left me her address when she came to visit,' I said, unhooking Monty's claws from the rope again. 'We write to each other. You must know that – you open half of my letters before I get a chance, in case it's someone sending me something weird. Beatrice is nice. She understands.' My spelling had improved dramatically in the months that we had been communicating. 'Dad, when can we see her again?'

But Dad wasn't listening. 'One of them's digging up my garden!' he said, dashing to the back window. 'He's ducked under the ropes! What on earth do they think they'll find? I'd better go and see them off.'

'Can I come?' I said, picking the cat up.

Dad paused on his way out. 'No, no, best not, Romilly. I think you should stay here.'

'But...'

'We don't know who they are. Let me talk to them. You can watch from the window.'

I slumped down grumpily by the window. Dad pulled the netting across, covering the glass before running out of the room.

'I can't see now!'

'Yes, you can, look through the holes!' he called, already at the back door.

I peered through the lace. He had appeared outside now and was talking to a man who had a small spade in his hand. Dad was gesticulating wildly. Then he pulled the spade from the man's hand, and started to dig. A group of tourists formed a circle around him so that he was hidden from view. Little flurries of soil were exploding into the air.

'If you can't beat them, join them,' I said to Monty. He struggled in my arms and jumped down, running from the room, only to reappear outside a moment later, uncharacteristically friendly, winding round the strangers' ankles. An old man bent down and stroked him. A woman lifted her camera and took his picture. Dad was shaking their hands now, nodding his head as they all dipped into little bows around him.

'Bloody tourists,' I said.

It was unfair that people could travel halfway around the world to look for the treasure, and yet here I was, the one the press had begun calling 'The Illustrated Child', shut in my house, unable to even go looking in my garden.

'It's not out there, you tomfools!' I yelled through the glass, but they were so caught up in their conversation with my father that they didn't hear. 'I know more than all of you put together,' I said quietly, watching as Dad led them down to see his mobiles. I went back to the windmill book, spinning the sails, watching the pictures sweep in and out of view and thinking of the windpump, far across the fields.

Slamming my hand on the sails to stop them moving, I whisked to the front window and looked outside. It was still busy out there: a man spotted me looking and lifted a camera to his eye. I jumped away, the net curtain falling back into place.

In the hallway I found one of Dad's caps on the floor by the door, filled with ripening conkers. Pulling my hair into a bun on top of my head, I emptied the cap and put it on, tucking the remaining strands of hair inside. I looked in the mirror, trying to see if I still looked like the girl in the books.

I liked how my eyes looked so much bigger with my hair tucked away, and my androgynous figure made me almost look like a boy. My mole stood out on my cheek like a clue. I found some face paint left over from Halloween and dabbed it on my skin. The person in the mirror gazed back at me, unknown and mysterious.

As I walked, I saw fewer and fewer people, and Braër got smaller and smaller behind me. Finally, I stood at the edge of the reed field, the beginnings of the boardwalk ahead of me.

The reeds were tall, high above my head. From here I couldn't see the windpump at all.

Dad and I used to walk this way when I was younger. More recently, Stacey and I sometimes ventured out along the planks that wound their way through the reeds, but we had never got as far as the windpump. There was something about the way the reeds closed over our heads, making us doubt which way was forward and which way was back. We always ended up coming jubilantly out of the reeds, certain we had found it, only to see the village coming into focus in front of us.

I met a dog walker and stopped to let them by, standing on the very edge of the planks, trying not to fall into the rainbow-lustred mud as she strode past. My head was getting hot and itchy under the tweed cap, but I kept it on, liking the feeling of being incognito.

As I walked, I thought about the sails on the front of the book: how if you lined two of them up with the clouds in the sky so that they weren't symmetrical, a flower appeared in the window, so small its detail couldn't be seen with the naked eye. For weeks I had assumed it was just a pale blue speck of dust, until I had been looking at the pictures with my magnifying glass, and enlarged it by accident.

The plank walk in front of me split in two directions, and I paused, unable to decide which way to go. As I stood there, a low rumble emanated from within the reeds. The wind dropped down, stirring the thin stalks, and for a split second the reeds parted. I peered into them. Deep within, a dark shape crouched, waiting.

The growl came again, and without thinking I took off. Something began crashing through the reeds behind me, but I dared not look back in case I lost my footing. I ran and ran, following the planks, twisting and turning through the reeds, until eventually I couldn't run anymore, and I slowed to a stop, my lungs screaming, and turned to face whatever was behind me.

All was still. I dropped my hands onto my knees in relief, trying to get my breath back. When I stood upright, the windpump was in front of me, as if it had been waiting all this time.

I climbed up the wooden steps that led to a grass bank next to the pump, checking over my shoulder every few seconds for movement. From the top I could see across the reedbeds, and I scanned them for a dark shadow, a flattened area, anything to prove the panther had been there, but there was nothing. If Stacey had been with me, she would have laughed at me, mocking me for imagining things that weren't there. But she wasn't, and without her I couldn't shake the feeling that something, somewhere was out there still, watching me.

I turned back to the mill, trying to put the panther from my mind. It was a huge, tall building, terrifying in its height, rising up, fat and round out of the reeds like a dormant monster. The sails looked tired and worn, rather like those in the book after my constant agitation. Despite the brisk breeze, they weren't moving, but they groaned quietly. There was a small window halfway up. It looked dark inside, the antithesis to the pretty images in the window of Dad's picture. I wondered whether if I swung the sails into action, a kaleidoscope of pictures would whir by in glorious Technicolor.

The mill was surrounded by a moat not unlike that of Braër, but the tiny, rickety plank of wood that acted as a bridge across it appeared far less inviting than our solid bridge at home. It looked like someone had thrown it across to gain entry. The heavy door stood partially open. Was it the swish of reeds I could hear, or the scurrying of rats inside?

I stood for some time, trying to work up the courage to go in. Eventually, I placed my foot on the thin plank. It wobbled and then settled. There was only enough space to put one foot in front of the other, and I grabbed at the reeds, foolishly hoping they would help keep me upright, and began the slow walk forward.

Halfway across, the plank wobbled precariously again, and I stood as still as possible, trying not to look down at the dark water below. Eventually I reached the other side, clinging to the door and turning to see how far I had come. It occurred to me that if the plank were to fall in now, I would be stuck, marooned at the windpump forevermore.

I pushed the door open and stepped inside. It took a while for my eyes to get used to the dark. I heard a scuttling, and something ran over my foot, making me jump.

As the light from the door filtered in, I began to make out huge cogs and great wooden beams. In one corner, the remains of a staircase wound upwards. It looked charred, as if someone had tried to burn it. There wasn't much room to move: the machinery took up most of the space, and I backed against the wall, feeling its friendly curve encircle me. I put my hands to it, grateful to touch something solid, and my fingers found a strange collection of bumps in the brickwork. I crouched down, feeling for the strange patterns, waiting for my eyes to get used to the dark.

Letters began to form underneath my fingers, words scratched into the bricks.

R O M I L L Y, I spelt out, a strange prickling at the back of my neck as I recognised my own name.

This is it! I thought, this is a clue! I frantically rubbed at the letters, trying to see what words had been written.

R O M I L L Y K E M P

I reached further along, my brain buzzing at the thought that my name existed in a place I had never stepped foot in before. I felt further along, working out the next word.

LOVES

I scrambled along the floor on my knees, my hands furiously scrabbling in the dark.

COCK

I dropped my hands to my sides. What did it mean? This wasn't a clue from my father, it was graffiti. Cruel words written about me by people searching for the treasure.

I was getting used to the dark now. All around me my name was coming into focus, dancing in front of my eyes. I walked around the windpump, my hands reaching out to touch my name wherever I saw it. Words had been etched onto the wooden joists that hung low across the room; there were words scratched into the brickwork; words painted on the floor.

DEVON TREASURE SEEKERS, one read, carved into the wood.

WE'RE GOING ON A TREASURE HUNT, WE'RE GOING TO FIND A BIG ONE, proclaimed another, winding its way round the curved wall.

I turned round and round in the little room, the words spinning around me.

SIMON AND TINA WOZ 'ERE

IV FOUND THE TRESSURE SO U CAN ALL BUGGER OF

WHERE'S THE GOLD MR KEMP?

Someone had painted, I ♥ ROMILLY in large, looping letters around the base of the huge cog in the centre of the room. Someone else had added, BUT WOULD YOU SHAG HER THOUGH?

I crouched down in the small space, feeling very alone. This wasn't the mill in the book. It was cold and dark and scary. I let out a little sob, running my hands through the dust on the floor.

With a shaking finger I wrote, ROMILLY WAS HERE. Then

I stopped. I could hear something outside. An assured tapping of footsteps, as if someone were walking the plank. I jumped up, just in time for the door to burst open, the silhouette of a large woman blocking out the light.

'Oh!' she said seeing me standing there. Her mouth, just visible in the grainy dark, formed a perfect o. 'You gave me a shock. I didn't expect anyone to be in here. Are you looking for the treasure too?'

I nodded, rubbing my message out with my toe.

'I didn't think I'd get over there—' she nodded back to the plank, '—I fear I may have cracked the bridge a little. Not to worry though, Bob'll help us if we get stuck. He's out there, doing a spot of bird-watching. There's the chance of an egret apparently.'

She walked into the room, the light still blocked by her impressive bulk. Taking a torch from her rucksack she clicked it on and shone it round the walls.

'Looks like plenty of people have been here before us,' she said. 'Oh dear, they do say some thoughtless things, don't they?' She kicked at an empty beer can on the floor. 'That poor little girl. I think some of them forget she's real.'

'How can they forget?' Dad sometimes forgot about me, of course, but that was different. He was Dad.

'Well, I suppose nobody really sees her, do they? There's that photo in the back of the books, but apart from that...'

'Maybe she's a ghost,' I said, thinking how I sounded like Stacey, and then, 'Do you think the treasure's real?'

'I can't see why not. I think Tobias Kemp would have told the press by now if it wasn't.'

'I can't find it, and I've been looking for years.'

'I expect it's like the Pools – someone who's never had a thought to finding it will dig it up one day, oblivious to all the hard work we've put in – just like that chap from Leeds who won a million the other week. Never played before.'

'That's not very fair.'

'Life isn't fair, is it? Look at that poor little girl, her name scrawled all around us.' She shone her torch around again. My name flared from the darkness. I patted my cap nervously.

'How do you know she's poor?' I said.

'Well, I bet she never asked for any of this. Rumour has it she doesn't even go to school. He keeps her locked up in that house day in, day out. I've a mind to report him to social services.'

'Who?'

'Tobias Kemp. From what I hear, he's a bit of a prima donna. And she's got no mum around to care for her, poor pet.' The woman tutted.

'Betty?' A voice from outside echoed across the water.

'That'll be Bob. Are you coming out with me?' She pulled a small trowel out of her pocket. 'I like to dig, whenever I find somewhere like this. Just in case. You want a go?'

We stepped outside and blinked in the light. Bob was standing on the other side of the bridge, a pair of binoculars on a strap round his neck.

'I thought you'd got lost,' he said.

'I was just chatting with this boy. He's a treasure hunter too.'

'There's no accounting for taste,' Bob said in a bored voice, and turned away, putting the binoculars to his eyes.

We edged round the thin stretch of grass that ringed the wind-pump, Betty teetering every now and again, her round shape not conducive to delicate climbing.

'Now, my logic says that if we find a place where the treasure might be, we may as well dig anywhere nearby. I never dig too often though – it's like picking wild flowers: one is enough. And I always put back the earth I've uncovered. I'll go first.'

She bent down on creaking knees and tucked the shovel into the earth. A sod came away, soft and crumbly. Together, we looked into the little hole it had made.

'Doesn't look promising, does it?' she said. She replaced the earth and handed the trowel to me. 'Your turn.'

I looked around. We were on the far side of the pump. Far off to the east, Bob was standing, binoculars to his eyes. Four silver-white birds flapped lazily through the sky.

The windpump soared above me. There was no graffiti on its brickwork here. I took the shovel from the woman and crouched down. The scoop sliced satisfyingly into the earth, and for a second my stomach clenched in the hope of finding the treasure. I lifted the trowel and looked into the hole that it left behind.

'You've got something,' Betty said, her wiry curls getting in the way, and before I had a chance to move, her pudgy hand had flown in and pulled out something small and shiny.

'Well, will you look at that.' In her hand was a tiny, hard-shelled insect, shining like real gold. 'Isn't it beautiful?' she said.

And it was. It was a perfect oval, its shell a metallic, all-consuming yellow gold.

'It just goes to show, there's treasure in nature too,' the woman said, placing the little insect in my hand, where it began to walk, exploring the crevices of my skin. Then, with a slow whir, its shell opened and two little wings extended, and it was off, flying lazily up into the blue of the sky. We watched it until it disappeared.

'Don't forget to replace the soil now, there's a good boy.'

I patted the soil down. A single blue flower was growing out of the grass that I had dug up. I hoped I hadn't killed it.

After we had navigated the plank of wood ('You go first, dear. Bob can rescue me if it all goes wrong'), I said goodbye to the woman and waved to the man, who was far away now in the distance.

In the garden, my head humming from all that I had seen and heard at the mill, I sank down by the moat and dipped my feet into its chill water. The garden was still busy, but no one seemed bothered by a boy in a cap sitting by the water. A silvery clinking heralded Dad's approach.

'I thought it was you under that hat,' he said, towering over me, beaming. 'Are you incognito? Good plan, good plan.' He sat down next to me with a huff of satisfaction. 'They're loaded, those nice tourists,' he said, putting his hand in his pocket and swilling the coins around. 'All I did was show them the mobiles and make them a cup of tea, and I got twenty pounds for my trouble.' He began rolling his trouser legs up. 'Look at these forget-me-nots,' he said, examining the tiny blue flowers half hidden in the grass.

'Beatrice brought them when she came to visit.'

'Of course.' He dipped his toes in the moat and let out a sigh. 'That hat suits you. I hope you haven't chopped all your hair off underneath. I need to make a start on the next book soon, and everyone'll get confused if I start painting a boy.'

I grinned up at him, and suddenly his eyes widened as he looked at me.

'Where's your mole gone?' he said, leaning towards me so quickly that I nearly toppled into the moat.

'I didn't want to look like me.'

He lifted his thumb and rubbed hard at my cheeks, wiping off the paint. When he had finished his breath rushed out in an audible whoosh. He studied my mole for a moment, then he stood, his legs dripping, and walked back to the house, the money in his trouser pocket clinking.

I looked down at the bank, and put a hand to my cheek to calm the sting. Leaning over, I inched forward to see my reflection in the moat, curious to see how different I looked with my mole covered up. But Braër's high wall cast a thick black shadow over the water, and all I could see when I looked down was an eerie silhouette that had no eyes and no mouth, and yet managed to stare right into me, penetrating to my very core.

Seventeen

In the spring before my thirteenth birthday, I dressed up as a clown and accompanied Dad to the village pub. Dad pushed the door open and I stomped in in my oversized shoes, my clown's wig falling over my nose. I had never been inside before. The carpet was a swirl of reds and greens. It stuck to my shoes as we made our way to the bar, the plastic handle of the collection bucket digging into my hand.

I could see men leering at me through my blue nylon hair as we walked, raising their glass tankards to their lips. The pub smelt of eggs. At the bar, Dad ordered a pint, and an orange juice for me. He handed it to me in the bottle, a thin straw bobbing in its neck.

'Don't mind if my daughter collects for Comic Relief, do you?' he said, attempting to sound local and friendly, but sounding like the posh Londoner he was. The landlord eyed me, his hand resting on the beer pump. A film of grease coated his face and slicked back his receding hair. I could see oily finger marks on the beer pump too. I had a feeling there would be a sheen of it on the top of Dad's pint, like petrol on water. He dropped a twenty pence piece into my bucket. It landed on the others, shiny and slippery. My fingers contracted in disgust and I resolved to wear gloves to count the money.

The pub dog, Bert, thrust his huge snout into my crotch as I walked past him. He was a large, overweight boxer, a guard dog that turned into a pathetic baby when you rubbed his belly. A pair of fat, hairless testicles swung between his back legs. He was known in the village as the local Romeo, the father of many litters of accidental puppies. He was allowed to roam free, leaving fat, squelchy poos in his wake, the result of the many chips shoved into his salivating chops by inebriated customers.

Dad found a seat by the window while I made my way round the pub, shaking my bucket and trying not to trip up on my huge shoes. The tip of my painted red nose was just within my sight, and I kept squinting at it, my eyes crossing.

'So this is where Tobias Kemp hides his treasure, is it?' one man slurred, putting his hand into the bucket and stirring his fingers through the coins. I left his table before he could put any money in.

A man at the bar dropped a five-pound note in. 'Is that Romilly Kemp under there?' he said, trying to look under the long blue curls of the wig. 'My daughter loves your books. Here, could you sign this?'

He handed me a beer mat and grabbed a biro from the bar. It had been a while since anyone had asked me to sign anything, and I grinned at him, enjoying the feeling of being recognised. I scrawled my name. The signature looked disappointingly ordinary, the ink coming out in gluey blobs, and I made a mental note to carry a proper fountain pen around with me, just in case.

As I started back to Dad, I felt the soft grip of the man's hand on my arm. 'You couldn't give us a clue, could you?' he was talking under his breath. The grip on my arm tightened. 'It's just, my daughter, she'd be made up if I could help her find the treasure.'

I could smell the beer on his breath. 'I don't know any more than you,' I said, pulling my arm away, but his grip tightened.

'Rumour has it the treasure's hidden in your bedroom,' he said, fingering the beer mat I had written on, looking at my signature.

'Beneath that big old bed of yours, that's what I heard. Don't you find it weird that everyone knows exactly where you sleep?'

I pulled my arm away again, and this time he let go, raising his hands innocently.

'Better be careful no one comes and searches for the treasure in the middle of the night,' he said, watching me as I made my way back to my dad.

As I hurried back, I passed a man reading a newspaper by the fire. It was open on the table, and a familiar phrase caught my eye. SHADOWY FIGURE PROMPTS INVESTIGATION INTO TREASURE HUNT AUTHOR, it read.

'Excuse me, could I have a look at that page, please?'

The man handed the paper to me without comment, looking at me strangely. When I took it, I saw why: the page opposite had a picture of a woman with no top on. I felt my cheeks burn red, and I ducked my head and walked away quickly, finding a spare table to read it at.

It was a short article, with no real information at all: the public were concerned about the shadowy woman in Dad's books, and one person had voiced the opinion that Dad might have murdered someone, and that was what he was hiding in his books. The paper quoted a psychologist as saying that it was probably an image of his mother, who had died when he was young. It took me a moment to realise they were talking about my grandmother. I'd never met my grandparents on Dad's side, but I had assumed they were alive somewhere out there. I didn't know how I felt, knowing at least one of them was dead. Surreptitiously, I ripped the page out of the paper, naked breasts and all, and scrunched it up. On my way back to Dad, I dropped it in the fire.

I slid into the seat beside Dad, thinking about the third book. I had found the shadowy woman as soon as the book arrived. She was on the first page, in the distance as before. She still had her hands to her face, but this time her knees were also bent, as if she were sinking to the ground.

Dad shook the collection bucket, listening to the clink of coins. 'Nice one, Roe,' he said, passing me my orange juice. Bert was lying on the carpet, stretched out, his genitalia leering up at me. He lifted his head at Dad's voice, his tail thumping on the floor. A pearl of white shone at the end of his penis, glinting in the firelight, and I looked away, feeling queasy.

Dad had set up a tattered game of chess in my absence. I hadn't bothered playing chess with Dad for a long time, as I got sick of him always beating me. But this time, as I sucked hard on the dregs of my orange juice, some magical alchemy began to happen. I moved my pieces thoughtfully around the board, chewing on my straw and taking his pawns in quick succession. After he had refilled his pint and, grudgingly, my orange juice, I jumped on one of his rooks, circling his king. His queen had gone off on a promenade around the edges of the board, no use to anyone. Perhaps she was drunk too, I thought, looking at Dad's crossed eyes as he sipped his fourth pint.

A couple of pickled eggs and a fifth pint appeared as Dad managed, at last, to overpower one of my bishops. Alas, it was too little too late as he plonked himself right in front of my queen. I made sure the end was gory.

Dad was sitting slumped at the table, his head on his folded arms. He was talking, but his mouth was attached to the cuff of his jumper and his voice was muffled. I leant closer, the better to hear him, and he lifted his head.

'I went out to the hazel wood,' he said, his mouth slack now that it was loosed from the wool of his jumper, 'because a fire was in my head.' He looked at me, his eyes squinting. 'I have a fire in my head,' he said, touching the tip of his finger to my forehead.

'Shall we go home?' I asked and he nodded, picking up my bucket and knocking the chess set to the floor as he attempted to get up.

It was a clear, dark night, the thin sliver of moon hardly lighting the way.

'They want a treasure hunt,' Dad slurred, 'but they don't understand.'

'What don't they understand?' I said, trying to steer him along the edge of the road.

'It's not for them.'

The spring moonlight seemed to trickle down the back of my neck, 'What do you mean? Who's it for?'

Dad stopped in the middle of the road. 'It's for me,' he said, 'and for you.' He pointed his finger at his chest and then tried to do the same to me, but he tripped on the grass verge. The collection bucket spilt onto the grass like a clown's water bucket at the circus. For a moment I felt terribly, terribly sad for my father, for even though I was the one dressed up, it was obvious that he was the clown. He dropped down onto his knees and started picking up the pennies.

'The silver apples of the moon,' he said, collecting up a handful of change and letting it slide through his fingers, 'the golden apples of the sun.' I knelt beside him and began to help, but his huge hand rested on mine, stopping me.

'What treasure is this?' he asked, turning to look at me again, his eyes full of tears.

Eighteen

I could always tell when the summer holidays began because my garden became off limits, not just at weekends, but every day. Families arrived bringing picnics and metal detectors. Little children carried buckets and spades as if they were going to the seaside. It was the day after my thirteenth birthday, and already my summer purgatory inside the house had begun.

'Stacey, why don't you go to school?' I said, drowsily. We were lying on my bed, staring out of the window over the tops of Dad's mobiles.

'You know why, Mum home schools me. Anyway, you don't go to school either.'

'I don't know if what Dad does could really be called home schooling. It's mostly art and ancient history.'

'Sounds nice.' Stacey picked at a scab under Monty's fur. He purred loudly. 'Is it the summer holidays yet? For people who go to school, I mean?'

'Only for private schools so far. Soon all the schools will break up, and then it'll get even busier, and I'll be stuck in the house, day in, day out.' I rolled over and looked at her. 'Did you ever think about going to high school?'

I had met a girl from my primary school while I was out walking the other day, and had been surprised when she told me she'd already been at high school for two years.

'Did you think we stayed at primary until we were eighteen?' she had said, looking at me with pity. It felt strange knowing all the children I had briefly met at the little school down the road were moving on in their education without me.

'Why would I want to go to high school?' Stacey said.

'To learn? Maybe we could go. If we both went, it would be OK. You could ask your mum…'

'Learning's overrated,' she said, lifting the edge of the scab. It came away with a few hairs attached.

I frowned. 'Well, maybe your mum could home school me too, then. For the stuff that Dad knows nothing about. Can I come to your house sometimes?' I knew the answer, I had been asking it for years.

'Nah. It's boring at mine. It's much more fun at your house.'

'No it isn't. It's so dull here.' I began picking at Monty too. 'What shall we do?'

The summer stretched before us. My usual excitement at this time of year had been replaced by a foggy malaise. My gaze settled on a flicker of green playing across the far wall. 'What's that?' I said, pointing to it.

Stacey got up and went to the light, following it back to a dish on my dressing table. She came back to the bed and opened her hand. My mum's emerald earrings lay in her palm. I picked them up, letting them dangle. The green light splintered and spun across the room. I wondered if Mum had ever worn them, and with that thought came a longing, a need for her that puzzled me. It had been two years since I last saw her, and then only for a short few days. Why did I suddenly need her now?

'Let's pierce our ears,' Stacey said suddenly.

'What?'

'You want to be able to wear your mum's earrings, don't you?'

'I suppose so,' I said, doubtfully.

'We'll need a needle and a candle,' she said, and I remembered a programme we had seen recently on Children's BBC about a girl who had done exactly that. I tried not to think about how she had gone to the doctor's afterwards because they'd got infected.

Stacey was rummaging around my room and came back with the surgical instruments. 'I'll do yours first,' she said.

'OK,' I said warily, eying the needle.

We lit a candle, and I sat on the edge of the bed, holding an ice cube to my earlobe, while Stacey put the end of the needle in the flame. As she approached me, I had a fleeting feeling of foreboding, and then she was pinching my ear between her finger and thumb, and pushing the needle into my skin.

'Ow!'

'Keep still.'

'I don't think the ice cube has numbed it.'

'It's nearly through now, stay still. Gosh, your skin is tough.'

With a jolt, I felt the needle exit the back of my ear. Stacey pulled it out, her hand bloody.

'Now the other one,' she said.

'No way, that was enough.' I backed away, onto the bed.

'You can't have just one ear pierced.'

'Why not?'

'It's weird.'

'I'm going to start a new trend. Anyway, one of Mum's earrings is bent. Your turn.' I took the needle from her, wiping the blood off on a tissue.

'No way. You think I'm going to go through that? Here—' She slipped the earring into the hole she'd made in my ear. It stung for a moment and then I could feel it dragging my earlobe down.

It was a strange feeling, wearing an earring. I felt lopsided. My whole ear burnt. When I looked in the mirror, my skin there was bright red, but I was bewitched by the sparkle of the emerald, the gleam of the gold. I wished Mum could see me.

Stacey lay down on the bed, picking at the wooden beam above her head, trying to coax a death watch beetle onto her finger. 'I forgot to tell you,' she said, 'I've found somewhere new: a secret place. I wanted to show it to you for a birthday present.'

Stacey never brought me material gifts. Her presents were places or objects she found out on her walks, and I treasured them always.

'I think it might even be a shrieking pit,' she added.

I turned to look at her. She hadn't mentioned shrieking pits for years, not since we went looking when we were nine and Dad had to pull me out of the mud minus my wellies. 'No way,' I said.

Stacey grinned. 'Get your shoes on, Rom,' she said.

'Do you think we're the same people we were when we first met?' I said to Stacey as we walked across the marsh. My earring swung wildly as I walked, brushing against my neck.

'I don't know,' she said, stopping to study me.

I was finding it hard to identify with the version of me in Dad's stories. Romilly in the books was forever nine years old. She had a talking cat and lived in a world where adventures happened as soon as she opened her bleary eyes. No spots marred the face of the storybook Romilly, and I was pretty sure she didn't need to wash her hair every day like I had to now.

Unlike my literary counterpart, I was growing like a weed, my body erupting with weird and embarrassing lumps, and my second patched denim dress hung in the wardrobe, too small and tight on my frame to ever be worn again.

I looked at Stacey. She was not quite as tall as me. Her shoulders were broader, and her hair was long and wavy. Everything about her was soft and rounded. It suited her.

'Do you remember when I used to think you were a boy?' I said, immediately regretting it as the smile dropped from her face.

Stacey turned and carried on walking. 'I wanted to be a boy,' she said, 'when I was younger. Still do sometimes.'

'Did you? Why?'

'I thought if I was a boy I could run away.'

I pictured her with her short, scraggy hair, a polka dot handkerchief tied to the end of a stick over one shoulder. 'Girls can run away too,' I said.

'I didn't know that then.'

We had reached the edge of the marsh now. It gave way to flat fields, shimmering with corn.

'Listen,' Stacey said, stopping suddenly so that I bumped into her, 'it's like singing.'

'What is it?'

'I think it's those trees. Over there in the middle of the field.'

'What do you think they're saying?'

'Probably telling everyone to bugger off.'

'Oh, nice.'

'Come on.'

Close up, they weren't a line of trees, but a circle. I stopped on the edge of the field, not daring to trespass through the corn.

'Come on, Rom,' Stacey said with a glint in her eye, 'dare you.' And she parted the corn like silk in her hands and waded into the golden field, her body swinging through it like a slow pendulum.

I watched her weave her way through, trying to decide whether to follow her, but then something black caught my eye, way off in the distance. It was the size of a large dog, but it moved very differently, slinking low to the ground, its long, slim tail furled out behind it. The panther, I thought with a shiver, watching it as it disappeared over the horizon.

'Stacey, wait for me!' I called, hurrying through the corn to catch up.

At the edge of the trees we stopped, a tangle of brambles blocking our path. Stacey ducked down to peer through.

'There's a way in here,' she said, pushing her way into it, holding the bramble cables so I could squeeze through behind. The trees above us were deafening. It was more like chanting than singing, but as we came through into the centre, it died off until it was hardly audible.

I gasped. A small, perfectly round lake lay in front of us, the water brown and brackish. We stood as if we were in a church, shivering, waiting for something. And then the sun broke over the tops of the trees and a ray of light pierced the water. The opaque lake became gold before our eyes, revealing the long, wet fronds of weed that lay horizontally on its bed.

'I bet people have drowned here,' Stacey whispered to me, and then she was pulling at her clothes, unbuttoning and unzipping until they fell in a messy crumple round her feet and she ran, plunging into the water, shrieking at its cold chill.

I couldn't help but stare at the change in her. Whereas my breasts were little more than tiny protuberances on my chest, hers were alive, rolling down towards her stomach, settling on the skin there, the nipples like eyes gazing into her tummy button, only to jump upwards and gaze at the sky as she bounded into the water. As the first cold droplets landed on her skin, her nipples shrank and darkened like sea anemones sensing an exploratory finger.

'Come on!' she shouted, the mad glint back in her eyes. And so

I did, pulling at my clothes in the same excited panic, running at the water as if my life depended on it.

Even in high summer the water was cold, and my nerve endings died a sudden, scissory death as I hit the water. Stacey and I dared each other to run in, taking it in turns to splash to the pool's centre, our feet caught up in mud and pondweed. The water swirled with a hurricane of disturbed silt, tiny filaments of dead leaves and insects and whirling vegetation.

After we had run and jumped and dived until our hair and skin was plastered with the lake's debris, we lay on the long grass, feeling the sun dry our bodies until the little pieces glued themselves to our skin.

'What kind of death frightens you most?' Her voice was quiet, rousing me from the beginnings of a warm dream on the bank. I squinted at her through my eyelashes.

'I dunno. You?'

'Drowning. But not on a day like today. Under ice, so there's no hope of getting out.' She had sat up and was staring out over the little lake, her hands encircling her knees.

A trickle of cold sidled across my skin. 'Why?'

'It's like a window you can't cross, isn't it? Your skin would get so stiff from the cold that it cracked, and all the time you'd be watching the world going on on the other side of the ice.'

She hugged herself. I felt the cold penetrate my bones, and I rubbed at the goose pimples on my arms.

'Let's make a potion,' I said, changing the subject.

Her expression changed too, like scudding clouds leaving the sun. 'Yes,' she said happily.

'What could we make it in?'

She pointed to an old glass bottle bobbing in the water, 'That do?'

The potion-making had become a ritual, started two years ago when we were eleven. It was something we usually did in the garden at Braër, hidden behind Dad's shed under the cool of the willow, but this time it felt different: secret.

We stood, as if in a trance, and collected blossom from the wild flowers that ringed the lake. Stacey waded out and picked a wilting yellow flag iris. We pushed them into the bottle, and filled it to the brim with lakewater.

Legs crossed, our knees touching, naked but for our knickers, we gazed at each other as Stacey swirled the bottle. The perfume was musty, like undiscovered attics, and it curled high into my nose and stayed there. The ritual had been perfected over the years: taking my hand, Stacey pulled it towards her and dabbed the perfume on my arm. I copied, pulling her arm to me and swiping the water over her wrist. Fragments of brown petal plastered themselves to her, mimicking the freckles on my own arm. We sat, looking into each other's eyes, our skin anointed. Stacey lifted a hand and tucked my hair behind my ear, watching my new earring catch the sun.

Sitting there, our skin prickling, we leant towards each other and touched nose to nose, mirroring what the other held out. It had always fascinated both of us, this game, since we'd first met.

Her nose was oily, slipping against mine. I could smell the darkness of her unwashed hair, hear the downy whisper of her top lip. We held the position for a second, our breath filling each other's mouths, choking our tongues. Finally we reeled back, exhaling quickly and rocking our bony bottoms against the ground. The tip of my nose felt greasy.

Stacey leant forward again and whispered about a wetness in the gusset of her pants, her breath hot and virulent in my ear. She spoke proudly of blood and pain and stains she couldn't remove. She placed my hand low on her warm stomach, and I felt the knotted muscles beneath the fat. Stacey showed me her pants, still damp from her swim. They had the echo of a dark stain in the warm bit that went between her legs. My own pants were stretchy and a little bit small for me, with cartoon flowers dancing across them.

In the golden light, amid the spiders' nests and tiny midges, we placed our hands together so that our palms were touching, warm and soft. My heart prickled in my tummy and my fingers flexed, wanting to touch more.

Quietly we let go, picked up our clothes and began to dress.

Nineteen

In November, the dew-covered spiderwebs on the lawn were replaced by creeping webs of frost. The beech tree was completely smooth now, the bark long since fallen away, and in the early morning frost it shimmered like a huge snake winding its way through the garden towards the house.

Dad and I lit the fire earlier each afternoon, and spent our mornings on long foraging walks, finding wood we could burn. Dad had developed a love of collecting conkers. They were piled into bowls and lined up on every window sill in every room of the house, burnished and fat, as if he wanted to stop an impending invasion of spiders.

One particularly cold evening, Dad was watching the news. A man was stepping out of an aeroplane into the wind and rain, waving at the waiting crowds.

'He is thinner and greyer,' the reporter said. I stopped on my way to bed, caught by the poise of the man as he stood, stooped in the aeroplane's doorway. He looked a bit like a skeleton. He was stumbling down the steps now, the skin of his face ashen, his eyes vacant and staring, despite the smile.

'Unsteady on his feet after being chained for five years,' the reporter continued.

'Who is he?' I asked, perching on the arm of the sofa.

'His name's Terry Waite. He was taken hostage for years,' Dad said.

'How did he escape?'

'They let him go.'

'Why?'

'I don't know. Maybe they ran out of reasons to keep him. Shh, Romilly, I'm trying to listen.'

Mr Waite was making a speech. He was wearing a thick coat, but still he looked cold. 'One thousand seven hundred and sixty-three days in chains,' he said, looking around at his audience. Something about his eyes scared me. What had they seen?

A picture of a postcard appeared on screen, a colourful stained-glass window. It reminded me of the circular window in my bedroom. The reporter explained how it had reached the hostage in prison, and on the back, the simple message, '*We remember. We shall not forget.*'

'Sounds like they'd already decided he was dead.' Dad chuckled. He had a sketch pad resting on his knee. He was holding a pen in his hand, absentmindedly tapping the nib against his head as he watched the TV.

'Dad, you're doing it again,' I said.

'What?' He put his hand to his head and felt beneath his hair. His fingers came away inked in blue.

'Damn,' he said, 'I'm so used to doing it with a pencil, I forgot it was a pen.'

'How about if you stop stabbing your head with sharp implements altogether?'

Yesterday I had come across one of his paintbrushes on the kitchen table, snapped in two. I had rolled it between my fingers, brushing it against my skin, dabbing it on my wrists like perfume. Essence of Tobias, I thought.

I looked at my dad now as he touched his fingers to his scalp, frowning at the blue glint that came away on his skin, and I realised with a pang of sadness that I missed the dad from my childhood.

The man sitting in front of me now was a different man to the one I remembered. His mood, always turbulent, changed now so quickly that it was like being caught in a storm that whipped up from nowhere. The father that drew me into his arms for a hug, that tucked me up at night, he had crept away months ago, stealing off into the night while I slept on, oblivious.

'Do you like toffee apples or candyfloss best?' Dad said, pulling me back from my thoughts.

'What?'

'Or those huge sweets that look like a baby's dummy. The ones you hang around your neck?' He was licking his lips now. 'Or donuts?'

As I watched him, he scratched his cheek with inky fingers, leaving a blue mark that looked like a bruise.

'What do you mean, Dad?'

'Romilly,' Dad barked, looking at me as if he had only just realised I was there. 'I wanted to ask you something. You know *Picnic*'s been out for a little while now? The *Observer* want to do a short piece on it to coincide with the paperback's release. They want a photo of you.'

He was referring to his latest book, the fourth in the series, entitled *Romilly and the Picnic*. In it, Monty and I took a picnic to a lake, where Monty fell into the water and I had to jump in and save him. I looked at Dad for a long moment, trying to work out if he was playing some macabre joke on me, but his face remained serious.

'Can't they just use a picture from the book?' I said eventually.

'That's the thing – they are. But they want a comparison shot. It'll be a nod to *Lolita*, I presume: I'm not sure whether to be flattered or disgusted. Anyway, it means you'd need to wear the denim dress again.'

'There's no way that dress would fit now!' I shuddered at the thought of fitting into it. It might squeeze over my hips, but it would definitely not cover my bum.

'I know, my love. But we can have a new one made.'

'I'm not nine years old anymore. I'll look…' I searched for the word, 'freaky.'

'It's what they want, and I must give them what they want. Especially if we want to fix the chimney before it collapses in the next high wind.' He turned to me beseechingly, his blue-stained cheek glinting. 'Will you do it, Roe?'

It struck me that his eyes were a bit like the man on the telly's — hollow, as if they had sunk into his skull.

I sighed and nodded. If wearing a pinafore was all I needed to do to make him happy, then of course I would do it.

Upstairs, I found Stacey lying on the bed, gazing dreamily out of the window. She often let herself in these days. She found the change in Dad's behaviour a little frightening, and she rarely spent time in his company any more. I would find her instead up in my bedroom, flicking through a book or lying on the bed staring at the ceiling, waiting for me.

I sat down at my desk and began a letter to Beatrice. We had kept up our correspondence, sometimes writing weekly. It had helped enormously with my handwriting and spelling. The letters often got lost in the sacks of fan mail we received, or else Dad opened them to check they were safe and forgot to pass them on straight away, but I always managed to extricate them sooner or later.

I had noticed over the months that Bea's writing was beginning to change, the words stretching across the page as if they were taking longer to leave her brain and travel down to the pen. Sometimes I could hardly read whole sentences, and I had to skip to the next line.

You mentioned your father, and how he seems to be changing, she wrote in her last letter.

I know it can be hard, finding common ground, especially as you enter your teenage years, but persevere. Your father is an unusual man, and he loves you terribly. It might not be him changing, but you. This is an important time in your life: you're transforming from a girl into a woman, and fathers especially find it hard to let go.

She was very good at advice, and I tried to take Dad's strange behaviour with a pinch of salt. After all, I must be hard to live with, too.

I finished my letter to her and licked the envelope closed. Stacey was still lying on the bed, her eyes closed, humming quietly to herself. I went over and sat next to her, holding my hand above her head, palm side down.

'What are you doing?' she said, opening her eyes and batting my hand away from where it hovered.

'You've had twenty-three boyfriends,' I said. I'd seen it on *Grange Hill* the other day. The bullies were doing it to a new girl. They'd counted to fifty-five before she noticed. Half the class had been sniggering behind her back. I'm like that girl, I thought. Thank God I don't have to go to school.

'What's the point of that?' Stacey said. 'Who cares how many boyfriends anyone has?'

I shrugged. 'Do you know who Terry Waite is?' I asked.

She shook her head.

'He's this man who was held hostage for four years, three years in solitary confinement. Can you imagine being on your own with no one to talk to for three years? And he didn't even have a window to look out of.'

'A bit like being stuck in your dad's shed,' said Stacey.

'But at least Dad has his paper and his paintbrushes,' I said, then I remembered the forlorn broken brush, and I thought that Stacey might be right.

'What's with your dad at the moment anyway?' she said, as if she could read my mind.

'What do you mean?'

'He's gone a bit weird, hasn't he?'

I thought of the *Grange Hill* bullies, how mean they could be. I thought of having to wear that stupid dress again. I was sick of being nice.

'He's probably got a brain tumour,' I said, wincing inwardly, but Stacey laughed heartily. Guilty adrenaline surged through me, leaving my body limp and spent, and suddenly I had an acute and inexplicable urge for my mother

'I wish Mum was here,' I said, looking over at the portrait of Mary Mother-of-God, my mind mixing the two until the memories of my real mum all had a golden halo round her head.

'I thought you didn't get on?'

'I just wish I had someone here who cared about me. Someone to talk to. Dad and I never talk any more, not about important stuff.' I sighed.

'You've got me.' She sounded hurt.

I reached over and wrapped my arms around her. 'I know. And I don't know what I'd do without you.'

'Romilly!' Dad's panicked voice shot up the stairs.

I sighed and got up off my bed. 'Here we go again,' I said quietly. Stacey giggled.

'What is it?' I said as I met him on the landing.

'My mobiles!' he said, bending over and gasping for breath. 'They're gone!'

Panic shot through me. 'How can they be gone?' I said, running to the landing window.

The mobiles were in the meadow, moving gently in the wind.

'They're there, Dad,' I said, nodding towards them.

'They're... oh. Oh goodness. There they are.' Dad sat down quickly on the window seat, narrowly missing a line of conkers, keeping his eyes on the mobiles. Or perhaps, I considered as I climbed back up my stairs to Stacey, he was fixing his eyes firmly on the horizon, as if he were on a listing ship, desperate to stay afloat.

Twenty

Over the following year, I made it my job to watch Dad, making notes of any unusual behaviour. But he spent so much time in his painting shed, it was hard to gauge. Dad had always been eccentric. Where do you draw the line between quirkiness and madness?

Beatrice came to stay for a few days in the spring, and I watched her watching him, her eyes following him as he went about his day. When she left, she pulled me into a hug.

'Keep writing to me,' she said, her eyes flicking meaningfully towards Dad, 'I'm there if you need me.'

On the morning of my fourteenth birthday, the doorbell went.

'Post!' came Dad's call from somewhere in the depths of the house. I opened the door.

'Slightly more than usual this morning,' the postman said, heaving a small sack over the bridge and dumping it on the doormat, 'you've got a large amount from America in there too.'

Stacey appeared behind him, edging across the bridge, her eyes popping at the bulging bag.

'Are there any for me?' I asked hopefully, 'I mean any cards?' I eyed the sacks warily.

'Your birthday is it?'

I nodded.

'The top layer's for you.' He prodded the sack with his toe. 'Happy birthday.'

I sighed and pulled it inside, Stacey helping. Most people wrote letters to Dad, but sometimes I got some too. Mine were usually from children, whereas Dad's were from the professional treasure hunters: those who had given up work to spend more time deciphering the clues in the books, or who were travelling round the world trying to find where *x* marked the spot. One man wrote every single day.

I had always been allowed to open my own letters until Dad realised it wasn't just kids writing to me. When I was eleven, a photograph had fallen out of a letter I was unfolding of something pink and squishy-looking. Dad had whipped it away before I could look at it properly, but from then on he took over the job of opening my mail.

'Miss Romilly Kemp!' My name unfurled out of Dad's mouth like a richly embroidered royal banner. He was marching down the stairs, a loosely tied bow tie round his neck, but no shirt for it to sit on. 'Like it?' he said, pulling on it ever so slightly so it began to unravel, 'It felt like an occasion. Fourteen years old: you're in your fifteenth year. Ah, I see the post's arrived.' He bent down and scooped up a pile of letters, spilling the sack all over the floor. 'What mad delinquents are wishing you salutations this year? Perhaps for your fourteenth birthday you'll get more than a picture of someone's flaccid penis.'

Stacey giggled.

'Dad! That's really inappropriate. And can't you put a shirt on? You look ridiculous.' I grabbed a wrinkled shirt from the radiator in the hall and helped him on with it.

'Sorry, daughter-mine. Manners.' He turned around so that I could button it up. I could feel his gaze scorching my face as I was doing it. With a pang I remembered how he used to help me button my own shirt up for school. I reached up and lifted his collar, correcting the bow tie, teasing and tightening until it looked right.

'There, all done,' I said, stepping back and admiring my efforts.

'I do wish *my* fans would send me pictures of their naked flesh,' Dad said, almost to himself. 'Well, the ladies, anyway.'

I turned in distaste, shaking my head, and stalked up the stairs. This was not how a birthday should start. Stacey ran after me. When we were safely on our own, she said, 'Do people really send you pictures of willies?'

'Come and see.'

We raced up to my room and re-formed around my loose floor-board. I opened it with the end of a ruler and pulled out a tightly bunched pack of letters.

'I thought your Dad opened your letters?'

'He used to, but sometimes he forgets. And in the summer he can't burn them on the fire, so he just chucks them in the bin.' I indicated a bit of egg yolk on the edge of one. Pulling the elastic band off, I eked out a photo and handed it to Stacey.

'Whoa.'

'I know.'

We looked at the photo together.

'What is it?' said Stacey, turning the photo upside down to see if it made more sense.

'I think it might be balls,' I said, and we both dissolved into giggles.

My birthday had fallen on a Saturday. Dad remarked that it was uncommonly hot, but when I thought back to past birthdays, they had all felt hot and sunny, draped in the sugary glow of birthday excitement.

Stacey wanted to show me something for my birthday. Last year's gift had been the lake in the circle of poplars. The year before, an oak tree with a type of fungus attached, a webbed nest below it full of gently pulsing eggs. The fungus had given us both itchy fingers for days afterwards. This year, she had a theory about the location of Dad's treasure.

'He started writing the books after he moved here, so something must have triggered it, and if we can work out what it was, we'll find the location of the treasure. Come on!'

As we walked south from the village, over the bridge and beyond, she was full of an almost palpable excitement, as if it would rip straight out of her at any moment and go shooting off into the sky like a firework.

'Bodies,' she said with glee as we perched ourselves on a fence that surrounded a small disused quarry. From this height the water below was a rich tan colour. Here and there you could see lumps in the water, floating lazily. They did look quite body-like.

The quarry walls were a harsh orange threaded with chalk, sloping down into the water. A pipe stuck out halfway, dripping rust.

'I was hoping we might spot the black panther,' she said, 'there's been another sighting.' She looked over her shoulder, 'Maybe it's stalking us right now.'

'I doubt it,' I said, but I glanced over my shoulder anyway. I hadn't told her about my own sighting last year near the lake. I sometimes felt like Stacey knew all my secrets – it was nice to have something just for me.

'You really think this is it?' I said, changing the subject. 'It doesn't look like somewhere you'd bury treasure.'

'But your dad isn't a normal person, is he? He'd never just go to a field and dig a hole and shove it in. He's more complex than that.'

I looked down at the water-filled quarry. Stacey was right, there was something about watery places that always made me think of the treasure hunt. With a shiver, I remembered the gargoyle, buried in our moat. Why had Dad been so keen to sink it from view?

'Look, see those trees?' Stacey said. There were two spindly tree trunks on the far sides, bowing to each other high up over the water. 'Wait till the sun comes out.'

We sat and watched as the clouds scudded across the sky. As the sun broke through, she pointed down into the water. The trees' shadows appeared across its surface, at angles to each other, criss-crossing in a perfect x.

'That's not possible,' I said, trying to work out how they could be casting shadows in different directions.

'It's the reflection,' she said, 'the water's reflecting the sun back again, like a reverse shadow.'

She was right. I studied the cross on the water. It was just off centre. 'That's too clever, even for Dad. It's just a coincidence, it's got to be.'

'It's not!' Stacey said angrily, pulling at my sleeve till I tumbled off the fence towards the quarry's edge. I climbed back on quickly, the chemistry of my leg bones dissolving to liquid.

'Come on, let's go down and see.'

I leant out a little, safe on the fence, and peered over. The drop was almost vertical. My feet tingled and I leant back quickly.

'I'm not going down there.'

'Come on, scaredy pants. Just follow me, it'll be easy.'

'No! We could break a leg, or… or fall in the water.' I looked at the unidentifiable things floating far below and shuddered.

But Stacey was already at the quarry's edge. She was standing on the very brim, and I could see how soft and crumbly the ground was, like a crust, her toes pressing into it, sending motes of sand cascading down.

'Careful, it won't hold your weight.'

'Wooo! Look at me! I'm going to fall!' She giggled, and then her expression changed as she arced slowly backwards, dropping over the edge, her mouth a silent scream.

'Stacey!' I shouted, jumping off the fence and rushing to the edge.

And she was there, crouched on a ledge a metre or so down, silently laughing.

'That wasn't funny.'

'Yes it was.' She uncurled herself and raised her hand for my help, but I turned back to the fence, anger boiling inside me.

'Why can't you be serious just for one day? It's my birthday, for God's sake.'

'Can't I have a joke now and then?'

'You're always having jokes.' I rounded on her, anger bubbling inside me. 'You're always trying to frighten me or tell me about ghosts or murderers. Why can't you leave it?'

'I thought you liked it. Anyway, it's who I am, I can't be someone I'm not just to please you.'

'Then maybe we shouldn't spend so much time together.' As soon as I said it, I regretted it, but it was too late, the words were out. There was silence behind me.

I turned. From here she was still hidden by the quarry's edge, and I had the feeling she had disappeared. But then her hand appeared, the knuckles white as she strained to pull herself up. Finally, her face emerged over the lip of the cliff, her expression immobile.

'What do you mean?' she said.

'Maybe... maybe you shouldn't come round so much anymore.' I kicked at a lump of grass with my toe, not daring to look at her, but she was silent for so long that I lifted my gaze.

Her expression was impassive, her hair whipping over her face as the wind blew, but she made no move to sweep it away. We stood watching each other and I wondered how long we could stay like this, staring each other out.

And then she let go. It was a simple move, the gentle raising of each finger as it left its nest safe up on top of the cliff. And then there was just the echo of her body shimmering in the air. I stood where I was, waiting for the inevitable giggle, but there was none.

'Stacey. This isn't funny.'

There was no answer.

I stepped closer to the edge and peered over, confident she was hiding just below, but the ledge she had been on was empty. I looked round at the edges of the quarry. Was she hiding, just out of sight, sniggering at the look of desperation on my face?

'Stacey!' I shouted, the blood pumping in my ears, my voice echoing out over the water. I looked down in desperation at the flotsam floating below, and tried not to see bodies.

'Stacey,' I said again, the deafening silence surrounding me as I tried to listen for any sign that she was there.

But she had gone.

Twenty-One

Beatrice had come for my birthday tea. We sat around the kitchen table, Beatrice pouring the Earl Grey from a high arc into tiny teacups that I didn't know we owned. I hadn't seen her for a few months, and she seemed more fragile than I remembered, her movements accompanied by a barely there shimmer, as if she couldn't quite keep still.

There was a space set for Stacey, but it was empty. Nevertheless, Beatrice poured her a cup.

Dad pushed a poorly wrapped present at me. 'From Stacey,' he said.

'But she's not here.'

'Well, she made this for you. She dropped it off earlier.'

Before our fight, he meant. Inside was a piece of paper, rolled like a scroll and tied with a ribbon that I thought I recognised from our fabric box. I unrolled it carefully. It was a sketch of me.

'I look so grown up,' I said, forgetting my anger at Stacey and studying the picture. I was leaning against a wall, Monty at my heels, and my face was turned up to the sky as if I was basking in the sunshine. I ran my eyes over the outline of my body. It was strange to see such a true representation of myself, so different to Dad's drawings of nine-year-old me.

'It's good,' I said, and it was. I never knew Stacey could draw. A rush of jealousy sped through me.

Beatrice had baked a huge Victoria sponge, and it stood at the centre of the table on a glass cake stand. There was a sense of expectation in the room: Beatrice and Dad had ceased their chatter, and they were both shuffling in their seats.

'Shall I cut it?' I asked, picking up the knife.

Dad and Bea shared a look.

'What?' I said.

'Well, there's a sort of birthday surprise,' Dad said, glancing out of the window.

Beatrice was looking at her watch. 'She should be here by now,' she said. 'She's not coming. I bet she couldn't convince them.'

'No,' Dad replied, 'she could convince anyone of anything, trust me.'

At that moment, the doorbell rang. Dad pushed his chair back so quickly, I feared he would knock it over.

'Who is it?' I asked, jumping up to follow Dad to the door.

'No, stay here, Roe, it'll be better...' He turned and left the room.

'Who is it, Beatrice?' But she just looked at me warily and mimed zipping up her lips.

I thought of Stacey, disappearing over the edge of the cliff. It was probably her at the door, this morning's incident just a silly stunt to make her entrance now all the more dramatic.

There were hushed whisperings in the hall. I tapped the knife on the edge of the table, waiting.

And then Dad came back into the room. For a moment I thought he was alone, the person behind him was so slim, but then I heard the click of her heels, and I froze.

'Romilly,' she said, standing in the kitchen doorway, and my heart jumped. She was thinner than I remembered, and smaller too, or perhaps I had just grown.

'Hi, Mum,' I said, and she beamed.

Mum took what would have been Stacey's place opposite me.

'You look so grown up,' she said.

Dad slipped into his seat. He and Beatrice looked like sentries at the ends of the table.

'I can't believe you came for my birthday,' I said, leaning across and taking one of her hands in mine. It was chilly, with the long, bright red nails I remembered so well.

'I wouldn't miss it for anything,' she smiled, 'you're a teenager.'

'She was a teenager last year, too,' Dad said.

I shot him a look.

'You look well,' Beatrice said to my mum.

'I am,' Mum said, nodding, 'it's been a good month.'

I had almost forgotten that Beatrice was my mum's own mother. It felt strange to be part of three generations all sitting around the table, the first time in my memory that we had all been in a room together.

'You've got so tall,' Mum said, turning back to me. 'You must be taller than me now. And look at your hair. I was always jealous of that red.'

'She's turned into a beautiful young woman.' Dad lifted his teacup high into the air. 'Cheers, Lidiya,' he said, then his eyes grew wide as he took in Mum, sitting across the table. 'Lidiya!' he said. 'What are you doing here?'

The room went silent.

'Who's Lidiya?' Mum said, her eyes narrowing. She looked around the table. 'Is this a joke?'

'Don't be silly, dear,' Beatrice said, putting a small hand over Dad's, 'that's Meg, Romilly's mother.' She spoke as if getting two people confused was the most normal thing in the world.

Mum was still looking from Dad to me, her eyebrows drawn together, her lips parted as if she wanted to speak, but she remained silent.

'Well, you could be sisters,' Dad said heartily, shaking his head, but I saw him shoot a glance at Mum when he thought she wasn't looking. 'I don't suppose anyone wants a little nip in their tea?' he said, looking over at the dresser where the whisky decanter stood, an inch of amber liquid at the bottom.

'You still like a drink, I see,' Mum said.

'Now then, Megan, don't be spiteful dear,' said Beatrice.

Mum breathed a sigh and nodded.

'Let's cut this cake,' said Beatrice quickly, pouring more tea for everyone, her voice softening the sharp silence like buttercream.

'Would you like to do it, Mum?' I picked up the knife and handed it to her. She took it, her hand so small that it looked like a huge weapon clenched between her fingers.

She pressed it into the cake, and cut three fat slices, and a tiny sliver for herself, licking the jam and cream from her fingers.

'Now it's mine and your mother's turn to give you your present,' said Beatrice, and she opened her arms and lifted her shaking hands to the table. 'Ta da!' she said. I looked around, confused.

'The tea-set!' she exclaimed, pointing to the tiny cup in my hand and waving with a flourish at the plates and teapot on the table.

'Really?' I looked at my cup. It was made of porcelain so thin you could see the swish of tea through its walls. Dad's cup in the crook of his hairy hand made him look like a giant. There was even a tiny pepper pot and salt cellar as well, and I picked them up one by one and admired their delicate cut glass.

'Of course, my darling,' Beatrice said, grinning so wide you could see a smudge of pink lipstick on her teeth, 'though it's really a present just from your mother, since she would have inherited it after I'm gone. It's all right,' she said, seeing me shoot a worried look at my mum, 'we've discussed it, and she wants you to have it too, don't you, dear?'

Mum nodded, smiling shyly.

'It's Meissen, I believe,' said Beatrice. 'It was left to me by an old uncle. Hardly any chips.'

'I remember this set,' Dad said, picking up the little salt pot. 'Beatrice used to serve me tea from it when I was first dating your mother, Romilly. I even painted it into *Romilly and the Picnic*. Isn't it strange how things come full circle?'

I looked around the table, feeling the warm glow of family.

'To Romilly,' Beatrice said, raising her teacup.

'To Romilly,' my parents chanted, and I grinned, looking at Mum, raising my teacup and tapping it to hers.

Mum stayed for the afternoon. As soon as we had eaten, I ran upstairs to find the emerald earrings she had given me. I tried to push the unbent one through the hole in my ear, but it had been months since I last wore it, and the little dot in my earlobe refused to open. Instead I looped the earring on a chain and hung it round my neck, running back down the stairs, taking them two at a time.

Sated with tea and cake, she and I sat by the moat, dangling our feet in the water.

'I'm afraid I didn't get you a present personally,' she said, 'it feels a bit tagged on, having a share in the gift of the tea-set.'

'But it would have been yours, so it's a present from you,' I said.

She nodded, picking a flower from the bank and twirling it between her fingers. 'It was touch and go as to whether I would be allowed to come at all.'

'I thought it was your choice whether you stayed at that place? Can't you leave whenever you want?'

'Well, yes, but it helps to get approval for visits. It shows willing.'

'What's it like? At the facility?' I imagined startlingly bright white rooms, food on little trays with compartments for main course and pudding.

'Is that what your father calls it?' Mum laughed, a musical tinkle that landed on the moat like spring rain. 'It makes it sound like a prison. Or an asylum.'

'It's not, then?'

'No. It's a... therapeutic retreat.'

'Do you live there?'

'Sometimes. Sometimes I live on my own.'

I leant back on my arms and gazed up at Braër, kicking idly at the water. The circular stained-glass window was bright in the afternoon sun.

'I hear you've been writing to my mother,' she looked across the garden to where Bea was knelt, pink gardening gloves on, attempting to bring order to a bed of weeds. 'Quite the little happy family while I've been away.' She leant toward me and lifted the earring from round my neck. 'And I see she's been handing out the family jewels, too.'

'But you gave me this.'

'Romilly, not this again. I promise you, the only thing I have ever given you in all the time we've been apart is that dress that made you famous.' Her words landed on the water in front of us, floating there for us both to see.

She sighed, rubbing her arms as if suddenly cold. 'He's made a career out of the saddest time of my life,' she said quietly, shaking her head. 'Not that I've seen a penny of the profits.'

I didn't know what she meant, but I didn't dare ask in case I angered her even further. I wondered if I would ever know her well enough to talk to her properly. 'But you sent the earrings with a card last year,' I said. 'For my birthday.'

'I didn't, I—' she stopped talking, realisation dawning on her face. 'Mum,' she said, looking over at Beatrice.

'What?'

'It must have been Mum. She said she'd send you presents when I couldn't, so you'd know I was thinking of you.'

'Beatrice sent them to me? It wasn't you?'

My mum nodded. 'She's been a good mum,' she said lightly, 'to both of us.'

I stared out over the water.

'I started my period a couple of months ago,' I said, speaking to the moat, my cheeks flaring red, 'I didn't know how to tell Dad.'

I chanced a quick look at my mum. She was staring at the moat, her eyes blazing.

'I didn't really understand what was happening, but I remembered something I'd heard about them on Radio Four. I didn't know what I was meant to do: I used old socks and bits of ripped-up sheet.'

Mum turned to me and I dropped my head, hiding my flaming face behind my hair. I felt her hand, cool and still, settle over mine.

'I chucked the rest of the bedsheet in the bin. I think Dad thought I'd been sacrificing animals for midsummer.' A giggle escaped my lips, and I turned to look at Mum.

She was watching me, a sad, searching look on her face.

'It's OK, though, Stacey got me some pads from the shop in the village.' I didn't add that she'd had to steal them since Dad didn't appear to have any money any more.

We both looked at the moat. The silence was deafening, as if it was filled with all the things I wanted to say but didn't quite dare.

'I'm sorry I wasn't there for you,' Mum said eventually, stirring her feet slowly in the water, 'I'm sorry I haven't been there for a lot of the important things in your life.'

I wanted her to say that she would be there for me from now on, that she was here to stay, but she went quiet again.

I kicked at the moatwater, feeling the chill of it settle on my bare legs. The water rippled out from us in ever expanding rings.

When it was time for Mum to go, we stood in a line in the narrow hallway. She gave Beatrice a quick hug, and received a kiss on the cheek in return.

'I'll see you in a few weeks,' Bea said, patting her cheek, and Mum nodded.

She said a very formal goodbye to Dad, and then she turned to me. She pulled me into an awkward hug, and I clung to her, breathing in the half-remembered smell of her beneath her perfume.

As we pulled away, I said, 'You could live here. We could look after you. We could all look after each other.' I looked from Mum to Dad.

'It's not that simple, Romilly,' Mum said, 'we've tried living together, haven't we?'

'But things are different now. I'm older, I could help more.' I could hear the pleading in my voice.

'It's a different sort of help I need at the moment,' she said, 'I'm sorry.' She was looking at the door like a trapped animal calculating its exit. 'I can't come back, not now.' She sighed, putting her hands to her face, covering her eyes as if she wanted us all to go away.

I clung to her arm, 'Please, Mum?' I looked wildly around at Dad. 'Make her stay, Dad, please. Tell her she can stay. She can have my room – her own floor of the house.' I turned to her again, 'It would be like your own flat. Please, Mum, please.'

But my mother was shaking her head, her hands still covering her eyes. When she took them away, her face was white.

'This was a mistake,' she said, walking backwards, her hand already on the door handle.

And then Beatrice was next to me. 'Let her go,' she said gently, 'let her go, Romilly dear.'

And then my mum was gone, and the hallway was silent, and I crumpled slowly to the floor.

Later, as I was climbing into bed, Dad squeezed through the door. He was carrying something wrapped in brown paper.

'Happy birthday, Roe.'

'No it isn't,' I said.

'Well, no, I suppose not.' Dad sat down heavily on the bed and placed his hand on my head, stroking my hair.

'I behaved like a five-year-old in front of Mum today,' I said, 'do you think she'll ever come back?'

'I'm sure she will. And in the meantime you can write to her, she left her address.'

'She did?' I pulled the duvet up to my chin. 'I think I upset Stacey today, too,' I said, 'I was rude to her.'

'Then you need to apologise. Stacey's a good girl, she'll understand.'

'But what if she doesn't?'

'Then... then it will be what it will be. You're growing up. We all move on. Here.' He tipped the parcel into my lap. It was tied with a plait of dried rushes.

'But you already got me a present.' The paints and paper I had asked for sat on my desk, waiting to be used.

'This is something else. Something I made.' He shifted on the bed. 'I know I haven't been the best dad in the world recently. I just... wanted to make you something to show how much I care about you.'

I lifted the parcel and shook it gently and a muted chime echoed from somewhere deep inside. I put it to my ear and listened. Did I imagine it or was there a quiet ticking sound? I pulled the paper off, and out fell a wooden box.

But it was like no other box I had ever seen before. It was almost rectangular, and carved from pale, honeyed wood. Here and there knots stood, with little twigs sprouting from them as if the wood was still evolving. I could make out tiny wooden hinges all over it, miniature doors that opened in many different ways. As I tilted it, things rolled around inside, hitting invisible walls as though they were trapped in the tiny rooms of a house. The ticking was louder now.

'Is it a bomb?' I asked Dad warily, placing it on my quilt.

'Not exactly.' He checked his watch. 'It should be about the right time. Look.'

And we looked. The ticking was more insistent now, a tapping of fingernails trying to get out. And then, just as I couldn't bear it any longer, it stopped abruptly, and a different sound started, a quick whirring of cogs. And then a tiny, tiny door opened stiffly on the side. There was the sound of a pool ball rolling through the workings of a table, and then a small silver orb dropped through the door and came to land on the quilt.

'It works!' Dad said with a clap of delight. 'The ticking will start again next year, just before your birthday.' He stood up and laid his hand on my head for a moment. Then he turned and left swiftly, climbing down the stairs before I had time to ask for an explanation.

I lifted the ball, and I realised it wasn't a ball, but a bell. It was small – about the size of my thumbnail, and it was attached to a shred of blue velvet. It chimed as it moved. Monty pricked his ears up, and I knew instantly where I'd heard the sound before.

'It's yours,' I whispered to him, letting him sniff it, and wondering where it had been all these years.

I woke with a start late into the night, the remnants of the familiar hushed voice lingering in my ears. It brought with it a swathe of memories: my bedroom in London, a pair of shoes with a red bow, a silvery toy hare staring, staring, seeing all.

'What do you want?' I whispered back, and the voice stopped, as if listening. I could sense something, an intangible presence floating just above me, so close that if I breathed in I might inhale it, silencing it forever.

I lay in bed, gazing into the dark, dwelling on the sound. It was a child's voice, much younger than me, quiescent and breathless, happy, even. Who were they? Why did they keep appearing, waking me from my dreams? I tried to understand the words they had whispered, tried to make sense of the strange, familiar language. I closed my eyes and I could see a soft, pink mouth like a little bow hanging in the dark behind my eyelids, just like the Cheshire Cat's smile, without a face to call its own.

In the dark, I looked for my birthday box on the window sill, the bell placed mutely beside it. I got up and pulled the curtain aside to let the moonshine in, and there was Dad, running past the beech tree towards the house, completely naked, his stomach and testicles bouncing up and down. As if he sensed me, he looked up, and seeing me there, raised his hand before turning and running back towards the mobiles, his bare bottom flashing in the moonlight.

Twenty-Two

As the summer reached its peak, the garden awoke from its green slumber. The delicate scent of soft pink roses and the stronger, fresher fragrance of the buddleia mingled over the moat, drifting up to my bedroom window, their combined smell at once sickly and comforting, reminding me of Stacey's Parma Violet sweets.

A group of people had started camping out on the common land that bordered our garden, and during the day I took to lying out on the beech tree, hidden from sight by the high hedges, listening to their treasure hunt discussions. Stretched out on the tree's sun-warmed surface, watching the armies of ants scaling its smooth trunk, I spent much of the summer dozing, half listening to their far-fetched theories.

The beech was getting soft in places, the wood eaten away by insects until here and there it had begun to look like lace. I listened half-heartedly to someone singing tunelessly round the camp fire, and pushed my thumb into the soft wood, making holes across its once beautiful trunk. How I would love to be out there, swigging from bottles of cider and discussing the mysterious Kemp Treasure, not trapped in here with no one – not even Stacey – to keep me company.

Dad didn't like me staying outside after dark. As soon as the light began to dim, and the flicker of the campfire was visible through the trees, I climbed down from the tree trunk and slipped into the soft hollow at the base of the tree where the roots had tipped over in the hurricane years ago. It was soft and mossy, and I could lie there, warm and dry, the roots curving round me like the arms of a chair, completely hidden from view. When Dad came out to find me, he did a quick scan of the garden, then went back inside to continue his search. If it rained, I would crawl right inside the hollowed-out trunk, watching with a bored sort of pleasure the hypnotic splash of water as it hit the bramble leaves and nettles outside.

This hideout worked for weeks until one evening, when Dad was calling my name (much to the excitement of the people on the common), and Monty found me, meowing so loudly that Dad was soon on his tail, escorting me angrily back indoors.

Eventually, Dad decided it was best if I didn't spend any time outside on my own at all. The summer holidays were in full swing, and with them had come hordes of treasure hunters, desperate for knowledge of when the next book – about which I knew nothing – was due out. I took to sitting each day, curled up on the window seat, gazing out at the forbidden garden. I wrote to Beatrice, demanding to know why she had pretended to send presents from my mother, but she didn't reply. When a month had gone by and I still hadn't heard from her, I tried telephoning her house, but the ringtone rang on for minutes before I finally put the phone down with a feeling of unease. I asked Dad if there was any way of reaching her, and he shut himself in his study and made some calls.

When he came out, his usually animated face was still and waxen, and I knew what he was going to say.

I ran to my bedroom and shut the door, throwing myself on my bed and soaking the duvet with my tears. I refused to come down to eat, going through her letters one by one, remembering our conversations as if she was perched on the bed with me, chattering away.

Late that evening there was a quiet knock on my door, and Dad climbed in through the little space. He had an envelope in his hands.

'I was just going through the fan mail from the last month. I found this. It must have got caught up in it.'

He handed me the envelope, the familiar writing even more loose and wavy than I remembered.

Inside was a photograph. It was old and cracked, as if it had been looked at repeatedly. It was a picture of Mum and me. I looked about four years old – around the time we went our separate ways – and I was sitting on her lap, clutching a toy hare, gazing up at her with rapt attention. She was pressing her lips into my hair, her eyes closed, and while she didn't look happy, she looked content, as if she was in the exact place she needed to be, right at that moment.

She may be ill, Beatrice had written, *but she is your mother. She loves you, Romilly, and that love will go on, long after I'm gone, long after we are all gone. Never forget that.*

When Dad came up later to say goodnight, he sat on my bed and brushed away my tears.

'She was very old,' he said, 'you met her at the end of a long and interesting life. She was so pleased to have got to know you again. There's a lot of her in you, you know.'

I remembered when I had first met her two years before, how I had envisaged her as part of the late summer garden; a flower that had already bloomed. I had known she wouldn't live forever, but still it was hard to take in.

In the bathroom mirror as I got ready for bed, my eyes were shrouded in dark circles. The whispered voice had become louder recently, keeping me awake. Each night it began around midnight, pulling me from my dreams, whispering to me deliciously, almost as if it were there beside me. Sometimes I felt a small, soft hand in mine and heard the soft drip, drip of water, but when I turned on the light, there was nothing there. When the voice left early each morning, whispering away like smoke, I felt it like a physical thing, tearing at my chest, pulling me in two, and I lay awake, not daring to sleep, desperate to hear it again.

That night as I lay there, waiting for the voice to visit me, I stared at the ceiling and wondered if Beatrice knew she was dying when she wrote me that final letter. I wondered if she was alone when she died, how long it was before anyone realised she was gone.

The child's voice didn't visit me that night.

The weeks after Beatrice's death shimmered by in a blur shrouded by lack of sleep. I no longer minded that I wasn't allowed outside. I was content just to sit in my bedroom. I didn't even have the energy to look at the treasure hunt books any longer. I sat at my window, gazing out at the reeds in the distance, thinking of the escaped panther. Sometimes I thought I imagined him stalking sleekly across our garden, bending his noble head to drink at the moat. More and more I preferred to live in the world of stories in my head, where nobody dies, but nobody is really alive either. I think things would have continued in this way, but for something that happened one evening towards the end of summer.

I could hear Dad downstairs, tinkering with the telephone. Someone had leaked our number a few days before, and we'd had a constant flurry of phone calls since. After one particularly vicious caller, I was no longer allowed to answer the phone.

With both Stacey and Beatrice gone, I felt like my whole world had shrunk down to the size of my bedroom. I lay, looking up at the little painting Dad had given me five years ago for my ninth birthday. It felt like a lifetime ago: before Mum had come to stay; before Stacey left. Back then, Dad had been full of colour and vibrancy, just like his paintings. Now, he was a spectrum of grey, and I didn't have the paints or the ability to put him right. -

I wondered what Stacey was doing this evening. Probably stomping over the fields with a torch in her hands, sods of earth clumped around her shoes. And what of my mother? I didn't even know where she was living. What did her bedroom look like? What paintings hung on her walls? What mug did she drink from? These were things a daughter should know. Did my mum know these things about Bea before she died? Did she yearn for her own mother in the same way that I was yearning for mine, right now?

Dappled moonlight streamed into the room, muting the colours of the painting above me so that it looked like a negative of a photograph. The moonlight was so crisp that even from here I could see three or four versions of myself holding onto Monty, stretching back into the painting, getting smaller and smaller as if I was in a hall of mirrors.

The clouds outside shifted, and the moonlight trickled brighter over the painting. I sat up. A pair of eyes had appeared in it, hovering on the blank wall as if they belonged to a disembodied ghost. Quickly, I stood up and went to the painting, but as I got closer, the eyes disappeared. Instead, where there was usually just a blank stretch of bedroom wall, a shadow had appeared on the canvas. It looked almost like damp, creeping across the picture. I took the frame down and laid the picture on my bed to look at it better. The dark patch was indistinct, but it mirrored the posture of Romilly in the painting so exactly that I thought it might be her shadow. I flicked my bedside light on. The dark patch disappeared, as if it had never been there at all. I turned the light off, and it appeared again, skulking next to the smiling nine-year-old as if it were about to envelop her and her cat completely. With a shiver I thought of the faceless woman in Dad's books: the same shapeless form; the same lack of features, and fear overwhelmed me. I turned the light back on and quickly hung the painting back on the wall.

I ran down the stairs, not daring to look back in case the shadow had peeled itself from the painting and was sliding across the floor, following me.

I found Dad muttering to himself in the small bathroom, the telephone in pieces in the empty bath. He was tapping the bell on it, an insistent ping ringing out each time.

'What are you doing?'

'Hmm?' He looked up. 'Ah, Romilly. Just the girl, come here and hold this.'

I edged into the tiny space and knelt beside him, replacing his finger with my own to hold a wire in place. I looked back into the hallway, my eyes searching for shadows that shouldn't be there.

'What did you girls get up to today? Anything nice?'

I bristled, stung that Dad had already forgotten Stacey didn't come around anymore.

'*I'm* not doing anything,' I said caustically.

But Dad was humming under his breath, concentrating on what he was doing, not listening to me.

'Is a bathroom the best place to do this?' I eyed the leaky tap sending droplets of water over the telephone's components.

'Yes, yes it's fine.' Dad's voice was muffled, a fat screwdriver in his mouth. He was still tapping the bell, cocking his head to listen as if tuning a piano.

He had a familiar twist of concentration to his face. I had seen it a few times recently, usually when he was so absorbed in doing something that he didn't notice I was there. It made him look different, not like my dad at all, and each time I saw it, my stomach gave an unpleasant lurch, as if I had just encountered a stranger in the house.

A few weeks ago, I hadn't seen or heard him for some time, and, like a mother searching for a naughty toddler, I went and spied at the crack in the study door. Dad was leaning over his desk, counting out some money. But the sheer amount of it made me catch my breath. Tens, twenties, even fifty-pound notes. Piles and piles of crisp, clean banknotes. I knew he must have earned some money from the books, but I had assumed it was frittered away on expensive feasts back when the first book came out. I thought about Stacey stealing the sanitary towels for me a few weeks ago; about measuring out sugar for my cereal so that I didn't use too much, and anger rushed through me. Why wasn't the money safely in a bank, for goodness' sake? I watched him put it away in a desk drawer, making a mental note to explore further when the opportunity revealed itself.

The sound of Dad tinkering with the phone brought me back to the bathroom, and I watched as that same twisted expression of concentration trickled over his face. 'What are you doing?' I asked again.

'Fixing the phone.'

'Was it broken?' It had certainly been ringing enough earlier.

Dad stayed silent, trying to screw the shell of the phone back together. When it was done, he lifted the telephone ceremoniously out of the bath and took it, dripping, to the hall where a phone cable lay waiting. Plugging it in, he lifted the receiver and a smile spread across his face.

'Fixed,' he said, walking off, lifting the screwdriver to his mouth like a victory cigar.

I knelt down and picked up the handset. Silence.

'Fixed,' I agreed. I glanced behind me, sure I had seen the edge of the shadow move. I put my ear to the phone again, a creeping feeling of dread filtering out of the handset and into my ear, as I listened to the sound of nothing where a dial tone had once been.

The incident with the telephone was the catalyst that awoke me from my malaise. Since long before Bea's death, it had felt as if a creeping fog was clinging to me, hampering my movements. In some ways it had been a comforting blanket, shrouding me from everything bad, but the ringing silence of the telephone brought me sharply back to reality.

Dad was a mystery I needed to unravel, and I tried to connect the incidents of his odd behaviour together, attempting to solve the puzzle that was Tobias Kemp in the hope that it would in turn help me to solve the treasure hunt.

As August gave way to September, and the people camping out on the common drifted back to their lives, my curfew lifted at last, and I was allowed to roam free. With my newly opened eyes, I spent every moment applying myself to the treasure hunt. It felt as if time was running out somehow: as if Dad's strange behaviour was part of a huge, unseen clock, winding down until eventually there would be no time left to find out the truth.

Sometimes I thought I glimpsed Stacey in the distance when I was out walking, but when I called her name she never turned. It was more likely just one of the village kids, people I didn't know any more and didn't want to befriend. I hadn't seen Stacey since our argument at the quarry almost two months ago, and in her absence, the books began to take up all of my time, the pictures whispering to me as I pored over the pages, trying to solve the clues.

I quite liked being on my own. There was more room in my head to think without Stacey's constant chatter. But occasionally, when the space around me was so quiet that it hurt, I missed her dreadfully. It reminded me of when we'd been younger and she'd disappear for weeks, even months. Back then I'd always known it was only a matter of time until she came back, but this time I wasn't so sure.

Downstairs, Dad was in one of his moods, racketing around Braër like a bear with a sore head. I locked myself in the bathroom with my books and my carved box, trying to block out his roars.

I opened up the latest book, *Romilly and the Picnic*. I raked my eyes over the picture of the picnic laid out on the rug, trying to find clues to something, anything that would tell me where the treasure was. I had done this so many times before, that it was hard to see it afresh. I tried to see what the fans saw when they looked at these paintings, and for the first time the illustrations seemed to glow, to take on a life of their own. They were colourful and bold, yet a second look revealed tiny details: brown mice climbing the reeds by the lake; half eaten cakes sitting on crumby plates; a pair of chattering false teeth biting into an apple. On one corner of the rug sat two hares, their noses twitching at the smell of cake. I began to appreciate Dad's talent in a way I hadn't when I was younger, and yet, as I turned the pages, I found myself looking, not at the beautiful paintings, but at the tiny silhouettes of me being chased by various animals at the top of every page. It still hurt to think that Dad saw me as someone who would run away from a challenge rather than turn and face it head on. With just a few drops of ink he had turned me into a slapstick comic strip for everyone to laugh at, and it stung.

I looked away from the little drawings, my eyes settling instead on a strange-looking brass contraption standing on the rug in the main picture. It was emitting little puffs of steam, and it had a handle and a spout, like an overlarge, ornate kettle. I wondered where Dad got his ideas from, which objects were important, and which were just there to put you off the scent. I so desperately wanted to believe there was a treasure hunt hidden in the pages, and I held the objects in my mind, analysing and dismissing each one before moving on to the next.

Sitting on the bathroom floor, my back to the bath, I picked up *Romilly and the Kitten* and turned to the picture of Monty as a kitten in my father's hand, the bell hanging round his neck. I was sure now it was the same bell that Dad had given to me, hidden in the box: the real bell had a shred of blue velvet attached to it, just like Monty's collar in the pictures. I picked it up, letting it roll around my palm.

I studied the box. What other objects were in there, hidden deep inside? I imagined myself small enough to climb in, and I crept through its carved walls into countless tiny rooms, worming my way through Dad's mind. Inside the box, all was ornate and glowing. Minute paintings hung on walls and rich red rugs kept my feet silent as I padded through. It was like a museum of my father, a memorial to a man I didn't understand anymore, and I didn't want to leave.

Dad's bawling roar brought me back to the damp bathroom and the cold metal of the bath against my back. I picked up *Picnic* again and turned the pages, searching for the person I was now in the paintings before me. I stopped briefly on the shadowy woman. She was on her knees by the lake in this book, as if she had fallen, her hands still over her face. I wondered if she was meant to be me. I turned the page quickly.

There was no summer potion in this lake story, no skinny dipping or staring at naked breasts. No Stacey whatsoever. The place between my legs trembled at the memory of her.

Downstairs, Dad continued to remonstrate noisily with the air. I got up, pins and needles in my feet, and stood in front of the mirror. I so rarely looked at my reflection nowadays that I hardly recognised the girl that looked back at me. There was something of my mother in my pinched face, and something of my father in my bushy eyebrows. I could even sense something Monty-like in my eyes, a sort of wistful, almond-shaped slant, and for a second I thought I saw another set of eyelids slide across my pupils. I blinked, and they had gone.

I remembered when I was small, and had just met Stacey, I had tried to conjure her to me. I screwed up my eyes and counted to ten, trying to summon her into the mirror.

'Romilly?' Dad's voice, cheerful now, drifted up the stairs to me.

I opened my eyes. My dull reflection looked back at me, brow furrowed, as if it were trying to work out what I was doing.

'Girls?' His voice was more insistent now, shouting almost. 'Some help?'

Girls? His memory was so poor at the moment. He had forgotten again that Stacey no longer came around. I frowned at myself in the mirror. It felt like he was deliberately rubbing it in, taunting me for my loneliness. I left the bathroom, shutting the door on my reflection and stomped angrily downstairs, ready to give him a piece of my mind.

Halfway down I stopped. 'Where on earth did you find that?' I asked, staring at the apparition in the hallway, a sort of bushy Christmas tree with Dad's arms and legs sprouting from it.

'Ah, Lidiya, it was in the churchyard. They won't miss it. I'll put it back.'

'Lidiya?' I said, stopping on the last step.

'Who? Grab the end, Roe, go on, there's a good girl, it's not too earthy.'

I took hold of the rooty base, looking at Dad warily, and together we heaved the tree into the snug, where Dad righted it and stood back to admire its gently shaking branches.

'It's for the new book.'

'What book?'

'The next treasure hunt book. The grand finale. It's a Christmas book.'

'But it's September.'

'Yes, and the book will be out in a month, time waits for no man.'

'You've already finished it?' I had known he was working on

something, he had been spending so much time in his shed, despite the rot that had set in around its base. It was a relief to know: the treasure hunters that I had encountered over the summer had been desperate for any hint of when the next book was due, but as always, Dad had kept me in the dark.

'Keep up, Romilly, goodness me. The publishers have asked for a painting to auction off for charity, but I'll be damned if I give them an original from the book. I thought I'd make a copy: a little extra something to keep my richest treasure hunters happy. Imagine what they'll pay for an original Kemp!'

I sat down on the sofa, trying to digest all that he had told me. The final book was already finished, the last piece of the puzzle, and the last ever *Romilly* story. I had had no idea.

'When will we get the proof?' I said.

'They sent it a while back. It's lying around here somewhere.' He looked around the snug as if expecting to see it propped up by his feet.

'They've already printed it? Why didn't you show it to me?' Dad had always given me the proof as soon as it was delivered so that I would have the chance to pore over it before anyone else did.

'Stop whining, Romilly, and grab some decos, there's work to be done.'

I got up grumpily and reached for the old cardboard box. Not even the sight of the glittering decorations filled me with cheer.

Christmas carols boomed out of the little room as we sweated in the stifling heat of the crackling fire, lifting our treasured decorations out and hanging them carefully on the tree. There were lopsided snowmen made out of cotton wool, and hand-painted angels, both of my own and my dad's making. His were made of thin pieces of tin, and so intricately painted they seemed almost real. Mine were made from little cones of paper. They had round, red-cheeked faces and yellow wool for hair. I was embarrassed to remember how pleased I had been when I made them, and I crumpled one up and threw it on the fire when Dad wasn't looking.

As the box became emptier and the tree more laden with glittering memories, I began to get that feeling of restive waiting that only comes on the nights before Christmas.

At the bottom of the box, on a soft bed of pine needles and the shimmering dust of baubles long since broken, lay one of my favourite decorations: a little gilt bird cage. Perched inside was a tiny bird, covered in fragments of real feathers. When you twisted the base of the cage, the bird's minute beak opened and began to sing 'The Holly and the Ivy'. I hung the cage on a prominent bough halfway up the tree and wound it up, sitting down on the sofa, humming to its tinny tune.

'Why does the fire have to be lit?' I asked, peeling off my jumper and wiping damp hair out of my eyes.

'It has to be authentic,' Dad said, a manic glint in his eye as he reached up and placed the star on top of the tree.

'Hey! That's my job!' I had been looking forward to doing it for the first time without the need of a chair or a pair of grown-up arms to lift me. I looked at the star as it wobbled. It wasn't even on straight. Dad just sighed huffily, leaning over to stoke the fire.

He set up his easel and blockaded himself in the snug with the whisky decanter and his paints, perfecting the shine of the tinsel and the glow of the embers with quick flicks of his brush. Christmas carols were replaced by cheesy Christmas pop as he worked, eventually overtaken by overtures of 'Auld Lang Syne'. The house smelt faintly of pine and linseed oil, and I thought idly of last year's crackers and if there might be some left over to pull.

We spent our evening in the snug, taking secret delight in its Christmas camouflage. The fire crackled away merrily, and Dad sat back in his chair with a sigh of pleasure, gazing at the Christmas tree. I noticed a bead of sweat running down his forehead. I watched it trickle into a crease above his eyebrow, and somewhere at the back of my mind I knew that what we were doing in this room was not normal; not right.

'When's lunch?' Dad said, taking a sip of his port and smacking his lips together.

'About five hours ago,' I said.

'How odd, I don't remember. Did we have Brussels sprouts? Pigs in blankets?'

I eyed him warily. 'No, we had jam sandwiches and a packet of crisps.'

'What a terrible Christmas dinner.'

'Well, it's not really Christmas, is it, Dad? It's September.'

He was looking down at his hands, his huge eyebrows furrowed so that I couldn't see his eyes. 'But I wanted presents,' he said quietly.

He picked up a fallen plastic decoration and dangled it in front of Monty, who immediately pricked his ears up and batted at it. Dad twitched it some more, chuckling gruffly, and then with sudden enthusiasm he launched it into the fire. Monty charged after it. I shot off the sofa, grabbing the cat just in time. The decoration hit the flames and collapsed immediately like a dying star, melting into a puddle on the grate.

'Dad! What on earth were you doing?' I stroked Monty furiously, checking his ears and whiskers in case he was singed.

'I was just playing,' he said. 'I didn't think.'

I finally found the proof copy of *Romilly's Christmas* the next day, wedged under a leg of the coffee table in the drawing room. I turned the pages slowly, mesmerised by the glow of the paintings within.

Perhaps it was just because I was getting older, but this book felt significantly different to the rest: the colours were richer, like paintings from the golden age of the Dutch masters. There was a depth to the artwork that I hadn't noticed in the previous books, as if something was hiding in the shadows just out of sight, some hidden meaning I couldn't quite penetrate. Each picture was lit with a warm, treacly light, like diffused candlelight, or the dim flicker of an open fire.

My heart leapt when I first saw the little silhouette of me running across the top of each page, for, finally, Dad had got it right. In this book I was chasing the animals, not the other way round. At first it was rabbits and frogs, but further on in the book the animals got bigger, and I was tearing after tigers and frightening off rhinos, until, on the last page, a wily old crocodile scuttled away from me as I charged towards him.

This new book was special in many ways. It was a winter book, and although every page felt warm and Christmassy, Dad had painted a small window into every scene, reminding us that outside, the bleak, snow-filled skies loomed on the horizon.

There was a sadness to the pictures. One page showed the kitchen, our little table covered in the trappings of a Christmas dinner. On first look it was wonderfully festive, but as I looked closer, I saw that the Christmas pudding, instead of being lit by a halo of blue brandy, was smoking as if it had been left to go out. The crackers had been pulled and the hats lay torn on the table. The turkey had been stripped of meat, its skeleton lying upended on a plate, and the cranberry sauce had been spilt, leaking red across the table. This was a Christmas meal where an argument had ensued. It was the *Mary Celeste* of feasts, the players having left a moment before, never to return.

The more I looked, the more I felt as if the pages were loaded with symbolism. Vases of flowers were arranged with random objects – a skull here, a dead pheasant there – like Victorian still life paintings, the light playing over them thick and caramelised. It felt like Braër House of a hundred years ago. And always, on every page, there was a jug of dusky pink roses, their petals turning, changing, beginning their descent into decay. There was a finality about every picture, a reminder that life does not carry on forever, that there always must be an ending.

The shadowy woman was on the final page. This was the only painting not set inside Braër. It depicted Monty and me laughing and grinning as we made a snowman in the frosty garden. But even here the snow was beginning to melt. There were dark pools of slush on the edges of the picture, ice dripping from the end of the snowman's nose.

I didn't see the shadowy woman at first. She was lying on the ground, half-hidden by the silhouettes of old logs and creeping brambles, but once I had found her, my eyes locked onto her, unable to stop looking. Her hands were over her face still, and she looked so desolate and sad. Something about her pose brought to mind a memory. I got up and found the other books, looking at her in each of them. The memory began to crystallise, and quickly I found some of Dad's tracing paper and a pencil.

I set to work, tracing each version of her onto a separate sheet, starting with the first book, where she was standing upright, and working through to the last, where she lay, her hands over her face. I stapled the pages together and lifted the edges with my thumb, letting them fall back slowly. I did it again and again, faster and faster, watching as she began to move under my hand, flickering into life at my touch. She stood serenely, her long hair flowing, then she raised her hands to her face, and her knees crumpled until finally she lay, defeated on the ground.

Again and again I flicked through the little book I had created, and again and again she put her hands to her face and collapsed to the ground. I could almost hear the sob emanating from her, the long, guttural cry of despair, and I knew I had heard it before.

It was the keening cry of my mother, the awful wail as she sank to the floor, her hands to her face, while I looked on, helpless, locked in the pantry.

When Dad had finished the painting in the snug, I helped pack it all away, feeling again the strangeness of a Christmas that had never been. The melted decoration clung to the grate, and I prised it off with a knife without saying anything.

Dad was humming 'Good King Wenceslas' cheerfully.

'It's Mum, isn't it?' I said, scraping at the grate with the knife.

'What is?'

'The shadowy woman in your books.' Dad stopped trying to untie the star and looked at me. 'She's sad about something, isn't she?' I said. 'She's crying.'

'How did you work it out?' he said.

'When she locked me in the pantry, the first time she came back, I watched her through the keyhole. She fell to her knees and cried, just like in your pictures. And when she came for my birthday tea a few weeks ago, she put her hands to her face as if she couldn't cope with what was going on. It's something she does, isn't it? You've seen her do it too.'

Dad sat down on the sofa, narrowly missing a bauble.

'Why is she so sad?' I said.

'Some people are born to be sad,' he said, 'and sometimes things happen to make them even sadder.' He picked the bauble up and held it in his hand, looking at his reflection in its shiny surface.

'What happened?' I said.

Dad breathed a deep sigh. 'You'll understand one day, I promise,' he said.

'You always say that,' I said crossly, 'I want to understand now.'

Dad had taken some more baubles off the tree. He was putting them in a line on the rug by his feet.

I watched him, waiting for his reply. Behind me, the fire crackled, hissing into the quiet room.

'Dad,' I said angrily.

'Help me, Romilly, I can't seem to count them.' He was staring at the baubles, his eyebrows furrowed.

'Why do you need to count them?'

'I... I don't know.' He began hurriedly collecting them up, his huge fists manhandling them so fiercely I thought their delicate glass might dissolve into powder in his hands.

'Here, Dad, let me.' I crouched down to help.

'No!' His voice was loud. Far too loud for the little room, and it pushed me to the floor with its force. Dad was looming over me, looking at the baubles in his hands as if they were something alien. I stood up warily.

'It's *my* job,' he said quietly, 'it's always been my job.' Then he looked up and saw me standing there and his face changed. A look of fear came over his eyes and he mouthed something, like an exhalation of breath.

'Ff...' he said, 'fff...'

And then his skin seemed to warp and change as if poison gas was siphoning over his features, and he shouted, 'Get out. Get out!' Throwing the words at me like grenades, their force pushing me back into the door. I scrabbled for the doorknob behind me. He was twisting around now, like a trapped giant. He took a step forward and his huge body knocked the tree over. It crashed down in the tiny room, the remaining decorations smashing to the ground.

A lone red bauble rolled towards me, and I ducked and grabbed it, before turning and pulling the door open and running.

Out of the snug, along the hallway, down through the garden and the meadow and into the mobiles. Forgetting they were dangerous. Forgetting about past accidents. Forgetting. Forgetting. Forgetting.

Dad found me hours later, sitting under the inky sky, the bauble cradled in my palm.

'Come,' he said, offering a hand, 'we need to talk.'

We sat in the snug, the tree still upended between us. Dad was Dad again, but a paler version. A cowed, fragile Dad, shrunken with shame.

'There's no easy way to say this, Romilly, so I'm just going to come out with it: your old Dad's not well.' I looked at him. He looked scared, as if he'd never spoken the words out loud before.

'What do you mean?'

'I have an illness called dementia. It's affecting my memory, my...' He shook his head, trailing off. His voice was infused with sadness. Where was my great bear, I thought, in this broken being before me? The edges of my heart began to curl inside my chest.

'Is it serious?'

He nodded.

'Will you get better?' I asked, dreading the answer. He lifted his eyes to meet mine and shook his head.

'No,' I said, standing up abruptly. Dad grabbed my hand, his huge fingers desperately stroking my own small ones as if this small gesture could make everything all right. My whole body trembled, the room a blur of colour as tears coated my eyes.

'I've... I've known about it for a few years,' he said, speaking faster now, as if now he had started, he couldn't stop until he had said it all, 'but it's never really impacted on our lives… never really been important, until now.'

The outpouring stopped abruptly. I stood over him, looking down at this man, my father. He watched me silently, his pale face a moon, orbiting me in the hot room. I could feel the cloying scent of terpene and pine resin coating the back of my throat. I felt sick. I turned to the fallen fir tree and plucked a pine needle from its branches, unable to look at Dad.

'It may not get any worse for a long time,' he said. 'And there'll be good days among the bad, I promise. Whatever happens, I'm still here. I'm still me, inside.'

The sound of his hand thudding against his chest made me glance up. He was covering his heart with his huge fist. The gesture made him look like he was clutching at his heart, as if it too had started to fail.

'Will you die?' I whispered. I could hear his inhalation of breath. I forced myself to keep looking at him.

Dad opened his mouth to speak, but only a quiet moan came from his throat. He lifted his arms to me and I ran to him, melting into him, enveloped by his warm grown-up smell, ignoring the sour tang clinging to his skin that I had never noticed before.

PART TWO

Twenty-Three

Over the following months, I watched my father apprehensively, mindful that his health might deteriorate. But he remained stable, and as spring turned to summer I allowed myself to forget momentarily that he was ill.

On the dawn of my fifteenth birthday, the box began to tick. I lay in bed, awoken by the sound, listening to its beat urging to me to get up, get up. I wondered if it had in fact begun its ticking exactly on the stroke of midnight. Childhood stories always speak of midnight as a liminal time, when the earth is balanced between the ghost world and ours, shimmering in unreality.

I looked at the clock. It was three in the morning – long past the witching hour. Nothing magical ever really happens at midnight, I thought. It's all a story to sate little children's appetites: princesses don't turn back into raggedy maids and witches' cats don't start to talk. The fairy tales have got it all wrong.

I got up sleepily and brought the box into bed with me, covering it with my quilt so that its tick was more like the heartbeat of a mouse, fluttering next to my skin.

I dreamt I was inside the box, inside the museum of Dad's mind. I was padding barefoot along the velveteen rugs, admiring the richness of the paintings all around me. The rooms each smelt different, cinnamon in one, candyfloss in another.

I came to a room where a summer breeze blew lightly, fragranced with the smell of meadow grass. A door ahead of me began to slowly close, and I glimpsed a familiar, dirt-encrusted foot retreating. At the same time, the smell of Parma Violets drifted across to me and I ran towards the door, but it closed just as I reached it.

'Stacey!' I called, pulling at the handle, but the door was jammed shut. I turned to leave, but the way I had come was blocked. Desperately I pulled again at the door, but it was disappearing behind twisting vines. The floor was pockmarked with rubble like an abandoned castle. The vines were growing quickly now, snaking round my wrists. I wrenched free and ran onwards. Every time I turned a corner I was met with a dead end. These weren't rooms, I realised, but a crumbling, disintegrating maze. I put my hand in my pocket and pulled out the bell, shaking it wildly, desperate for someone to hear its ring amidst all this destruction.

I woke up. The bell was by my ear on the pillow, the echo of its peal still hanging in the air. I slept fitfully till morning.

I awoke to pale early morning sunlight filtering into the room, and thought of Dad sleeping on the floor below, probably oblivious to the fact it was my birthday. I thought of Bea, and the letters she used to send me. It was nearly a year since she had died: nearly a year since Dad told me he was ill.

My mother had come to visit this time last year. I remembered saying goodbye to her in the hallway, clinging on to her, trying to anchor her to Braër when all she wanted to do was escape. I pictured her waking up this morning, wherever she was. I doubted she remembered it was my birthday either, and with Beatrice gone, there would be no one to send a card or present.

It was too early to get up, but I felt wide awake. I sat up and found the carved box next to me in the bed, the tip of a bright pink feather poking out of a new opening in its base. I reached over and pulled it out. It was sparse and bedraggled, as if it had been left out in the rain a long time ago. I touched it to my cheek, and a shimmer of glitter cascaded through my mind: a majestic horse flaring its nostrils and tossing its head, pink feathers nodding on its brow.

Could this be the same feather from the circus all those years ago? I remembered how envious Stacey was that I had gone. How she had grabbed the feather from me and tucked it jauntily behind her ear to make me laugh.

A feeling of loneliness overwhelmed me. Oh Stacey, I thought, where are you? I went to the window and looked out, hoping I might spot her marching across the fields. I inhaled deeply, trying to recreate the smell of Parma Violets from my dream, remembering the way her mouth sucked lazily on the sweets, rolling them around with her tongue as she grinned at me.

From my window I could see a group of treasure hunters' tents on the common land. Their number had grown in size this summer. I don't know if it was because all of the books were out now, and they thought they had a complete set of clues to crack the code, or if the public had got wind that Dad was ill, and wanted to snatch a glimpse of him to see just how bad he was. Whatever it was, the police sometimes tried moving them on, but they always trickled back, new tents popping up here and there. A handmade banner had been stuck into the grass. It billowed in the breeze, proclaiming proudly, KEMP TREASURE FOREVER, in tie-dyed patches of red and gold. As I watched, a man crawled out of his tent and stood and urinated up against our hedge, the stream arcing high and falling against one of Dad's mobiles that stood, neglected and beginning to rust. I stared angrily as the plume of liquid forced the mobile into movement.

I felt a sense of restlessness as I looked out of the window. What was Dad hiding in his books? I had better access than anyone to all of the clues: I spent my days in the treasure hunt house, I cuddled up at night to the treasure hunt cat. Cracking the code should be easy, so why couldn't I work it out?

I got up and padded downstairs to make myself a cup of tea, the feather tucked into my hair for safekeeping. There was a pile of letters on the doormat that neither of us had bothered to pick up yesterday. I bent to collect them up, still half asleep, hoping someone had sent me a birthday card amid all the fan mail. But there was no card: everything was addressed to Dad.

In the middle of all the letters was a paper flyer with a picture of a circus on the front. I blinked, my eyes still gummed with sleep. Was this the same circus we had visited years ago? The same circus that Dad painted in his book? My stomach flipped in excitement. I scanned the list of places the circus would be performing at. The nearest was a village a few miles away, a place called Terringstead. I closed my eyes and remembered standing on a hill, the smell of animal sweat and candyfloss all around me. My hand went to the feather in my hair.

Perhaps I was so deeply entwined with Braër and all that it represented that I couldn't see through it to the truth. Maybe what I needed was some distance: to get away from all I knew so that I could scrape together some semblance of scale.

It wasn't running away, I told myself as I ran back upstairs to get my rucksack, my cup of tea forgotten. It was just space, so I could see the wood instead of the trees. A fact-finding mission, I thought as I ran through the details in my head, collecting together a bus timetable and an ordnance survey map.

With a flash of inspiration, I tiptoed downstairs to Dad's study. The key hadn't hung next to the door for years, but I tried the handle anyway, knowing how forgetful he had become.

The door clicked open, and I slipped inside, remembering vividly the day I saw him counting the money on his desk. I had checked on it often since then, carefully watching where Dad kept the key to the desk drawer, and unlocking it now and again to make sure it was still there. He rarely ate into it, occasionally nipping into his study and coming back with ten pounds for me to take to the village shop to buy essentials. Once he had come home from an auction with a clanking suit of armour, and when I checked the drawer later, some of the fifty-pound notes had disappeared.

Now, as I slipped into his study, I stopped.

Dangling from a rope in the middle of the room was one of Dad's wooden mannequins – the little models he used to help him draw people. It was hanging from the ceiling, revolving slowly in the air, its head drooping.

Feeling slightly sick, I took a step forward, and my feet crunched on the carpet. I looked down. The whole study was strewn with sawdust. For a moment I thought it was an elaborate anti-burglar system, but then the woody smell drifted up to me, and I was transported back to our day at the circus.

I approached the model, sawdust clinging to my feet, and let out a breath of relief. The rope was not around its neck, as I had feared, but around its chest. It was dressed as a trapeze artist, wrapped in ribbons of silk, its arms and legs stretched gracefully outwards. I tiptoed around it, still feeling nauseous, and hurried to the desk, fumbling the drawer open, wanting to be away from the strange, silent scene.

I skimmed the surface of the money, peeling off layers of notes and tucking them into my pockets. I put a few into my rucksack too, and then I left the study with a quick glance back at the room.

Out in the garden, I slipped deep into the beech tree and tucked the money away. I backed out and blinked in the haze. The garden was alive with birdsong, louder than I had ever heard it before. I propped my rucksack on the beech and rummaged around for a bus timetable I had grabbed from the kitchen. The first bus was at seven o'clock – two hours' time.

Stacey would have loved an adventure like this, I thought. She would have relished travelling across the country, experiencing new places and meeting new people. I looked across the garden, staring far out at the horizon, past marsh and reed. My mind made the decision for me: before I knew it, I had jumped down from the tree and begun walking towards the gate. Perhaps today I would find her.

I set a course across the fields: we had always spent our time outside, on the outskirts of the village, exploring and playing, so it made sense to start my search there.

It had occurred to me to try to find Stacey's house, to hammer on the door until she let me in, but she had rarely talked of home in the years I had known her, and all I knew was that she lived in one of the council houses on the other side of the village with her mum. When I was younger, I had set out on more than one occasion to surprise her at home. It was a very long, straight road, a line of regimented red-brick houses on one side, a crescent of small bungalows on the other. There had often been a skinny dog chained up in the front garden of one of the first houses, and I could never quite muster up the courage to walk past it. I always consoled myself, as I walked home, that Stacey spent as little time as possible at her house, and she was probably not there anyway.

The farmer had cut the corn early this year, and the stubble lay in regimented rows across the field. I scooped up a handful of soil and sniffed it. It was sweet and rich in my nose like the crumbs of the birthday cake I would not have this year. Beneath my step, the warm crust of earth crumbled, and I recalled Stacey and me walking this route before, our feet turning to leather from going without shoes all summer long.

Was she barefoot this year, like in my dream? She might even have crossed this field recently, leaving soft footprints in the soil for me to follow. I bent and removed my own shoes.

Halfway across the field I stopped: far away, where the sky met the fields, a black cat trotted. I tried to focus on it as it merged with the shimmering horizon, to decide if it was domestic or wild, but it evaporated before my eyes. I began to walk again, heading for the circle of trees and the little lake within.

At the ring of poplars I turned one last time and surveyed the field. Clouds had appeared in the east now, moving fast as if a storm was pursuing them. Huge swathes of land were covered in shadow interspersed with light. I turned and passed into the cool of the trees, pausing for a moment, reminded of another glade, another magic circle, trying to remember where I had seen it. A place where woodland animals came, where the drip, drip of water never ceased. As I pushed through the last of the undergrowth, I half expected to see a deer standing at the water's edge, drinking, but there was nothing there but me.

It had been two years since I was last here. The ground was clotted with marsh marigolds, dipping their tiny golden heads into the lake. A dog rose wound its way through the trees, swaying in the ripening breeze. My head was aching now. I sat down in the shade of the poplars and dipped my toes into the cool water.

A twig snapped somewhere within the bushes.

'Stacey?' I said, peering through the branches, trying to spot movement. Something plopped quietly into the pool. I shifted back to look, but the lake was completely still, no rings rippling its surface.

'Stacey, stop it,' I said, angry now, my head pounding. 'I'm sorry if I upset you, I really am. I miss you. Things aren't as fun without you.'

I stopped and waited. The ring of trees was silent. The lake was still.

'I came to tell you that I'm going to find the circus in Dad's books,' I called over the water, feeling mildly stupid. 'I want to see if they can tell me anything. I just... I just need to get away. Will you come with me?'

I could hear the echo of my words drifting away from me, and then there was nothing but the sigh of air over water. It had been pointless to search for her. She was still angry with me. I stood up and turned to go, tripping over something in my haste. An old glass bottle lay half submerged in the long grass. I kicked at it. Dried petals had pasted themselves to the inside of the glass, the remains of the summer potion from two years ago. Bending down, I pulled at the long white grass roots that had wrapped themselves around it and levered it up.

With all my strength, I hurled it into the centre of the lake, hoping she was watching. I paused to listen to its satisfying splash, watching as it bobbed for a moment or two and then sank without trace.

Twenty-Four

Back in my bedroom, I dropped my rucksack on the bed and pulled opened my chest of drawers, trying to decide what to pack. Monty jumped up and began kneading a jumper of Dad's that I had secreted away, the thick yarn catching at his claws.

'Monty!' I lashed out, grabbing him by the scruff of his neck and flinging him off the bed. A fistful of fur came away in my hand, and immediately I felt guilty. I rubbed it between my fingers and tucked it quickly into the front pocket of my rucksack. Monty stalked off, eyeing me from the far side of the room, then he stuck his leg in the air and began to wash.

I picked up Dad's jumper, smoothing the plucked fibres. His smell was in it like the ripeness at the centre of a fruit, and I pulled it over my head, immediately feeling cocooned and protected.

My thoughts drifted towards him, lying in bed on the floor below me. He spent a lot of time in bed now. I tried to encourage him out, to sit in the garden with his sketch pad, or else wander down to the meadow to admire his beloved mobiles, but the enthusiasm that used to burst from him like the jewel colours of his paintings had waned since he told me the truth about his illness. It was as if he didn't need to keep the pretence up anymore.

I wondered how he would react if he saw what I was doing. I hoped that a small part of him would be proud that I was finally going on a treasure hunt. Maybe, just maybe, he would worry for the safety of his daughter. But in reality, I knew he wouldn't understand or care. Not anymore. I banished the thought and turned back to the rucksack.

I wrapped a small trowel in a balaclava, just in case, and tested its weight in my hand. Dad always said that it only takes three digs to bury treasure, but a thousand to find it. I figured I had to start somewhere.

In the midst of my packing I caught sight of the painting, hanging on the wall by my bed. The version of me in it was looking up at the painting above her, unaware of the drama unfolding in the room she was hanging in. I remembered the shadow that had appeared in the picture last year. In the intervening time I hadn't dared look at it on moonlit nights. I got up and stood in front of it. The little girl in the painting was so much smaller than I was now. She could hardly reach up to touch her picture, whereas my own eyes were level with it. I touched the blank stretch of canvas where the shadow had been. Just above my finger I thought I saw again the glimmer of a pair of eyes, the wet reflection you see when someone is crying, but then it was gone.

I went back to my bag and stuffed the circus flyer inside, and then I turned to the bed.

The feather and the bell lay next to each other on the quilt. You can choose one, I told myself sternly, a talisman for the journey. I picked up Monty's bell, and it lay in the crease of my palm, glinting. But then the feather caught my eye, and I quickly grabbed that too. It was sparser than I remembered, the once soft strands spiky and discoloured in places. I touched it to my face, remembering how the feel of it used to soothe me to sleep, and I threaded it through the buckle of my bag, taking care not to bend it. The bell went into the front pocket, safely ensconced in Monty's fur.

All that was left now were Dad's books.

I lifted them, hugging them to my chest, their familiar weight a comfort. Opening the first one, I turned to the back page, and there we were: Dad and me, the black-and-white photo making our teeth look unnaturally white.

I studied my ten-year-old self. Somewhere in there was the teenager I was to become. I drank her in, this pretty little girl, jealous of her innocence, her contentedness that life would always be this way. I stroked the thick paper, tracing our faces, then I ripped the photo from the book and slipped it into my rucksack.

I was ready.

I looked for Monty, heaving the rucksack onto my back. He had settled in my armchair, watching me warily. In the gloom of the bedroom his usually blue eyes were sloe-black, shining out of an alien face. I walked over to him and offered my hand for him to assess. He sniffed it cautiously then began to purr. I stroked him, massaging the bare skin where I had grabbed him. It was damp from licking.

'Look after Dad,' I whispered, and he chirruped an assent, forgiving me easily my earlier violence. I crouched down to his level and touched my forehead to his, trying to channel the resonance of his purr deep inside me, white noise to block out my thoughts.

And then I stood and looked around at my bedroom – at the bookcase beneath the window sill, at the floorboard so often lifted that it stuck out permanently – telling myself not to be silly, that I would only be away for a day or so.

On my way out of the room, I caught sight of Dad's carved box on the window sill, and I wondered for a brief moment what would happen if I didn't come home in time to hear its next tick. If I didn't come home at all.

The early morning bus was empty but for an old woman sitting near the front. As I stepped on, my stomach prickled with nerves. I shot a last glance back at Braër, half hoping Dad would see me getting on and come running, yelling at me to get off.

As I went past the old woman, she pulled her handbag closer to her, eyeing me suspiciously. I sat down near the back, my chest tight, and pulled out the flyer for the circus, trying to focus on what I was going to do. The picture on it was a mixture of red and gold, striped and colourful as a stick of rock. The circus was due to perform in Terringstead. I knew the name: there was a poster pasted onto a telephone pole near my house advertising a car boot sale there. I looked out of the window, watching the hedges and fields rush by.

The pale morning light was beginning to trickle into the bus as we pulled up by a bank of grass in the middle of nowhere. I got up unsteadily and made my way to the front, the woman with the handbag resolutely ignoring me now.

'Is this Terringstead?' I said to the bus driver.

'It is.'

'Is the circus here?'

'Lord knows, dear. Why, you running away to join it?'

I ignored him and got off the bus. What *was* I doing here? Maybe I should join the circus. What was the point of going home now? And then I thought of Dad, wasting away alone, and guilt surged through me.

The bus pulled away, leaving me in the deserted lane. I stood on the little square of grass between a cross section of country roads, a war memorial in the middle. Past the church to the west was a hill, rising up like an island. I thought I could see the red-and-white stripes of a tent on the very top. It was a long way away. I pulled my rucksack onto my back and began to walk.

The field at the bottom of the hill was empty of cars. No tyres had yet spoilt the smooth green of the grass. As I reached the brow of the hill a village of caravans came into view behind the circus tent. They loomed closer as I walked the circumference of the tent's huge red-and-white walls.

The ground here was churned up and muddy. I inhaled an animal smell from somewhere nearby and turned my head, trying to locate its source. Here and there piles of horse manure lay amidst the mud, clouds of yellow flies sitting like lazy kings on the plump brown balls.

It was eerily quiet all around. A light shone from the window of the nearest caravan. I knocked on the door, gently at first, and then louder when nobody came.

The occupant took a long time to get to the door, I could hear them stomping heavily across the floor. The door swung open. A huge man with a bull neck stood there, looking down, his eyes bloodshot and bleary.

'Yes?' he said.

'I'm... I'm looking for the lady who rides the horses. I think she might be called Lidiya? She's foreign, she's...' I came to a stop, realising I had hardly anything to go on. The last time I'd been to this circus was six years ago, if it even *was* this circus. I looked around me, a swooping sensation in my stomach, and I felt suddenly foolish: my memories of that night were almost nothing, all I was basing this search on was Dad's books. What if this wasn't the right circus? I cleared my throat and began again. The man was looking at me with an amused expression.

'She's very pretty. Lots of sequins. She's got pink feathers in her hair. Like this one.' I swung my rucksack round and pulled the feather out to show the man. He squeezed his eyes so that they looked like little holes in his face.

'This way,' he grunted, and I let out a sigh of relief.

He stifled a yawn as he stepped down onto the grass, swearing as the dew coated his bare feet. 'It's too early for this,' he said. 'What do you want with Lidiya anyway? Another treasure hunter, I s'pose. She won't like you asking for her autograph this early in the morning, I promise ya. You can have mine though if you want it.' He grinned lasciviously as we wound our way through the caravans. When I didn't answer, he said, 'Quiet, ain't ya? You haven't come to join the circus, have you? We could call you the Mysterious Mute.' He laughed at his own joke.

'My dad knew her, a few years ago,' I said instead.

'Lots of people's dads know Lidiya, she's that kind of lady.' He sniggered.

We had arrived at a large, old caravan. It was much prettier than his, with a great curved roof and a floral chrome pattern round the windows. It felt familiar, but then, there was a caravan just like this in *Romilly and the Circus*. How often had Dad been here, I wondered?

The man knocked on the door, surprisingly lightly for someone with such huge hands, and my stomach churned unpleasantly.

'Someone to see ya, Lidiya,' he called.

The door opened quickly, and a waft of scented air billowed out, momentarily stunning the man so that he blinked and walked off without another word. The woman standing in the doorway looked familiar. She was wearing a thin oriental silk robe, wrapped tight around her body. Her make-up was heavy and smudged in the pale morning light, but beneath it, her skin was white as if she were looking at a ghost.

'Romilly Kemp,' she said, beckoning me in without smiling.

I sat down nervously at a small table attached to the floor. Lidiya sat opposite me. She poured me a cup of tea from a teapot. The scented steam billowed from the spout, making me drowsy. In a corner of the caravan a wardrobe stood open, and I glimpsed a fragment of pink sequined fabric. Its sparkle threw out a spool of memory, connecting me to my day at the circus with Dad, and I turned to her again, remembering.

She had the same slim face and high cheekbones, but the skin was somehow thinner and the bones so much more prominent. Without her headdress, she looked small, like a child or an old, old woman.

'How did you know it was me, at the door just now?' I asked.

'I have been waiting for you,' she said with a shrug, the hint of an accent collecting in her throat along with the smoke from a thousand cigarettes. 'You still look like your pictures, even now.'

She reached for my hand on the table. It felt weird to be touching a stranger, but I kept it there, trying to be polite. We sat in the quiet caravan and looked at our hands joined together, mine with bitten nails and freckles, hers long-fingered and stained with nicotine.

'So, Romilly Kemp, why are you here?'

I wanted to explain about the pink feather appearing in my wooden box, about my hunch that the circus — that Lidiya — was important somehow, but I didn't know where to begin, or if it made any sense at all.

'I don't know exactly,' I said. 'In every book there's something to do with the circus. I remember Dad was painting pictures of you way before he made the circus book. I feel like everyone in the world has tried searching for Dad's treasure except me, and now I want to have a turn. I know he'll never tell me the truth, and you were the only person I could think of who might be able to help me.'

'You are determined, like your papa,' she said, 'you will find it, Romilly, I am sure.'

'I used to dream of being famous, like you,' I said shyly. 'When Dad started writing the books, he asked me if I wanted to be famous, and I thought of you in the ring in your sparkling costume, and everyone watching you. I didn't really know what fame meant back then. What it can do. I didn't believe you were real when I met you.' I trailed off, thinking back to all those years ago, her glittering silhouette in the dark after the performance, long eyelashes blinking luxuriously like the wings of a rare insect.

She dropped my hand and swept her hair from her face. I noticed bluish hollows under her eyes, picked out by the glare of the caravan's overhead light.

'Oh, I am real all right,' she said, 'but you were never like me, *dorogaya moya*. You had a father who loved you. And besides, my small fame is incomparable to yours.'

'Dad says he and I followed the circus for a while, when I was about four.'

'That is correct, but you came to see us first when you were two or three. All of you.'

'All of us? Mum too?'

Something about her smile changed. It dropped from the edges of her mouth. 'The whole family,' she said, sipping her tea thoughtfully. When she lowered her cup, her smile was back in place, flickering in the steam from her cup.

'You were young, you probably do not remember. And then you came many times, just you and your papa. You followed us round the country — you spent many evenings in this caravan.'

I looked around the small space, feeling through my memories, trying to locate the caravan in the tangle of past that I had long forgotten. Lidiya gazed out of the window. Her face had a hard prettiness about it. I watched her forearm flexing as she placed the cup on the table, the muscle born of years of manual work.

'My dad's ill,' I said, watching her expression, the lack of surprise on her face confirming what I suspected: she already knew.

'I am sorry.'

'He's… not himself very often anymore. Sometimes he thinks I'm you.'

Lidiya didn't answer straight away. She pulled a pack of cigarettes from a pocket in her silk gown and offered me one. I shook my head. She put one to her lips.

'He is a good man, your Tobias,' she said at last, lighting the cigarette and inhaling, gazing out at the colourful bulbs on strings that hung between the caravans. 'What will you do?' she said, pulling her eyes away.

'What do you mean?'

'You should not look after him on your own. Where is your mother?'

'I don't know.'

'Surely you cannot be expected to care for someone at your age? How old are you, fifteen, sixteen?'

'I'm fifteen.'

'The same age as I was when I came to this country.'

'Were you alone?'

Lidiya nodded. 'I thought I had left all the bad men behind in Russia, but there are a few in this country too, it turns out. Be careful, Romilly.'

'But you're safe now,' I said.

She shrugged her shoulders imperceptibly. 'This life is probably better than the one I left behind, so I don't complain.' She exhaled in a sigh and gazed at me through the smoke. 'You are very lucky: your father loves you very much. Besides,' she picked a bit of tobacco from her teeth, 'everything happens for a reason: without torture, no science.'

Her words flowed over me with the smoke, their sound like poetry or song. There was a knock on the caravan's door, an insistent tapping

'It is like Kings Cross station round here this morning,' Lidiya said irritably, getting up and opening the door.

A sheepish-looking middle-aged couple stood outside. The woman was wearing a thick fleece with a picture of a wolf on the front.

'Can I help you?'

'It's her, Don!' the woman said, nudging the man next to her, her voice loud in the hush outside. 'It's you, isn't it? You're the circus lady.'

'O' course it's her,' the man said, smiling up at Lidiya and throwing out his hand. 'Don and Patty Mason of Missouri, USA. Nice to meet you.'

The couple hadn't seen me yet, dazzled as they were by Lidiya in her silk robe. I quickly slipped through a door into the bedroom. From here I could still hear Patty's loud voice booming through the caravan.

'I told Don, it must be the right circus. We're members of the Kemp Treasure Hunters US division. We've set up a website on the World Wide Web and everything! Don here is a whizz with technology. But I bet you don't even know what that is, do you dear? Why, you can't even have a computer out here in this mobile home, can you?'

Don began speaking now, his voice softer than his wife's but just as enthusiastic. 'We have a message board forum so that we can all keep abreast of any developments. I can't wait to tell them we've met the circus lady.'

I wondered how they would react if they knew Romilly Kemp was sitting metres away. I prayed Lidiya wouldn't let on.

'Would you like an autograph?' Lidiya's voice was resigned.

'Oh yes please!' I could hear the delight in Patty's voice. Don seemed so starstruck he had stopped talking.

There was a pause while Lidiya signed something, and then Patty spoke again.

'It's real nice to speak with you today. Thank you for being so accommodating.'

'It is my pleasure.'

I heard the door click shut, and I came out of the bedroom and slipped into a seat at the table, sitting low to avoid the windows. Lidiya sat down, laughing quietly through her nose.

'I am plagued by treasure hunters,' she said, 'always, people asking for autographs, trying to break into my sleeping car to find the gold. What gold, I ask you? Your father has no idea of the effects his books have had on the lives of others.' She looked out of the window, at the sky that had lightened so much in the time I had been there. 'They are harmless, mostly, the treasure-hunting people, but they are tiresome.'

'Do you know anything about the treasure hunt?'

She shook her head.

'You must know something.' I heard the desperation in my voice, but I was unable to stop. 'You knew my dad so well. Did he tell you anything? Anything at all? However insignificant?'

'All I know is that this treasure hunt does not contain gold or jewels. It is not something that just anyone can solve. Your papa said he was going to give you the clues, and when you have them all, you will be able to solve it.'

With mounting excitement, I reached for my rucksack and pulled the pink feather from the buckle.

'Do you mean this?' I said, handing her the feather. 'Is this one of the clues?'

Lidiya's eyes lit up at the sight of it. She took it, twisting it in her bony hands, her breath stirring its strands.

'I remember this,' she said, 'I told you you were a pretty girl. And I was right. You have grown into a beautiful young woman.'

I blushed and ducked my head behind my hair. Nobody had ever called me beautiful before.

'Dad made me a box for my birthday. It's mechanical – clockwork – and each year it delivers another gift. So far it's given me a bell, and your feather.'

'Then these must be the clues he was talking about. This is the start of the treasure hunt.'

A shiver licked at the back of my neck. 'Do you know what the other things are? The other objects he's hidden?'

Lidiya shook her head, 'He told me nothing else.'

I pushed the feather across the table. 'Here, it's yours.'

'What? No, I…'

'I think Dad would have liked you to keep it. I know how much you meant to him, and I think he meant a lot to you as well.'

Lidiya's cheeks flushed slightly. She took the feather, twisting it round her slim fingers. 'If you are sure?'

I nodded.

Lidiya cleared her throat and stubbed out her cigarette, tucking the feather away in a pocket of her robe. For a moment I wanted to grab it back, but then it was out of sight. Abruptly, she stood, motioning for me to follow.

We walked across the damp grass, Lidiya incongruous in wellies with her silk robe. People were stirring in their caravans. I could smell bacon frying somewhere close by.

'What are your plans now? Does your father know you are here?'

I shook my head. 'But I'm not going back, not yet.'

'Where will you stay tonight?'

I shrugged. I hadn't thought that far ahead.

'OK, I will help, but will you promise me something? If I let you stay tonight with us, will you go home, back to your father tomorrow?'

Reluctantly, I nodded.

'Good. You will watch the show later? For old times' sake?'

'Yes please.'

'Excellent, let's find some breakfast. Are you hungry?'

Twenty-Five

As the day grew dark, we sat again in Lidiya's caravan. The customers had left, satisfied with their brief glimpse into the circus' world. Outside the caravan, toffee apple sticks and sweet wrappers attempted acrobatics in the mounting breeze.

Lidiya was coaxing an old metal urn into life. It creaked as it began to boil. Circus folk came and went, stopping briefly to chat in the doorway. A woman dressed head to foot in bells leant in to shake my hand.

'They all know you from your books,' Lidiya said, pouring a splash of tea into two glass cups. 'You made this circus very famous for a while. Even now we still get many fans: you saw how many autographs I gave after the performance.'

The urn was making a quiet whooshing noise, rather like a boiling kettle with too little water in. Lidiya ignored it.

'Sometimes people snatch feathers from my headdress; from my horse's headdress even. My horse, he is head-shy now. He hates the ring. And yet, if I get another horse, the same thing will happen. It has been a blessing and a curse, this fame. I cannot imagine what it has done to you. At least I am able to move on every few days. You are trapped in that house.'

The tea's smell, acrid and strong, surged into my nostrils. I thought about Braër. Was I trapped? It felt safe, and yet sometimes I felt so isolated, with the world going on, untouchable outside my window. This was my first real taste of a treasure hunt. If I had made the connection with the circus sooner, I thought crossly, I might have gone looking earlier. Why did all of Dad's clues have to be so cryptic? I lifted the cup to my lips, my thoughts twisting and knotting.

'Not yet,' Lidiya said, putting her hand out and laughing softly. She took the cup from my hands and placed it under the urn's spout.

'This thing takes time.' She filled the cup to the brim with boiling water. Droplets of it splashed onto my hand, little pinpricks of pain. Noticing, she said, 'And waiting is painful too, no?' She pushed the cup to me, repeating the process with her own.

The urn wheezed again as the boiling water poured from the tap, little clouds of steam puffing from the edge of its lid. I found I couldn't stop looking at it.

'Lidiya,' I said, 'there's an urn like this in *Romilly and the Picnic*.'

'Yes, it is my samovar in the picture.' She reached up and pulled the book down from a shelf above us, flicking through until she found the page. 'Here,' she said, sliding it across to me.

It was exactly the same urn, down to the vine-like detail of the tap's spout.

'Do you remember the little doggy in *Romilly and the Circus*?' she said.

I nodded. 'Tula,' I said. He was a fawn-coloured poodle. In the story he had chased Monty round the ring.

'That was my dog. He was a circus dog until he got too old, then he spent all his time lying on a little velvet pillow in my caravan like a prince. I think once when you were here, you fell asleep in his basket,' she said, laughing.

I smiled. There was so much of Lidiya's life in the books. How often had Dad and I been here? How much had she meant to him?

'I am glad you have seen us perform again,' Lidiya said, peeling a false eyelash from above her eye. 'It felt like Tobias was here with us too.' She stiffened suddenly, and I turned to see a small man in a red overcoat standing at the door. Immediately I thought of the nasty-looking rat dressed as a ringmaster in *Romilly and the Windmill*, and I was amazed all over again at Dad's ability to capture people's characters.

'Well, well, Romilly Kemp, I heard you had deigned to walk among us. And how did you enjoy my circus?' His eyes were small and shrewd, watching me carefully. He lifted his top hat, revealing a huge shining pate ringed by dark, luscious hair. I could see Lidiya's reflection in the urn. She was very still.

'Very much, thank you,' I said, and he smiled. 'It was strange to come back without my dad though.'

'Ah yes, the inimitable Tobias Kemp. I hear he is not all he once was.' Noticing my expression, he added. 'Gossip travels fast in the circus, my dear.'

He lifted his leg onto Lidiya's step, a move that felt possessive, as if he were coiling his way around the caravan, slowly contracting his grip. I noticed Lidiya move back imperceptibly.

'Forgive my impertinence, Romilly, but your father fascinates me.' His voice was something like a fox's bark. 'Most people are more fascinated by *you*, I think – the child who never grew up. But for me it's all about him. For instance, how did he keep making those books when he knew his mind was dissolving into jelly?'

I put my cup down, determined not to look away. 'Did you know him, then?' I asked.

The man shifted position in the doorway. 'Know him?' He gave his barking laugh again. 'I gave him permission to use my circus in his book. I met him many times.' He said this reverentially, as if the man he was talking about was God and not my dad.

'Roberto, I...' Lidiya interrupted, but he cut her off, still staring at me.

'Do you think on some level you were your father's experiment?' he said. His face remained expressionless.

'I... I don't know.' I looked around the caravan, and my eyes settled on Dad's book on the table from earlier, the familiar sight nourishing me. I looked back at the man, my head held a little higher. 'Do *you* think I was an experiment?'

'Undoubtedly. Of course, I think *you* are a work of art, Miss Kemp. You know, there will always be a place here for such a work of art, should you wish to be on display. Now if you'll excuse me, there is work to be done. It was a hard crowd today,' he said, looking pointedly at Lidiya, 'farmers are extremely careful laughers.' Then he slipped away into the noise of the night. I took a sip of tea, but it failed to warm me.

'I am sorry,' Lidiya spoke finally. She had relaxed her pose again and was running her finger around the rim of her cup. 'It is his circus. Sometimes it feels as if he owns us performers too.'

She lifted *Romilly and the Circus* down and opened it to the page where her doppelgänger galloped around the ring. I noticed there was a crease in the corner where it had been folded to mark the page.

'It is so strange seeing one's self in a book,' she said, 'it makes me feel like I am made up, somehow, like I am just the fabric of someone's mind. I don't know how you have coped with being in book after book. How do you know what is real anymore?'

'I don't know if I do,' I said, pulling *Romilly and the Picnic* towards me and opening it up, the spine cracking. I flicked to the picture of the picnic by the lake. The rug was spread with all kinds of food: boiled eggs in eggcups, a flask of tea, three different kinds of cake. There was the urn, sending plumes of steam into the air. A minute mouse poked its nose out from behind a biscuit tin. Another was lifting a tiny salt cellar, sprinkling salt onto a pork pie. I marvelled at all the objects Dad had painted into his pictures. So many of them had meaning, so many belonged to the people that he loved.

'I've always been fond of this picture,' Lidiya said, stroking the china plates, tracing the tiny rose pattern on their surface. 'So very British. I have never been for a real picnic – it is something I think one can only do with a real Englishman. I always wanted to sit in the sun by the water and eat tiny sandwiches and slices of the best Victoria sponge. One day I will. I will wear a hat, a huge floppy hat to shade my skin from the sun.' The expression on her face was unreadable.

'Your father promised me a picnic, you know,' she said, closing the book. 'I thought he meant a real one – he and I, sitting by a lake, but now I look back, I think he was meaning this picture. When I am sad I look at it, and then I am not so sad anymore. After all, this picnic goes on forever, a real picnic lasts for only a few hours.'

I didn't know what to say to this. In my embarrassment I rummaged in my bag, looking for something to change the subject, and my fingers touched the bell. I placed it on the table, where it rolled slowly, its tiny peal barely audible over the samovar's hiss.

'Montgomery's bell,' Lidiya said, lifting it up and putting it to her ear to listen to its chime. 'This would fetch a lot of money, you know. And the feather too,' she said, realisation dawning.

She stood up and went into her bedroom, coming back with the feather in her hands. 'You gave this back to me, but I cannot accept. It is too precious, it is worth too much money. Please, you must take it back.' She tried to push it into my hands, but I pushed it back, closing her fingers around it.

'No, Lidiya, it's yours, please.'

She nodded, looking down at it, stroking the sparse barbs into place, then opened the drawer by the table and tucked the feather inside.

The bell was still on the table. My reflection frowned back at me, tiny and distorted.

'Perhaps each item is linked to someone I know,' I said slowly, trying to work it out. 'I mean, the bell belonged to Monty...'

'That makes sense,' Lidiya said.

'But I won't be able to find out for a long while. It's my birthday today: I have to wait a year before it will open again.'

'Many happy returns,' Lidiya said. She slid off her seat and went to the little kitchenette that ran down one side of the caravan. When she came back, she was carrying a cupcake, the kind they sold before the performances, and on top she had placed a lit candle. She passed it to me and I blew the flame out. She cut it in two and passed me the bigger half. It was bright pink and very sweet: a poor imitation of Beatrice's Victoria sponge from my last birthday, but the gesture was so well meant that I found it hard to swallow.

'You could try to guess the other objects in the box,' Lidiya said between mouthfuls. 'Who else is important to you, and what have they given you in the past?'

She was looking at the picture of the picnic again. Her face had a faraway, sad look.

'I wonder what will be next,' she said, tapping the bell so that it rolled across the book. 'These must be the key, the key to it all.'

Lidiya made me up a bed on the sofa of her caravan. The circus went to bed late, and it had been dark for several hours before I climbed between the sheets.

'Lidiya,' I asked, my stomach churning at the question, not sure I dare ask it, 'can I stay here?'

'You are staying, silly girl.' She patted the sheet around me. It was a hot night and the caravan door and windows were open. People walked past, chatting in a language I didn't recognise. I caught a glimpse of a clown, his arm around a girl in a leotard followed by two tiny dogs dressed as elephants.

'I mean stay forever.'

Lidiya sat on the edge of the bed with a sigh. 'I am not your mother, Romilly,' she said.

'I know you're not. It's just, you feel like family. Sometimes it feels like I've blocked out a huge part of my life before moving to Braër, including you, and I can't work out if you're familiar to me because of the books, or because of the memories I have of you from when I was little. But this place—' I looked around the caravan, breathing in the herby scent of the tea we had drunk earlier, '—it feels like... home.' I pushed myself up on my elbows, searching her face. 'I could look after the horses. I'm strong, and good at cooking and cleaning. Maybe one day I could ride in the ring?'

Lidiya put her hand to my face, smoothing the hair from my forehead. 'And what about your father?' she said lightly. 'What about your house?'

I looked down at the blanket tucked around me, focusing on the crocheted squares.

'You have too many threads joining you to this part of the world to go travelling with us right now,' she said. 'One day you will realise this, and then you will be free to make that decision. But not now. Now, you sleep.' She got up and went through to her bedroom.

'Lidiya?' I called again. She appeared in the doorway, looking exasperated.

'Was there a panther here, when I came with Dad? Did it escape?'

'We have never used wild animals,' she said, 'never. Now sleep.'

That night, lying in an unfamiliar bed, I dreamt I was watching the performance again, with Dad by my side. We were sat high at the back, eating toffee apples, but as I tried to eat mine it turned to gold.

'Lovely treasure, this,' Dad said, holding his golden apple so it glittered in the light and biting down on it until his teeth fell out, one by one.

Twenty-Six

The next morning, I woke to the murmur of the hushed voice from my dreams. Even here, away from Braër, it was following me. I ought to feel scared, but the familiar sound comforted me in this unfamiliar bed, and I lay, listening as it chattered away.

'I don't understand what you're saying,' I whispered, conscious that Lidiya was asleep on the other side of the paper-thin wall. The voice paused in its chatter, and I could hear its breathing, little gasps of air that made my own breathing stutter for a moment. Then it began again, the same words, the same sounds. I tried to capture the trail as it evaporated into the air: it felt like a magical language, something half remembered, a mixture of English and a whispering, powerful spell, but it disappeared before I could make sense of it.

I got up quietly and, tiptoeing to Lidiya's room, peeked inside. She was still asleep, a dark mask over her eyes. Quietly I packed my rucksack. I pulled open the drawer she had put the feather in, listening all the time for any noise from her bedroom. The feather wasn't there. Disappointed, I let myself out of the caravan.

The sky was a clear deep blue above, but below the hill all was a sea of golden mist. Nobody was up. A horse whinnied from somewhere behind the caravans. I set off down the hill, plunging into the mist, watching it dissolve at my touch.

The bus took me further away from home, through countryside that became so flat I could see for miles. Long dykes ran alongside the road, stretching away into the distance, and swathes of green fields surrounded us on all sides.

This time, the bus dropped me a mile from where I wanted to be, and I stumbled across fields, through woodland and along footpaths, the map growing ever more creased in my hands as I bent and studied it.

I saw the church's tower long before I reached it. It was an old church, almost a ruin. Trees and saplings had grown up around it so that it felt like it was growing too, sprouting shoots in numerous places, ivy trailing through cracks in the stonework. There were few gravestones remaining. Some had been moved and were propped in a line against a far wall. Others were leaning at dangerous angles, lichened and worn soft from years of weather. I found Beatrice's immediately: the stone stood out, polished and neat, so very like Beatrice herself.

I hadn't wanted to go to Bea's funeral, and Dad had agreed, saying it was better to celebrate her life by toasting her with the Meissen tea-set rather than attending a dreary church service.

The words on the gravestone were very simple.

BEATRICE ARCHER
1917–1992

At the top of the headstone were two tiny hares facing each other, their long ears pointing upwards, their little noses almost touching, and below them, the simple phrase, *Beloved Grandmother.*

The soft mound of earth was covered in little blue flowers — forget-me-nots, I realised — their perfume rising in the warm slants of sunlight that dappled over the grave. It was a peaceful, happy place, and I sat down, content just to be there.

Eventually, when the sun had moved so far that it was blocked from view by the church's tower, I pulled myself up, my joints cold and stiff.

Leaving home had given me the distance I needed to see things clearly, but I couldn't solve the treasure hunt just by going away. If, like Lidiya and I had discussed, the objects in the box were linked to the people I knew, then I needed to be in my own beloved Braër to be able to put all of Dad's clues together.

It was time to go home.

I arrived at Braër starving, last night's meagre supper long ago in my memory. I ran across the road from the bus stop, vaulting the side gate and grabbing the tiny bud of a new pear off the tree as I went. Biting into it, my teeth punctured the hard skin, the expected sweetness painful in its absence. I spat out the hard, grainy flesh, my stomach twisting from hunger.

As I crossed the bridge to the back door, something made me stop. I turned around, looking at the garden, trying to understand what had changed.

The bank of the moat, usually green and verdant, was a swathe of blue, just like the flowers on Bea's grave, and I remembered the tiny forget-me-not plant she had given me all those years ago. Over the years it had grown and spread, covering the bank in a blanket of blue and yellow.

I looked around at the rest of the garden with fresh eyes, as if by leaving Braër I was able to see it all anew. The beech tree was lying across the garden as it usually did, but something about it, too, was different. I approached it cautiously. Along its length, a thin crack had opened up, as if its spine had finally dissolved. Hastily, I checked that the money was still safely hidden away, and then I stepped back and gazed at the tree. It no longer looked alive. It was a skeleton, a collection of bones enclosing dark shadows, and the joy I had felt on seeing Bea's flowers trickled away. I looked up at the sky, where years ago the tree used to stand. The gap there was huge and yawning, and terrible in its blankness, and I turned and walked swiftly to the house.

Inside, I ignored the smell of the dirty dishes piled up in the kitchen sink, and stepped over a pile of cat sick, drying on the carpet. I found Dad where I had left him yesterday morning, lying in bed. The sharp smell of urine drifted up from the sodden sheets beneath him.

'Oh, Dad,' I said.

He lifted his head and smiled at me. 'Hello, daughter-mine,' he said. He had slowed down so much in the last few weeks, even his voice lagged, like a pocket watch whose spring has unwound beyond repair.

I cleaned him up and brought him tea in one of Mum's china cups. The teacup trembled in its saucer as he took it from me. I noticed how bulbous his knuckles were, how thin his wrist was before his pyjama sleeve slipped down, covering it from view. I was conscious of my messy hair and my unwashed smell, but he didn't seem to notice.

'You two always look after me, don't you,' he said, warmth in his voice. He sipped his tea, unaware he had said anything unusual, his cracked lips lifting at the edges in a smile. At one point he stilled, looking at something over my shoulder, his cup coming to a stop in mid-air, then he blinked and focussed back at me, smiling again, the rattle of the teacup shrill in the quiet room.

When I finally had a moment to unpack my rucksack, something right at the bottom tickled my fingers. I upended the bag onto my bed, and among the underwear and old toffee apple sticks, the pink feather that I had given Lidiya fell out onto the quilt.

I picked it up, trying to work out when she had slipped it back into my bag without me noticing. I thought of the wooden box; what clues might be in there? Downstairs, the one person I loved above all was barely surviving, his brain shutting down in fits and starts, with no way of telling me what this was all about, even if he wanted to.

I thought about Braër, wandering its rooms in my mind, trying to think where my dad might have left clues, intentionally or not. And then it came to me: the one place I had never set foot in. I went to the window and looked out. Dad's painting shed stood, half covered by the branches of the weeping willow, leaning precariously into the boggy ground.

I went downstairs quietly, not wanting Dad to hear where I was going. In the garden I took a spade that was leaning up against the cart shed, and I stood in the shifting morning light, studying the shed. The moatwater was uneasy today, rippling and fractious behind me, reflecting my mood.

When I was younger, the shed had been painted in garish stripes of red and yellow, but the paint, applied by my dad in a fit of enthusiasm, had been meant for indoor walls and as such had run and dissolved over the years. Small specks of gold and crimson still clung to crevices on the weathered boards, giving the shed a freckled appearance. As I approached it, I lifted my hand automatically to my own freckles, smattered across my skin, and onto the mole on my left cheek.

The picture of the circus tent that had been nailed above the door had come partly away, swinging round so that it was upside down, like a macabre ship. The key to the padlock had been lost a long time ago, but it didn't matter since the door had rotted around the metal loop that held it in place. The only reason the door didn't hang open was the great slick of muddy ground that enveloped the bottom half of it.

Up close, the shed appeared to be almost to the point of toppling over. I stood and observed it. Tiny creakings offered up from somewhere near its base, and water dripped from the rotted roof, though I couldn't remember the last time it had rained. A good foot of the shed was below the earth. It had been sucked down over the years at an imperceptible pace.

Dad's shed had once been a thing of beauty. He had written and painted most of the books in the tiny wooden space, but almost as soon as he had built it, it had begun to sink into the boggy ground. Where the farmhouse managed to stay afloat by clever use of a pump to draw water away into the moat, the poor sedge-ridden garden had no such luck. At some point whilst illustrating *Romilly and the Picnic*, Dad had noticed a slight list to the right. If you look hard enough at the pictures in *Picnic*, you'll notice everything is at a very slight angle. By the time he began painting *Romilly's Christmas* two years ago, he had corrected it by nailing wedge-shaped planks to the floor.

I don't think Dad had stepped inside the shed for a long time. He certainly hadn't painted anything in there for over a year. He didn't paint at all now. I tested the weight of the spade in my hands and thrust the blade into the earth. The ground parted satisfyingly, and a huge sod of swollen earth settled, quivering, on the glinting metal. After half an hour of excavation, I was able to reach my fingers under the rim of the door. It opened a crack, and I peered inside. The shed's windows had been boarded up after the panes of glass began falling out. A line of sunlight pierced the room, settling on the edge of an armchair and a curling wad of paper. Motes of dust danced in the air. I felt a thrill run through me.

Setting to work again, I clawed at the earth with my hands, spraying handfuls of wet dirt into the air behind me like a dog digging up a bone. At last the door began to come free and I pulled it open enough to squeeze inside.

From deep within the shed, a breath like the exhalation of a sleeping child flickered over my face, and I paused on the threshold, hesitating.

Inside were memories, some of them private to my father. But the pull of those memories was so strong: the robust, colourful dad of my childhood, full of stories and self-possession. I needed to remember him. I looked behind me, towards the house. Dad was a crumbling ruin now, a watercoloured echo of his former self.

I took a deep breath, and stepped inside.

The first thing that hit me was the dark: it was almost black inside. The wooden floor was littered with dead leaves. It felt soft underfoot as if it had recently been underwater. I stood for a moment to let my eyes get used to the dark. Eventually shapes began to form. A small desk, an armchair, horsehair sprouting from its seat. Pencils and paints lay on the desk as if their owner had left moments ago. Eraser rubbings were dotted across a piece of paper, the faint outline of a girl's face that looked like mine sketched lightly upon it. I found the rubber lying nearby, a large grey thumbprint on its surface. I picked it up and pressed it to my lips.

I perched on the corner of the desk and observed the armchair, squinting my eyes, trying to see Dad through the fuzz of my eyelashes. A shadowy figure etched itself onto my retina, crammed into the chair, his hands working fast with the pens scattered around him.

I looked at the drawing he had been working on. It was full of movement and life, as if the girl he was sketching was dancing, her hair flying out in a messy braid behind her. The crack of light from the door shone straight onto the paper, and in its bright beam I thought I could see something else. I moved closer, my eyes inches from the paper, bringing my hand up to touch it.

Where the paper should be smooth and flat, soft bumps were impressed into it. I took my finger away and looked again. I could make out an imprint of words winding their way across the little girl's smiling face, as if Dad had written something on another piece of paper, and the impression had carried through to the drawing, loping down the desk in his familiar handwriting.

I bent close again, my nose millimetres from the desk. It was some kind of a list. There were five words, each below the next.

As I read the first two words, the hair on the back of my neck stood up.

'Montgomery's bell,' I whispered to myself, 'the pink feather.' The two objects Dad had given me, concealed in his carved box. I read the rest of the words quickly, my eyes flicking down the list with mounting exitement. It was as if Dad was sitting at the desk with me, hunched over the page, sharing in my discovery.

I found a pencil and hastily made a note of the words on a scrap of paper. My mind was racing. I took one last look at the shed, at the chair and the desk and the half-finished drawing, and slipped out into the summer sunshine, the scrap of paper held tightly in my hand.

Twenty-Seven

Bell

Feather

Bauble

Forget-me-not

Salt cellar

I was back in my bedroom, the books spread out over my bed. I ran my eyes over the words in the list. They resembled a potion bottle on the scrap of paper: a stoppered vessel, waiting for me to unleash the intoxicating answers within.

I thought of the people that were linked to these items, each one important to me, each one a special part of my life. The bell had belonged to my beloved Monty, the feather had been Lidiya's. The bauble I knew immediately was Dad, round and jolly like him, a reminder of our Christmas tree decorating. The forget-me-not was inextricably linked to Beatrice, its delicate smell reminding me of the perfume she wore, and now of her grave in the woods with the two little hares.

I frowned at the salt cellar. Where had I seen one before? I flicked through the books, searching, until I found it in the picnic scene by the lake, a little mouse shaking salt over a large pork pie. I looked closely at the cut glass sparkling in the sun, and I remembered at last:

it was from the Meissen tea-set that my mother had given me for my fourteenth birthday.

Five objects, each one from someone I loved.

Outside, the pale morning sun had reached my stained-glass window, and the coloured light painted itself across my duvet in thick, luscious strokes.

I pulled *Romilly and the Windmill* towards me and turned to the picture of the windmill at the centre of the book, its four sails pointing to the four corners of the page.

In the topmost window of the mill, my young face peeped out. Monty was sitting at the open door, looking up at a butterfly dancing just above his head. The grass around the windmill was choked with clouds of tiny blue flowers – forget-me-nots. A mouse in one corner of the picture had picked one and was sniffing it delicately.

Hidden within the picture – as with all of the pages of Dad's books – were words, beautifully written in a bold italic script.

'It must be to do with these,' I muttered, finding the words and running my finger over them. They formed a list of the picture's contents: sails, mouse, butterfly, forget-me-not, windmill.

Forget-me-nots were my link to Beatrice. They covered the garden with their little blue flowers just as they covered her grave. Had Dad chosen that flower because he knew she wouldn't always be there for me? Reminding me never to forget her? Or perhaps it wasn't just to do with Beatrice. Was Dad worried *he* would forget *me* as his illness overtook him? Or – and at this I let out a cry of anguish – that I would forget him after he was gone?

The word 'forget-me-not' in the picture was hidden in the brick-work of the windmill, its twisty letters disguised in the crumbling mortar. I looked at the little blue flowers that flooded the scene like a foaming sea, their swell surrounding the mill. I ran my finger over the word, thinking of Dad downstairs. Did he really think I could ever forget him?

My carved box was on the table next to me. Had he put a forget-me-not in there? Wrapped delicately in tissue paper, his huge thumbs slipping against its petals as he tucked it safely away?

I looked again at the word. It was written in masterful calligraphy, the letters sloping along in pale grey. As I peered closer, I noticed The *n* of 'not' was a slightly darker hue, more of a charcoal colour. I took out my magnifying glass and looked at each of the hidden words in turn.

In each one, a single letter was a slightly different shade: the word 'windmill' was painted onto one of the sails, hardly distinguishable from the white wood it was written on. But one letter, the *i*, was a pale ash blue. I began to flick through the rest of the books, finding slight differences in the colour of one letter in every word hidden on every page.

I went from book to book, searching for the five words on Dad's list, realising as I did so that each book contained one object from the list.

The bell was in *Romilly and the Kitten*, on the page that showed Monty lying curled up in Dad's hand. It was written delicately into the chocolate brown at the end of his tail. The word 'feather' was formed in sawdust on the circus floor in *Romilly and the Circus*, with Lidiya riding gloriously in the ring above it.

In my excitement I went to nudge Stacey. 'This is it!' I whispered frantically, remembering too late that she wasn't there. How she would have loved to be in on this discovery, I thought. I could almost see her, leaning in to look, her hair tickling my ear, her hands frantically running over the pink feather in anticipation.

The salt cellar was in *Romilly and the Picnic*, the word winding around the edge of a plate full of cupcakes. The word 'bauble' was in *Romilly's Christmas*, written in glittery tinsel on the tree.

I picked up my pen, making a note of the different coloured letters from each of these important words.

n

a

e

f

e

Naefe. What did it mean? Quickly, I tore around each letter, making five little papery tokens. I tried putting them in different orders, remembering as I did so the way I used to try to slot the last few pieces of jigsaws together, my brain never quite seeing how to do it until the picture was almost complete.

Anfee

Efane

Feean

I stared hard at the words as I rearranged the letters. I was getting closer: something about them felt familiar. I tried to make my mind relax, my eyes hazing over until the letters danced in front of me. Slowly they changed position, like an unhurried waltz until they stopped again, forming into a word I knew.

A word I had not spoken or heard for eleven years.

A name.

The morning sunlight was beginning to disappear from the garden when I finally made my way back downstairs. The great girth of the house blocked out the sun's rays from soon after lunchtime in summer, and during the winter the huge swathes of yellow grass hardly saw the sun all day. I checked on Dad, snoring in his armchair, before pulling on a pair of wellies that stood by the door, and trudging back to the shed.

The pale trickle of light made the shed shine silver as I approached the door, and the garden seemed to whisper, the closer I got. Montgomery followed silently behind me, winding round my legs as I came to a stop. We stood, studying the shed, the breeze lifting my hair. I shivered and stepped forward, my hand on the door, my body squeezing through the small gap. Montgomery stayed, sentry-like, outside.

It was easier to see this time, as if my eyes had memorised the small space perfectly. A plan chest stood in one corner. There was a muffled sound coming from it, a hushed sigh that I thought I recognised, rising like vapour from the drawers. I shifted round in the tiny space, balancing precariously on the edge of the desk, and pulled at the top drawer. With a wet screech it began to open, jamming halfway, and the voice from my dreams was there, rushing into the air and settling around me, whispering to me, as if she had been hiding inside all along, waiting for me to let her out.

I reached inside the chest. Folder after folder of drawings met my fingers. I pulled out the top one and settled into the armchair.

Dad had drawn many preparatory sketches: picnic hampers, plates full of sandwiches, a small oil painting of Monty holding a teacup with the claw of his paw stretched out like a little finger. I spent a long time examining a sheaf of pastel drawings, all of a huge black panther. There were hundreds of sketches of me, running, sleeping, eating.

The girl continued to whisper all around me, her voice encouraging me, urging me on.

And then, quite suddenly, I came upon the painting I had been looking for. It was in a drawer marked '1987'. I remembered the first time I had seen it, a year later, the day Dad had brought the book home fresh from the publishers. It was a close up of my face, my red hair brighter than a fiery sun, blazing like a halo around my head. It was an iconic painting, one that had been used in adverts for all of the books.

I studied the original. It was far more beautiful than the print in the book. I was sucked into the little girl's world, captivated by the light that played across her face.

My face.

At this thought, the whispering voice became more insistent, chattering at me, babbling in a language I couldn't yet grasp. I looked hard at the picture, feeling the voice around me become a tangible thing, a solid presence in the tiny shed.

The light in the painting was fluid, trickling over the brushstrokes that made up my skin as if reflected from water. In the painting I was looking slightly off to the left, an expression of something like joy turning to laughter.

Then I noticed the mole.

In the pictures in the books, my mole had often been on the wrong cheek. I put my hand to my left cheek unconsciously to check, feeling the familiar bump, just above the cheekbone. The girl in the painting had a mole on her right cheek. Her left cheek was smooth and blemish free.

The girl in the painting was not me.

The murmur in the shed was louder now, calling to me, spilling over in excited childlike laughter as I reached into the plan chest again and pulled out folder after folder, searching through them feverishly, not caring if I ripped them or dropped them on the wet floor. Hastily I pulled out another batch of sketches and paintings, trying to find something, anything to prove what I was thinking.

These ones were early: drawings of my mother looking young and ridiculously happy, a gruff self portrait of Dad in brown pastel. I slowed down, forgetting for a moment why I was here, examining each one.

I could hardly remember my parents like this. Mum's face was full of wonder. Her deep lidded eyes were looking up, and raindrops fell on her softly smiling face. I stopped to look properly, enraptured.

This was a different mum to the one I knew, a mum from so long ago that I could allow myself to love her a little. The woman I knew, I realised now – the mother who flitted in and out of my life – could never be the mum I needed, and with that thought, I felt lighter. Bringing the drawing close, I kissed her forehead gently before putting the sketch back into the chest, knowing I was strong enough to begin to let her go.

The girl's voice had quietened while I looked at the pictures of Mum, but as soon as I put them down it began to babble again, muttering feverishly in excitement, and at last, as I listened properly, I began to understand what she was saying. The meaning behind her words was penetrating me, appealing to something deep within me, something instinctive and ancient. It was a language I had forgotten, a language that came back to me now, lost many years ago.

'This way,' she was saying, 'this way, Romilly,' her words urging me on and on.

As the early afternoon light began to disappear from the shed, I pulled open the last drawer with some difficulty, drawing out a final bundle of sketches tied with string, and her voice, wherever it was coming from, began to sigh with excitement.

'Look,' she whispered, 'look.'

I flicked through the sketches in my hands.

And there, on the last but one piece of paper, I found it. A small drawing in charcoal, sketched very quickly so as not to wake the subjects. The child's voice that had filled the shed stopped with a sudden hiccup, and in the silence that followed, I stared at the drawing.

Cradled in the arms of my mother were two babies. Two heart-shaped faces, two rosebud mouths. Each child had a mole prettily stamped on her cheek, and they were gazing into each other's eyes, mirror images of each other.

Twenty-Eight

Dad was still in his armchair when I came in, an empty whisky glass on the table next to him.

As soon as I saw him, a bittersweet burning sensation ignited deep in my chest, a flickering, peppery heat, dangerous and addictive.

I was still holding the sketch, and I dropped it into his lap. When he didn't wake, I kicked him hard in the ankle. He awoke with a snort and, seeing me, smiled. Then he noticed the piece of paper.

'What's this? Have you been drawing?' He smiled again, his mouth crinkling so that his face was all beard. Slowly, his expression changed.

'You've been in my shed,' he said, his words tinder to my combusting chest.

'Yes.' My voice felt strange, as if I had swallowed the word and it had caught alight somewhere near my lungs.

He took a deep breath, letting it out slowly through his nostrils as he looked at the drawing.

'You made a mistake in your planning,' I said, and with each word I spoke, my chest got hotter and hotter until I could feel the heat rushing up through my throat and coming out as sparks in my voice. 'You left a list of all the objects, and I worked out the clues.'

Dad put his hand over his face and rubbed hard. 'You weren't supposed to find out yet,' he said eventually.

At his words, my heart caught alight, a pyre of burning meat inside me. 'It's not a game, Dad,' I said, 'it's not a treasure hunt with a deadline and a prize. It's my dead sister.'

He flinched at my words.

'She is dead, isn't she? I haven't got that bit wrong? She's not locked up in a tower somewhere? Or lying comatose, waiting for her prince?' I was pacing the small room now.

'You're too young,' he said, his words hardly audible.

'Too young for what?' My whole body was on fire now, I could feel flames leaking round my eyeballs, fire-hair licking about my head. 'Too young to take care of myself? Too young to feed us, to look after us? I run this house, Dad, I take care of *you*. But I'm too young to know about my own dead sister?'

'You've had so much else to deal with——' he looked at me imploringly, '——I didn't want to add to the load.'

I grabbed the sketch from his lap, and sat down opposite him, looking at the drawing. The babies' faces were identical, nestled close to my mother, but even in this quick sketch I could see one was fractionally smaller; less plump, less healthy.

'It meant "small fawn",' Dad said quietly. He was leaning back in his chair as if winded. 'Feena,' he whispered.

At the sound of her name I felt a cooling in my chest, a drip, drip of water quelling the fire. I stayed studying the picture, not sure I could look at him without it re-igniting.

'Feena,' I repeated, the first time I had spoken her name out loud. It sounded strange, not like a name at all. A little creature came into my mind. A long-limbed, spindly deer, nervous ears swivelling. A woodland creature, dipping its head to drink.

'Your name means "strength",' Dad said. 'She was always smaller than you. Always delicate. You romped from the moment you could move, but she... she was born blue and thin as porcelain. You could almost see inside her, like she was made of glass. I tried to capture her organs pulsing and beating in a painting once, but your mother got angry. Ripped it to shreds.'

'How old was she? When...'

'Four. You were both four.'

I tried to picture this tiny version of myself, delicate and fragile. It was impossible.

'What happened to her?' A sudden feeling of dread began spreading over me. 'Was it me?' I asked, trembling. 'Was it something I did?'

Dad shook his head. 'She caught a chill, that's all. She was always catching chills. This one was just nastier than the rest. She couldn't fight it.'

'Why didn't you tell me about her?' I said. 'How could you let me forget?'

'Do you remember the story I told you once, about your parrot and the little girl?'

'This isn't the time for stories, Dad.'

He lifted his hands. 'Just hear me out. It was how you were after Feena died: shattered, like you had dissolved into a million shards.' He was looking at me, his eyes so sunken that they looked black. 'How could I keep talking about something that was tearing you apart?'

I slumped down onto the sofa, trying to digest all that he was saying.

'With your mum gone and me already starting to forget things I just... decided we would forget. You stopped asking about her, and we carried on. And then I got the idea for the books, and it seemed like the right way to leave clues for you: so you could understand when you were old enough.' He paused. 'The books help me to remember her, too, you know,' he said. He was fumbling for his whisky glass, searching the room for the decanter.

I got up, pacing the small space, not sure what to do with this new feeling of revulsion I had towards him, not understanding where it had come from, or the power it had over me. I stared at my sister in my hands, refusing to look at my father. And then something came to me, something from the story Dad had told me all those years ago.

'In the story, the father poured the remains of the girl into the moat.'

Dad looked down at his hands. 'Yes,' he said.

'Feena,' I whispered, rushing to the window and looking down into the moat's dark waters, imagining my sister down there, just below the surface.

'You don't understand, Romilly,' Dad said behind me, 'this thing in my brain, it's eating away at me. And it's *always* hungry and it's *always* getting fatter, and every day it's eaten something else, some memory, or word, or feeling. I can feel it pushing at my skull even now. Do you have any idea how frightening that is?'

The worry in his voice made me turn. He had abandoned the search for the whisky, and he had his hand at the back of his head and was grabbing at his skull as if he wanted to pull the illness out of him. A wisp of hair came away in his fingers instead.

'You can't mourn with this disease because it steals away the very thoughts that allow you to grieve. Sometimes I look at you and my mind says, *Feena*. And sometimes I see you and my mind says nothing at all. And sometimes I wake in the middle of the night and I see you at the end of my bed, but you're not actually there at all. And I don't know if it is the ghost of my dead daughter, or the ghosts of my memories coming back to haunt me.'

He leant forward and took the picture of the two little sleeping newborns from me, lifting the sketch shakily to his lips, and kissing the cheek of each baby in turn.

I seized it back, relishing the way he flinched at my touch. 'Don't, Dad. You can't just give me this information and then snatch it away again.'

'I am so sorry, daughter-mi—'

'Stop,' I said, the fire beginning to snarl inside me again.

'If I can do anything, anything to make it better.' He sounded so pathetic.

'You can,' I said. 'You can go to the shed and find every picture of Feena and of me. Every sketch, every painting that you made when she was alive or when she was dead—' he flinched at my words, '—collect them all together and take them up to my bedroom. They're mine now. They're all I've got left.'

He nodded.

'Do it now,' I said quietly, my heart beginning to turn to ash.

Dad got slowly up from the armchair, and I tried not to notice how browbeaten he looked, how frail.

At the door, he stopped. 'If I could go back,' he said, 'I would have done things differently. And if I could get rid of this illness then I would. But you must believe me that everything I have done has been for you.'

He was staring, wild-eyed around the room, and I wondered which of us he was talking to: the living, breathing daughter in front of him, or the small, dead one captured forever in the drawing.

And then he was gone.

I noticed the whisky decanter on the mantelpiece. I went to it and pulled out the stopper, pouring the contents into the empty fireplace.

I sank back on the sofa and picked up the sketch, tracing the curve of our little skulls in the picture, like fragile eggs in our mother's hands.

Our mother. For a desperate moment I wanted to talk to Mum, to let her words soothe me, but I pushed the thought aside furiously, the fire inside me igniting again. She had known all along, and she had never told me the truth. She had lied to me too.

I looked at the drawing, glimpses of my former life beginning to hit me like little shocks of electricity: another house, another life. Two of everything: two beds, two dolls' houses, two little girls clutching two little toy hares.

And her voice. I could hear her voice again now. It was a hushed, breathless version of my own. I had heard it throughout the years, in my sleep, and when I woke, but I had never before been able to understand.

'This way,' she was saying, 'this way, Romilly.'

Feena, my twin sister, speaking words that only we two understood: our very own code, secret and special, impossible for anyone else to crack.

It was a magical language that I had no use for anymore, for I was the only soul on earth who spoke it.

Twenty-Nine

I sat cross-legged in the middle of my bedroom. Every surface, every bit of floor, was covered with pictures. Frames and pieces of board leant against the walls. Scrolls of paper were spread across my bed.

I rested my hand on the collection of Dad's books stacked next to me, reassuringly familiar in the midst of all these new paintings, and suddenly I needed to open them, to lose myself in their familiarity, to forget for a moment everything I had learnt.

I picked up *Romilly's Christmas*, and ran my hands over the sleek dust jacket. It was the only one of Dad's books to have a removable cover, and I slid it off, admiring the cloth-bound hardback beneath.

I opened it to the first page, where the publication details were listed, and my breath caught. Here, at the very top of the page, was the usual little silhouette of me, chasing an animal across the top of the white paper. I had seen it a hundred times. But now there was something else.

In the left-hand corner, where the dust jacket had covered it up, there were two hares, embossed in silver. At first I thought they were boxing, but as I peered closer, I saw they had their arms around each other in a hug. The one on the left, slightly smaller, slightly more fragile, looked as if it had just stopped running: its willowy legs were still outstretched, and its ears were trailing behind it as if they had not had time to settle. There was something human about these hares, something child-like too, and suddenly it struck me: they were meant to be Feena and me.

I thought about the silhouette of the little girl that appeared at the top of the page in every book. In the first four books she was running away from the animals as if scared, but in the fifth and final book, she had begun to chase them away, and at last I understood. The silhouettes in the first four books were meant to be Feena, the ones in the last book were me. Dad couldn't have drawn us together; it would have been too much of a clue. Instead, at the beginning of the final book, he had transformed us into animals that he knew I would recognise; the stuffed toy hares that had watched over us in our bedroom in London, and in this drawing, he had given me the chance for one final, tender moment with my sister.

I looked at the two silver hares, my eyes blurring, and their shining fur swam in my vision. Dad *hadn't* doubted me: he hadn't turned me into a comic strip to be laughed at; he had been trying to define us, to illustrate our differences amongst our similarities. I was the strong twin, the brave twin, looking out for my timid, gentle sister. I gazed at the picture, seeing how desperately we were holding onto one another, and it occurred to me that it might not be a welcoming hug, but a hug goodbye, one final touch before I went on with my life, leaving my sister behind, trapped in the pages of a book.

'Romilly.'

I looked up, blinking away tears. In the silence of the room, her voice seemed loud.

'Feena?'

There was a giggle. 'This way,' she whispered, 'this way, Romilly.'

Those words again. I closed my eyes, and there she was, my sister, standing waiting for me, one hand outstretched. Her other hand was clutching the ears of her toy hare, small and silvery, soft from years of love. I looked down, and found an identical one in my own hand.

'This way,' she said again, taking my hand and turning, her long, red plait spinning out behind her.

'Where are we, Feena?' I asked, looking around. 'Where are we going?' But she put her finger to her lips.

This place was familiar. It was a green place, filled with nature: tall, bristling monkey puzzle trees sprouted from the ground, yews in the shape of peacocks loomed in the distance. As we walked, I could hear the laughter of a hundred ghost children following behind us like the wind, and I knew all of a sudden where we were. I had read about it in Beatrice's book.

'This is where she lived,' I said, 'where Bea lived. This is the garden in her book.' And with that realisation an unknown terror gripped me. I planted my feet into the ground, not understanding why, but knowing that to go on was to see something I had tried for years to forget.

But Feena only glanced at me, her eyes solemn now, and pulled me onwards. 'This way,' she said again.

We had been here before, I remembered now, really been here. Mum had taken us, a trip to visit grandma Bea's old house, the house she had written about in her ghost stories; the house that Mum had grown up in. It was open to the public now, and we wandered the chilly grounds, buttoned into winter coats, our breath misting before us.

But Feena wanted to see the fountain from the book, the one with the woodland animals drinking out of a huge leaf. There was a fawn in it, she said, just like her. When Mum wasn't looking, she pulled me off the path, disappearing into the bushes.

'Feena, I remember,' I said, feeling her little hand tug me along, 'you don't have to do this. Please.'

But she kept on pulling me onward. We clambered over the huge mossy roots of a rhododendron, a green leafed roof above our heads. Feena put a hand in her pocket, pulling out a packet of Parma Violets, and offered me one. The sickly smell of them hit me in the back of my nose, and I shook my head, knowing now why I hated them so much. Feena placed one on her tongue and twisted the packet closed.

We began, again, to walk.

We pushed through the rhododendrons, stumbling over the soft ground, until the branches opened onto a little clearing, and in the middle was a fountain.

'Look,' Feena whispered, pointing.

The fountain was huge, ancient and green, towering over our heads. It was in the shape of a curling leaf, and around the edges were statues of woodland animals, their heads kissed by frost. It felt as if they had stopped, frozen in time, just as we entered the glade. The giant leaf was filled with water, its surface mirror-still, and I realised as I looked at it that the water was iced over, freezing cold and forbidding.

The feeling of terror intensified as I took it all in. I knew this fountain. I had looked at the drawing of it often when I was little, and again when Bea had given me my own copy of the book, three years ago.

'Feena!' my sister said, pointing, and I looked up, confused. On the fountain, next to a hare with cold, staring eyes, was a fawn, standing stiffly near the edge.

'Feena,' I repeated, remembering. Of course, her name meant *small fawn*.

Then my sister was off. She ran to the fountain, clambering up the snaking vines that sparkled in the winter sun, reaching for the statue of the deer that was her namesake. As she scaled the top, her hand reached out to touch the curve of the fawn's ear, and she leant too far. I stood, re-living the memory, frozen to the ground as her small knee slipped against the frosty edge of the fountain, and she fell forward onto the ice.

For a moment, I thought it would support her weight, but it was thin, barely a skin over the freezing water, and with the sound of splintering glass, she fell through.

The water wasn't deep, and I heard a splash and a peal of laughter. Relief and strange terror mixed in my chest, and I started forward. I climbed the fountain easily, pulling her out of the freezing water, her little face a mirror of my own shock, and then she laughed again.

Crossly, I tried to pat her dry, aware that she was shivering. I was always the serious twin, the protective twin. It was a cold day, and she was frail, not strong and solid like me. She let out a wheezy little laugh again. It rattled in her lungs.

'Don't tell Mummy,' she whispered, her coat dark with water, mischief gleaming in her eyes.

She lifted her hand to wipe her hair from her face, and I saw how blue her skin was, as if she was turning to metal, becoming part of the fountain. The dark little mole stood out on her pale cheek, and her teeth began to chatter. We slipped down from the statue and climbed back through the rhododendrons, and out of the memory.

I opened my eyes.

The book was still lying open in front of me, the two hares hugging goodbye.

'Feena,' I said.

By the time we had found Mum again, Feena had begun wheezing, the crackle in her chest turning to a bubbling that kept exploding out of her mouth in little wet coughs.

By the time we got home, her temperature had peaked, and she was shaking.

She stayed in bed for days. I tucked my hare into her bed to watch over her. I wasn't allowed to stay with her, but I sat, sentry-like outside our bedroom door, listening, waiting.

Eventually she began to improve. Her skin lost its blue tinge. She began to chatter and babble and I was allowed to sit on her bed for short bursts and talk to her. She had lost a lot of weight, and her face looked, for the first time, different to mine. The last thing I remember was being allowed to nap next to her, falling asleep with her sweet, shallow breath trickling over me.

I had thought she was going to be all right.

I closed the book in front of me. I couldn't look at the two of us together any longer. Next to me on the floor was a huge painting on a stretched canvas, and I looked at it instead, trying to lose myself in the thick swirls of oil paint.

'Don't think of her,' I thought to myself, 'don't think of Feena.' But it was no good: now that I had remembered, she was everywhere.

I went to the window instead and opened it, desperate for some air. The moat sat gleaming below me, and I leant out, looking down.

Even here, I was reminded of her, for this was her final resting place. I looked at the water, trying to imagine my sister, drifting, becoming a part of it. Instead, the ugly face of the gargoyle shimmered up at me through the pondweed. I remembered the day Dad had destroyed the gargoyle fountain. Had it reminded him of that other fountain? Is that why it now lay at the bottom of the moat?

I latched the window closed, nearly knocking over my old stuffed parrot, Jasmine, who sat on the window sill. She looked so forlorn these days, her stuffing swollen inside her like an exploded bulrush, her once green feathers a flea-bitten, cobwebby grey.

The telephone was sat next to her. Weeks ago, I had taken it from the hallway and brought it to my room. Hours of fiddling with it had finally rewarded me with the sound I craved: a dial tone. It had been like music, connecting me with the outside world.

My hand went to the phone, my thoughts turning to my mum. I had so many questions. Mum would answer them honestly, now that the truth was out. She wouldn't care about protecting me, like Dad had. My hand hovered over the receiver.

But what if she blamed me? What if all her pent-up grief and anger came bubbling up out of her, and she directed it straight at me?

I turned back to the room, and the large painting on the floor caught my eye again. I crouched down next to it. This picture had been the centrepiece in *Romilly's Christmas*, a double-page spread depicting the snug on Christmas Eve. It was very similar to the painting Dad had made the night he told me about his dementia. That one had been auctioned off, raising thousands of pounds for a charity that helped bereaved children. At the time I hadn't understood why he had chosen that particular cause. Now, the irony of it hit me full on: that I was a bereaved child, myself, and yet no charity had stepped forward to help me.

I looked at the Christmas tree and the roaring fire in the painting in front of me. In the past few years, Dad often painted copies of his original pictures, versions of old paintings, as if his brain would no longer allow him to come up with anything new. Sometimes I found seven or eight sketches scattered across a table, all exactly the same. Was the painting he had made that night in the snug the start of it: an image dredged up from a part of his brain that still remembered?

I looked at the painting on the floor. The girl was reaching up to wrap tinsel around the tree. I could make out the mole on her left cheek: it was definitely me. The tree was covered in decorations, amongst them, a tiny pair of shoes with red bows — shoes I now remembered had once belonged to my sister – and the crimson bauble I had rescued after Dad's outburst, just before he told me he had dementia. Perhaps it was this bauble that was locked inside my wooden box, one of the clues to Feena's name.

I looked closer at the tree. Hanging among the decorations were all the other clues, too: the silver bell on a strip of blue velvet, the pink feather, the forget-me-not, and the little glass salt cellar. The painting was so large that everything in it was magnified to ten times the size I was used to, and in the sparkling glass of the red bauble I saw my sister, reflected back at me, gazing into the room.

I stood up and walked around my bedroom, finding the original paintings from all of the books. I lifted and sifted them until they were grouped together in two equal piles: one pile contained me, with a mole on my left cheek, and the other, Feena, with a mole on the right. And now I could see differences between myself and my twin, things that only a man who had lived with us and loved us both would see: my lips were slightly fuller, my hair straighter. Feena's eyes sloped down at the corners more than mine did, and the freckles on her nose were more pronounced.

But there was more. In each picture that Dad had painted of me, I found Feena, tucked away, invisible if you didn't know where to look. He had hidden her at the centre of a flower; in the pattern of Monty's fur, and even – most confusing of all – in the pendant of a necklace hanging from my own neck. She was there, hidden in plain sight, gazing out at me everywhere I looked: my lost sister.

There was a knock on my bedroom door, and Dad poked his head round.

'Can I come in?'

'It looks like you're already in.'

He climbed into the room, and I noticed how his hand shook as he tried to pull himself up, his joints creaking. He looked around at the paintings, nodding at the way I had divided them.

'It's why Mum left us, isn't it?' I said, looking down at the face in the bauble in front of me. 'Because Feena died.'

Dad sat down heavily on the bed. 'It is,' he said.

'I wasn't enough for her,' I said, staring round at all the pictures of me and my sister, 'I wasn't her favourite, and every time she looked at me, she saw her dead daughter. I get it.'

'It wasn't that, Romilly. Your mother had been ill for years. Your sister's death sent us all off on different tangents. Even you.'

I began to object, but he lifted a hand to silence me.

'Yes, even you.'

I looked down at my hands, not daring to look at him, in case the expression on his face made me cry.

'You went into yourself. You became – all of a sudden – just like Feena, as if you missed her so much you were trying to *be* her. I think it was this that got to your mother so much. She would come into a room and encounter a vision of her dead daughter.'

'So it's my fault then.'

'It's nobody's fault. Your mum stayed for a while. We tried to work our way through, but in the end we weren't strong enough. And so we had to find a new way.'

'Without Mum.'

'It was her choice to go, Romilly, and I believe it was the healthiest thing to do. She gets the help she needs where she is. And she does need help, more than you or I.' He stood, walking over to the little painting that was hanging on the wall, the one he had given me when I was nine years old.

'I wanted to show you something,' he said, lifting the picture off the wall.

'What are you doing with that?' I asked nervously. Dad had been known to snap paintings in half before.

'I just...' he trailed off, shaking his head, then he stumbled over to the window, and held the painting up to the glass so that the light shone through.

With a shiver I saw the shadow on the wall appear in the picture, darker than before. I stepped closer. It was a silhouette, the delicate shape of a person, but with the light passing through it I could see that muted colours were painted into it too: a pair of eyes looked out at me, a little hand clung to the hand of Romilly in the picture. There was nothing shadowy about this person. It was my sister, standing in the picture, holding my hand.

'She was always here,' Dad said, 'watching over you.'

I leant closer, looking at Feena. She had been covered by a layer of paint so that she was only visible when a strong light shone through her. 'I thought she was a ghost,' I said, 'she only appeared at night.'

Dad moved as if to hug me, then stopped himself. 'The last thing I meant to do was scare you,' he said, 'I wanted to give you comfort: it was the only way I knew how.'

I couldn't take my eyes off the painting. We were holding hands, and she was looking at me and smiling. Dad passed the picture to me, and the further it got from the light, the fainter she became until she disappeared once again, and I was alone. I stared at the blank stretch of wall, unseeing. When I looked up, Dad had gone.

I placed the painting on the window sill so that Feena appeared again, and I went to the bed, where Dad's early sketches lay, mottled with mould and curled at the edges. These were the drawings of us together, when we had been too small to crawl away. In one, our eyes were open and we were staring at each other as if looking in a mirror.

I studied it for a long time, my eyes blazing, and then I scrunched it into a ball and held it to my chest, feeling the tears come.

I went and stood over the Christmas painting on the floor, seeing in my mind Dad standing at his easel, a paintbrush in his hand, carols blaring out of the cassette player. I kicked hard at the frame, but it just creaked, a flake of wood chipping off, so I lifted my foot and stamped, hard, right at its centre.

My shoe went through the canvas, and a rip seared across the pine tree, through the painted reproduction of me, through the bauble that held my sister's face. I kicked and I kicked until the painting lay in tatters, an implosion of multicoloured paint curling like a dying flower at the centre of my bedroom.

I crept into the kitchen. Dad was standing by the sink, his hands submerged in steaming washing-up water. He was gazing out at the garden. I watched him for a moment, caught by his stillness, waiting for him to turn. His hands reached blindly for the hot tap, injecting a bit more warmth into their bath.

As he stood by the window in the pool of light, he appeared to grow younger, his hair gleaming, his skin changing until I convinced myself that he had become the dad who used to carry me over his shoulder up the stairs to bed, the dad who made toffee apples so hard and sugary that I broke a tooth on their curved golden shell.

Perhaps the warm, sudded water was sustaining him, flowing up through his fingertips to tenderly massage the follicles of his scalp, turning him into the father I remembered, the father I wanted him to be again.

I was the same height as him now, I realised. Not just because I was growing, but because he was shrinking. His back had begun to curve, the arc of the spine visible under his shirt. If I stretched up

I could just make out a tiny bald patch on the top of his head, hidden by a fine layer of hair. Where had the jolly, impish man from my childhood gone? Maybe this man wasn't my father at all, but a clever imposter, a wicked uncle.

As I watched him, he stirred the water with his hands, gazing not at the garden, I realised, but back into the past, watching himself long before his twins were born, long before one of them died, to a time when he was happier. I drunk him in and my stomach squirmed. I wanted to cry out, to run up to him and hug him and kiss that tiny patch on the top of his head. I wanted to tell him that everything was going to be all right.

But I didn't. I stayed where I was, feasting my eyes on the pale, stubbled skin beneath the beard, and his wrinkled, hairy hands as they splashed back and forth in the soapy water, wishing that this quiet, nostalgic version of my father would turn and see me and smile with love in his eyes.

'She was so cold,' he said suddenly, startling me out of my reverie. He turned his head, catching my eye for a moment.

'She had been asleep for so long when it happened, you both had. I hadn't checked on you – I was enjoying the peace. Your mother was out shopping. It was the first time she had dared leave Feena since she got ill, but she had been getting better, so...

'I went to your bedroom and you were both there, curled around each other, and she was blue.' He stopped and breathed in sharply, his face a frightening grimace. 'I scooped her up and rubbed her skin, just like they tell you in the books and at the hospital, just like they did when she was born.' He let out a long, painful sigh that disturbed the foam on the water. 'There was a breath. A tiny, rattly breath, and then, nothing. Oh, her blue lips!' Dad lifted his wet hands and covered his face, water streaming down his wrists.

'Dad.'

'I tried to cover her mouth with mine, blow my own soul into her, but it was too late, she was gone. My poor little darling doll.'

'Dad,' I crept forward and placed my hand on his wrist.

The effect was immediate – his arms flew up and he slapped me across my face, his eyes heated. I jumped back, my cheek flaring with pain.

'Get away from me,' he said, watching me as I held my sore cheek. Turning back to the sink, he said, 'You stayed asleep throughout, of course.'

'Dad, I—'

He reached out a hand to me again, and I tried not to shrink from his touch. 'You look just like her,' he whispered, stroking my cheek, 'and yet you're not her. You're a copy.' He touched the red mark he had made, his finger moving on to the mole that defined me from my sister. 'You were born first, did you know that? You always pushed in front. And she always followed you in everything you did. She would have been like you now – tall and beautiful. But far sweeter. She was always so much more thoughtful than you.'

He dropped his hands, suds dripping to the floor and returned to the sink, staring out of the window as if nothing had happened. Cautiously I took a step forward and followed his gaze, looking at the garden, my cheek still stinging.

The shed door stood open, as if it were screaming silently at me, its mouth wide open. Pieces of paper drifted across the grass, stirred by the breeze.

'We'll sort this out, you and me, Romilly,' he said, 'we'll find our way through.'

The sinkwater sloshed over the side, covering our feet as we stared out into the garden together.

Thirty

If you had stood outside Braër House and looked at it, really *studied* it, in the year that followed, you might not have thought that anyone was living there at all. The door remained unanswered to knocks, the curtains remained closed, the grass in the garden grew long and barbed. A window pane at the front of the house was broken by an over-enthusiastic fan who threw a stone at it. It stayed that way for months, cracked and splintered, until I eventually boarded it up with layers of cardboard.

When the final book had first been published nearly two years before, back when Dad had been well enough to care about it, there had been an excited buzz from fans and press alike. People believed that once the last book came out, everything would slot into place and it would only be a matter of time before the treasure was revealed.

But as the months wore on and nobody was able to crack the code, the fans became disillusioned, becoming interested in other things; new fads to get their teeth into. The treasure hunt obsession began to wane, and people started to forget.

With the decline in sales came a reduction in royalties. The cheques that used to come regularly from the publishers dried up, and things that we used to buy whenever we needed them became luxuries. The money I had stashed in the beech tree started to run out too, and I spent the daylight hours digging a vegetable patch in the garden, and foraging for food and firewood in the countryside. I grew potatoes and carrots, things that would sustain us over the winter, filling us up and keeping us warm.

In the spring, the trickle of money from the publishers dried up completely. I searched the beech tree for the last remaining notes, but they must have rotted along with the tree trunk, or else been blown across the garden in a winter gale. Life became even harder. I took to rummaging in bins, stealing milk left on doorsteps, taking eggs from our neighbours' hens, hunger driving me onwards.

I think Braër existed for other people only as a shell at that time, a prop where the lives of the girl and her cat had their adventures. I don't think they believed we were actually still in there, trying to survive. We were growing smaller and smaller in their memories until eventually we shrank from their minds altogether.

On the morning of my sixteenth birthday, I could sense the box beginning to tick before I became fully aware of it, rather like a hard to reach itch that I desperately needed to scratch. I luxuriated in the space around me, my feet stretching in the coolness of the sheets until my toe touched the tip of Monty's nose at the bottom of the bed. He gave a shake of his head, and purred, waiting impatiently for the early morning sun to curl round the corner of the window and lick at his ears.

I closed my eyes and tried to get back to sleep. There was no hurry to get up, it was still so early. But as I lay there, my mind began to wonder what the day would bring. No longer did Dad make a special effort on birthdays. No longer did we feast together on quirky banquets laid out on the kitchen table. Dad's appetite had shrivelled up. He seemed to survive on watery tea and the apples that I had stored in the pantry from last autumn. I knew not to expect a present from him, let alone a birthday cake. I fantasised about the giant Victoria sponge Beatrice had brought for my fourteenth birthday. Even last year's pink cupcake from Lidiya seemed far beyond the realms of possibility now.

At six o'clock, Monty and I left the box in my room to tick alone, hoping that when we came back it would have revealed a new gift, nestled on my quilt like a freshly laid egg.

Dad was already sitting at the kitchen table, a milky coffee in his hands. He smiled at me as I sat down warily, the cat winding his way around my legs.

'Now, I know you. Remind me again?'

I sighed and picked up a piece of bread, buttering it before placing it in front of him. 'I'm Romilly.'

His frown melted into understanding, and he nodded. I touched his coffee mug. It was stone cold. Lumps of coffee powder floated on the surface.

Dad lived now in a world of smoke and mist, lumbering through it until he strayed into a pool of lucidness, and there he would try to stay, his hands clinging to the edges of the fog to keep it at bay. Sometimes I was able to anchor him there for minutes, hours, or even days, speaking gently, reassuring him that everything was all right, but always in the end the mist evaporated between his fingers, and he would be powerless to stay, sucked back into a world of shifting thoughts and memories.

Today was a day of thick fog. I could see it swirling in his eyes.

'Yes,' he said, nodding slowly, 'that's right, we've met before. You're my daughter, aren't you?'

'I am.'

'And there's something special about today, isn't there?' He was looking at me quizzically. My heart leapt.

'There is,' I said, beaming.

'That's right. *Stars in their Eyes* is on later, I think. Shall we check?'

I swallowed painfully. 'Actually, I was thinking we could go for a *birthday* walk. And then…' inspiration struck me, eyeing the last remaining egg on the kitchen worktop, 'maybe when we get home I could bake a *birthday* cake.' There might still be enough flour in the pantry, I thought hopefully, as long as the weevils hadn't got there first.

'A birthday stroll, what a marvellous idea. Is it my birthday?' His face was childlike in his excitement.

'No, Dad, it's mine.'

'Of course it is.' He ran his twinkling eyes over me and placed his huge hand over mine, smiling warmly. 'Where shall we go, daughter-mine?'

We stomped over the fields, crossing the little bridge under which Stacey and I had found our magical brooch oh so long ago. Condensation trembled on the wooden balustrades, and my bare arms tingled from the cold morning air. In the distance, the quarry that Stacey had shown me two years ago glimmered, full after unseasonable July rain.

We made our way out onto the boardwalk that wound through the field of reeds. Far away I could see the tips of the windpump's sails, moving assuredly in the breeze. Dad marched on ahead, stopping now and again to pick a gently swaying reed. He had developed a fascination with collecting things. At first it had been conkers, but now his pockets were always brim-full of stones and leaves and snails' shells, just like a schoolboy's.

I caught up with him and took his arm, noticing the reeds he had collected were falling from his grasp like a trail of breadcrumbs.

'Stacey and I used to walk here when we were younger,' I said, 'when we used to go exploring.' I remembered how she had purposefully stepped off the planks and into the petrol-sheened mud, grasping the reeds for support as the mud sucked at her trainers.

A line of drool hung from my father's bottom lip. He snapped off a stalk and examined the tip of a reed. As I watched, he edged his overlong fingernails under the layers so that pale husks floated down onto the wooden planks. A piece got caught deep in his nail and a flush of blood bloomed. He didn't seem to notice.

I pulled at his sleeve, dragging him along. 'Come on, Dad,' I said, and then, when he didn't respond, 'Come on, Tobias.'

At his name, he lifted his head and smiled properly, the bags round his eyes crinkling. He took my hands in his, and I could feel the fragments of reed crushed beneath our skin as he beamed at me, nodding and smiling like an automaton.

As we walked through the village on our way back, I stayed behind, seeing him afresh. His walk had changed over the last year, the pattern of his steps imperceptibly different. He shuffled along now, occasionally stumbling as if his brain could not keep up with his feet.

It was still early, cool and peaceful. At the centre of the village there was a triangle of green with a solitary oak tree grown deeply into it. Dad had stopped to pull a branch towards him, tracing the curves of the leaves, picking the best ones. It would have made a beautiful painting, I thought as I watched him silhouetted next to the tree, but he hadn't picked up a paintbrush in over a year.

'Dad, this way,' I said, tugging at his arm, wanting to get home now, but he planted his feet stubbornly on the grass, refusing to move.

'Psithurism,' he said, staring upwards, still pulling the branch towards him.

'Dad, come on.'

But he just carried on repeating the word, gazing at the tree. Angrily, I stalked off. I would leave him on his own. He could find his own way back. A small voice told me that he might get lost, but I shoved it aside in my annoyance and stomped up the road.

At the post box I paused and looked back.

'Romilly Kemp, I presume?'

A man was standing nearby. He was unnaturally tall, curving with pleasure over me.

'I'm a huge fan,' he said, standing a little too close, his voice slightly gravelly. 'Do you mind if I take a picture?' He lifted the camera, the lens flashing in the sun. Something about it dug at a long-forgotten memory.

'I—' The camera clicked before I could give my answer. I took a step back, feeling suddenly vulnerable.

'Thank you, dear. May I shake your hand?' Not waiting for permission, he leant in and clasped my hand, bringing it to his lips fleetingly and kissing it. His mouth was cold and wet.

'Is that your father over there?'

Dad was reaching far up into the branches of the tree, smiling at something the man and I could not see. He had an armful of leaves already, chartreuse and deep green cradled like a baby in the crook of his arm, and I felt suddenly embarrassed by him.

The stranger's hand was on my elbow, stroking it gently.

'How is he, your father?' he said, leaning towards me, 'The *great* Tobias Kemp?' The glint of his camera lens caught my eye again, blinding me for a moment.

'I heard he's going a bit mad?' he continued. He was close now, close enough that I could see a tiny piece of blood-soaked toilet paper clinging to his skin where he had cut himself shaving. He ran his eyes over my body, his fingers still stroking my elbow, and in that instant, I had the sensation that my whole world was transforming, tipping onto an axis I couldn't quite comprehend.

Desperately, I looked over to Dad, but he was still near the tree, gazing with love at the newly acquired leaves in his arms.

'Dad!' I called.

I was suddenly aware of my chest beneath my thin T-shirt, the shape still so new to me that I had forgotten to put a vest on underneath. I reddened, and at the same time the man lifted his hand from my elbow, eyebrows raised as if he were asking my permission, and then he leant forward and stroked his hand down the front of my top.

My brain refused to register what had happened. I took a step back, the feeling of his hand on me still. In the same moment I became aware of a sort of pained whine roaring towards me like a fine-tuned missile. Dad's bellow, as he barrelled into the man, was something otherworldly, as if his soul had ripped from his body and was rushing into the very depths of the man to destroy him from within.

The force of the blow sent me off balance, and I landed heavily, banging my head on the post box as I went down so that everything appeared in twos. Two dads, two horrid men. Two Romillys, I thought with a drunken giggle. Falling oak leaves were spinning down all around me. I tried to sit up, but my skull felt like it had been compressed in a vice, and I lay my head back down on the cool pavement. From this angle all I could see were two pairs of ankles and feet dancing a macabre tango around me.

My eyelids closed. I could hear the soft patter of oak leaves falling nearby, and then the sudden thud of a body falling to the ground.

'Dad,' I whispered, opening my eyes and trying to see who had fallen, my voice reverberating painfully through my skull. The standing man lifted his left leg and aimed a hard kick at the lifeless body on the ground.

'My... dad,' I pleaded again. Again, the leg lifted, and again it kicked out, like some sort of clockwork device that cannot work out how to stop. There was a spattering of blood on the standing man's trouser cuff now.

I tried to raise my head again, the double vision clearing, but now blackness was pulling into my sight from every edge, and everything began shrinking down into a small circle, as if I were looking through a telescope. Dad's face was in that circle, and to my relief he was upright, standing over the other man, pacing, muttering, his hands sweeping over his beard and his hair. There was a smudge of blood on his cheek in the same place as my mole, and I tried to reach up, to point out we were now twins, but then he turned to the wall and, drawing back his fist, smashed it into the brick repeatedly, the skin of his knuckles mashing into the wall so that I couldn't tell if it was blood or brick dust coating his knuckles. I tried to shake my head, but it would not move, and instead I found my sight locked onto my dad as he lifted his head high, looking for a moment towards the bright, bright summer sky. And then, with an ursine roar he brought his head down against the brick, his forehead meeting the wall with a dull thud.

'Dad!' I shouted silently, the telescopic view shrinking further until I could hardly see at all, but I could still feel the sickening thump of his skull ringing in my ears. I lay my head down so that the fallen man was in my vision, still and silent on the floor, his camera shattered beside him. A droplet of blood landed on my hand, and I focussed on that instead, turning away from the stranger and my dad and the pained animal sounds he was making. The drop of blood lay on my hand, quivering, and in it I could see the whole world.

From out of the shadows, dark paws emerged, padding towards me, huge and velvet.

The panther stopped by my side and slowly shook his magnificent head as if he had all the time in the world.

'Now sleep,' he said, exhaling his warm, somnolent breath over me, his damask tail twitching. I closed my eyes obediently.

'Sleep,' said the panther, melting back into the shadows, and I did.

Thirty-One

I woke up. Stacey was sitting on the end of my bed. She was wearing my denim pinafore dress with the large red buttons. The dress was dotted with patches of white fabric, each one spattered with blood. I turned my cheek to the cool of the pillow. Everything went black.

I woke again. This time my mother was sitting in a chair pulled up to the bed, resting her high heeled shoes on the duvet next to me, her bag of cat-skins on her lap. She smiled, her teeth sharp like a panther's.

I slept.

When I next opened my eyes it was the middle of the night. Beside me, on my little table, was Dad's carved box. A small round door had opened in its side. A shiny red bauble sat like a fat robin just inside.

My throat hurt, my head pounded. I put my hand to my hair and felt a mountain range of tender stitches on my scalp, bristles of scrappy hair sticking up between my fingers.

I closed my eyes again.

My bedroom became my whole world. Dreams and reality interwove: Monty jumped onto my white duvet, becoming a polar bear padding across Arctic lands; the man in the moon hung in the circular window, his evil eye spying through the muted coloured glass; my father ambled past the bed on all fours, his hands and feet grizzly bear paws preserved in salt.

I ached to be able to get up, to be normal again. Stacey was spending a lot of time on the end of my bed now, watching over me. It was beginning to creep me out.

As soon as I was able, I left my bedroom behind and made the precarious journey down two flights of stairs to the kitchen in search of my father. In the hallway I paused, bracing myself to see what sort of dad I would find today.

He was standing at the sink, looking out over the garden. At the sound of my shuffling footsteps he turned.

'Romilly,' he said, and I let out a breath of relief.

'Hi, Dad.'

'I'm glad to see you up. It's been rather lonely without you.' His face crinkled into a smile. I sat down at the table, and he placed a glass of milk in front of me.

'I've been to the shop,' he said proudly. 'I got milk and bread and eggs and bacon.' There was a dressing on his temple, surrounded by a circle of shaved skin. It looked stupid, like a bald spot that had slid out of place, and I felt angry at the nurses for not just shaving all his hair off. I reached up and felt for the bump on my own head. The landscape of stitches curved like the spine of a fish.

I lifted the milk shakily to my mouth and took a sip. It tasted good, and I gulped it down, feeling the liquid strengthen me. I couldn't remember the last time I had eaten.

'The thing is,' Dad said, sitting down at the table, 'while you've been having these mammoth teenage lie-ins, I've been thinking.' He pointed to the dressing on his head. 'This can't happen again.'

'It won't, Dad,' I said, wiping the milk moustache from my upper lip. 'I'll look after you better, I promise.'

'It's not that. What I mean is, it's not up to you to keep me safe. And I certainly can't do it. Thank goodness someone saw what happened and called an ambulance, otherwise...' he trailed off, his face ashen. 'The point is, I've been looking at this place.' He produced a creased leaflet from his shirt pocket and pushed it towards me. 'Briar View' it said above a glossy picture of white-haired dears sitting around a table playing cards. Inside were other photos: a smiling, laughing grandmother with her equally happy granddaughter. A dapper be-suited old man with a carnation in his lapel. I looked at Dad.

'What do you mean?'

'It's only a few miles away. It's on a bus route. You could visit.'

'No.'

'I thought the name sounded a bit like Braër.'

'No, Dad.'

'You can't look after me forever, Romilly, I'm too far gone. And I can't look after you. What if it's you I attack next time, thinking you're someone else? I've made an appointment with the GP later this morning to discuss getting admitted. I'd like you to come – in case I get a bit forgetful.' He smiled shiftily, scratching at the dressing on his head, and then remembering and pulling his hand away.

'Why did you do it, Dad?' I asked, nodding at the shaved patch of skin.

'Who knows. I suppose I just wanted it all to end.' He heaved a sigh. 'For what it's worth, I'm sorry.' He leant forward and pushed my fringe up off my face, cupping his cool hand to my forehead.

'Now, I'll cook us some bacon. You must be starving. But best you stay in the kitchen, just in case I go a bit gaga.' He crossed his eyes for a moment, and I giggled.

'I've been living off cold baked beans for three days,' he said, getting up, 'thank goodness you're up and about to keep an eye on me.'

He stopped in the middle of the kitchen and gazed at me, and for a moment I thought he had dipped back into the fog of dementia. But then he said, 'I'm so glad we've had this talk, Romilly. I can rest easy knowing someone is going to take care of me.' His habitually puzzled expression melted into something more at peace and he smiled.

The doctor's surgery was a fifteen-minute walk away. Dad maintained his sobriety all the way, chewing on a handful of leftover bacon rinds as he went. He sat quietly in the waiting room while I flashed glances at him out of the corner of my eye, searching for signs of the fog descending. Bacon fat churned unpleasantly in my stomach.

In the doctor's room, we sat together whilst the GP surveyed us through thick-lensed glasses.

'And do you think this is the best solution?' he said, turning to me. I nodded, my stomach somersaulting queasily.

'Who will be looking after you, young lady?'

'Her mother's back to take care of her,' Dad said, leaning forward and patting my knee. I looked at him, unable to determine how close the mist had encroached. The doctor nodded and scribbled something on his pad.

Once we were outside I said, 'Is Mum really back?' I had a hazy memory of seeing her in my bedroom. But then I had also had a conversation with Mary Mother-of-God, so I couldn't be certain.

'Your darling mother is a gem,' Dad said, picking at a bit of bacon rind stuck in a molar. 'Nursed me back from the brink when I was ill with the influenza. She'll look after you well, trust me.'

The edge of his dressing had come loose and was flapping in the wind. I reached up and pressed it to his head again, but not before I glimpsed the soft dent in his skull underneath.

PART THREE

Thirty-Two

Dad left for Briar View in a taxi a few days later, with me waving him off from the gate.

'I want to settle in before you visit,' he said, 'make it homely. You do understand, don't you?'

I nodded, swallowing my tears down, not wanting to make this harder for him. But however hard I tried, I couldn't see his logic: surely it would be homelier if I were there. Surely home for both of us was when we were together.

I came inside, wrapping my arms tightly about myself. Braër felt cold and still, as if a pulse no longer beat beneath its crumbling skin. I went to the kitchen, hoping to scrape the last of the Ovaltine from the jar to eke into a mug of warm milk. All I wanted to do was curl up in bed and never get out.

I stopped.

Stacey was sitting at the table, looking at me warily.

My skin prickled in shock. 'Stacey,' I said, holding onto the wall for support, 'I thought I dreamt you.'

'Nope,' she said, 'it's really me.' A hopeful smile hovered over her lips. Her hands were stroking the rim of the teacup in front of her as if she didn't know what else to do with them.

'What are you doing here?'

'Your dad asked me to come. He thought you could use some

company. And he's right: you look awful.' The old merriment glittered in her eyes for a moment.

'Thanks,' I said, sitting down feebly and pulling my knees up to my chin.

We stared at each other across the table, soaking up the changes in our faces. She looked older: more grown-up. The roundness in her face was gone, and newly emerging cheekbones accentuated the delicate slope of her nose and her large, unusual eyes. Next to her I felt shabby in comparison. I put my hand to the scab that had formed on my head, feeling for the stitches, scratching at the dried blood in my unwashed hair.

'You're shaking,' she said.

'Yes.'

She stood up and poured a glass of water from the tap.

'I just… I can't believe you're really here,' I said. 'I dreamt about you, but I never thought you'd actually come back.'

'Well, I am back.' She shrugged, sitting down and pushing the glass towards me. 'You don't have to get all emotional about it.'

She lifted her tea again, looking at me over the edge of it as she sipped. I noticed the little painting of the virgin Mary was on the table. Behind her, the pantry door stood open, and I thought of the time I was shut in there when I was little; the touch of Stacey's fingers on mine through the grate. Outside it began to rain.

'How are you feeling,' she asked, 'after what happened?' She indicated the cut on my head.

'I'm OK. Tired, mostly.' This was an understatement. The real world and the dream world had merged while I was recuperating up in my bedroom, and now their strands were so knotted that I couldn't summon the energy to separate the two.

'Have you been eating?'

'I'm not hungry.'

'I bet your dad hasn't helped. I can't imagine he's been much good at looking after you.' She twisted a lock of hair, looking at me, 'He doesn't make much sense now, does he?' Her voice was loud in the quiet room, the mischievous grin I remembered so well playing over her face.

'What do you mean?'

'Well, he was always a bit gaga, but he's royally messed up now, isn't he? He could hardly get a word out when he spoke to me earlier.'

She put her cup down. A droplet of tea slopped from it, landing on my cheek, like an old tear. I wiped it away.

'He's ill.' My words came out sharper than I had intended.

'OK, sorry, I didn't mean to upset you. It's just, we used to laugh about him, you know, before. Your dad the "loony"?'

'Of course I remember. But it's not funny anymore.'

'Well, he's gone to the best place then. They'll take care of him properly.'

'*I* took care of him properly,' I said.

'Calm down, Romilly, I'm on your side!' She had picked up the picture of Mary and was trying to sit it on the table, but the stand had been broken long ago and it kept falling down with a clatter. The noise jarred in my head.

'I'm going to visit him soon,' I said, 'he might be well enough to come home for a bit, the doctor said dementia slows down sometimes.' I could hear the pathetic hope in my voice.

'But it doesn't get better.' She had abandoned the picture now. Her elbows were propped on the table, and she was leaning forward, looking at me intently.

'No.' I had forgotten how all-encompassing her attention could be, how it lasered into you, engulfing you until you felt submerged in it, unable to breathe.

She placed her hand on mine. The movement was so quick that I hardly saw her do it.

'Don't visit him yet,' she said, 'let him settle in first. You don't want to make him feel guilty for abandoning you.'

'He didn't abandon me,' I said, pulling my hand away.

She looked round the kitchen theatrically. 'Where is he then?'

'That's not what I meant,' I said. 'I can look after myself.' The unfairness of what she was saying billowed around me, and yet I knew she was right. Stacey had an uncanny way of pointing out the truth, the things shrouded in shadows in my head.

The beginnings of an ache threatened at my temple, and I reached up and touched my sutures again, running my finger over the rigid threads. 'Why do you always pick arguments with me?' I said.

'I don't pick arguments. We just don't see things the same way. You said yourself that he's ill,' she said, 'he's not going to get better. He's never coming home, so it's time to move on. It's simple, when you look at it like that.'

I picked angrily at the scab, edging my nail under the tight stitches. How was any of this simple?

'I've had a really hard time over the last couple of years,' I said quietly.

'Is this going to turn into a woe-is-me story about how we stopped being friends, just when you needed me most?'

Her words landed in my chest, igniting the fire that had been smouldering there quietly for months.

'Real friends don't just drop each other like that,' I said. 'It was two years ago, Stacey. I was pissed off, and I'm really sorry if I upset you, really I am, but it was just a comment. Why did you leave? Why didn't you argue back?' Anger like white hot sparks was shooting through me now. 'You have no idea what I've had to deal with.'

'I've had to deal with stuff too,' she said. She was looking down at the picture of Mary in her hands, stroking the golden halo around her head, 'And I didn't go far. I was always nearby if you needed me.'

'Like the time I went to the lake, you mean? That's what friendship's about, is it? Stalking someone?'

'Yeah, well you weren't a great friend either!' she said, her face full of the stubborn anger I remembered from when we were young.

She had bunched her fists up, her cheeks bright red, and I realised that deep inside she was still that child, with the same hopes and fears that an eight-year-old has, and all of a sudden I was jealous of her. Jealous of her lack of responsibility, of her lack of complexity. I stifled a sob.

At the sound, her anger abated as quickly as it had come. She sank back against the chair, drooping like a wilted flower. Her hair had changed in the two years she had been away. It was streaked with highlights from the sunshine, and it hung over her face as she looked down at the picture in her lap. She curled a lock of it round a finger, twisting it tightly.

'Do you remember when we thought her name was Mrs Mother-of-God?' I said, touching the picture.

A smile spread slowly across Stacey's face.

'Maybe... we could start again?' I said. I pulled my chair closer and touched the hand that was frantically braiding her hair. 'I missed you.'

'I missed you too,' she said, an uncertain smile still flickering over her lips. She pulled out a worn packet of Parma Violets and offered me one.

'You don't still like those, do you? They taste like rotten flowers.'

'At least my breath doesn't stink like yours.'

'It doesn't smell!' I licked my teeth, conscious of the fact that we'd run out of toothpaste weeks ago.

'I can smell it from here,' she said, putting a handful of Parma Violets in her mouth and crunching gleefully.

I took a sweet and put it in my mouth, bracing myself for the feelings the taste of it would spark. But the flavour wasn't as strong as I remembered. We sat, grinning at each other, rolling the sweets around our mouths.

'Did you go to the circus in the end?' she asked.

'You heard me asking you to come, then, that day at the lake?'

'Course I did. Did you go?'

'I did.'

Stacey's eyebrows lifted imperceptibly. 'Wow. I didn't think you had it in you.'

'Thanks,' I said. 'I found out something: a clue to the treasure hunt.'

Stacey's eyes widened. 'No!'

'I have so much to tell you. I nearly didn't come back.'

'What? You mean you nearly joined the circus?' She looked at me, unsure whether or not I was joking.

I nodded.

'As a clown, or a bearded woman?' she said, shaking with silent laughter, and then we were both giggling, enjoying the familiar ring of our voices together, inhaling the smell of Parma Violets that surrounded us, thankful that we had finally found each other again.

Thirty-Three

Stacey supported me that evening as I climbed the stairs on wobbly legs, despite my protestations that I could do it on my own.

'Whoa,' she said as we came to my bedroom.

It was the first time she had seen all the paintings. I tried to see it for the first time: my face staring out at us from every corner of the room, the eyes, painted in oil and watercolour or sketched in charcoal and pencil, following us as we walked across the room.

'This would give me nightmares,' she said, avoiding looking at them as she ushered me back into bed, 'how do you get any sleep?'

'I like it,' I said. I could feel Feena's benevolent gaze beaming into me from all corners of the room.

Stacey turned her back on the pictures and began tucking me in.

'Stacey,' I whispered when she had finished, 'I'm scared.'

'About what?'

'About Dad. About living here without him.'

'But you've practically run the house singlehanded for years. What's the difference? And at least now you're not having to deal with your dad's piss-soaked knickers.' A sardonic smile lifted the corner of her mouth, and she began patting the covers around me.

I tried to smile too, knowing she was only trying to cheer me up. I didn't want to be reminded of my dad now. I looked over at the telephone on the window sill.

'I should call my mum,' I said. I could suffer her anger and sadness now, if it meant seeing her again. If it meant I could hear stories about my sister that my dad's brain could no longer hold onto. I thought of Mum's red nails, her sad eyes creasing into a smile as she stroked my face until I slept.

Stacey stopped fussing round me. 'What do you need her for?'

'I don't think I can do this on my own. I need her help.'

'But I'm here,' she said. '*I'm* helping. That's enough, isn't it?' She sounded hurt.

I reached up to pick at the scab on my head. The stitches were the kind that melted away, but they were still there, clawing into my scalp. My brain was whirring over everything that had happened since Stacey went away. 'I have so much to tell you,' I repeated.

'Shh, it can wait one more day. You look exhausted. Here, take this.' She shook a small white pill onto her palm. 'It'll help you sleep.'

I took it, and she lifted a glass of water to my lips. As the bitter pill slid down my throat, I thought again of my mum. I could always call her tomorrow. Perhaps.

'You're right: you do need looking after,' Stacey said. 'You never were very good at taking care of yourself, were you?'

There were those words again. Truthful, but barbed. She sat on the bed and took my hand in hers. Her fingernails were short and chewed, just like I remembered them.

'Why does everybody leave me?' I said.

'I didn't leave you.'

'Yes, you did.'

'Well, I came back.'

'Eventually.'

Stacey sighed. 'Don't start again, Rom. I'm here now.'

'What's wrong with me?' I asked quietly. 'Why can't I cope?' I could hear the whine in my voice, magnified tenfold by tiredness and the pill she had given me. My hand was back at my head, scratching, picking. The scab felt huge now, taking over my whole scalp, a bumpy landscape for my fingers to explore.

Stacey sighed again, gazing out of the window. 'I don't know, Romilly, what *is* wrong with you?'

My breath caught at the cruel words, and I edged my nail deep beneath the stitches, prising the scab away. Warm blood rolled suddenly over my fingers.

'Shit,' Stacey said, jumping up from the bed. Finding a towel, she pressed it tightly over the cut.

I leant into her touch in spite of myself. 'I'm so glad you're here,' I said, laying my fingers lightly on her wrist, smearing blood across her skin.

She flinched.

'I'm sorry, I—' Tiredness was beginning to overwhelm me now, I couldn't form the words I wanted to.

'Shh, I'll take care of you now.' Her words were long and drawn-out like a record on slow play, hardly recognisable as words at all. 'It's not your fault you're so pathetic, it's how you were brought up. People who do as they please their whole lives tend to be selfish and thoughtless.'

Each word was like a little pin in my skin, as if I was a voodoo doll she was stabbing with relish.

'But I...' Sleep was folding me into its barbed arms now. I curled up in the bed, pulling my knees to my chest, my eyes heavy. 'I didn't...' I murmured, but she patted the duvet, pulling it close around me.

'It's OK, you don't need anyone else anymore. I'm here now. I'm enough.'

'I...'

'Shh, sleep now, we'll talk more in the morning.'

My eyelids closed, and the room melted into nothingness around me.

A white feather was dancing in the corner of my bedroom window, caught in a cobweb. I lay in bed, watching it.

It had been a week since Dad went, a week since Stacey came back. A week of bedrest and sleep, punctuated by dreams deadened by the little white pills that Stacey had found. The bottle was on my bedside cabinet now. It had my father's name on it.

The police had just called, the telephone's ring so loud it had made me jump, pulling me from my drugged sleep. The man Dad attacked was out of hospital. He was not pressing charges. He probably didn't want the world to know he was a sick pervert, I thought angrily.

I rolled over and my eyes rested on the red bauble that Dad's box had delivered on the day of the attack. I leant over and picked it up. It fitted perfectly in my palm, and I remembered the night Dad told me about his dementia, when I had run to the meadow with it, and he had found me in his mobiles, and led me back to Braër to tell me the truth about his illness.

This bauble formed a part of Feena's name in Dad's clues. I thought of the complex web that Dad had created to lead me to the truth about my sister, how his brain must have worked so hard, knowing that at any moment he might start to forget.

'Feathers appear when angels are near,' Stacey said, climbing through the door with a cup of tea and making me jump. She put the tea on the bedside table. I looked over at the window. The feather was still there.

She had ordered me to stay in bed for the past week, bringing me food and drink, and frowning if I tried to get up. My legs felt weak whenever I padded to the toilet, my skin hot and feverish. Stacey had listened, entranced, as I recounted the last two years: Dad's slow decline, the hunt for the clues, the raiding of his shed. When I got to the part about Feena, she had looked over at the paintings, frowning. 'But they all look just like you,' she said.

Now, whenever she came upstairs, she sat in front of them, gazing at the girls within.

'This is definitely you,' she said now, sitting cross-legged in front of a small watercolour of a girl making a daisy chain.

'How do you know?' I said, distracted by the movement of the feather in the window.

'It just feels like you, she's got a cheeky face. And she's a bit fat.'

'I'm not fat!'

'No, but next to the pictures of Feena you have a certain chubbiness.'

'Don't you need to go back to your mum's for a bit?' I said. 'Or your gran's? I'm well enough to cope on my own now.'

'Oh no,' she said, turning and fixing me with a sweet smile, 'I live here now, with you.'

The feather was swaying hypnotically in the window, like a pendulum. Nausea swelled up into my throat, and I swallowed it back. I got up, ignoring Stacey's protestations, and pulled down the sash, but the feather took off out of reach into the air, high up above the house and over towards the road at the front.

I made my way shakily towards the stairs, climbing precariously downstairs after it, Stacey's calls ringing in my ears.

What kind of angels could possibly be near me? A white feather was supposed to tell you that loved ones in heaven were thinking of you. But the only person in heaven was my sister, and why would she start thinking of me now after all these years?

I crossed the bridge and climbed awkwardly over the gate, craning my neck back to look for the feather. A dot of white appeared, swirling down towards me and I reached out my hand. It helixed down, straight into my palm as if, after all, it was meant for me. Tiny and perfect, it pulsed gently in the wind, and a rush of exultation went through me. I examined the soft downy hairs, wondering who was looking out for me; who cared enough to send me a sign.

'They're everywhere,' Stacey said, following me from the house. I looked up, and with a sinking feeling I saw she was right. The whole road was covered in white feathers. Quite a few were swirling in the air, but most lay on the ground. I kicked at them, narrowly missing Stacey's foot. Further away across the road, a whole heap of them lay together, lifting and dropping like seaweed in a tide.

We approached the pile of feathers cautiously. In its midst, a white dove lay, its beady black eye staring up at us. When it saw us coming it tried to scramble up, but only its head rocked back and forwards, its body staying still.

'Its neck must be broken,' Stacey said.

The bird continued to stare at us, its eye a swirl of smoke, as if it had already begun the slow descent into death.

'We can't leave it,' she said.

'What do you expect me to do?' I asked, rubbing the feather anxiously between my fingers.

'You've got to kill it.'

I looked up at her. 'I can't kill it! You kill it.'

But she just shook her head, staring at the bird.

I looked up at the sky. A sleet of feathers danced around us. One had landed in Stacey's hair.

'We'll... we'll just let it die.' I turned my back on the dove, but the feathers were everywhere, a scurf of white falling in front of Braër's windows like snow, as if the dove was shedding its life, layer by layer.

'You've got to help it, Romilly.' Stacey's face was white. Her eyes resembled the dove's, grey and marbled and swirling with something that might have been tears. I couldn't remember ever having seen her cry before.

I looked down at the dove. Instinct made me want to crouch close to it, to stroke its warm breast, to calm it in any way I could. But I knew if I did I would see the terrible truths of the world brewing in its eye. I stayed standing.

'How, how do I——?' The dove was watching me still, its breast moving quickly in and out.

'I don't know. Quickly?'

'With what, though?'

Stacey looked about. 'Maybe… your foot?' I looked down at my feet. I was wearing wellies. Ready-made, washable, bird-killing shoes. I shuddered.

I looked again at the dove. It wasn't struggling to get away now. It was watching me with quiet acceptance. It blinked its eye slowly, the lids slipping over the glassy eyeball, covering the world within.

'On the count of three?' I asked, and she joined in as I began.

'One, two,' I lifted my boot high into the air. 'Three.' I brought it down.

It became obvious that something had gone wrong the moment I slammed my foot down. I felt a silent pop as my heel hit the dove's stomach. In the second that I lifted my foot back up I knew I hadn't killed it, merely damaged it further. Skeins of intestine were attached to my boot, ribboning out of its burst stomach, and still it eyed me, its lungs fluttering delicately, inflating in a liquid chest that was half destroyed.

'What did you do?' Stacey said, stepping back, reeling away from the damaged bird.

Memories of broken snails twisting and turning in silent pain flooded my eyes as I stared at the poor mutilated animal.

'You need to stamp on its head!' Stacey said, miming her boot going down. 'Its brain. You need to crush its brain! Quickly.' She was staring in fascinated horror at the dove, its little head twitching now, its beak partly open.

With a huge effort I lifted my foot again and brought my heel down sharply on its head. With a crack, it stopped moving.

Feathers swirled about us as we stood by the side of the road. Stacey sat down on the verge and looked at the little bird on its bed of feathers. She reached a hand out to stroke its gleaming, twisted neck.

'There are no angels,' I said to her, wiping my foot on the grass and walking back to the house.

Thirty-Four

When I was well enough, I began planning my journey to visit Dad. It had only been a matter of weeks since he left, but as I began to gain the strength I had lost after so much bed rest, the need to see him intensified. I needed to hug him and smell his particular smell, to check he was all right, and see that he was being well looked after.

I dressed quietly and slipped out of the house when Stacey was on an errand, waiting nervously at the bus stop, hoping she wouldn't come back early and find me there. I was reminded of when I took the bus to the circus, how I had wished Dad would see me and pull me back to the safety of Braër. I looked up at the house. It didn't feel so safe now.

The bus took a slow, circuitous route, winding through country lanes I had never been down before. Throughout the journey, I held onto the pink feather, running it through my anxious fingers until it lost its silky feel. My head pounded, radiating out from the stitches on the top of my scalp, pulsing through me until my whole body ached.

Was Stacey home by now: had she discovered I was gone? Let her worry, I thought savagely. A part of me hoped she would find the pillows wedged under my duvet, plumper than the real shape of my body. A part of me quailed at the thought of her anger on my return.

As the bus continued onwards, I thought about the day Dad and I got hurt.

It's strange, but I don't remember the blood or the violence or the pain. I don't even remember the man that touched me.

I remember green oak leaves floating silently down. I remember huge, velvet paws padding away. And I remember Dad's fingers tenderly stripping the stalks off the reeds, the pieces sighing to the ground, where they stayed, like a trail marking where we had been.

Perhaps silence was what my father had craved when he hurt himself on that wall: a reprieve from the constant twisted assault of memories in his mind.

Eventually, the bus dropped me off at the end of a long driveway, and I began to trudge between the leafy hedges. The stillness and silence suited my mood, and I wanted only to continue walking here forever, knowing as I did that each step was taking me closer to my dad.

I stopped walking. Briar View loomed ahead of me. My first impressions were of a sad, tired place. It looked like the house of someone quite grand who had passed away. It was vacuous and yawning. All the windows and doors were closed, and yet a smell – something between the brine of tinned tuna and the grease that coats old carpets – leeched out from between the bricks. Its smell seemed to diminish the hope that had sprung up in me on the bus journey here, and I wondered for a brief moment if my mother lived in a similar building; if that was why she was so unhappy.

I tucked the feather away and looked up to the first floor where Dad resided. The windows glinted darkly in the sun. Here and there I could see the snowy heads of patients sitting within. It looked as if to live at Briar View you must be grey-haired. I started walking up the ugly concrete steps.

A care worker showed me to a large day room with a selection of white-headed men in it. I recognised two that I had seen from outside, sitting in wipe-clean chairs near the large windows, their hands occupied with knitting, the sharp needles sitting lifeless in their loose grip.

I looked for my dad, searching out his salt-and-pepper hair in a sea of white. He wasn't there. I turned to the carer, and he pointed out a man sitting regally in a chair in the corner. I blinked. It was Dad. He sat proudly, his back a little straighter than the others, his chin a little higher. His hair was almost completely white.

A chair had been left for me. I walked over to him, unable to take my eyes off his hair. His face was paler than I remembered too. He had lost that ruddy glow, his skin taking on a damp pall instead. Someone had shaved him badly, missing a patch of stubble on his upper lip and nicking his chin. His cheeks looked virginal in their whiteness. I wondered if they had given him a tablet to change the colour of his hair so that he might feel more at home amongst the white-haired men.

Because that was the sad thing; he *did* look like everyone else in there. I looked around the silent room. They all had the same look in their eyes; a look that made you realise they could see things you couldn't, a common shared film playing in all of their heads. It was such a good film that one or two of the patients' jaws hung open, saliva pooling behind their bottom lip, occasionally spilling over onto their chins and their necks and the grey bibs that they all wore.

I sat down in front of Dad, thankful at least that he didn't have a heap of knitting in his lap.

'Hi,' I whispered, leaning forward so that my chair creaked. He looked up sharply at the sound, and I knew today was a day of fog. A gleam of sunlight caught the wound on his temple. The dressing had been taken off, and the newly formed scar tissue glowed red and concave through his grizzled hair, as if a slice of his head had been scooped out.

His eyes sought mine for a moment before settling on something just to the right of my face, near my ear. I moved slightly, willing him to look at me again, but his eyes dropped downwards, breaking the spell, and I let out a breath of frustration.

Gazing round the room, I took in the wheelchairs, the oxygen cylinders. I let the tinny sound of Glen Miller wash over me as an orderly fiddled with a CD player. A man in the corner was sitting in a chair, his overlarge skull in his hands. A nurse crouched by him, supporting him as he rocked backward and forwards.

With sudden inspiration, I pulled Monty's bell from my pocket and, leaning forward, placed it in Dad's lap. His breath rattled in his throat, inflating his cheeks as he lifted an overlarge hand and let it rest precisely over the bell. It chimed quietly beneath the skin of his palm. He jumped imperceptibly and looked up suddenly, almost lucidly at me.

'Romilly?' he said, his voice unsure. His breath quickened, little flecks of snot shooting from his nostrils, his eyes flashing from left to right, from the bell to my face.

I smiled and opened my mouth to speak, but before I could say anything, he stood quickly. His body unwound, his shrunken frame expanding, growing upwards, no longer cramped by the clinical armchair. He towered over me, his head whipping one way then another like a bear disturbed in hibernation. The wound on his head flashed like a beacon, and then a huge bellow erupted from the bottom of his lungs, his eyes rolling backwards, and his arms began to lift and swipe at the air. I jumped back in my chair, staring up in horror. Workers came running over, white-aproned and mechanical in their movements. They calmly pulled him down into his chair, where he sat, moaning to himself, little breaths of air puffing from his nostrils.

I stood up shakily, watching as the nurses worked their magic, stroking his leathery hands until the trembling began to slow.

'I think I ought...' I whispered lamely, pointing to the door, but no one turned to me. No one cared. I walked quickly across the room, my heart beating fast. At the door I looked back. My father was sitting in his chair. He looked at peace, almost as if it had never happened. He mouthed something as he stared at the wall. I turned to go.

As I walked back along the driveway, I imagined the tall hedges drawing together behind me, Briar View disappearing behind them like some mystical fairy tale tower, holding my poor broken dad captive.

It wasn't until I was halfway home, sitting on the bus, lost in thought, that I realised I hadn't picked up the bell. I scanned my memory for it, trying to remember it falling onto the floor, but all I could see as I thought back to that room was my father's great yellowing hand closing over it, and the sad echo of its chime as it was swallowed beneath his skin.

Thirty-Five

At the beginning of August, I was woken by the slow whir of Dad's carved box kicking into life.

I struggled to surface from sleep, trying to understand how a year could have gone past already when I had no memory of autumn or Christmas or spring.

'Is it broken?' Stacey said, stretching next to me. She had taken to watching me fall asleep each night. Often I would wake in the morning and she was still there, propped up on one arm, her eyes travelling over the shape of my body under the sheet.

'I don't know,' I said. The ticking was deeper than when it had last ticked, two months ago on my sixteenth birthday; the day of the attack. I lifted the box into my lap and sat, watching it warily. Perhaps it was beginning to go wrong, just like Dad's brain.

'What do you think it will be this time?' Stacey asked in excitement. She had never seen it open before.

I looked at her, curled up next to me, and shrugged. I could feel her body heat radiating towards me.

We took the box, still ticking, to the lake with us. The grass within the circle of trees had grown and collapsed with its own weight, forming clumps of golden hay. There was a hum in the little glade, a cacophony of heat and insects and dragonflies dancing over the water.

The box's ticking felt quieter outside, as if it were listening beneath the chirrups of birds for a less complex language it could understand.

After our first, freezing swim, I walked around the edge of the lake, my hands brushing the velvet bulrushes that ringed the water as I watched Stacey collecting flowers for our potion.

'Do you think we'll do this every year?' I asked, indicating the swirl of petal-water in the jar.

'You mean, when we're a hundred?' Stacey said, and we giggled at the thought of us both, naked and wrinkly, descending into the lake with wildflower-water on our wrists.

Stacey stretched out on the grass and dipped her toes into the water. I was beginning to get used to the curve of her bare skin now, but my eyes were still drawn to the buttery shadows beneath her breasts and the gentle swell of her stomach.

'I'm so glad we have this time,' she said, 'just the two of us. It feels special, doesn't it? Important.'

I nodded, looking out at the lake, at the damselflies flitting over its surface. 'It's a shame it can't last forever,' I said.

Stacey turned her head. The sun shone straight into her eyes so that all I could see was a reflection of blue. 'But it could,' she said. 'There's no reason we can't carry on like this. We don't need anyone, else Romilly, we have each other.' She reached over and touched my hand. 'It's like we're linked somehow,' she whispered, 'like twins.'

Next to us, the box's tick was a metronome, providing rhythm to her voice. I lay back on the grass, staring at the sky, trying to unpick the meaning in her words.

The box continued to tick, dictating the soporific rhythm of the day.

'Do you ever think what it would be like to drown?' she asked suddenly.

I turned my head so that I could see the line of her eyelashes against the sky. 'Not much fun, I shouldn't think.'

She picked a thick blade of grass, and held it above her to block out the sun, pressing it into the pad of her thumb.

'You'd think it would be easy to swim up to the sunlight,' she said, 'to kick at the weeds and escape.' She swiped the sharp edge of the grass across her thumb, and the skin parted. Bright red blood bloomed around the stalk. She put the cut to her lips.

'Death is just veiled from view,' she said, turning to me, her lips crimson. She touched her thumb to my mouth too, and without thinking I leant forward and pressed my lips to hers.

We had forgotten the box. In the loud silence, I sat up. The mechanism had wound down. Right at the centre, where the top came to a smoothly curved peak, a circle of wood had swung open. I dipped my finger into the waiting hole. Cold links of metal tickled my skin, fine as gossamer. I pulled out a golden chain with a locket dangling from it.

'If that's not treasure, I don't know what is,' Stacey said, a trace of jealousy in her voice.

The locket was tiny, and my fingers stumbled over the catch. It swung open with a delicate click. Inside, a pale blue flower was set behind a sliver of glass.

'It's the forget-me-not,' I said, thinking of Bea, of her kindness and friendship, her welcoming acceptance of me after so many years.

My breath misted the locket so that the flower was hidden for a moment, and as the fogged glass caught the light, I thought I could see vestiges of Dad's fingerprint on it, but then the moisture cleared and it was gone.

It struck me that the box might not be broken – perhaps Dad had set it deliberately to open now because he knew I would need him. But how could he have known?

'Let me put it on for you,' Stacey said, taking it and lifting my hair so that she could hang it around my neck. I looked down at the little locket resting on my bare skin.

'It's beautiful,' she said, replacing my hair.

We got dressed slowly, separately, and began the walk back to the house in silence. Stacey reached for my hand and we walked, deep in thought, our shoulders brushing occasionally, our fingers linked.

Braër was bathed in sunlight as we approached from the road, but as we entered the garden, the sun was cut off immediately by the house. We stood in the shade, looking at the house's towering walls, at the opaque depths of the moat. I thought of the dark rooms inside, so like my dreams of Dad's box, and I shivered, the locket cold on my skin.

Down on the edge of the moat, almost submerged by the water, a snippet of blue flashed at me. I stooped to look. It was the last of the summer's forget-me-nots, a tiny pinprick of bright blue in the dark shadow of Braër. I turned to point it out to Stacey, feeling the ghost of her fingers slip in mine, but she was already walking away from the house, down towards the meadow and into the sunshine.

In early autumn I woke up late and wandered downstairs to find Stacey cleaning out the pantry. Jars and bottles were cluttered on the kitchen table, rusty lids and faded labels written in a hand I didn't recognise.

'I don't think those are very fresh,' I said.

'Thank God. I wasn't looking forward to a lunch consisting entirely of vinegared produce,' she said, spearing a piece of pickled beetroot with a fork and wrinkling her nose at it. 'Fancy a cuppa?'

I nodded, and she busied herself in the kitchen, making a fuss of taking out my tea-set and warming the pot. I would have been perfectly happy with teabags plonked in mugs, I thought. I caught sight of a jar of pickled eggs, and I was instantly transported back to the village pub, that night, a lifetime ago, when Dad had tripped and fallen drunkenly on the way home, spilling the bucket of collection money as if it was water. Looking back, it was so easy to see the illness grabbing hold of him, even then. I thought of him as I had last seen him in the care home, and gulped down the shame I felt at having left him there, alone.

'I know you went to see your dad,' Stacey said idly, as if she could read my mind. She was rubbing a tea-towel over a cup again and again, not meeting my eyes. 'Just after I came back. I know.'

'I am allowed to. He's my dad.'

'Did it go well?'

I looked up at her. She was still polishing the cup, running the tea-towel over and over the same spot.

'Thought not,' she said, 'you would have told me if it had gone OK.' She placed the cup on its saucer and poured an arc of tea into it. 'Did it feel good, upsetting him?'

A charge of electricity passed through the room, making the bare bulb in the ceiling flare noisily for a moment.

'That's not fair,' I said.

'What's not fair? He might have thought you were your twin sister, back from the dead, poor man.' She poured milk into the cups and took a sip from hers, pushing mine across the table. 'You should listen to me next time.'

'I needed to see him, Stacey. To check he was all right.'

'And was he?'

I thought back to Dad's cavernous eye sockets, his strikingly white hair. I remembered him standing over me, his eyes thrown back into his skull so that only the whites showed.

'He's never coming home,' Stacey said, 'you might as well try and forget him.'

The light bulb began buzzing above us, like an angry wasp. 'Why is it doing that?' I said.

'Why does anything in this broken old house ever do anything?' she said. She took a sip from her cup, draining it. 'I don't think you should go and see him again,' she added, putting her cup down, 'at least, not without me.'

'Fine,' I said, squeezing my teacup so tight in my hand I could hear the porcelain groan.

The bulb above us exploded, showering us with fragments of glass.

As the cold autumn nights drew in, Stacey haunted the downstairs rooms of Braër as if she owned them. I stopped on the threshold of each room before entering, trying to sense her presence on the other side of the door. Often she would sit in silence, waiting for me like a spider waiting for its prey, and I began instead to light the little fire in my bedroom, preferring to stay high up on the second floor rather than spend time in her company.

On a particularly chilly November night, Monty and I sat in my bedroom, leaning close to the fire's glow, shivering until the flames took hold. The damp smoke twisted past me up the chimney, and my stomach growled with hunger, remembering the smoky taste of baked potatoes cooked on the bonfire when we were children.

Monty stretched his long body out by the hearth, preening himself, his loosened hairs dancing across the room. I sat down at my desk and opened up *Windmill*, desperate to feel the spark of happiness that Dad's pictures used to rouse in me. The phone was on the window sill next to me. I looked at it for a long moment, my hand hovering over it, daring myself to pick it up. But who would I call? I thought. Who would care?

A step on my staircase creaked, and I pulled my hand away from the phone and pretended to be reading the book. Stacey climbed through the little door, not bothering to knock. She looked around the room, taking in the books spread out on my desk and Dad's box on the window sill. She walked over to it and picked it up, idly running her fingers over its knots and burrs.

'It seems so long ago that we used to hunt for the treasure,' she said, 'something little children do. I wonder if it'll open again?' She put it to her ear and shook it hard before dropping it back on the window sill.

She went to sit cross-legged on the bed and began picking at the skin around her fingernails. There was a vase of late roses on the bedside table that I had cut yesterday. They were a dusky pink, veined like butterflies' wings, just like the ones that wove through every page of Dad's last book. Stacey reached over and swirled them lazily with her hand, then she took a petal between her finger and thumb and squeezed it so that its moisture spread, darkening to a deep red.

'Stacey, don't, I just cut them.'

The liquid, dark as blood, dripped down the flower's stem. I couldn't take my eyes off it.

She chuckled. 'You're so easy to scare, Romilly.'

She stood and went over to my dressing table where I kept all my candles. Choosing one at random, she took it to the fire and lit the wick in the flames, then she set the candle down on the hearth.

'Come here,' she said.

'Why?' A thrill of fear passed through me. I looked at the candle, flickering in the ashes.

'Just do it.' Her voice was commanding, and I went over and knelt next to her.

'Give me your hand.'

'Stacey, please,' I said, feeling a familiar swooping sensation in my bladder not borne since childhood.

'We're best friends, aren't we?' she said. 'And best friends seal their friendship with something that will last forever. Look, I'll do it first.' She placed her hand over the flame.

The thought of the flame touching her skin sickened me, and I lifted my gaze to her face, searching her expression for any sign of pain, but it remained impassive. Seconds ticked by and still she held her hand over the candle.

And then, a smell began to rise from her hand, accompanied by a wisp of twisting smoke. It was the unmistakable stench of burning meat. There were pinpricks of red on Stacey's cheeks now. She was holding her breath, fighting the pain, her eyes glassy as the smell enveloped the room.

'Stacey, stop it,' I whispered, mesmerised, unable to move.

Finally she pulled her hand away, exhaling in a gasp and shaking her hand in the air to quell the pain.

'Your turn,' she said, and she reached out her unhurt hand to me.

'Stacey, I...'

'I did it,' she said softly.

And as if I was hypnotised, I held out my hand.

She took it, lovingly caressing the lines of my palm. Then she turned it over, stroking the back where the fine hairs had risen in panic.

Gently, she pulled it over the flame, and trustingly, I let her.

At first it felt warm, like holding a cup of tea, but then the flickering flame found the centre of my hand, and stayed there, pulsing violently upwards, forcing its heat through my skin.

'Stacey,' I said.

The pain was hot and sweet, as if it were worming its way through me, bypassing bone and muscle, finding only soft fat and flesh to dissolve. I was vaguely aware of Stacey holding it in place, squeezing my fingers.

'Stacey, it's hurting, please.' I tried to pull my hand away, twisting my body this way and that, but she held on, her own hands shaking now.

The room was flashing, great white-hot bursts obscuring everything but the guttering candle in front of us. I realised that she had let go of my hand. I pulled it towards me, cupping it gently in the crook of my elbow. My palm was red and raw. Already, liquid was pooling in a blister at the centre. Fire was spreading up my arm, pulsing through my body like a heartbeat.

I collapsed onto the floor, my cheek hitting the hearth, a puff of ash erupting around me.

Stacey was kneeling by my side, the vase of roses between us. She held the sharp stems, and trickled the water onto my upturned palm.

In the eaves, deathwatch beetles tapped, and starlings chattered, unaware of the violence unfolding within.

Thirty-Six

The fire flickered on the drawing room walls, and Monty purred on my lap, my bandaged hand catching on his bony spine as I stroked him. *Romilly and the Kitten* was open on the velvet sofa next to me, and I gazed into the eyes of my namesake, rubbing the cat's fur between my fingers reflexively like a comfort blanket.

A day had passed since Stacey held my hand over the candle, but still the pain pounded ferociously like a heartbeat along my arm. I stared at the book, concentrating on the paintings, trying to blank it out.

I cupped Monty's neck in my hand, feeling for the purr in his throat. It vibrated against my finger. I pressed harder. Monty's head twitched, as if he were trying to shake me off, but he stayed put, trust in his eyes.

The cat's throat felt delicate beneath my fingers, as if I could push deep into it, breaking the skin apart like paper. I pressed again, the thrill of danger mounting as my finger found the tiny bones and cartilage beneath. His throat made a gagging sound, and he struggled, trying to escape. Horrified with myself, my heart pounding, I let go, then grabbed him and held him close to me, kissing his head and whispering to him, closing my eyes to the images in the book, my fingers far, far away from his silent, bruised neck.

Far away at the other end of the house, there was a knock at the door. I heard Stacey's feet running down the hall before I saw her. She came to the threshold and stopped.

'It's someone official. She has one of those ID cards round her neck.'

'What do you think she wants?' I had jumped up as soon as I heard the door. 'What if she wants to take me into care?' We were whispering.

'We can pretend your mum's just gone out for a walk. Isn't that who the doctor thinks you're with?'

I nodded.

'Go and let her in. I'll get the kitchen set up.'

But as I turned to walk to the door, her hand shot out, gripping my arm. 'We don't need any help,' she said, 'we agree on that, don't we?'

I balked at the blackness of her eyes.

Her grip tightened on my skin. 'We need to stay together, Romilly, that's the only way we'll survive.'

I nodded.

'Go!' she wafted her hands at me, and I broke into a run, pausing as I reached the back door to tuck my hair behind my ears and check my face in the mirror for smudges.

The woman knocked again. I could see the top of her head through the frosted glass, trying to stand on tiptoe to look through. I opened the door.

'Oh, hello. You kept me waiting! You must be Romilly.'

I nodded.

'My name's Barbara. I'm from social services.'

We stood opposite each other, taking each other in. I held the door half closed. I could feel my heart pounding in my chest.

'Do you think I could come in? Perhaps have a glass of water?'

'Of course.' I fixed a smile on my face and pulled the door open.

'What an interesting house,' she said as she pulled the heel of her shoe out of a rotten plank and stepped inside. 'Is your mother at home?'

'No. She's gone out for a walk.'

'Will she be long?'

'I don't know. Probably.'

I steered the woman towards the kitchen. Stacey had laid out two teacups.

'We were having tea, and she likes to go out after a cuppa,' I said, nodding at the tea-set on the table. Stacey had managed to print a lipstick mark onto one of the cups. I was impressed. I saw the woman glance at it as I poured her a glass of water.

'Shall we go and sit in the drawing room? That's where my mum always takes the guests.'

We trooped along the hallway. I couldn't see Stacey. I thought I could hear quiet sniggering coming from upstairs: she was probably hiding on the landing, listening hard.

A fresh log had been added to the fire and a vase of pink roses had appeared on the coffee table. They smelt cloyingly sweet as we entered the room, mingling with the woodsmoke, a sour edge to them as if they were just beginning to turn. A pale petal had got stuck to the curve of the glass. Sunlight shone through it, shooting a lick of pink across the table towards me.

The social worker sat down on the sofa and I put her glass on the table and sat opposite her on an old wooden chair that Stacey must have put there for that purpose. It was so hard I could feel a pulse flick nervously across my buttocks and up my spine.

'I'm just here to check everything's OK with your mum and you after your father went into the care home. It must have been hard for you both.' She leant forward and took a sip of the water, leaving a lipstick mark on the glass.

'Your lipstick's similar to my mum's,' I said.

'Oh! Yes. It's a nice colour. This one's a bit cheap though, you have to keep reapplying it, it comes off on everything.' She laughed, a tinkling giggle that sounded a little nervous. 'Does your mum find the same?'

I nodded, adding, 'I don't know when she'll be back. She loves going for walks, especially in autumn. It's the leaves, she loves the colours of the leaves. She could be gone for hours.' I closed my mouth.

'That's fine. It means we can have a good natter.' She smiled. There was lipstick on her teeth. I licked my own teeth automatically.

'Is there anything you'd like to begin with?' she said, pulling out a clipboard.

She looked so normal and nice. The burn on my hand pulsed painfully, and I thought of all the things I could tell her: I thought about the candle flame eating into my skin, the possessive gleam in Stacey's eyes. I thought about how cold and hungry I always was. Last night I had looked at myself in the mirror when I got undressed. My ribs were so close to the surface now that I could dig my fingers underneath them. If I pressed hard enough, I wondered, would they snap, one by one, sending me falling to the floor like a puppet with its strings cut?

Just one word from me, and everything could change. Hot meals. Warm baths, kind people. Someone to hold me as I cried. Fresh sheets on a fresh bed. Care and warmth and the satisfaction of feeling full.

The social worker stayed silent. She was practised at this. I opened my mouth and looked up.

Stacey was standing in the hall by the door, out of sight of the social worker. She was staring at me, no trace of a smile on her face.

The fire crackled behind me, giving out little warmth.

'How did you hurt your hand?' the social worker said suddenly.

I glanced down at the bandage. 'I burnt myself on the oven.'

'Sometimes we do things to help relieve the pain we feel inside.

Sometimes by feeling pain on the outside, we forget about the pain inside. Do you think it was that kind of burn?'

'I burnt myself on the oven.'

'OK.'

I stared at the flowers. The edges of the petals were crisp as if they were beginning to die before my eyes.

'It must have been hard, seeing your father go into a home. And it must be strange, just you and your mum on your own now. How are you coping with the treasure seekers? I've heard a lot about them. Do they still come?'

'They don't bother us much,' I said. 'Not since they realised there isn't any treasure. They hung around for a bit before Dad went into care and the story was leaked about the attack, but they left as soon as they realised they weren't going to get anything new.'

'It must be hard, having to deal with that on top of everything else.'

I shrugged, picking at the edge of the table. I thought of the reeds that Dad had dropped on our last walk, leaving a trail behind us, and I wanted all of a sudden to retrace that trail, follow it back to before the books began, before everything started to go wrong.

The pink reflection of the petal had moved. It was stretching towards me on the table. I leant forward and placed my finger at its tip, noticing how long my fingernails were now. I had a feeling the social worker was watching me, examining me, trying to penetrate inside my skull with her stare.

'You're doing a grand job, Romilly,' she said at last.

'Am I?'

'What I see before me is a young woman who has suffered terrible losses in her life, and has had to live them out in the public eye. But on the whole you look like you're coping admirably.' She smiled at me. 'I will need to speak with your mother. Can you get her to give me a call, and we can arrange another time to meet?' She ripped a piece of paper from her clipboard and handed it to me.

At the door she turned to me, giving me the same searching look.

'Try to eat a bit more,' she said. 'I'm a great fan of your books. But you look a lot skinnier in real life.'

When she had gone, I shut the door firmly and waited for Stacey to appear. As soon as we heard her car start up and drive away, she dissolved into giggles.

I smiled. 'That was scary,' I said, clutching my chest.

'You're a good actress, you could make a career out of it.'

'The lipstick was genius. Where did you get it?'

'In the bathroom cabinet. Maybe it really did belong to your mum.'

'And the flowers were good too.'

'Weren't they? I took them from your bedroom, I hope you don't mind. They're at that perfect point between life and death, just as if your dear darling mother had bought them for you to cheer you up a few days ago.'

I stopped laughing abruptly, thinking of the roses I had given my mum when she came to stay all that time ago; the way she had dumped them unceremoniously on the compost heap.

'And then there were two!' Stacey was singing, looking in the mirror and applying lipstick with inexpert precision. 'Hello, dear Romilly, I'm your long-lost mummy. Give us a kiss!' She planted her lips on my cheek, smearing the make-up over my skin.

'Get off.' I pushed her away and walked down the hallway.

'Where are you going?'

But I didn't answer. Rubbing at the lipstick on my cheek, I pulled the back door open, and slammed it behind me, wanting to be anywhere that Stacey was not.

I walked on my own far from home, over the steps, across the bridge and onto the marsh. Pulling the bandage off my hand, I let the chill autumn air get to the wound, examining the blister as I went. It was yellow and bulbous, like a strange, round pebble. It seemed separate to my hand, as if I had placed it in my palm and could drop it any time I wanted. I prodded it gently and winced.

I thought of the social worker, and what she might be doing now. Probably writing up a report on how well the famous Romilly Kemp had turned out despite such trying circumstances.

I looked up. A skylark had risen nearby, and was singing high above me, a tiny dot in the blue. Far across the water meadows, a white van pulled up haphazardly, and two people got out. I stopped walking, feeling vulnerable on the flat stretch of land, the tiny bird hovering above me like a sentry. One of the people was scanning the marshland through a pair of binoculars. As I looked, she lifted her hand and pointed at me. At the same time, the other person raised something long and black, lifting it to his shoulder.

It was a rifle.

I dropped to the ground, my heart racing, a clump of sedge jabbing me in the face. The skylark continued to sing, oblivious.

Who were they? I lay as still as possible, hidden in the tall grass, my nose inches from the ground. I could hear their voices now, far off, drifting towards me across the grassland.

And then I sensed it rather than saw it, behind me, dark and looming, padding across the marshy grass.

The panther.

I turned my head a fraction. He was huge, his lithe body well-muscled from living in the wild for so long. Close up, his coat was threadbare like worn velvet, white hairs sprouting here and there, pocking its surface.

He was ambling through the marsh, dipping his huge head to sniff calmly at the ground.

He hadn't seen me.

One of his ears was torn, flapping gently as he walked. I stayed as still as I could, holding my breath. I could see the luminous blue-grey of his eyes now. He blinked sleepily. And then his head shot up, his ears swivelling, looking in the direction of the two people across the marsh.

A shot rang out, the crack of sound reverberating across the field. The panther lurched sideways, his ears flat to his head. And then he sprang up and suddenly he was rushing blindly at me, running at full pelt, his jaws gaping as he roared in pain. Desperately, I tried to scramble out of the way, but my limbs were frozen as if time had slowed. Bunching his muscles together, he leaped, soaring over my head. For a moment his black belly stretched above me, so close I could have reached up and touched it, and then he was gone.

I collapsed back into the sedge, gathering myself, trying to quieten my breathing, and then I peered over the grass.

The panther had not got far. He was a little way away, weaving drunkenly in a way that reminded me of my beloved three-legged Monty. I could see something sticking out of his thigh, and I understood: he had been tranquilised.

I stood up and crept forward. The people were in the distance, crossing the field too. When they saw me, they stopped and shouted, waving their arms at me, but I strode on.

The panther had stopped walking now. He was panting, his head and tail low to the ground. I crept forward slowly. As I reached him, his back legs gave way, and he sank down, collapsing onto the ground, a plaintive roar echoing from deep inside his chest. He looked so out of place, lying in the middle of an English water meadow, and I swallowed back a gulp of surprised laughter.

I crouched by his head and tentatively reached out a hand, my breath catching in my throat as my fingers came into contact with his fur. I stroked him gingerly, aware of the huge teeth below the peeled back lips. I could feel the hardness of his broad skull beneath the fur. His skin felt so fragile, so old.

'It's OK,' I whispered, my voice catching in my throat, 'it's OK.'

He was so still, so watchful. His eye stared up at me. Close up it was a clear, liquid blue, full of a familiar intelligence, as if I had known him forever.

But, of course, I had known him, I thought. Hadn't he been there in some form, whenever I was in need? Hadn't he kept me company in my darkest moments, while I waited for help to come?

The people came skidding to a stop, breathless from running.

'What on earth are you doing?' the man said, laying the tranquiliser gun down and quickly securing the panther's legs together.

'You... you can see him?'

'Of course we can see him, he's a bloody huge panther.' The man looked at me strangely as he tied the cat's paws jerkily, pulling at them roughly to check they were secure.

'Be careful with him,' I said, 'he's so old.'

The panther's eyes were unseeing now, his mouth slack as if he were mid roar. He looked so sad. I cradled his soft, grand head, dropping a kiss on his torn ear.

'It's OK,' the woman said, crouching next to me. 'He'll be all right. We know what we're doing, I promise.' She gently prised my hands from him, and the man pulled a muzzle over his head, pulling it tight so that the straps bit into his skin. It was the final insult: he looked so dejected, trussed up and still.

'What will you do with him?'

'He'll go to a zoo. He'll want for nothing.'

'But he won't be free.'

'No, he won't. But he'll be safe and looked after. He's elusive, this one. We've been hearing about him for years.'

Between them they lifted the lifeless body into a cage and carried him back to the van. I stayed, crouched on the ground, my hand stroking the imprint of the panther's body, the empty tranquiliser dart discarded on the ground next to me.

That night, despite the first frosts outside, my bedroom felt claustrophobically hot. Stacey and I lay without clothes, the thinnest sheet over our bodies.

With a flick of her wrists, Stacey lifted the sheet above us, the cotton billowing in a huge arc and floating down gently onto our skin. As it fell, I caught a glimpse of our bodies lying together: the hills and valleys of Stacey's warm skin, her dark pubic hair rooted and twisted like vines in a musky woodland. I turned to look at her, and saw she was looking at my body in the same way. She took my hand in hers as the cold sheet came to rest over us like a coating of frost. We lay in the middle of the huge bed, facing each other, our foreheads touching.

'All these years I dreamt of this,' she whispered. 'We're so lucky, to have each other.'

I squeezed my eyes closed, and felt a fat, oily tear run down my nose onto the pillow.

'Why are you crying?'

'I don't know,' I said in a small voice. I laced my fingers deeper into hers under the sheet. 'Everything is changing,' I whispered, my voice breaking as the words left my lips.

'No it's not, it's staying the same,' she said. 'All our memories are here, watching over us, keeping us safe.' She sighed and turned to look up at the cavernous ceiling. 'I've always wanted to live here,' she said, 'in this house, in this bed. And now I do. With you.'

I pulled the sheet up under my chin, suddenly cold. She had always understood me, but it felt as if that link, that connection, were loosening. It was coming unstitched as surely as the edges of the old, frayed sheet around us.

I closed my eyes and felt the memory of the panther's soft fur under my fingers, his poor torn ear against my lips.

Stacey lifted her hand and wiped my tears away with her thumb.

'You'll get through this,' she said, pushing a half empty bottle of pink liquid into my hand. It had my father's name on the label. I put it to my lips. It tasted of cough mixture. A warmth spread from my shoulders down to my stomach, and I shivered and stopped crying. We passed the bottle between us, Stacey taking little sips that stained her full, ripe lips, while I dozed fitfully, my eyes fixed on her softly sucking mouth.

'I'll look after you,' she said, exhaling the words, her breath whispering over me like perfume.

I sipped at it greedily.

Thirty-Seven

In late December, the snow came. The small amount of traffic that passed by Braër's windows stopped altogether, and drifts of snow banked up against the house, muffling the outside world.

I rarely saw Stacey. I don't know where she went during the time of snow. Her mother might have needed her at home, or perhaps she was hidden away in one of Braër's many rooms, avoiding me. I wondered if she was sorry for burning my hand; if at last she had understood how much pain she'd caused me.

One chill evening, when the snow outside was covered in crystals of sparkling ice, I went to check on the fire before going to bed. I stopped in the doorway. Dad's old chess board had appeared in the drawing room, set ready for a game. I gazed at the black and white squares for a moment, then I sank down onto the rug and lifted a pawn.

We played, Stacey and I, just as Dad and I used to – never together. Each time I came into the room she had made a move, and so I countered it with my own. At first it was comforting, reminding me of games with my dad, but as the game went on I began to feel that there was something else to this contest; its result would have consequences that reached much further than the confines of the house.

And outside, the snow continued to fall.

I liked the snow, it felt as if the world had stopped. Somewhere out there, I thought, Dad was sitting propped up in his wipe-clean chair, frozen in time, a dewdrop turning to an icicle at the end of his nose. Somewhere far away, my mother was wrapped in a stiffly frozen jumper, her eyes staring out of a window at a different skyline. Only in Braër was there movement: chess pieces slowly playing out an important game, a cat slumbering next to a fire, a teenage girl walking from room to room, her misty breath preceding her.

On the day I took Stacey's king, the snow stopped. At the precise moment its crown hit the chequered board I felt a soft whoosh in my eardrums and I looked up to see stillness settling outside. It settled inside the house too. Dust that had been floating in the air landed. Dripping taps stopped. Even Monty's purrs dropped like frozen pebbles onto the floor.

'I've won,' I called out, but the house was silent.

On Christmas morning I was awoken for the second time by the unexpected tick of Dad's box. The house was freezing, and my breath clouded into the rafters as I scooped the duvet around me and walked to the window, shivering. Stacey hadn't slept in my bed for days, and I peeped through the curtains, wondering where she was.

The box's tick on the window sill was more melodious than when it had ticked for my sixteenth birthday. It was slower too, as if it was growing tired of having to work so hard. I pulled the curtains open properly. The world was obscured by swirls of ice, fractals distilling across the glass. I touched my fingertip to it, and the cold ran through the bones in my hand like a shock of electricity. I rubbed my finger and picked up the box, returning to bed.

I turned it over in my hands. It was smaller than I remembered. Less significant. Was this to be my only Christmas present? I tried to conjure the excitement I always felt when I first heard the tick, but it didn't come today. I looked at the box: it wasn't as pretty as

I remembered. It was gnarled and old. Dust had caught in the cracks and joints, and suddenly I didn't want it anywhere near me. I threw it across the room and it hit the wall. The ticking slowed and stopped.

We had no tree this year, but I had gone out and cut boughs of fir and ribbons of ivy, trailing them along the banisters and over the mantelpiece above the fire. I had found some fresh holly trembling with red berries, and I placed sprigs in jars all over the house, recalling something my father had once said about dwellings and holly and safety.

As I climbed carefully down my stairs, the duvet still wrapped around me, I paused to listen for Stacey. The house was cold, holding itself still as if any movement would crack the thin layer of frost that bound it together. Once downstairs I pulled on my trainers and stepped out into the garden.

Everything was white, but not the white of a Christmas card, an ethereal translucence that held onto echoes of the colours beneath. The moat had a layer of ice over it, thick enough to trap the fronds of pondweed so that it looked like a green willow pattern. I stood by its edge squinting my eyes, trying to read the future in its jacquard whirls. I put my foot tentatively on the ice. It creaked ominously, the first sound I had heard since the box's tick. It felt good to my ears.

I stopped at the remains of the beech tree on my way back inside. It was part of the garden now, sunk into the earth, overtaken by cables of bramble. And yet, as I crouched down and pulled at a piece of ice-coated wood, a whole world of teeming insects beneath it skittered away from the light. Heat emanated from the rotted trunk, rising into my nostrils in a vegetative waft, warming my hands against the chill of the frozen garden.

Back inside, I tiptoed down the hallway. In winters past we had barricaded ourselves in the snug, the little space getting warm quickly, but now the room felt synonymous with Dad's Christmas book, and the memory of him telling me he was ill. The door remained firmly shut. I crossed instead to the drawing room and knelt to light the fire. It was still smouldering from last night, wisps of smoke curling into the chimney.

'Merry Christmas.' The melancholy of her voice belied the words she had spoken, and my heart sank. This was how it had been for weeks on the rare occasions we saw each other: the first words she spoke would set the mood for the day. Today was to be restive, I could feel it already.

She was sitting by the window, the cat on her lap, one hand encircling his throat. There was something threatening in the way she did it, a sign of ownership; of power over him, and with a wash of guilt it reminded me that I had done the same, the day the social worker came to visit.

Monty began wriggling beneath her grip, and at last she let him go. He jumped down, skidding under the sofa and peering out, his eyes huge.

Stacey lifted a hand and trailed her finger over the ferns of ice on the glass. The warmth of her skin melted a line through them, patterns and zigzags blooming within the swirls.

'Are you Jack Frost now?' I said, trying to keep my voice light. It was Christmas, after all. She didn't answer, her finger continuing to spiral. 'You can ignore me if you want, but you'll have to talk to me eventually, you always do.'

'Did you open your dad's box?' she said.

'How did you know it was ticking?'

'I was watching you. When you slept.' She looked at me for the first time, and smiled. A small, secretive smile. Something about her eyes was different. They were darker, more reticent.

'I threw it against the wall,' I said, thinking of the little box, forlorn and broken on the bedroom floor. 'It stopped ticking.'

'What would your dad think of that?' her voice was low, without cadence or emotion.

We sat in the room, an uncomfortable silence growing between us.

The fire was catching, and I knelt back and let the crackle of flames warm my frozen fingers. 'Let's call a truce,' I said. 'Please, Stacey. It's Christmas Day. Let's go for a walk later. We could visit the lake like we used to.' I got to my feet.

Stacey stood up from the window seat and came over, stopping millimetres from me. I could feel her breath on my skin, threateningly close. She reached for the locket around my neck, and I tried not to flinch as she eased it open and looked at the flower within, a trace of a smile raising the corners of her mouth.

'He was always ingenious, your dad,' she said.

Up close, her eyes were even darker. They had a density about them, like coal before it turns to ash, and I had a sudden urge to pull us both outside, to let the sun penetrate her eyes so that I could check it was really her.

Instead, I looked down at the little flower at my neck. The colour had leached out of the petals over the past few months, and it was pale and ghostly as if it had shed its bright summer clothes and dressed instead for winter.

She snapped the locket shut, making me jump, and dropped it so that it knocked against my collarbone, then she settled onto the sofa. And it was then, almost imperceptibly, that I heard it: quiet at first, like the familiarity of my own breathing; a ticking, pulsing gently through the house.

'Can you hear that noise?' I asked. I looked around the room, searching for its source. It was like the ticking of my box, but softer, less like clockwork. I went to the window, rubbing my hand against the glass to remove the ice.

'What noise?' Stacey said.

'The ticking.'

'What ticking? I can't hear anything.'

'Can you really not hear it? Listen.'

We both stilled, ears straining. It wasn't loud, but it was insistent. I spun around on the spot, trying to imagine the sound, to make it solid. It wasn't the familiar sound my box made, this was a different tick. More of a thump, a beat.

A beat.

I put my hand to my chest, and I could feel it, deep inside me. I tried to slow my breathing, to listen to its rhythm, but the blood was rushing in my ears and pounding through my arteries.

'It's in your head, Romilly,' Stacey said in a bored voice. She hadn't moved off the sofa. She was looking at me coldly, as if I were an ugly exhibit in a museum.

The beat became louder, filling up my head. Stacey opened her mouth and spoke, but her voice was cancelled out by the clamour in my ears, and suddenly I couldn't breathe. My vision was filled with popping white stars, and there was a roaring in my ears, competing with the sinister pulsing beat that tore through me.

'Help me,' I whispered dizzily, and I sank down on the floor, touching my forehead to the cool of the floorboards.

Above me, Stacey's face appeared. Her skin was milk-white. She was staring at me. She said something, but I couldn't focus on her words. I clenched my fists, feeling the echo of the burn on my palm, and the pain of it made me focus. I looked at my hand. The remains of the blister were still there, encased in a thick rind, half scab, half new skin. The beat seemed to be coming from within it, rhythmic, like cogs whirring just beneath the surface. The scab was lifting at the edges, begging to be pulled.

I grabbed at the corner of it and, with gritted teeth, I yanked it away.

It ripped from my palm, new skin and all. The pain as it tore away obliterated the beat in my head, and I collapsed back onto the floor, my hand bloody.

The silence that followed was deathly.

I closed my eyes to the room, basking in the calm behind my eyelids. When I opened them, Stacey was standing over me still, eyes narrowed, as if she was seeing me for the first time.

'Why are you always trying to spoil things?' she said, her face pinched with vitriol, 'why do you always make everything about you? First the game of chess, and now this.' She crouched down and I flinched, but she only pushed my hair away from my face. 'Were you trying to scare me? To give me a taste of my own medicine?'

'I didn't mean—'

She grabbed my wrist and began to pull me up.

'What are you doing?' I said, scrabbling to stand upright.

'Your mother did the right thing, putting you in there.'

'In where?'

She had me by the forearm, one arm round my waist. She was half carrying, half dragging me out of the room. The last thing I saw as I stumbled over the threshold was Monty, his pupils huge, his normally sleek tail erect and bristling.

Stacey dragged me along the hallway. As we got to the kitchen, I grabbed onto the doorframe, the pain from my hurt hand almost whiting me out, but she prised my fingers from the wood and pulled me towards the pantry. She yanked open the door, shoving me towards it. I saw a flash of dark shelves, brown bottles and jam jars with gingham lids.

'Stacey, no!' In panic I scrabbled at her face with my free hand and I managed to grab a handful of her hair. For a second, her grip on me loosened a fraction, and in the gap between our flailing limbs I thought that I saw Stacey and myself through the kitchen window, young again, running down towards the mobiles.

I grabbed at her hair again and pulled. She made a noise halfway between pain and anger. We were teetering on the edge of the pantry now, both about to spill over into its dark mouth. Patches of Stacey's skin flitted in and out of my vision, clouds of her hair choked at my mouth. I could feel our bodies tipping, gravity pushing us both forward.

At the last minute, I spun my body as hard as I could, shoving her across the threshold, and I grasped the edge of the door and slammed it shut, the sound of falling bottles and breaking glass rising up from inside. I rammed the bolt home and took a step back, staring, horrified, at the door.

'What have I done?' I whispered, my hand to my mouth. Stacey's muted shouts strained through the cracks, accompanied by the pummelling of fists on wood. I backed away.

'What have I done?' I said to the empty room.

But there was no one left to answer.

Thirty-Eight

I paced across my bedroom. Even from up here I could hear her. There was a crash as more bottles and jars were sent smashing to the floor. Her voice ebbed and flowed through the house like a spring tide, bringing with it a jetsam of memories: Stacey, crushing the snails; Stacey telling ghost stories; Stacey, obsessed with the dead and the dying; Stacey, Stacey, Stacey. She was feelings and touches and scents remembered, and as I listened, the anger built inside me like a wall, prohibiting me from running down to let her out.

I waited until morning, listening as the screams finally died. Then the pleading started. The cajoling, the whimpering. As the weak sun began to rise over the distant fields, I tiptoed downstairs and put an ear to the pantry door, listening.

In the cold, dark silence, I thought I could hear breathing. Assured by the sound, I crept away.

That evening, I tiptoed back into the kitchen and knelt by the door. 'Stacey,' I whispered. 'Stacey, are you OK?'

A quiet breath, soft as air over teeth, drifted through the gap under the door.

'Help,' she said. 'Help me.'

I found an open tin of beans in the fridge.

Spoon by spoon I fed her, easing the jellied beans under the pantry door, taking the spoon back, licked clean.

'Let me out,' she whispered. 'Let me out, I promise I won't hurt you again.' A thin finger edged under the door, touching my foot and making me jump. The spoon clattered to the floor.

'I can't,' I whispered, backing away. This time I closed the kitchen door behind me too, and turned the key.

On the third day I was so hungry I crept outside and searched for windfalls in the garden, biting into their soft bellies and wincing at the squelch of rotten fruit against my teeth. I foraged for the seed potatoes I had discarded earlier in the year, old and rubbery, and piled them up, wondering how desperate I would need to be before I ate them.

By the fourth day, all was quiet. I sat with my back to the kitchen door, listening intently.

How long can a person survive without water? I remembered the bottle of vinegar I had drunk from, all those years ago. When you're desperate, everything looks like water. I imagined Stacey, tentatively unscrewing the cap, holding her nose and closing her eyes. I shivered.

I got up and turned the key to the kitchen door. I put my hand on the round brass handle, comforted by its familiar dents and scratches. With a deep breath, I pushed the door open.

Sunlight bathed the kitchen. Next to the sink, a china cup half filled with tea stood as if someone had recently left it. The room was quiet and peaceful, and for a moment it felt like nothing terrible could possibly have happened. The pantry door stood, firmly closed, across the room.

The walk across the kitchen was slow and syrupy, as if in a dream. I reached up to the bolt and slid it across. The sound it made as it ricocheted back was deafening, and I waited, half hoping to hear her stir behind the door, but there was only silence.

Slowly, I lifted the latch and pulled. The door creaked open. Stacey wasn't inside.

The glass jam jars and bottles were neatly lined up in rows on the shelves, the floor clear of broken glass. I stepped inside and lifted the bottle of vinegar, its top neatly screwed on. My face in the glass stared back at me, eyes dark and deep like Stacey's, reflecting back my own emerging realisation.

She had never been there at all.

I sank down onto a chair, staring into the dark corners of the pantry, as if she could be hiding in there still, small and quiet as a mouse. The kitchen felt darker now, and all around me I could see encroaching shadows, as if the clouds had obscured the sun.

I kept the pantry door closed, glancing at it every time I went into the kitchen. Upstairs, I found my carved box on the floor where I had thrown it. I went to pick it up, noticing a new door had opened in its base. What remained of the salt cellar from *Romilly and the Picnic* nestled in glass shards on the floor next to the box.

I missed Stacey desperately. I began to unpick all of my memories, the good and the bad. I thought of the donkey and the snails and the dying dove. Was this violence, this obsession with death not really Stacey's at all, but my own?

Over the next few days, I slowly ran out of food and stopped eating altogether, taking little sips of cold water straight from the tap to fortify me instead. I plaited my long hair and stroked the concave hull of my belly, feeling hollow within, like those thousand-year-old bog bodies you see preserved with only a handful of grains in their stomach. I relished the feeling of power that starvation had on me, surging through my body, an energy more visceral than anything food could provide.

Being truly alone had a calming effect on me, a feeling of control. I had always been alone, really, this was just one step further. I spent my evenings stroking Monty, sitting close to the fire, trying to understand what had happened. I thought of all the times Dad had talked to Stacey, all the times he had set her a place at the table, referred to us as 'the girls'. Had he been humouring me, playing along? Or was it his dementia, simply forgetting that he no longer had two daughters?

Questions flew through my mind, back and forth, back and forth, but I had no answers because the only place I would find them was with Stacey, and Stacey was gone. I had made her disappear, I knew that now, and with a craving in my gut, I knew that I must go after her, to conjure her to me one last time.

I unplaited my hair, lank and greasy, and brushed it out, ignoring the snow-like scurf that fell around me. Pouring a basinful of water, I stripped and splashed it over my body, taking vicious pleasure from the sting of the ablutions to my skin. I secured Dad's forget-me-not necklace around my neck and re-plaited my hair.

Pulling on a thin nightdress, I belted an old coat over the top. There was no need to wear warmer clothes; I hadn't felt the cold in days. Monty wove round my ankles, and I crouched down and dropped a kiss onto his soft head. He was looking skinny too. The kitchen floor was littered with the last tins of tuna, opened and licked clean.

'Go catch a mouse,' I said, pushing him away and straightening up.

The back door was frozen shut. It took all my energy and a kettleful of boiling water to ease it open.

As I walked out into the silence, the cold took my breath away, and for a moment the brightness bloomed so white it had a song of its own. I wavered on the doorstep, swaying to its celestial ringing, then with a huge effort, I picked up my foot and took a step forward.

Thirty-Nine

The world had changed since last I stepped outside. I couldn't get my bearings, and I stood at the front of Braër House, lost. But then a distant line of poplars came into focus, like a tiny pencil sketch on a piece of pristine white paper, and I started forward.

I had made this pilgrimage before, but never at this time of year. The going was slow, the snow so deep that at times my wellies sank into drifts, filling with flowers of snow that wilted against my skin.

A thin, leafless sapling was growing out of the snow ahead. I focused on it as I trudged across the ground. A shimmer of snowflakes flew from its branches, forming something like a swan's wing in the air before disappearing.

Feathers appear when angels are near.

Did Stacey have wings? I wondered. Was she a terrible angel, sent to watch over me?

Or perhaps everyone had got it wrong, and *I* was the imaginary one – not the little nine-year-old version of me, trapped in Dad's colourful treasure hunt, but the Romilly Kemp of now, imprisoned in the pages of a black-and-white story, the words crisp and cold as winter.

'It's not all about you, you know.' Her voice was so close that I jumped. I turned, expecting to see her next to me, but she wasn't there.

'I know it's not,' I said, feeling lightheaded. Her voice had an echoing quality to it. She sounded, for the first time, unreal. I began to walk again.

I could make out the familiar circle of trees in the distance now. I remembered the time I had walked there without Stacey. She had been there, waiting for me, haunting me. As I reached the poplars, I pushed through carefully, unsure what I would see on the other side.

The lake was invisible under a covering of snow. No footprints scarred the little glade, and for a moment it was as if I was looking at a different circle, a different glade: one with an ancient fountain and a small metal fawn bending to drink at the edge of a giant leaf. I shook my head, trying to banish the image, my memories merging, my thoughts confused.

'Stacey, where are you?' I called. A cluster of crows took off from the tops of the trees, and she was there, standing at the centre of the lake.

'I knew you'd come,' she said, and she opened her arms to me. Desperate to reach her, I ran forwards. The ice crackled beneath the snow.

As I reached her; as she pulled me into a hug, for a moment I glimpsed her face, and it was like looking into a mirror.

'You're so cold,' she said, 'and so thin. When did you get so thin?'

'I'm all right,' I said between chattering teeth. She rubbed my arms, trying to force some warmth into them.

And then the ice began to groan.

I pulled away from her, unsteady on my feet.

'We need to get off here,' she said, panic in her voice, 'it's not safe.' She took my hand and pulled.

'No,' I said, the decision making itself as the word left my mouth. I planted my feet deep in the snow.

'What do you mean? Come on, Romilly! It's cracking!'

I looked around at the little glade, everything soaked in snow. It was beautiful. 'I'm staying here,' I said, my legs suddenly unable to hold me, and I dropped down onto my knees, the snow burning my skin.

'Romilly,' Stacey pleaded, 'remember our first summer here? We swam in the water, with the bees buzzing in our ears and potion on our wrists. This is our glade, our lake. There'll be more summers just like that. Please.' She was pulling at my arm, begging me to get up.

'No there won't,' I said, 'you're not real, Stacey. You never were.'

The groan of ice beneath us was loud now. I could see terror in her eyes, but, *it doesn't matter*, I told myself, *I'm home now*.

'Lie down,' she shouted urgently above the whip-roar in my ears, 'it won't break if you lie across it. Here.'

Slowly, carefully, she pulled me down until I was lying on the snow, the ice juddering beneath us. The floor shifted, then stilled. Far below us came a moaning, as if the ice was impatient to move.

'We just need time,' she said, as if to reassure herself, 'it just needs to settle, that's all.' She was sitting next to me, her knees drawn up to her chest. She reminded me of the tomboy I had met when I was eight years old.

'I'm so cold,' I said, though the words came out in shuddering gasps. Stacey rubbed at my shoulder, and I realised I couldn't feel her touch.

Time and silence drifted together like snow.

'I'm so sorry,' she said at last, 'I didn't mean for this to happen.' All around us, the poplars seemed to be leaning in, listening to her confession.

'Will it hurt?' My breath was coming in little gasps now. My body kept making involuntary movements.

'It's just like falling asleep,' she said, stroking my cheek. Little puffs of snow-haze were billowing from her into the air as she spoke, so that I wasn't sure if she was there at all, not really.

'Will you stay with me?' I said. 'To the end?'

She nodded, tucking my hair behind my ear, stroking my cheek with gloveless hands.

And the ice began to sing.

It was a haunting sound, an electrified murmur, its song reaching inside me, winding its way round my bones. As my eyes became drowsy, Stacey's face began to shift in front of me, becoming younger: there were smudges of dirt across her cheeks, pale brown marks that could be freckles. Her hair was short and messy. I drank her in longingly; her upturned nose, her unusual eyes.

'Were you ever real?' I asked, but I wasn't sure if I said it out loud.

Her face changed again, blending with my own until we had merged into one person. Before my eyes she began to evolve, to grow up, as if I were seeing each day of our life, flitting from the child I had known to the adult we would never become.

'I thought perhaps you were an angel,' I whispered. 'What will happen to you, if I go?'

The figure that had been Stacey shrugged, the gesture so reminiscent of the girl I knew that I laughed. Her face was indistinct now. Part ice and part air, but there was still something of the girl I had loved in the form of snowflakes before me.

'I'll miss you,' I said, the words pale and insubstantial. I was squinting against the sun now, hardly able to make her out in its brightness.

She reached out a fog-soft hand to me, and I lifted mine, needing to feel her touch one last time. But as our hands clung to one another, and desperately I tried to hold onto the tiny crystals of ice, she vanished.

I dropped my head, tears melting into the snow, and I realised I could no longer feel my body. I was becoming part of the lake, part of Stacey, and I cried openly now, knowing what it meant. I closed my eyes and waited.

'Romilly.'

I was sitting by the fire in the snug, a Christmas tree strung with tinsel nearby. Monty was chasing a bauble, and Dad was standing at the mantelpiece, hanging up stockings.

'Romilly,' he said. His beard was bushy and almost black. He had streaks of green and gold paint across his cheek, and he was peeling a tangerine and dropping the rind into the fire. The smell of citrus and woodsmoke and pine was all-consuming.

'Romilly, this is not how it ends,' he said, straightening up and looking me in the eyes. His voice was buoyant, amused even, as if he knew I was only jesting with him.

He took down a bulging stocking and handed it to me. 'For you,' he said.

I took it and peeped inside. There were five objects in there, one on top of the other. I recognised them as I pulled them out one by one: the bell was small and bright and attached to a brand-new collar. The salt cellar was no longer a pile of glass, but whole and filled to the brim with salt. As I pulled the feather out, its soft strands rustled, thick and luscious, the deepest of candyfloss pinks.

'Keep going,' Dad said, humming in excitement.

The forget-me-not necklace came next, the colour that had leached out of it restored. Lastly, I pulled the bauble from the stocking's toe, smooth and shining, reflecting my sister's treasured face back at me.

'Look at them all, Romilly,' he said with satisfaction. 'Each one was given to you by someone who cares deeply for you. Think of the love that comes with such gifts.'

I cradled the treasures, and finally I understood.

'You are loved, daughter-mine,' Dad said, 'both you and Feena are loved. All of these people hold memories of you and your sister. They have been a part of this treasure hunt, because, in some ways, they are the treasure. They are the link to your life ahead, and the link back to your sister. Let them in, Romilly, and you will never truly be alone.'

I thought about what he was saying, my fingers touching the objects one by one, naming the people they stood for, and I knew he was right: I would never forget my twin because she had always been a part of me, and so a part of every person that I had ever loved.

'It's time to go, Romilly,' Dad said, popping a piece of tangerine into his mouth and chewing thoughtfully, the juice frothing at his beard, 'you can't stay here forever.'

'But I like it here,' I said, stretching in the warmth.

'Get up, Romilly. Get up. There is still treasure to be found, and this is not where it is hidden.'

Nearby, Monty mewed, but the mew sounded strange, like the cawing of a rook…

'Romilly…'

I awoke, unsure how long I had been lying there. I was shivering violently. The snow clouds had broken and I could feel the sun warming my back. I tried to remember what had woken me.

'Romilly,' someone whispered in my ear.

'Dad?' I said drowsily. I tried to open my eyes, but my eyelashes were knitted shut. I lifted my head, and my cheek parted painfully with the ice.

I squeezed my eyelids together and pulled them open, looking around. I was alone in the glade.

I pulled myself up slowly, my coat crackling with frost, my body numb from the cold. Without Stacey I was lighter somehow, and I crawled across the lake's surface, the ice so silent I wasn't sure if it had ever really cracked.

I pushed through the tangle of trees, marvelling at the whiteness all around, and began the tentative journey home.

Forty

As soon as I stepped across the threshold, I felt a peace within Braër that I couldn't name. It was a comforting peace, and it spoke to me in hushed tones as I climbed, exhausted, into my bed, my mind wandering before sleep. It was a nourishing peace: when I woke, it directed me to the pantry, a place that no longer looked dark and dangerous, and showed me countless jars of homemade jam. It gave me the strength to wrest off the lids and scoop handfuls of sweetness into my starving mouth.

When I was sated, Braër's peace gently nudged me, touching my hand to my forget-me-not locket, and bringing to mind my dad, reminding me that my journey was not yet done.

My father was sleeping quietly, slumped in the chair of his tiny nursing-home room. His bony head rested against one plastic wing, two clear prongs fitted neatly into his nostrils. A pretty walnut bureau that I remembered from home stood next to him, supporting an oxygen canister. There were no pictures or photos.

I stood in the doorway, rubbing at the numb tingle in my burnt hand, knowing it meant it was healing. I watched my father as he slept, a ray of sunlight shrouding him like a thin blanket. His eyelids flickered and a pulse twitched in his cheek. His hair was thinner than last time I saw him, with more scalp shining through, and his eyebrows had lost their bushiness. His slightness, his paleness seemed to glimmer in the room, and the longer I stood there, the more it felt as if he belonged to another world, as if he were crossing some unseen border, turning from solid flesh and blood and beating heart to something I couldn't touch.

With a small snort he woke up, going so quickly from asleep to awake that before I knew it he was blinking at me, alert and interested. I smiled.

'Hi, Dad,' I said, sinking down to crouch by his chair. He smiled back, his thin mouth stretching into an echo of the grin I used to know.

'I wanted to tell you. . .' I tried to form the right words, but I didn't know where to start. What did I want to tell him? That I had been on a treasure hunt of my own? That Stacey had only been gone for a few days but already I struggled to recall her face?

'I wanted to tell you. . . that everything's all right,' I finished, taking his hand in mine. He jumped at the touch, then bent his large head to look at me. Lifting his free hand, he touched it to my face, sweeping back my fringe and placing his cool palm on my forehead, just like he used to.

'I'll keep visiting you, I promise, as often as I can. And I'm going to visit Mum soon too: on my birthday – because of course it's Feena's birthday too – I think she'd like that.' Dad didn't seem to understand my words, but he smiled, and that was enough.

We sat in the shaft of sunlight, Dad drifting in and out of sleep, our hands entwined as his head gently lolled, meaningless murmurs drifting from his lips.

My rucksack slithered off my shoulder, spilling the *Romilly* books all over the floor, and Dad awoke with a start. I bent down to gather them up, but my father's hands were already there, long-fingered and yellow. He was clasping at them, drawing them slowly towards him. The movement reminded me of something; a gorilla I had once seen at the zoo. Dad was reaching out shyly, his hand flashing out daringly, fleetingly, only to withdraw to his side as soon as he saw me looking.

'It's all right, Dad,' I said, placing the books on his lap and opening up *Romilly and the Circus*. He pulled the book towards him, stroking the glossy paper. The hairs on his hands were white now.

'You made these, Dad. Look.' I leant forward and pointed to the red-haired girl on the page, 'Romilly.' A drop of saliva landed on the glossy denim of the girl's dress. I wiped it away.

'Fee... na...' he said. It sounded like longing. I looked at the little picture, wondering which of us it was meant to be.

Suddenly, Dad's hand was at my neck, and I jerked back, realising at the last moment that he was reaching for my necklace. With expert precision he deftly flicked the locket open. He stared at the flower, rolling it between his fingers, his eyes travelling over the tiny petals. Trying not to move, I reached for my rucksack and pulled out the feather, placing it in his lap.

Dad made a sound, somewhere between a sigh of longing and a groan of sadness. He dropped the locket and picked up the feather.

'It belonged to Lidiya,' I said, watching his face for any sign of recognition. 'She helped me solve your clues.'

I pulled the carved box from my rucksack, placing it on top of the books in Dad's lap. The feather fell to the floor. Dad was staring down at the box, his mouth moving, a soft clicking coming from his jaw. He picked it up in his huge hands, and it fitted perfectly between them in a way it never had in mine, melding with the shape of his palms as if he had grown it from his own skin. His fingers sat obediently in small dents in the wood that I had never noticed before. Dad closed his eyes and pushed gently, and the box began to change. It evolved before my eyes, slots of wood moving like pieces of a puzzle. From inside came a mechanical whirring, as if time itself were speeding up. He was concentrating on the box, grunting slightly under his breath, and then he flicked his wrists as if he were unscrewing a jam jar, and the box came apart cleanly in his hands.

Inside was a maze of little compartments, each with its own door to the outside world, each one empty. Near the centre, a ring of tiny cogs was clicking away, like the movements of a clock, and right in the middle of this was an oval cavity, shaped like the shell of an egg, but this segment had no exit, no way of escape. Deep in here, something glimmered.

Dad was staring at the opened box. I leant closer to see what was nestled inside, but his hand got there first. A glint of gold, and then it was gone.

For a moment I worried it would go the same way as Monty's bell, but the trembling hand that had snatched it was drawing closer to me. He pulled my small hand into both of his own, looking into my eyes and nodding. When he drew away, I felt something solid beneath my curled fingers. I looked down. A coin lay there, thick and gold as custard, shining brightly in the beam of sunlight. I traced the relief of the man's head, my thumb running over the laurel wreath in his curly hair.

'This is old, Dad. It's...' Something about it was familiar. I tried to remember if I'd seen it before, like so many of Dad's gifts.

Dad was humming, the little prongs in his nose vibrating with the sound. He was looking fixedly at the wall to his right, the books and box on his lap forgotten. I quietly packed away my possessions, tucking the coin into my pocket for safekeeping. I leant forward and kissed him softly on his forehead, the edge of my mouth brushing the scar that he had got saving me that hot summer's day. Beneath the antiseptic tinge of medical soap, I caught the real smell of my dad, warm and cinnamon, and I breathed it in.

As I crossed the hallway, I looked back at Dad through the open door. Two figures were crouched by his seat. I blinked. Dad was no longer looking at the wall. He was smiling at the girls, for that is what they were: two girls, one about my age, and one much younger with long, red hair, and all three of them were shimmering in the afternoon sun, so that none of them looked real.

The older girl turned to me for a moment and smiled.

It was Stacey.

I raised my hand in a gesture of farewell and she did the same, her other hand gently clasping my father's.

The little girl by her side looked up for a moment, her smile coy and shy, yet filled with a knowing wisdom, and I knew who she was immediately. She was like me, but she was not me. She was her own, whole person, stopped in time.

She was Feena.

I returned her smile, standing in the hallway, a sense of peace drifting over me, watching them together.

They did not need me anymore.

I pulled myself away and started down the stairs.

Forty-One

At home, I sat on my bedroom floor, my back to the bed, the coin spinning next to me. I had examined it on the bus ride home. It was Roman, made of real gold. I wondered where Dad had found it.

The floorboard seemed to be goading me. *Lift me up*, it whispered. I studied the plank, trying to remember all the things I had placed under it over the years. Did it still contain echoes of the Romilly I had once been?

I took hold of the board and pulled, peeking into the black hole. It trembled with dust. I lay down on the floor, dipping my arm in up to my shoulder, scrabbling around with my fingers. For a long moment I felt nothing but cool, gritty air, and then the tips of my fingers snatched at something.

The remains of a snail shell came up in my hand, half a bright pink star painted onto it. A thin strip of hay came next, bringing with it the touch of velvet tickling my fingers.

I pulled sheaves of brittle paper up to the light; signatures with hearts littered about them. An awkward looking sketch I had done of Stacey stopped me for a moment. I laid them all on the floor, and reached in again, my fingers trailing over the rough wooden joists.

I was looking for something specific. It was futile, really, just a tiny memory from so long ago, but the brightness of Dad's coin had ignited something that stung at the back of my mind. The meadow. A glimmer of gold.

As I pulled each object out and the collection mounted on the floor next to me, I felt a pang of disappointment. I put my hand in again, stretching my fingers until my joints cracked painfully, stroking the bottom.

A cold nugget teased the end of my index finger, and my heart jumped. This was it. I used the tip of my finger to slide it against the wood and up towards the light.

My heart sank. It was just an old, broken brooch, blue-green with mud. Was this what I had been thinking of? I rubbed disappointedly at its surface until the dried mud crumbled from the little lattice holes all over it. Something about it made me think of water and mire, and then of Stacey. I closed my eyes and held the brooch tight, my breath floating down into the empty cache.

I thought back to the child that had hidden these special things over the years, the stories she had made up, the adventures she'd had. She was so much more complex than the paper-thin girl in Dad's books.

The girl in Dad's books wasn't really me, or my sister, I realised. She never had been. And I certainly wasn't her.

If I were to tell the story of my life, I thought, where would I start? *With treasure*, a small voice whispered. Not Stacey's voice this time, but my own, heard for the first time, hidden deep within me.

Treasure.

One last time, I pulled the floorboard back. I dropped my arm in, and reached as far as it was possible to reach. Something in a far corner met my fingers, quickly this time, as if it had grown impatient with this game and wanted, finally, to come out. It was surprisingly warm to the touch. I could feel the smooth frill of its edge, the bumps and curves of a face. I pulled it out.

It was identical to the coin Dad had given me, and just as beautiful. The gold was duller — there was earth caught in the crevices of the man's face and between the laurel leaves on his head. I had thought it was toy money when I dug it up in the meadow all those years ago.

I walked to the low window and knelt down on the window seat, examining the two coins in the sunlight. Was it just a coincidence that Dad and I had both found a gold coin? Might there be more out there, hidden in the meadow? Perhaps a whole hoard of treasure trove, patiently waiting for me under the earth.

I looked out over the garden. The snow had melted away as quickly as it had come. The moat lay thick as tar below me, a rainbow sheen on its surface. Occasional bubbles rose slowly, popping with a wet smack that sent droplets of slime onto the grass. In the furthest point of the garden, almost hidden now by a mass of hemlock, Dad's sunken wooden shed stood, its door half open, caressed by the leaves of the weeping willow. In the distance, the rusting shells of Dad's mobiles stood motionless against the skyline.

The phone was on the window sill next to me. Tucked underneath it, a half-forgotten piece of paper poked out from one corner. I pulled it out and looked at the number written on it, complex and meaningful like a mysterious code.

The two coins burned like eyes in my palm. On impulse, I spun them both, one after the other.

Heads I call the number, I thought, tails I throw it away.

The first coin landed quickly, the face of the man staring regally up at me.

I tried not to look as the second coin spun on, but my eyes kept glancing back, drawn to its glinting dance.

The coin staggered and fell. The long, aquiline nose and the pointed chin of the second man's face winked up at me.

I lifted the receiver and began to enter the number; the slow drag and pull of the telephone's dial foreign to my finger.

On the third ring, there was a click, and a familiar woman's voice said, 'Children's services, Barbara Clarke speaking.'

'Barbara?' I said in a small voice. I could picture the regimented ID card around her neck, the lipstick on her teeth as she spoke her name.

'This is she.'

'It's Romilly Kemp.' I left my name hanging in the air, listening to the silence on the other end of the phone.

Eventually, 'Romilly? Are you all right? You sound like you're crying.' Her voice, both reassuring and authoritative, flowed over me like a balm.

I clung to the receiver, pushing it close to my mouth.

'Help me,' I whispered. 'Help me, please.'

After I replaced the receiver, I dried my eyes and picked up the coins again. Holding them tightly, I ducked through my little door and went downstairs, almost tripping over Monty, curled up on the bottom step. He yawned, showing off clean, white teeth, and attempted a scratchy meow. I lifted him up and draped him over my shoulders, where he clung on, purring happily into the back of my head, his paw clenching near my ear.

Stopping only to grab a trowel, I threw open the back door and went through the garden, down to the meadow.

Up close, the eroding skeletons of Dad's mobiles were scarred and pitted with rust. I wound my way through them, noting how they felt so much smaller now.

I came to the middle of the meadow, and turned full circle, making sure I was in the right place.

Braër House looked so small from here, like a witch's cottage in a fairy tale. I thought for one moment I saw someone standing at my bedroom window, watching me, but then I blinked, and she was gone, and I knelt down in the cool, damp grass, with my cat by my side, and I began to dig.

The End

Acknowledgements

Whilst daydreaming, I have written acknowledgements in my head for years, the list getting longer and longer the more people who have helped me on the way. It feels very strange to be writing one for real.

First of all, thank you to you, the person reading this book. It has been an extraordinary journey bringing it into your hands, and I hope with all my heart that it takes you on an extraordinary journey reading it, too.

To my parents, who listened patiently to my first attempt at a novel twenty years ago, and who have listened ever since. Also, my sisters Lucy and Jo — three is a magic number, and we three have a very special bond.

I want to thank Bear for being such a big part of my free-range childhood. Those searches for sweets hidden in the maize field started a lifetime love of treasure hunts for me. I wonder if there's still a fruit salad chew buried somewhere in a Suffolk field?

Teachers played an important role in my becoming a writer, among them, the inimitable Miss Pirrie - the kind of English teacher who sets your brain on fire. At the time of writing, I don't know if she is still alive — when I was ten, she seemed very old and grey-haired, as most teachers over forty did!

To Lee Cozens, Vicky McKenzie and Rachel Cogman, thank you for all your support. Also, to everyone at my Book Club: you always bring the best cheese and wine - what else is there in life? Cathryn Baker, Jenny and Mark Sheldrake and Nic Bouskill, thank you so much for all your help. And finally, Lucy Geering, who appeared in my life just before all of the wonderful things started happening, and whose wise words set me on a strange and magical path. I have a feeling you might be my fairy godmother.

On to those I have met on this writing journey: Lisa O'Donnell, whose clever, often dark ideas helped Romilly appear; Felicia Yap and everyone at Curtis Brown Creative; all at The Bridport Prize.

An awe inspired thank you goes to my agent Juliet Mushens, who I idolised for an age before daring to approach, and thank goodness I did! Huge love to my editor Clio Cornish, whose creative mind and kind, insightful words helped keep me grounded when I began to feel as if I were caught in the hurricane of '87. Massive thanks to Kate Mills for your enthusiasm and brilliant ideas. Thank you also to the HQ Design Team for the incredible cover, and to Joe Thomas, Joanna Rose, Claire Brett and everyone at HQ for all your hard work behind the scenes.

The seed of this novel germinated when I heard about Kit Williams' book, *Masquerade*, an 'armchair treasure hunt'. If you haven't read it; do. It's rather marvellous.

When heady dreams come true, it is sometimes hard to keep your feet on the ground. Thank goodness for my two boys: my husband, Matt, and our son, Seb. There is so much laughter with you two, and I love you both dearly. This book is dedicated to you.

And finally, to Dali, my ancient Oriental cat, and my muse. He sat patiently on my lap whilst I wrote, purring and blinking those huge blue eyes as if to say, keep going, Polly, we're nearly there.

Don't miss the stunning new novel from Polly Crosby
The Unravelling

When Tartelin Brown accepts a job as a PA to a reclusive lepidopterist, she finds herself on a wild island with a mysterious history.

Tartelin has been employed by Marianne Stourbridge to hunt for butterflies, but she quickly uncovers something far more intriguing. The island and Marianne share a remarkable past, and what happened all those years ago has left its scars.

The island has a strange effect on Tartelin, too, finally allowing her to confront her own, painful, memories. As she does, Marianne's story begins to unravel around her, revealing an extraordinary tale of two girls, an obsession with pearls, and a truth beyond imagination.

Atmospheric and deeply emotional, *The Unravelling* is a captivating novel about the secrets we can only discover when we dare to look beneath the surface.

Turn the page to read an extract from *The Unravelling*...

Prologue

Marianne

1955

Marianne bent over the ragged remains of the poor butterfly's broken wing. The insect held still, as if it knew she was only trying to help.

The wing was damaged beyond repair, and she gripped the tweezers in her left hand and, with great care, lifted the replacement silken waxed wing she had made, stopping to consider it in mid-air. It was a perfect match to the quaking peacock butterfly's remaining wing, even down to the glittering dust that coated its surface.

She painted a fine dab of clear glue onto its edge and brought it fluidly in to the broken wing, holding it in place with motionless hands. Four shimmering blue eyes aligned on the wings and gazed up at her, and she allowed herself a small smile.

Carefully, she opened the tweezers, and the butterfly lay pulsing on the desk, unaware it was free.

'Go,' she said, wishing it upwards.

Slowly, delicately, it lifted its wings, both the real and the manu-factured, until they closed above it. Marianne frowned as the silk wing lagged slightly, but then, with sudden weightlessness, the butterfly took off.

It flew around the great panelled room, and Marianne sat back in her chair, following its path with her eyes, a surge of joy bursting through her as she watched it in its jagged, miraculous flight.

Turning back to her desk, she began to clear away her work. The remains of the damaged wing lay like a spent husk on the leather surface. It had been torn away, almost down to the core, the pattern of the two eyes smeared and disfigured and, for a brief moment, she had the feeling that it was looking at her, the eyes penetrating her in a way that she didn't understand.

Above her, the repaired butterfly danced high in the air, unaware that anything was wrong.

Chapter One

Tartelin

Summer 2018

'I do not require nappy changing, I do not require spoon feeding, I do not require my ego massaging. What I do require is someone with a deft pair of hands. I asked for someone with experience in dealing with little things, delicate things. A scientist, perhaps. Is that you?'

I nod.

'Show me your hands then, child.'

I hold them out, palm side downwards, and she wheels herself over and inspects them. Her own hands, I see now, have a tremor.

'You're a pretty girl,' she says, her eyes drifting over my face, glancing off my cheek, and I feel my skin redden. 'Not very robust though. Are you sure this is the right job for you?' I open my mouth to speak, but she cuts me off. 'What did you do, before you came here? How is it that you are suited to this vacancy?'

I frown. We went over all this in our letters, back and forth, back and forth. Written on paper, not sent by email, each one signed 'Miss Marianne Stourbridge' in her regimented, barbed-wire scrawl. My life back home was the reason she chose me. But then she is old, and she can't be expected to remember everything.

'I grew up around my mother's artwork, helping her out in her studio,' I say, more loudly than I mean to. 'And then I went to art school myself. Mum's work was focused on found objects … making art from bits of nature: feathers, leaves and twigs—'

'Lepidoptera aren't "bits of nature", Miss Brown.'

'She also made sculptures out of grains of rice in her spare time. I helped her.'

'Why on earth would anyone do that?' She leaves the question hanging in the air and turns her chair abruptly, wheeling herself back to her desk.

The chair is made from cane. It looks like an antique, and I'm surprised it still works. It must be exhausting to propel.

'It's a shame you don't have a scientific background, but now you're here, you'll have to do. Here, hold this.' She lifts a pair of gold tweezers into the air and I hasten forward and take them. 'No, not like that. Pinch. Gently. That's it.'

I adjust my hold, and feel how the spring of the tines is like an extension of my fingers and I'm back with my mother and she's saying, 'Careful Tartelin, don't squeeze too hard, feather barbs bruise easily.' But before I can use this new-found body part, the tweezers are whisked away from me, and she's turning again to the desk and bending over her work. I stand by her side and wait, wondering if I'm allowed to go. The clock on the mantel chimes loudly. I count eight. I look at my watch. It's ten past two.

'Miss Stourbridge? Shall I adjust your clock?'

'No point. It'll only go back to eight o'clock.'

I look over at it, frowning. The second hand is juddering in jerky movements. It makes me dizzy to look at it, as if it's measuring a different kind of time. I turn back to my employer.

Miss Stourbridge is so still as she works. I can see her teasing the body of a dead moth from a cocoon, her fingers moving infinitesimally slowly. I look around the room. It is lined in dark panels of wood, and every surface has frames and frames of butterflies and moths, glinting pins plunged into husked bodies.

'Did you catch all these butterflies?'

She is silent, and at first I think she hasn't heard me. But then I see she's holding her breath so as not to disturb the moth's delicate wings. I watch closely, the clock ticking behind us. I'm looking, not at her work, but at her ribs, waiting for them to inflate, waiting for her nostrils to swell, anything that shows air is passing into her chest. My eyes sting from the pain of staring. She is so still that she has become a part of the chair she sits in. Only her finger and thumb move achingly slowly, and the minutes tick by.

When I was young, I used to try to be as still as she is now. My mother would sit me on her knee and tell me stories, and I would hold myself as still as a statue, bewitched by her tales.

'Long ago,' she always began, in a voice that was reserved only for when the moon was rising, 'I was a tiny jellied spawn, no bigger than a pearl, floating in the earth's great oceans. The fish nibbled and swallowed my brothers and sisters up, snap, snap, snap, and I was left, coming at last to rest on the pebbled shore of a beach. And that is how I came to have these,' she would say, waving her hands in front of my face, so close that they skimmed my eyelashes and all I could see was the thin layer of webbed skin between each finger. To my unprejudiced four-year-old eyes, the webs were not a deformity: they were beautiful, useful; magical, and I wished with all my heart that I could be like her, could be from the sea.

I take my eyes from the poor moth on the desk, and look over Miss Stourbridge's head to the picture window that frames the sea beyond, and I remember anew that the sea surrounds us here, like a comforting arm holding the world at bay. A feeling of calm settles over me.

However strange this woman is, whatever my job might entail, it was the right decision to come here, I can feel it.

I had seen the advertisement in one of Mum's ornithological magazines. Mum bought them for the photographs. She particularly liked the close-ups of the birds' eyes and feathers. The magazines were littered throughout our house, spattered with drops of paint, pages ripped out and twisted together into the vague forms of gulls and robins, so that every surface was covered in paper birds made of paper birds.

But the latest magazine had landed on the doormat, pristine and untouched, and when I shook it from its clear plastic covering, it had fallen open on the advert.

PA required to assist lepidopterist. Must be able to start immediately. Must not be squeamish.

When I had written to ask for more information, the return address had intrigued me.

Dogger Bank House, Dohhalund.

Dohhalund. An unusual word, not English-sounding at all. A bit of research showed me that it was a tiny island off the East Anglian coast, the long thin shape of it reminiscent of a fish leaping out of the water. Its heritage was a mixture of English and Dutch. Looking at it on a map on my phone, it had looked so small that I imagined you could walk its circumference in only a few hours. I had tried to picture what kind of an island it would be: a cold, hard rock grizzled with the droppings of thousands of seabirds, or a flat stretch of white sand, waiting for my footprints? Whatever it turned out to be, the isolation of it appealed to me.

Miss Stourbridge's letters had been vague about the position she was offering, but she did tell me, rather proudly, that the island had belonged to her family for hundreds of years. While I wait, I look about the room, searching for photographs, evidence of other people. Where is her family now?

I shift my weight carefully from foot to foot and I glance at my watch. Two twenty-three. Thirteen minutes. I wonder if I'm being paid to stand and do nothing. I look around the room. Next to the desk is a large clear glass box. Inside hang rows and rows of cocoons of all different shapes and sizes. One or two are twitching. I turn away with a sting of shame, feeling somehow as if I've looked at something I shouldn't have.

Over by the window, there is a huge black telescope on a stand. Unlike everything else in this place, it looks very modern. Next to it on the windowsill sits a battered pair of binoculars on a worn leather strap.

Quietly I back towards the chaise longue in the corner and lower myself onto its tattered silk cover. It's the first time I've sat down in hours, and my body sings with relief. I edge my hand into my pocket and pull out my phone. It's switched off: the battery ran low somewhere off the coast of Norfolk at around the same time that the signal disappeared. The lack of signal hadn't worried me: I'd been looking forward to charging my phone when I arrived, tapping in Miss Stourbridge's Wi-Fi code, the friendly glow of my phone's screen a comfort in this new place.

I look around for a socket in the room, and with a sudden slick shiver I find I can't see any. There must be electricity here, surely. But if not … realisation runs through me like a thrill: if there's no electricity in this house, there won't be any Wi-Fi either. And with no signal, there's no way of contacting the outside world. No way for the outside world to contact me. The roar of the sea appears to amplify through the thin glass of the window, rough and crashing, as if it is rushing towards me like a tsunami. Suddenly England seems very far away.

I look down at my phone and contemplate turning it on. I have a desperate need to open the photos app, to gaze at a familiar face in order to find an anchor in this strange new world. I touch my finger to the button, trying to remember how much battery I have left. Two per cent? Eight? My finger rests lightly on the button, undecided, the screen black and glaring.

Across the room, Miss Stourbridge sits back against her chair, and I tuck my phone away and approach the desk. I can feel it pressing against my skin, pulsing against me like the beat of a heart that isn't mine.

Miss Stourbridge sighs, her breath ruffling the damp wings of the newly hatched moth in front of her.

'Dusky brocade,' she says, nodding at the tiny brown body, 'they have such beautiful names, moths. They may not be as pretty as butterflies, but the names we have given them over the centuries means even Shakespeare was a fan. Beauty isn't everything, it turns out.'

I see her looking at my cheek as she says it, and for a moment I'm disappointed. Surely here, on an island in the middle of the North Sea, I am away from prejudice? It had been part of the reason the job appealed to me: to be able to stride across this island without the worry of others' stares. Or perhaps I'm naïve, and intolerance breeds in isolated outcrops like this, running within its very seams.

She sets down the delicate tweezers at last and, turning awkwardly in her chair, looks me in the eye for the first time since I got here. Her eyes are a deep grey-brown, not dissimilar to the moth on the desk. They are full of a cataclysmic wisdom, as if a fuse has been lit but the spark is not rushing along as intended.

'So, Tartelin, do you understand what I am doing, here on this island?'

'You're a lepidopterist.' I say, remembering the word from the advert. 'You catch and study butterflies and moths.'

'Yes and no. I think that's probably the closest term for what I'm trying to do. Dohhalund is a good place for finding the butterflies that get lost, the ones that get blown over from the Netherlands and Denmark. They rest on the ships, you see – and on the trawlers and Dogger boats the island is named after. But in the last few years I've dedicated my life to mutations. Do you understand what that word means?'

'Yes.' I bite my tongue. Who doesn't know what a mutation is, living as we are in a world where viruses mutate in our bodies and on our screens every day? I think of my mother's webbed hands. I go to touch my face, but stop myself just in time.

'Take me over to the window,' she orders.

I push her across the uneven floorboards and she wobbles in her chair like a marionette. The room is large. It might once have been an upstairs sitting room, but now it is a workroom: a vast empty space of floorboards and wooden panelling. The desk, a huge, unfashionable mahogany lump inset with green leather, sits in front of the window facing the sea. A small Chinese cabinet on ornate legs has pride of place beneath a wall of pinned butterflies. There is an upright piano near the door, and the tattered chaise I sat on looks as if it's been pushed unceremoniously into a corner, as if to get it out of the way. Other than that, the room is empty, as long as you don't count the hundreds of pairs of butterflies' eyes watching you from the walls.

'What could cause mutation, Tartelin?'

'I … I'm not a scientist, Miss Stourbridge.' Panic begins to set in. This feels like an interview, but surely I already have the job? I've come all this way. With a prickle of tension, I wonder if she'll send me back on the next available boat.

'When I came back to the island two months ago,' she says, leaning forward and indicating I should open the large bay window, 'I saw a little white bird over the sea. Just there.' She points with a shaking, liver-spotted hand.

Struggling to follow the darting direction of her thoughts, I edge past the telescope and unlatch the window. Immediately, the wet breeze skims off the North Sea and bursts into the room. A pile of papers ripples on the desk, barely held down by a lump of unpolished amber the size of a human skull.

'Swallows always return to the same nest, year after year,' she says. 'I remember the swallows nesting here when I was a girl. Their descendants are there now, just above the window. Have a look.'

I sit on the edge of the window, careful not to knock the binoculars off, and lean out, looking up. Immediately the wind wails in my ears. Just above the window frame a line of mud nests are glued to the eaves. Tiny voices can be heard from within.

'You've seen swallows before, I take it? You know what they look like?'

I lean back in. 'Of course.' I'm getting used to her short, sharp way of talking, like a schoolteacher to a child. It must just be uneasiness at having someone new in her house, a way of setting boundaries. I hope it will mellow with time.

'Tell me then.'

I think back to Mum's magazines. 'They're quite small, dark birds with a long, forked tail.'

'Good girl. Keep watching.'

I lean out again. The baby swallows are poking their heads out now. Three little navy blue and pale peach faces. With a faint whoosh the mother swoops in, narrowly missing the top of my head. Her body is white from head to toe. The fledgling swallows' mouths open, gaping wide. A fourth baby pops its head out, squealing for food. It, too, is white. I've never seen anything like it before.

'The term for an abnormally white bird is "leucistic",' Miss Stourbridge says. 'It's strange that she was able to find a mate. Most leucistic birds never manage it. They are considered freaks, and freaks are rarely accepted, even in the avian world.'

I watch the mother ignore the tiny white dot in the nest, shovelling dead insects into its three siblings' beaks instead. I have a feeling Miss Stourbridge is studying my cheek again. I stay on the windowsill, looking up, avoiding her gaze.

'I suspect there have been changes to a few species on this island since I was last here. Notably the winged ones. This is why I need you to catch some butterflies for me: so that I can know for sure.'

A movement out of the window catches my eye, and I stiffen.

'Is that your dog?' I point to the ground below the window, where a thin, swollen-nippled bitch is trotting across Miss Stourbridge's garden, her five puppies straggling behind.

Miss Stourbridge leans forward to look. 'No. The dogs here are wild. Presumably some were pets once.' She lifts the binoculars and peers more closely at the dog. 'There's something rather wolfish about her, isn't there? It's funny, humans have bred dogs for thousands of years, turning them into sick caricatures of themselves, but leave them to their own devices and they flourish. We don't always get it right, playing God.'

The mother dog sits suddenly and scratches her ear with a hind leg, the puppies pouncing on her floppy belly and suckling voraciously. Behind her, the garden ends abruptly at the edge of the cliff. A house this size would surely have had a much bigger garden. I look at the cliff edge, at an oak tree that grows precariously out from it, gnarled roots reaching into empty space. The garden must have eroded over time. How long until the rest of it disappears, devoured by the sea?

I lean further out of the window and look to the left, along the length of the island. There are more wild dogs in the distance, packs in groups of three or four, lithe and skinny, trotting over the brambled ground.

'In order to explore, you'll need to understand the layout of the island,' Miss Stourbridge continues. 'This house is situated on the most south-easterly point, the highest part of Dohhalund. On a clear day you can just make out the coast of Holland from here. To the north,' she points to the left, 'on that long spit of shingle, is the military base.'

I look in the direction she's pointing. Far away I can see what look like buildings, hazy on the horizon. I'd like to look through the binoculars, to get a better view, but they are still in her lap, her hand on them protectively.

'To the west of us of course,' she says, gesturing loosely behind us with a wave of her hand, 'is England.'

I think of the map I saw of the island, of the way it looked like a leaping fish, long and thin, a sharp spit of land at the north like a flicking tail and a soft curve of beach at the south like a head. I look down into the garden again. The mother dog is still there, stretched out in the sun.

'Are they dangerous?' I say, nodding at it.

'The dogs? Oh, I shouldn't think so. Only when protecting their pups. They might follow you if they think you have food, but I'm sure they'll do you no harm.'

'And am I right in thinking there's no electricity on the island?'

'That is correct. There used to be a generator at the military base, as I recall, but I doubt it works now.'

'And is there a phone signal anywhere?'

She regards me with those sharp, wise eyes. 'I have no idea, having never owned a mobile telephone.'

I look out at the island again, scanning the land. She hadn't warned me about the dogs before I came, or the lack of electricity. She'd hardly filled me in on the nature of my job at all, as if she wanted to trap me here so that I had no choice but to give it a go. As I stepped off the fishing boat earlier, gripping the handlebars of the ancient bicycle she had left for me at the station, I realised with a sense of queasiness left over from the boat ride that this wasn't an ordinary island, not a holiday destination certainly, and not really beautiful at all in the traditional sense of the word. It was a land covered in pebble and concrete, sewn together by weeds that twisted like rough stitches across its surface.

The fisherman had silently pointed a weatherworn finger when I asked where Dogger Bank House was. I couldn't read his expression, his heavy-lidded eyes drawn like a shutter to repel years of salt water. He hadn't wanted to stay around and help me with my bags to the house. I got the sense that he rarely brought his boat into these waters, that he avoided stepping foot on the island as much as he could.

'It's been sixty-three years since I left Dohhalund for the mainland,' Miss Stourbridge says, bringing me back to the darkness of the room, 'and still this island is changing.' Her voice softens as she says this, and I pull myself in from the lure of the sea to hear her properly, latching the glass closed against the spray.

'As well as finding butterflies, you will help me with menial tasks in the house: light the lamps for me, run my baths, cook my meals.

You will also wind the clock each day.' She nods towards the mantel clock as it ticks erratically.

'But I thought it—'

'The key is in place. Twelve clockwise turns. No more, or you will break it.'

But it's already broken, I think.

'Above all else, Miss Brown, your job is to observe. Observe the island. Observe what I do. You are my eyes and ears, and you cannot begin to help me until you have submerged yourself here. Island life is very different to mainland living, this island more so than others. Now, do you have any questions?'

'Why did you leave the island?'

Miss Stourbridge looks at me as if I have said the wrong thing.

'We were told we must,' she says simply, her hands gripping the bony wheels of the chair so that her knuckles whiten unpleasantly. 'Do you have any questions about your role here?'

I flush, realising my mistake. 'Why did you choose me?' I say, grabbing onto the first question that offers itself.

'Honestly? Because you could come immediately.'

I am affronted by this answer. That's it? My timing? Not my CV, or my artwork, or the care I have given my own family?

'From our correspondence, I also suspected you would be a good fit. You have something of the islander about you, I can sense it. You're astute, and you keep your emotions closed in. I like those qualities.'

Are they qualities? To me, they sound like faults.

'I don't want an emotional snip of a thing that flees at the first sign of my scalpel. I've had two like that already. Third time lucky, I think the saying goes.'

She glides back over to her desk, and leans over the glass box containing the cocoons. Lifting the lid, she reaches inside, and carefully detaches a chrysalis from its delicate fastening. It pulses as if it knows what she is going to do. She settles back at her desk, sitting the cocoon on the scratched leather surface, and picks up a scalpel. I realise the conversation is over.

'Is it safe?' I blurt out, thinking of the rough sea and the barren landscape and the isolation of it all.

Miss Stourbridge pauses, looking up. 'Safe?'

'Out there.' I point to the window, to the evening sun slanting across what remains of the garden.

'Yes, on the whole. Make sure to avoid the areas of inland shingle, we don't know what's beneath it. And don't get too close to the military base on the spit. Remember, we are, to all intents and purposes, alone on this island, Tartelin. There are no hospitals here. No police. Even the safest places can be dangerous for one who is *too* carefree.'

In the brief moment before she turns back to the moth, I see something else in her eyes, a darkness like ink spreading in water. Then she hunches over the insect, and I realise I'm dismissed.

I cross the room, taking one last look at the frail, bent woman in the wheelchair, before going out through the door onto the landing. As I begin my descent of the stairs, her voice drifts down, following me where her body cannot. The authority of it ties me to the stair.

'You'll find your rooms and the kitchen on the ground floor. I take my evening meal at seven o'clock — there is a whole sea bass in the ice box. You can gut a fish, can't you?'

I clutch the polished banister in my hand as I descend.

ONE PLACE. MANY STORIES

Bold, Innovative and
empowering publishing.

FOLLOW US ON:

@HQStories